PRAISE FOR *RISE*

'A gritty and steamy post-apocalyptic novel. Written with an intentionally rough and raw pen, where every scene feels packed with the potential for explosion, this is a bold and gratifying read for action, romance, and dystopian fans of all kinds, especially those drawn to the darker edge of genre-hopping romance.'

Self-Publishing Review

'Harley is an entertaining character with sharp wit, excellent dialogue, and a thirst to prove she doesn't need the protection of others.'

Independent Book Review

RISE

THE IRON FISTS

Margot de Klerk

MdK

COPYRIGHT

Copyright © 2023 Margot de Klerk

ISBN
978-1-9196213-4-0 (ebook)
978-1-9196213-5-7 (paperback)

Book Cover Design by MiblArt

Dedicated to my brother, who reads all of my books, even when they're a genre he doesn't like.

Keep on being awesome!

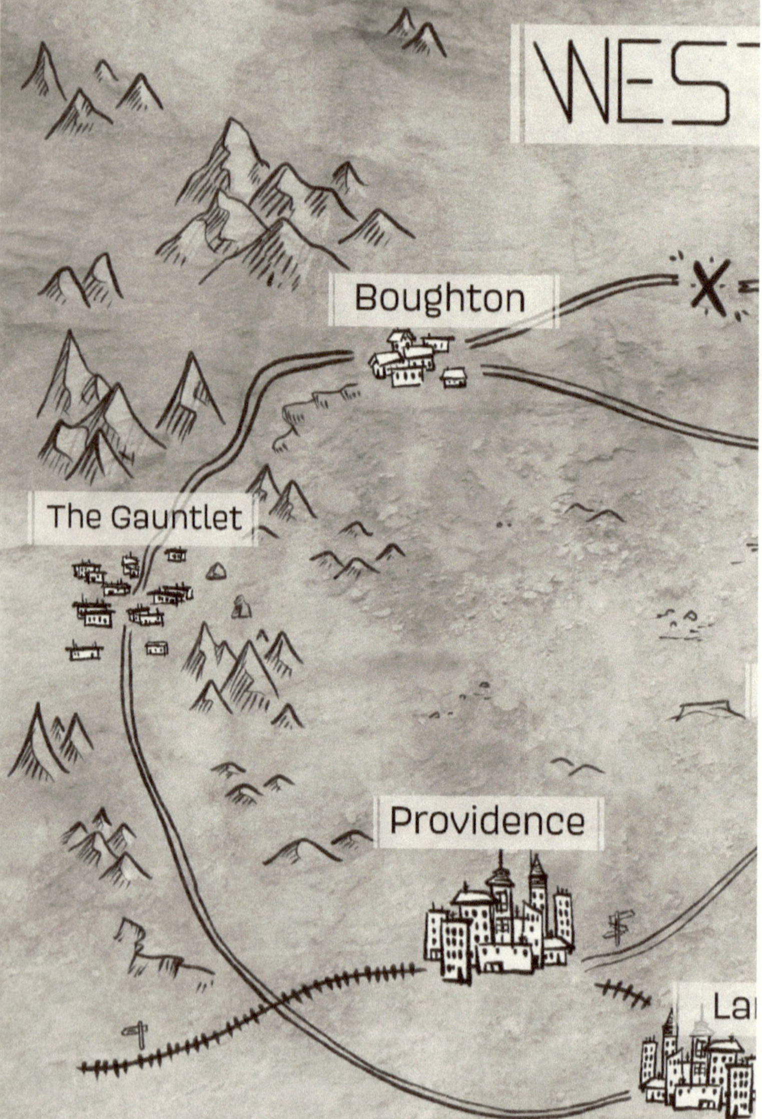

WES
Boughton
The Gauntlet
Providence
La

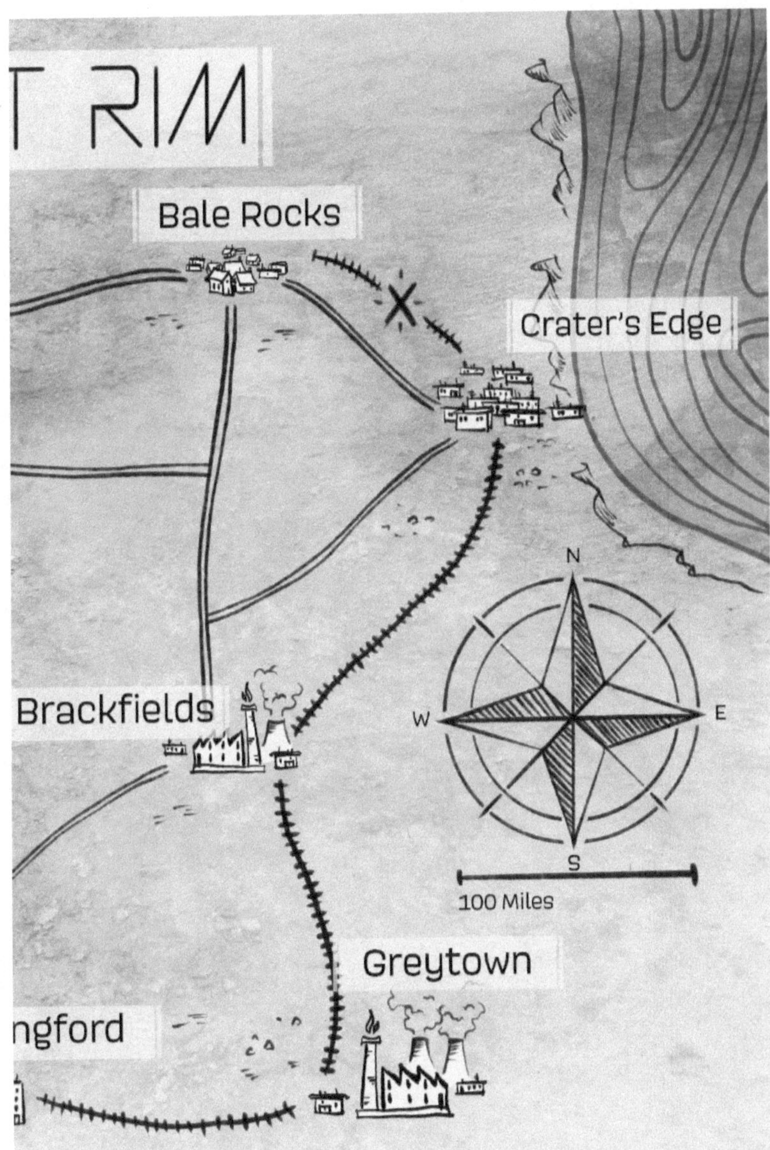

T RIM
Bale Rocks
Crater's Edge
Brackfields
Greytown
ngford
N
W
E
S
100 Miles

AUTHOR'S NOTE

Dear reader,

Thank you for embarking on this journey with me. *Rise* is the first in a four-part post-apocalyptic slow-burn romance series. That means that the steam level develops slowly over the course of the four books. In the meantime, you're in for an exciting ride. This is a no-holds-barred world full of threats, and the main character regularly has to fight for her survival.

I believe in fully warning my readers. This novel (and the whole series) contains the following potential triggers:

- Violence, firearms usage, and gang warfare
- Drugs
- Swearing
- Sexual content, including non-consensual sex, consent under duress, and sexual harassment
- Slavery

It is recommended for readers over the age of eighteen only.

If this is not your cup of tea, feel free to give this one a miss. I have cleaner reads available as well.

If this is exactly up your street, that's great! Without further ado, let's get cracking.

Margot

It is difficult to fight against anger, for a man will buy revenge with his soul.
—Heraclitus, 500 B.C.

PROLOGUE

AFTER THE ORANGE GLOW OF THE TUNNELS, the old bottling plant was full of spooky shadows, jagged silhouettes, and strange noises. I hated coming through here, especially after a long shift. It was too quiet. Even by day, it was eerie. By night, it seemed like some graveyard full of old war machinery, long abandoned by humanity. I hurried through the main hall and emerged out of the doorway into the yard.

Nights in winter always seemed darker than in summer, and tonight was darker than most, the moon obscured by thick clouds. The only light came from the guard's hut on the gate, a hundred yards ahead of me.

'I hate this place,' Posy muttered, picking her way over a pile of rubble a few feet behind me.

I squinted towards the gate again. 'There's no truck waiting.'

'What?' Posy drew up in the shadow of one of the soot-covered outer walls, peering towards the gate. In the darkness, her black hair looked like a pool of ink, and her pale skin seemed to glow. 'Fuck me, you're right. Where is Mike?'

We, along with a few of the other girls who danced in the underground club located on the north side of town—had cut a deal with one of the truck drivers to make sure there was always someone there to pick us up.

'Tina's going to be pissed.' Posy's breath fogged in front of her mouth. I dug my hands into my pockets, suddenly spooked.

The only thing that would be worse than having to walk through the old factory was having to wait in it. You never knew what sort of people might have decided to camp out here for the night—renegade gang members, homeless people, or slavers lying in wait to capture pretty girls for the brothels out west.

I curled my fingers around the handle of my knife. 'Let's walk to the road. Maybe he's just running late.'

'Fine, but if he's not there, I'm going back in,' Posy said. 'I'll suck one of the guys off for a lift home.'

Posy might be willing to do that, but I certainly wasn't about to. The only guy I liked was Marco Ellery, but he treated me like I was his kid sister. Besides, he was a member of the local gang, and I didn't want to get involved with a gang member. Even if he was really sweet.

'Let's just see,' I insisted.

We picked our way across the yard, between mounds of junk and piles of stone that had crumbled off where the building had started to collapse. The gate hung off its rail uselessly, guarded by a stern man with a rifle slung over his shoulder.

Posy walked right into the middle of the pockmarked asphalt and turned three hundred and sixty degrees, taking in the desolate road and the ruined buildings that lined it. We were in the middle of the wasteland, the town nothing more than a dim glow on the horizon.

'Nothing.' She turned to the guard. 'You haven't seen our taxi-truck?'

'Nope,' he said around his cigarette.

'Fucking hell.' She turned back towards town, staring down the road as though she could will our ride to appear out of nowhere. 'Should have known we oughta have paid him less. Fucker probably ran off with the money.'

I scuffed my toe through the dirt. 'Are you going to go back?'

'I dunno. Are you?'

I shook my head.

'You want to walk to town?' Posy groaned. 'That's going to take half an hour, at least.'

'There'll be taxi-trucks once we get to the outskirts.'

'*Maybe*. If we're lucky.'

I shrugged. 'I'm not sucking anyone off for a lift home. You know I don't do that stuff.'

Posy sighed exaggeratedly. 'Well, fine. Come on, then.'

'I thought you were going back.'

She rolled her eyes. 'I can't let you walk on your own, can I?'

'You could. I don't mind.'

'Come *on*, Harley.' She whirled around and began marching down the road. I sprinted after her, my dance bag smacking my hip with every step. My thighs burnt as I fell in beside Posy. Running after a whole shift of dancing *sucked*.

'Maybe Mike left late and we'll meet him on the road,' I suggested.

'I hope so.' Posy stuffed her hands into the pockets of her bulky coat. 'Though that would suck too because we'll have to come back here to pick up Tina and the others.'

'We should have left a message for them with the guard.'

'He'll tell them where we went.' Posy kicked a loose stone. It skittered across the asphalt and landed on the grassy verge.

We'd left the bottling plant behind, and now the darkness surrounded us. I found myself glancing around uneasily. You never knew what might be hiding in the darkness—or who. As a kid, I'd used to get nightmares about all sorts of monsters, but as an adult I knew better. Earth didn't need monsters. Men were capable of much worse.

We came to a turn-off, and Posy turned left, still walking in the middle of the road towards the distant glow of the town. It was perfectly safe; we'd have heard a car from a mile off. But the only sound was our footsteps.

Above us, the moon peeked out from behind the clouds, finally lighting up our surroundings. We were leaving the old industrial area behind. After the bombs had fallen, most of this area had been abandoned. The factories further south were still operational, but here the damage was too great to repair. A lot of the buildings had fallen down entirely, and between the ones that still stood were giant fields of rubble and scraggly bushes.

Nothing grows here but concrete, my dad used to say.

I bit the inside of my cheek. I didn't like thinking about my dad.

'There's someone there,' Posy whispered suddenly.

Ice crawled down my spine. 'Where?'

'Just ahead. Look.' She pointed just off the road. I followed her arm. A vehicle was parked about three hundred yards in front of us, shiny under the moonlight. I could see several bulky figures walking around it.

'They weren't there earlier, were they?' I mumbled out of the side of my mouth.

Posy shook her head. When I looked at her face, her eyes were wide with fear. 'We need to hide.'

I glanced around. We were in the middle of one of the rubble fields.

'Where?'

'We have to hide, Harley!' Posy's voice was fraught with panic. 'If they see us—'

'I know, but *where*?'

Anyone who was wandering around this far out of town in the middle of the night was bad news. If they saw us, who knew what they'd do? It might be anything from offering us a lift back to town to shooting us in the heads so we couldn't tell anyone we'd seen them. You really never could tell.

'Let's lie on the ground,' I muttered. I grabbed Posy's wrist, dragging her off the road. 'Here. The rubble will hide us.'

I lay on my belly behind a large chunk of concrete. Hopefully, anyone driving along the road would miss me in the dark. After a second, Posy squatted beside me.

'They're on the road to the old railway station,' she mumbled.

'I know. Lie down!'

She went on her knees, then eased herself down on her stomach. 'This is super uncomfortable. Ugh.' She flicked a few stones to the side.

'Hopefully they'll drive off soon.'

Silence fell. There was no noise whatsoever out here, apart from our breathing—nothing was alive except for us. I could hear my heartbeat in my ears.

For lack of anything else to do, I watched the men moving around the car in the distance. They opened the back and hauled a bundle out, throwing it on the ground. They seemed to be moving around a lot, though I couldn't tell what they were doing. Finally, they hauled the bundle up again, and I realised it was a person. He stumbled drunkenly, and one of the men hit him. The clap of flesh on flesh carried over to us.

Posy jerked in shock.

'Shh,' I mumbled. 'If we can hear them, they might hear us.'

'I know.' Posy tensed beside me.

In the distance, one of the men took something from his belt. The object glistened in the moonlight.

A gun.

He lifted it.

BANG!

I yelled out in shock. Posy grabbed my biceps, pressing herself against me. 'Harley! Keep quiet!'

She was shaking, or maybe I was—I didn't know. Her breathing was harsh against my neck.

'He shot him!' My heart was pounding. 'We have to do something.'

'Don't be stupid, they'll shoot us, too.'

BANG!

A second gunshot went off. I jerked against Posy's arms, but this time I managed to keep quiet.

BANG! BANG! BANG!

Surely he was dead by now? I swallowed hard. My eyes were stinging, my throat aching with the effort to hold back sobs of fear.

Under her breath, Posy was whispering, 'Please spare us, please don't see us, please, please, please.'

The gunshots stopped. The silence was almost louder than the gun had been, an oppressive stillness. I realised I'd never heard a man die before.

The roar of the engine cut through the silence. I looked up in time to see the car turn and drive back to the road, bouncing over the uneven ground. It veered in our direction and accelerated rapidly. Within seconds, it had whistled past us. I followed it with my ears until I couldn't hear it anymore.

'Do you think it's safe to move?' Posy asked once the sound had faded.

'I... I don't know,' I muttered. 'What if one of them stayed behind?'

I peered through the debris, but I couldn't see any sign of movement.

'We have to get back to town. We can't stay here all night!' Posy's voice was shrill.

'I know.' My chest felt tight, every breath rasping down my throat. Pieces of gravel stabbed into my stomach and ribcage. I tried to turn onto my side, but that hurt worse.

In the distance, I heard another car engine.

'Oh God, are they coming back?' Posy whined.

'I don't think so. It's coming from the other direction.' I wiggled forwards on my stomach and squinted into the distance. *Please be someone friendly...* A vehicle appeared, bulky against the night sky. The blocky silhouette was familiar.

'I think it's the taxi-truck,' I said.

'Oh, *please*,' Posy said fervently.

'It is.' I could see it more clearly as it approached. 'I think it's Mike. Come on, we need to flag him down.'

I scrambled up off the ground.

'Be careful, Harley!' Posy hissed. Ignoring her, I ran to the road, waving.

'Mike! Mike, over here!'

The truck had almost reached me when it braked, the tyres squealing. A moment later, it stopped in front of me. The window rolled down, revealing Mike, the elderly man who drove us to and from work every night. I'd never been so glad to see his whiskery face before.

'Harley? What are you doing all the way out here?'

'Mike! You were late—we started to walk—'

'Mike!' Posy lurched up beside me. 'You irresponsible fucker. Where the hell have you been? You're late!'

'Ey, you two aren't my only customers,' Mike grunted.

'We pay you to be there to pick us up,' Posy snarled.

'You don't pay me that good, princess.' He jerked his thumb towards the back of the truck. 'Get in and pipe down.'

'Fuck you,' Posy spat. 'I've a right mind to walk.'

Mike shrugged, uncaring. 'If you want.'

'Posy, stop it.' I grabbed her arm. 'Come on, let's get in.'

I pulled her around the back of the truck, and we climbed the built-in stairs into the back. There was a bench on either side, and the floor was roughly carpeted. I sagged onto one of the benches, and Posy collapsed opposite me. A second later, she leaned over and thumped the partition. Mike pulled the truck away from the kerb.

'We are never walking again,' Posy declared.

'Fine,' I mumbled. 'But... who do you think that was?'

'I don't know, and I don't care.' Posy nudged my ankle with the toe of her boot. 'And if you know what's good for you, you won't care either. Men who go shooting each other are bad news.'

'All men are bad news.'

'Yeah, but those ones are worse.'

I didn't have an argument against that, so I fell silent as we drove into the night.

ONE

'OOOH, LOOK.' ANNA LEANT IN, her eyes wide. 'The new boy's here.'

It was a slow, hot summer evening. We had the windows open to the square, letting in the warm, humid air and the sounds of the market closing up. Clem and his buddies were playing bridge next to the windows, and a couple of businessmen in the corner had paid us to ignore the deal they were doing. Apart from that, the bar was empty. I paused in wiping down the bar top to glance at the doorway to the hotel lobby.

'Huh, he's pretty.'

He was around my and Anna's age, twenty-four, with fluffy black hair, golden-brown skin, and green eyes. He was dressed in a suit, with the jacket thrown over one arm.

I'd been hearing whispers about the new boy all day, ever since he'd rolled up in his truck and parked on the square—not that I needed gossip. The Kranikovska, where I worked, was the only decent hotel in town; every newcomer walked through our doors eventually. Where else would they stay?

'He checked in at lunch,' Anna confided. 'Lou was on. She said he's paid upfront for a month.'

'Longer than usual.' There wasn't that much to do in our town.

'She said he told her he was here for business.'

We cut our gossiping short as he reached the bar. I tossed my long brown hair over my shoulder and offered him a saucy smile. 'Hey there, new boy.'

He smiled cautiously in return. 'The lady in the lobby said you serve dinner.'

'Dinner and drinks. We're open to two AM Sunday to Thursday, and weekends until four.' I bit my lip, looking coyly up at him. 'What's your name, then?'

'James Maddock.' He held out a hand over the bar. 'Nice to meet you.'

'And you, Mr Maddock.' I fluttered my eyelashes at him, purring, 'I'm Harley.'

I had a good name. It was sexy without any silly nicknames.

'Like the bike?' he asked.

'Vroom, vroom.' I smiled slyly. 'I ride like one, too.'

He laughed. 'I'm sure you do.'

His response took me aback. Most men were all too happy to flirt with me when I made comments like that. I leant back, assessing him. Well dressed. No ring. Polite, respectful gaze. He hadn't stared at my chest once, despite my low-cut top. *Hmm.*

'I'm Anna,' Anna chirped, waving. 'What can we get you?'

'I heard a rumour that Bale Rocks was known for its whiskey.'

'You've come to the right place, then.' She pulled a bottle off the shelf. 'My uncle stocks the good stuff. Best whiskey in the West Rim.'

'I'll take a double, thanks.'

'So polite,' I teased.

Maddock laughed. 'You're not the first to call me out on that today. I'm starting to think the ladies round here prefer their men rough around the edges.'

'Keeps things interesting.' I winked. 'Cash up front, hot stuff. Standard policy.'

He wasn't entirely comfortable with my flirting, I could tell. He hid it well, but I was good at noticing these things: the subtle shift of weight, the slight grimace that scrunched his nose. This one was going to be a tough nut to crack.

But I was game for a challenge. I got to everyone eventually.

'That's alright.' Maddock pulled a wallet out of his pocket. Even before he opened it, I could see it was stuffed with cash. 'How much for dinner and a drink?'

'Three NP for the drink, seven for food. Tonight is chicken burgers or veggie stew.' I rested my elbows on the bar, leaning forwards so he had an unobstructed view down my top. 'Water's free, if you want. We filter it.'

'I'll have the burger, thanks.' Keeping his eyes on my face, he held out a twenty. 'Keep the change.'

Rich and free with money. I took it before he could realise what a stupidly large tip that was, exchanging a glance with Anna. She widened her eyes and waggled her brows at me as she recapped the bottle of whiskey.

'Have a seat. I'll bring you your water.' I made a show of sliding the money into my top. He shuffled back a step, averting his gaze.

'Thanks.'

Anna and I watched him flee with shared looks of amusement. 'Don't scare him off,' she chided.

'I promise I'll be good.'

Anna rolled her eyes. 'You're never good.'

'Flirting gets good tips.' I shrugged.

Maddock had found a table on the far side of the bar from the window, under the tarnished antique mirror. Well, Tom called it antique, but by the strict definition, everything in our dilapidated town was antique, so the mirror was hardly special. Antique was a nice way of saying old, grotty, and essentially useless. The mirror certainly didn't do any reflecting.

I set a water jug on my tray, and Anna added a tumbler of whiskey. 'I'll call in the dinner order.'

'Okay.'

I made my way across the room to set my tray down on Maddock's table. Cocking my hip, I flipped over the water glass and filled it from the jug. 'So, what brings you to town, James Maddock?'

'Just business.' His voice was friendly. He rolled up the cuffs of his sleeves, exposing his strong, corded forearms. He wasn't as soft as his clothing implied; he had the lean muscles of a dancer—or a fighter. And no tattoos, at least not that I could see. Tattoos were a whole language of their own around here—without a mark to go by, I had to rely on my wits to figure him out.

'Business?' I set the whiskey in front of him and laid out cutlery. 'What sort of business are you in?'

Maddock smiled sheepishly. 'It's not very interesting, I'm afraid. Wholesale trading for the construction industry.'

'Construction?' I raised an eyebrow. We had a couple of new developments—the mayor's attempts at cleaning up the city—but mostly around here everything was make-do-and-mend: clothes, houses, medical care...

'Real estate and commercial.' He studied my face, his grey-green eyes intent.

'Are you working with the Godfreys, then? They're building a new dev in the southeast, right?'

'That's the one.' He leaned forward, his shirt gaping open to show the start of a scar at the base of his neck. 'Why all the questions?'

'Just curious. We don't get many new people round here.'

'It's a hotel.'

'In town.' I lifted my tray. 'In case you hadn't noticed, we're sort of the end of the line.'

'Maybe you need to build a new line.'

I laughed. 'Maybe you can sell the Godfreys that idea. See you later, new boy.'

'It's Maddock,' he called after me as I sashayed away. Halfway across the room, I looked back. He wasn't staring at my butt. *Hmm.*

Maddock remained the biggest topic of gossip in town over the next few days. I saw him again on Tuesday when he wandered into the bar around dinner time.

'Ooh, look, the new boy's back.' Anna twirled a strand of hair around her finger. 'Susie thinks he's going to stay.'

'They never stay.' I shifted the jug onto my tray. Condensation ran off it in little rivulets. We were in the dog days of summer, which always seemed endless—until they ran out suddenly. 'The city always draws them back.'

'I didn't think he was from the city,' Anna said sceptically. 'I guess he's got the manners of a posh boy, though.'

I was spared having to reply when Maddock reached the counter. 'Evening, ladies.'

'Good evening,' Anna called flirtatiously.

'Maddock,' I greeted. 'How's business?'

'Business is wonderful. At least, Mr Cornelius is pleased.' When he smiled, he looked younger, as though some heavy weight had slid off his shoulders. 'Could I get a whiskey?'

'Sure. Have a seat; I'll bring it to the table.'

He left a twenty on the counter again and headed for the same table as last time. He sat with his back to the wall. I watched him as Anna prepped his drink. 'He looks like a city boy to me.'

'Susie overheard him saying he was from Brackfields.'

Brackfields was an industrial area, hours away, and a pretty dangerous drive. You had to cross the territories of three different gangs. I cast a glance at our new boy, with his suit and his kind manners. 'I doubt it.'

'He's nice, anyway. And a bit of mystery is fun, don't you think?' Anna topped his whiskey off. She'd poured a bit too much. 'He likes *you*. He asked after you yesterday.'

Uh oh. That was the last thing I needed.

'Maybe just because he doesn't know anyone else in town.' I shrugged. 'City boys are always bad news.'

'You're so jaded.' Anna waved me off. 'Go flirt.'

Rolling my eyes, I picked up the tray and made my way to Maddock's table.

'How're you finding town?'

He leant back in his seat. He'd thrown off his jacket and rolled up his sleeves. It was another humid day; we were all suffering from the sticky heat.

'Not bad. People have been welcoming.'

'Oh, we're good at welcoming strangers.' Or rather, their money. Bale Rocks wasn't a wealthy town by any stretch of imagination. 'That's us, excellent hospitality.'

'Either that, or you're all bored and hoping I'll provide new gossip material.' A smile played about his lips. I smirked.

'That goes without saying.'

Maddock laughed. 'Well, this town isn't alone in that, I can assure you.'

'You travel a lot?'

Between the gangs that blockaded the roads and the slavers who picked up anyone who strayed too far from the town limits, the roads were pretty dangerous. These days, to travel, you needed one of three things: a good car, a good security detail, or a good gun. Preferably, all three. And luck, not that there was much of that left in the world. We hadn't had much in the way of luck at all since the meteorites had hit centuries ago.

'On and off. Someone has to sell things, and I happen to be good at it.'

'I bet.' I picked up my tray again. 'Will you be having dinner?'

'Yes, the meat option, please.'

'Alright, I'll be back in a few.' I stepped away.

'Before you go, can I ask you something?' Maddock's tone was guarded.

I turned back, curling my fingers around the edge of my tray. 'Depends on what sort of question it is.'

He looked me up and down, slow, searching, but not sexual. I knew sexual looks. I was wearing shorts so tiny they were hidden behind my apron and a top that swooped low, baring my cleavage. I didn't have much in the way of curves, but I knew how to direct a man's eye. This was not a sexual look.

'It pays to listen to gossip when you're new in town,' he remarked.

'I'm sure. Great way to get the lie of the land.'

'Exactly. And I've heard a few whispers, for example, that one of the waitresses at the Kranikovska used to be a dancer in a very specific club.'

My spine stiffened. It took every ounce of focus I had not to react to that. Someone had been telling tales, and if I found out who, I would flay them. 'I'm sure I don't know what you're talking about, Mr Maddock.'

'Of course not.' He knew. Somehow, he knew it was me. Someone had given him my name. 'But if you did know who it was… and I were to ask that person… say, if I were interested in fighting someone…'

Interesting.

There weren't many reasons people came out to our neck of the woods. Business was one reason—not that there was much in the way of business out here. The alcohol trade was the other. And the last was the fights. Those drew the most people, everyone from hardened mercenaries to soft city boys, all hoping to try their luck, and maybe win big, in the cage.

Except I hadn't pegged Mr James Maddock for the sort.

I made my eyes wide and my voice breathy. 'I didn't think businessmen went in for fighting.'

'Everyone has a bit of a warrior in them these days, don't you think?' Maddock's eyes never left my face. 'There's no other way to survive.'

Especially out here. We were a long way from the cities. 'True,' I murmured.

'So,' Maddock prompted, 'if I were to ask how one goes about buying into the fights… and you happened to have overheard the right sort of gossip, what would you tell me?' He slid a twenty across the table and tucked it into my apron pocket.

I bit my lip and fiddled with my hair whilst I thought. He wasn't the first person I'd given directions, but this felt different. He wasn't asking the same questions. Somehow, in a few short days, he'd found out that I not only knew how to get access to the fights, but that my last job had been in Sayle's bunker, the exclusive cage fighting club run by the Iron Fists.

The thought didn't sit well. I'd put those days behind me. It had been eighteen long, blissful months, and I didn't need the past rearing its ugly head now.

'If you were to ask,' I said tentatively, 'and you happened to find someone in the know, that someone would most likely direct you to a pub on Busker Street.'

'Busker Street?' His eyes glinted hungrily.

'That's right. The Arsonist. If the right person were to pay the right fee, they might be able to persuade the bartender there to let them buy in.'

Maddock's leant in eagerly. 'And if I were to buy in, what would I be required to do?'

We'd dispensed with any pretence. It was obvious that I knew what I was talking about—as obvious as it was that he wanted into the cage fights.

'Fight, of course.' I ran my finger over the edge of my tray. 'Don't expect it to be easy.'

'And if I win at The Arsonist?'

'It's not about winning, Mr Maddock.' I leant in. 'It's about impressing the right people.'

'Ah. And the right people may—if I'm lucky—be watching at The Arsonist?'

The right people were watching right now. Always watching. Always listening. But they wouldn't take action until Maddock gave them what they wanted: proof, either way. That he was an asset... or a threat.

'I wouldn't count on luck. Luck's never your friend out here.' I squeezed his shoulders, letting my fingers linger. 'Go tomorrow.'

He met my gaze head-on. 'On a Wednesday?'

'You get one tip. Seeing as you paid for it. That's it. Go midweek.

It'll be quieter, easier to get a slot. Play smart, not hard. One fight only.'

'I'm not here to play games,' he said flatly.

'But it is a game, Maddock. If you don't play, how can you win?'

Heavy footfall echoed on the tile floor of the lobby, a second before a group of men entered the bar, all dressed in black fatigues, young, fit, and built like fighters.

Sayle's enforcers, the men tasked by the local gang with keeping order on the streets.

I stepped away from Maddock's table. 'I'll order your dinner. Have a good evening, Mr Maddock.'

I felt his sharp gaze on my back as I moved behind the bar. Across the room by the window, the four men pulled out chairs, the legs scraping the floor, and sat down with loud chatter and boisterous laughter. It was an act, a deliberate game to fill the room, so no one could ignore them.

Everything was a game in this town. The faster you learnt the rules, the greater your chances of survival.

I straightened my apron.

'I wish they wouldn't come here,' Anna whispered anxiously.

'You know it's for show,' I mumbled out of the corner of my mouth. All the gangs in town loved to make public appearances—that way the common folk couldn't forget who was boss. The Kranikovska was considered neutral territory, so we often saw members of all the local gangs, either using our bar to conduct their illicit business, or else trying to throw their weight around and intimidate their rivals.

'Will you be okay?'

'Of course. I can handle them.' I tossed her a smile before leaving the sanctuary of the bar and crossing the floor.

Technically, we had three gangs: Moriarty's Black Hands, Percival's Aces, and Sayle's Iron Fists. But it was Sayle who had swept into town, gunned down the corrupt law enforcement, and taken over. It was Sayle who'd turned the town around and brought order to our streets. And it was Sayle who ruled with an iron fist.

I reached the table. 'Evening, boys.'

'Harley, baby,' Briggs purred. Of all of Sayle's enforcers, he was my least favourite. Handsome, but a pig. He ran a hand the size of a dinner plate up the back of my thigh, squeezing my bum. I leant away from the touch.

'Always so hands-on, Briggsy.'

'You need a firm hand, love.'

I giggled and pouted at him. 'I'm not so bad.'

'Oh, you're the baddest of bad.' Marco Ellery leant in across the table. 'Naughty, naughty kitten.'

Ellery was the only one allowed to call me kitten; he was the golden boy of Sayle's men—both my favourite, and the one I feared the most. Ellery was dangerous; not just because I'd seen him shoot a man point blank with a smile on his face, but because he was fun. He flirted and complimented. He was kind. He drew you in like a moth to a flame—and then he stabbed you in the back.

I blew him a kiss. 'Always bad for you.'

Ellery laughed, tousling his blond hair with a hand. He was broad-shouldered, not too tall, and had the build of a farmer: strong muscles earned from hard work. I'd known him for years, and I liked him more than I should have, though I'd never admit it to anyone. That was the sort of vulnerability I preferred to keep to myself.

'Quiet today, isn't it?'

'Mm, it's been nice.' I lowered my lashes, offering him a coy smile. 'Hope you boys aren't going to ruin it.'

'Aw, we'd never make trouble for you, kitty cat.' His suntanned skin crinkled as he flashed me a grin.

'I don't believe that for a second.' I turned my smile on Kade, the third man at the table. He was one of the youngest of Sayle's enforcers at around nineteen, a tall, lean black man. Fast, too. I'd seen him run. He ran a hand over his shaved head, the tattoos on his arms catching the light: a mermaid that was highlighted green and gold on one arm, and a lion on the other. He offered me a polite smile.

'Evening, Miss Harley.'

'Hello, Kade.' I liked Kade, even though I didn't know him well. He hadn't yet developed the cocky swagger the others had spent years honing.

The last man at the table was unfamiliar. Chestnut hair, olive skin, and eyes so green they looked like flecks of bottle glass. I'd never seen him before, which was interesting because I'd thought I knew all of Sayle's men.

Two new boys in my bar in the space of a week? That had to be an omen.

'Who might you be?' I ran a finger playfully up his bicep and bit my lip. His arm felt like steel.

He caught my hand and steered it back to my tray, squeezing hard enough that I knew it was a warning. I wrapped my fingers around the edge of the tray, and he let go.

'Bas.'

'Not interested in playing?' I fluttered my eyelashes at him.

'No.' His gaze was unwavering and totally devoid of humour. 'Flirt with someone else, *kitten*.'

'Harley.'

His mouth twisted angrily. 'I don't care.'

Most women would have taken a hint, but it had always been my weakness: whenever someone pushed, I couldn't resist pushing back. I rested my boot on the edge of his seat, watching as he tensed.

'Aw, but I'm super fun. Ask anyone.'

'If I wanted a whore, I'd pick one up outside.'

I dropped my foot back to the floor. 'I'm not a whore.'

'Then don't act like one,' he sneered.

Wow, okay, ouch. This guy really didn't like me. That was new. I wasn't bragging when I said I was popular with the boys.

'What can I get you, then?'

'We'll have whiskeys for the table. And privacy,' Bas said stonily.

Dismissed. *Wow.* Very, very rarely did I have customers who weren't good for a little flirting. It was considered part of the service.

As I stepped away, Briggs ran his hand up my leg and pulled me back onto his lap. I fell back with a gasp.

'Briggsy!'

'Don't worry, pet. The rest of us still enjoy your company.'

'Aww, that's so sweet.' I dragged a finger down his thigh, hard muscle under rough cotton. 'But don't enjoy it too much, yeah, baby? Or I won't be able to get your drinks.'

The boys laughed—except Bas. He looked as unamused as if he were watching an execution.

'Get your head out of the gutter, Duncan,' he snapped.

'Chill out, man.' Briggs pressed a damp kiss to my temple. 'It's just a bit of fun. Harley's one of the sweetest dancers we ever had at the bunker. She does this thing… Show him, baby.'

He made a crude gesture at Bas's lap. I gritted my teeth.

I really didn't feel like showing off dance moves—but it had nothing to do with Bas, and everything to do with Briggs. Briggs had given me plenty of reason to hate him in the past, though I hid it well. 'Nahhh,' I drawled. 'If he doesn't want to play, I won't force him.'

'Might help with that stick up his arse.' Briggs slid a banknote into my top, before releasing me. 'Alright, baby. Off you go. We gotta talk.'

The men wanted to talk, and off I was sent like a little girl to her bedroom. I stood, glancing at Ellery. He'd been up for flirting earlier. Now, he was watching me silently with a frown on his face. What was going on?

Bas's stare told me I was overstaying my welcome, so I headed back to Anna. It ought to have been a relief to be able to just serve without any demands for social interaction, but instead, it unsettled me. Ellery and the boys were always good for a bit of flirting; most of them liked to cop a feel, as well. Whoever this new guy was, he was upsetting the order of things.

I didn't like people who didn't play along.

'I don't know how you face them so calmly,' Anna muttered as I slipped behind the bar again.

'They're just men.'

'Rapists and murderers.'

'Not so different from every other man, then.'

'Not all of them.' Anna's eyes rested on Maddock. He was watching Sayle's men with, in my opinion, too sharp a gaze. Those were the last people he wanted to make enemies of, and even looking at the wrong person could be dangerous in this town.

'Don't,' I warned. 'You don't know him.'

The most dangerous thing a woman could do was build up a romantic fantasy. Those never worked out. It was the fastest way to get yourself raped and left for dead, killed, or worse, caught by the slavers. Keep smart, and trust no one. That was the way.

'I know.' Anna sighed wistfully. 'Anyway, who's the looker?'

'Bas. And he doesn't play.'

'Rough night for you! So many boys who won't pay extra for you to show off.'

I made a face at her and grabbed the bottle of whiskey we reserved for Sayle's men. Only the best for them.

I was always hyper-alert when Sayle's boys were in. Sometimes they had their jackets off and were in a relaxed, jokey mood, but that was a lie. They were never off-duty. Today, they had dropped the façade. Bas sat stiff and alert, Kade's eyes kept scanning the room, and even Ellery wasn't as laid-back as usual. Something was up.

Things had been quiet in town lately. We were probably overdue trouble.

The night chugged on slowly. Midweeks were always slow. An elderly couple came in, as well as a few rye farmers who supplied the whiskey distillery. There was a lull after dinner was finished. I brought Ellery and the boys another round, then wandered over to Maddock's table to fetch his plate.

'Did you enjoy your meal?'

'I did, thank you.'

'Can I get you anything else?'

'I wouldn't mind another whiskey.' He tilted his head towards Ellery's table. 'You know them?'

I affected a disinterested tone. 'They're enforcers for the Iron Fists. One of the local gangs.'

He raised an eyebrow. 'Wouldn't have thought the hotel would want people like that in the bar.'

'Tom's an equal opportunist. If you're thirsty and you have the money, he'll serve you.' Tom was the owner. I owed a lot to him—he'd given me a chance when not many people would have. Anna was his niece, and I was sure part of the reason why he'd taken a chance on me was because I was the same age as her.

'Except you're the one doing the serving.'

'Well noticed.' I balanced my tray against my hip. 'Maybe I'm an equal opportunist, too.'

'Maybe,' he said neutrally.

Maddock didn't want to play games, either. I frowned. 'Let me get that whiskey for you.'

'Sure.'

I had just delivered his whiskey when Ellery's trouble arrived: Jackson, one of the Iron Fists' lieutenants, accompanied by two guys I recognised peripherally. Jackson was in his forties, with a weathered face and cold eyes. He regarded me dismissively as I approached. Of the other two, one was a grizzled man who reminded me of a bear, and the other a redhead who was around my age.

'Evening, gents. What can I get for you?'

'Ales for me,' Jackson said. 'Gentlemen?'

'Ale is fine,' the boy said.

I reached over the table, turning over their water glasses so I could pour. The bear leant in and groped at my arse, almost making me spill the water.

'How much for your company?'

'I don't offer sexual services.' I straightened up and pasted on a smile. Before I could turn, the bear grabbed me, dragging my back against his chest and sending the jug crashing to the floor.

'Aw, come on baby, don't be shy.' He pawed at my chest. 'We'll make it worth your while.'

I tensed, biting my cheek against a wave of revulsion. 'My job is to serve drinks.'

He put his face close to mine, his rancid breath wafting over my ear and cheek. 'Dressed like that, I don't know who you think you're fooling.'

Behind the bar, Anna met my eyes and flicked her head upwards. *Do you want me to get Tom?*

I shook my head slightly, reaching into the folds of my apron. No one could handle this for me. I had to be the one to fight my battles.

'Unhand the lady.'

For fuck's sake. My captor turned us, affording me a view of Maddock. He looked ridiculous in his suit—not at all capable of fighting off several men who were quite likely to be armed. I suspected he'd try, though. Damn him and his stupid manners. Meeting his gaze, I lifted my hand, showing him the handle of the sturdy hunting knife hidden beneath my apron. His eyes widened in surprise.

'Please let go of me,' I said calmly.

The bear laughed. 'You know who I am, girlie? Or Jackson, there? We can get you in trouble with people straight out of your nightmares—'

I slammed my foot down on his, then jerked my head back, whacking his chin. He yelped, his grip loosening.

'You little bitch!'

I jerked away from him and spun around so I could see him. He was reaching for a weapon inside his jacket, but before he got close, he froze. Bas stood behind him, a gun held to his head. So much for being a gun-free bar.

'The fuck, man?' The bear's voice had gone high and shrill.

'This is a bar, not a brothel,' Bas said coolly.

'It's all good, man. I'm just here to do my business.' The bear eased his hands away from his jacket, holding them loosely in front of him. I kept a close eye on them. They were still awfully near his jacket and whatever weapon he had concealed there.

'Then sit down and do your business.' Bas gestured towards the empty chair with his gun.

Slowly, the bear shifted his weight and slid into his seat. He kept his hands above the table. 'No harm done, see?'

Bas's expression remained ominously blank. He tucked his gun back into the holster at his hip. 'As you were, then.'

Without sparing me a glance, he sat once more. I pursed my lips. After two deep breaths, I smoothed down my apron and picked up my tray. 'Let me get a towel to clean up this mess.'

My shift wound down around ten, when Brenda got in. Brenda was fifteen years older than me, a mother of two, and all-round fierce. She kept the bar in line a lot better than I did.

'Any trouble?' she asked as I untied my apron.

'Nothing out of the norm.' Anna shot me a pointed look from the other end of the bar, though fortunately, she made no attempt to refute my words. 'Bit of gang argy-bargy. You know how it is.'

'The boys get restless in the summer.' Brenda rolled her eyes, surveying the room. Maddock had left, asking me if I needed a lift home on the way out. I'd waved him off. Jackson and his lot had moved off, too, to my relief. Ellery was still there—Briggs was so deep in his cups that one of them was going to have to carry him home.

'Who was checking weapons on the front door when you came in?' I asked.

'Benny's on tonight. Why?'

That explained it. Benny was so crooked, it wasn't even funny. 'Reckon someone slipped him cash to turn a blind eye.'

Brenda pursed her lips. 'Thanks for the warning. Is that a new boy with Sayle's lot?'

'Bas.' I shrugged. 'He's hard. Maybe you can crack him. See you tomorrow night?'

'Always, darling.'

I slipped past the kitchen and emerged into the sticky night air.

Music drifted out of the bar, filling the square. A few girls were lurking along the line of crumbling buildings, some of them smoking to pass the time, and a couple of taxi-trucks idled to one side, waiting for passengers. Krani's had one of the best spots in town, overlooking the square—but in some ways, it was also one of the worst spots. Everyone in town came through there eventually, both the honourable and the troublemakers.

I lived a twenty-minute walk east, but I took a detour. It was never wise to walk through the open streets at night—and I had an errand to run.

I'd delayed a few nights, which was excusable, but now Ellery had been into Krani's and seen Maddock for himself, and that meant that I had to do my job. I slipped down the side streets, weaving through the shadows and taking a circuitous route to make sure I wasn't followed to the drop point. There, I slid a scrap of paper out of the pocket of my heavy coat. I'd scribbled on it:

New boy wants into the fights. Sent him to TA. H.

I'd bought my freedom over a year ago. I supported myself. But there was a fine line between a waitress and a whore these days, and if I wanted to stay above that line, I had to play Ellery's game. That was the price of freedom.

He'd got me my job, and in exchange I passed him information about what happened in the bar. That was how the gangs kept their power. Even the freest people in this town were owned.

I tucked the paper into the old mailbox and headed for home.

TWO

TWO STREETS OVER FROM the drop point, I noticed someone following me.

My boots slapped the broken cobblestones, almost, but not quite, covering the echo that bounced off the close-packed old buildings. I turned my head to look, fighting a wave of panic that threatened to close my throat up.

There. A dark shadow against the even darker buildings.

It was every woman's nightmare to be followed walking alone at night. Best case scenario, you survived the encounter. Worst case—well, no one would help if they heard me screaming. No one ever did. You walked on by and pretended you hadn't noticed.

Especially if the perpetrator was a gang member.

I wanted to run—but I knew better than that. It would only make things worse. My breath came in short sharp bursts, but I kept my pace even as I slid my hand into my jacket and found my hunting knife.

I was more than just a pretty face.

It was a nice knife, a solid, reassuring weight, expensive and well-made, with a blade about four inches long. It also wasn't mine. I'd slipped it out of Ellery's belt one day after my old one had been nicked by a beggar. I considered it the price for flirting with him: I played his game, and in return, he didn't ask for the knife back.

Good thing, because I couldn't afford anything half so nice.

I gripped the handle and forced myself to breathe slow and easy. This had happened before. I could deal with it. I always dealt with it.

I turned abruptly down a side street, slipping into a boarded-up doorway. The shadows slid over me like an old friend. I held my breath. *Please, let him pass me by without noticing me.*

But this man was no amateur. He moved almost silently from shadow to shadow, like he was part of the night. Not a homeless guy looking to steal my tip money.

He paused in the entrance to the alleyway.

My breath was frozen in my chest, my palm sweaty against the knife.

Move on. Please. I'm not worth it.

I pressed my back into the door, my heart racing.

The man approached.

The first time my father had given me a knife, he'd told me, *it's better to have it and never use it, than not have it and need it. But Harley, remember the most important thing: If you draw it, you must be willing to use it.*

I was willing. There weren't many people in this town I wouldn't fight to the death for the right to survive.

I closed my eyes, took one deep breath, and opened them again. Then I pounced.

We slammed together against the opposite wall, and for several glorious seconds he was off balance and I had the upper hand. Then he got his hand around my wrist, driving my aim off, and threw me against the wall. My head thudded against the bricks, and he managed to yank my arms behind my back and press my chest to the wall.

'Naughty kitten.' His breath was warm against my ear. 'You could have hurt someone.'

Ellery.

For several moments, I couldn't speak. My breath came in fast, harsh pants, and my heart pounded so hard I thought it might jump right out of my chest. The rough bricks scraped my cheek. Finally, I managed to relax, making my body soft in his arms. He released my wrists, sliding his hand over mine so we were both gripping the knife.

'Threatening me with a knife? Bad, bad girl.'

'Following me at night?' I croaked, my voice a far cry from the seductive whisper I'd been aiming for. 'Anyone would think you had impure intentions.'

'Oh, my intentions are wholly impure.' He held me bodily against the wall, bringing my hand up until the knife pressed under my chin. 'Someone's been very naughty.'

I could feel his hips against the small of my back, the hard bulge of his cock. He was getting off on this.

I leant into him. 'You like it when I'm naughty.'

Ellery laughed. His lips were right by my ear, his breath touching my cheek. I shivered.

'Put the knife away, kitten,' he purred, nipping my ear. Against my will, I felt hot. He released my hands, and I slid the knife back into my belt before turning around against him so we were front to front.

'Why were you following me?' I trailed a finger down his chest, keeping my gaze on his collar.

He slid his hands beneath my coat and cupped my hips. 'Shouldn't be walking alone at night, kitten. You never know who might be lurking in the shadows.'

'Then maybe I was right to threaten you.' I lifted my other hand, locking my fingers through his belt loops. He responded immediately, pressing closer, his erection a heavy pressure against my left hip.

I felt warm all over. This was why Ellery was dangerous. This, right here, right now. He engulfed me in his arms, his lips against my hair.

'Come back to the bunker, kitten. We miss you.'

'No thanks.' I worked his vest free of his trousers, my fingers touching smooth skin, taut over strong muscles. Ellery tensed against me. He lifted one hand to my chin, cupping it, tipping my head backwards so I was looking up at him: a statue in the moonlight.

'I'd make it worth your while.'

He was going to kiss me, and I couldn't allow that. If he did, I might break. But I'd found what I wanted. I withdrew my hands, taking one of his knives with me, and pressed it sideways against his abdomen.

'No. I'm not playing, Ellery. I'll never go to that place with *you*.'

'Aww.' Ellery laughed. 'Sheathe your claws, kitten. I don't mean any harm. I'm just playing.'

'Playing with knives?' I pulled my hands back under my coat, shifting his knife into my belt. A moment later, he backed off, taking his warmth and his erection with him. A part of me missed him, but I suppressed it ruthlessly. The sticky night felt cold all of a sudden. 'Why were you following me?'

'I had to make sure of your loyalties.' Ellery stepped back further. The heat of the moment vanished, his posture changing with it. Time to do business. 'You delayed.'

'I wasn't sure until tonight.'

'You're supposed to notify us straight away, kitten. Not after we come to the bar to see for ourselves. Sayle's already heard the rumours there's a new boy in town. You want him to wonder why his girl kept mum?'

'I'm not his girl.' I was free. It paid to remind them of that, sometimes. 'Does Sayle want me to drop a note in the box for every Tom, Dick, and Harry who wanders through the bar?'

'You know it's not like that.'

'I wasn't sure,' I insisted. 'Not until he asked about the fights.'

Ellery searched my gaze. He'd fuck me if I let him, but he'd still kill me if he thought I was disloyal. I knew better than to trust one of Sayle's men; they were all murderers. I met his gaze determinedly.

'Be quicker next time,' Ellery said. 'I like you. I don't want you getting in trouble, Harley.'

Harley. My name sounded like honey on his lips.

'Was starting to think you didn't know my name.'

A bitter smile crossed his face. 'Oh, baby, we all know your name.' He cupped my chin, pressing the pad of his thumb against my bottom lip. 'Be careful.'

'I'm always careful.' Daringly, I nipped his finger with my teeth. Darkness filled his eyes. I was pushing a boundary I knew I shouldn't. I drew back.

'Who's your new teammate? Never seen him before.'

'Bas. Stay away from him,' Ellery said shortly.

'He's one of you.'

'It doesn't matter. Stay away from him.' His gaze was sharp. 'You know not all of us are good news.'

'None of you are good news,' I corrected.

Ellery smiled. 'Go to bed, kitten. It's late. You need your beauty sleep.'

'You need it more than me.'

Ellery's composure cracked; he laughed long and low. 'Go. I'll be right behind you.'

It made me uneasy, having Ellery shadowing me. No one would make trouble with me if they saw him; no one picked fights with Sayle's men unless they wanted a bullet in the head. But I didn't want people to think I was with him. I wasn't a member of the gang, nor was I one of their whores. I didn't want anyone to get the wrong idea. Ellery wouldn't be around to protect me tomorrow. Nor the day after.

But we saw no one on the walk to my flat. In the doorway of my building, I glanced back. Ellery was little more than a dark shadow in the doorway opposite. There were no streetlights—we were lucky if we had electricity in this town. My flat did, most days, but I tried not to rely on it. It was expensive, and besides, if you got used to it, it made it harder when you lost it.

Recklessly, I waved to him. He didn't even shift, but he also didn't leave. He was still there when I peered out of the first-floor window in the stairwell.

My flat was on the top floor, tucked under the rafters in the attic. When I opened the door, the flat was dark, and the bedroom door closed. I navigated by moonlight and memory, pulling food out of the fridge. Savannah would long since be asleep. Occasionally, she left food out for me, but most days she came home exhausted from working at the clinic, picked up a honey roll on the way, and fell into bed the second she got through the door. That was okay. She did much more important work than I did.

Would Maddock go to The Arsonist? I wondered as I changed for bed. It was a silly question. Everyone tried their luck. I'd seen streams of men passing through, all hoping for a go. The Arsonist wasn't the goal; it was just a stepping-stone. If you did well at The Arsonist, you got noticed. If you got noticed, you might get invited to the bunker. The cage fights in the bunker were run by Sayle, but all the gangs went there to fight, do business, pick up whores… it was the centre of Sayle's empire, and a critical source of money for our town, what with the betting that went on, and the people who came here for the fight nights.

I wasn't naïve. Maddock was like all the others—he wanted into the bunker. But he'd been more subtle than some of the others. Subtle was dangerous. He'd taken his time to figure out the lay of the land. And he'd said he was here on business. Did that mean the cage-fighting was a hobby? Or did it tie into his reason for coming here? Or was he here to fight, and the business was an excuse?

I suspected he'd make it. He might act like mister nice guy, but he had a lithe, compact body, strong muscles, and a hardness to his gaze.

I didn't see Maddock at dinner the next night, and I would have bet money—if I had any to bet—that he'd gone to The Arsonist.

I kept my eyes and ears to the ground. Ellery and the boys thought I was just a pretty face, good for a few tipoffs and nothing else, but I wasn't stupid. I was pretty sure that the men Jackson had been entertaining were from one of the rival gangs. Something was brewing.

I saw the redhead who'd been with Jackson the other night chatting up a hooker on the square on my way to work on Thursday, but I gave him a healthy berth. I knew better than to get dragged into whatever was stirring.

My interest was strictly to do with avoiding trouble.

Maddock was back that evening, ordering his usual drink, sitting in his normal spot. Thursday evenings were always buzzing in the bar—more and more people came in towards the end of the week, desperate to drown their sorrows—but there was a lull after dinner ended and before the evening drinkers arrived. I made my way over to his table to refill his water glass.

'We missed you last night, Mr Maddock.'

Maddock laughed. 'Did you? I didn't realise my presence was that sought after.'

'Well,' I said breathily, 'who else are we going to gossip about?'

He chuckled again. 'Who indeed?'

I flicked my gaze around the room. All the tables nearby were empty, leaving us with a little bubble of privacy. Leaning in, I asked, 'How did your errand go?'

He quirked an eyebrow. 'Who said I was running an errand?'

'I can't think why else you'd miss the joys of our company.' I rested my hip against his table, smiling mischievously. 'Or did Mr Cornelius keep you late? So much buying and selling to do in our little backwater town.' I pouted.

Maddock laughed again. 'Alright, you got me. You like to play games, don't you, Miss Harley?'

'I don't know what you're talking about, Mr Maddock.'

'Oh, I think you do. I think you like buttering all the men up with your silver tongue. I'll bet they queue up to tell you all sorts of tales.'

'Oh no, I think you've got the wrong girl.' I twirled a lock of hair around my finger. 'I'm just a waitress, Mr Maddock.'

His smile said he wasn't fooled, but then, I wasn't trying to fool him. It was all part of the game. The rules shifted constantly, but the end goal remained the same. Trust me. Tell me your secrets. Let me control you.

When I'd started dancing in the bunker, over seven years ago now, one of the older dancers had taken me under her wing. One piece of advice had stuck with me to this day:

The best way to control a man is to become his fantasy. Figure out what he wants and give it to him. If you control his fantasy, you control him.

Words to live by.

Ellery and his boys were easy. They wanted a pretty face, a flirt, a bit of fun to pass the time. It was a small price to pay for the privilege of living and working in relative safety. Maddock was harder. I didn't know what he wanted yet.

But I'd figure it out.

'So?' I touched a finger to my lips, smiling against it. 'Did you go to The Arsonist? You can tell me… I can keep a secret.'

'I'll bet you can.' Maddock propped his muscular forearms on the table. He'd rolled his sleeves up against the heat again, and I could make out a few distinctively placed bruises. He'd got them blocking punches. 'Until someone pays the right price.'

'My services can't be bought.' I feigned offence. 'I'm a free woman.'

'Is that how it is? Tell me, how can one be free and have worked for a gang? From what I've heard, it's not possible.'

I resisted the urge to roll my eyes. *Nice try.* 'By not working for them in the first place?'

Maddock chuckled. He picked his whiskey up, swishing the glass so that the amber liquid caught the light. 'Yet you went from dancer to waitress. Is that a promotion?'

'I couldn't say.' I didn't like this conversation one bit. Figuring Maddock out was harder than I expected; he kept wrongfooting me.

'Can't think that your daddy likes you working here too much.'

'Can't think that he cares.' My voice was prim. 'Seeing as he's dead.'

Maddock raised an eyebrow. I cringed. I'd given away more than I wanted to there. 'I'm sorry. Your mother?'

'Also.' I shifted my weight and affected a heavy tone. 'The sickness got her when I was nine. Daddy was shot—wrong place, wrong time. I was seventeen.'

His brow creased. 'Now you're on your own?'

There it was: pity. Flirtation wasn't the only tool in my arsenal. I ran a finger up his forearm. 'Now it's your turn. These bruises didn't make themselves, new boy.'

He glanced at his arms. 'Ahhh, you got me. Fine. I may have fought a round or two at The Arsonist last night. Just to test the waters.'

'Of course you did.' I offered him a confident smile. 'Tell me you won. I'd hate to think I took a chance on a loser.'

'That'd be telling.' He rolled his shoulders. 'I've been invited back on Friday, so they must like me.'

'Wow, you are special.' I grinned. 'Gonna be a hard week, fighting twice. You'll need someone to take care of you.'

'I'm good at taking care of myself.' He took a sip of his whiskey. 'Could do with medical supplies, though. You don't happen to know a place where I could buy?'

Good luck. Medical supplies were a luxury around here.

'That's a tall ask, new boy.' I watched his frown. 'But… I might know someone who could help you. There's a clinic on the north side of town. A lovely lady by the name of Savannah works there. She's good at cleaning people up.' I winked. 'You'll know her when you see her.'

'Oh, really?' Maddock quirked an eyebrow.

'Just trust me.'

'How mysterious,' he responded with a grin.

'You look like a man who likes a good mystery.' I straightened up. 'Enjoy your evening, Mr Maddock.'

'You too, Miss Harley.'

His tone gave me hope. I may not have cracked his shell yet, but he was playing the game. I just had to make sure he didn't play me.

The weekend passed in a blur. Weekends were always terribly busy. For a town as poor as ours, I was always surprised how many people were willing to scrape together the cash for a drink. I certainly wasn't—and I didn't think my wage was lower than a market worker's. Maybe my priorities were just wrong.

Maddock reappeared on Sunday, and now there was no hiding he'd been in the fights. For once, he was without the suit, wearing jeans and a plaid shirt that highlighted the clean lines of his features—and the black eye. He smiled when he saw me.

'You are naughty, Harley. You never told me you had a twin.'

'I'm full of mysteries.' I tossed my ponytail over my shoulder. 'Did she fix you up good?'

'Oh, she has magic hands.' Maddock grinned. 'You two are very different. You didn't think of going into medicine?'

'Savannah is the clever one, not me.'

'I wouldn't be too sure about that.' He slid a note onto the table. 'The usual? Are there chips? The chips here are phenomenal.'

'Careful, or we'll convert you.'

'It's a slippery slope. First, you get me hooked on the chips, next thing I know, it's been six months and I just never left.'

We both laughed. Anna slipped in from the backroom. 'Oh, hi James!'

'Hello, Anna.'

'Whiskey?' she asked, already grabbing the bottle.

'Yes please.'

I gestured to a barstool. 'You could sit here for a change.'

Maddock glanced around the room, his mien suddenly uneasy. The bar was mostly empty; he was early. Give it an hour, and it would be packed.

'For a little while,' he conceded, sliding onto the stool. 'I was meaning to ask you something, anyway.'

'More questions.' I set a glass of water in front of his place. 'You are eternally curious, Mr Maddock.'

'You can call me James, you know.'

'James.' I made his name a sexy little purr, but he didn't even shift. Steely composure, this one. 'Whaddaya wanna know, James?'

'If I were considering staying,' he rested his arms on the counter, 'and were in the market for affordable lodgings, would you know who to speak to?'

Interesting. 'So the chips have converted you?' I winked.

'Oh, absolutely.' He smirked, picking up his whiskey to take a sip.

'Depends on your budget,' Anna said, leaning against the bar beside me.

'Modest. I'm more concerned about security.'

Security was a big deal. Shakedowns were commonplace, burglaries even more so. The best way to get security was to live in a building owned by one of the gangs—but of course, those places came at a steep price. Otherwise, you took care of your own security—or you paid protection money.

'I'd have thought the Godfreys would be willing to look after a potential supplier,' I said coyly. 'Don't tell me you've broken faith with them?'

'Of course not.' He matched my easy tone. 'I prefer not to mix business with my personal life. It creates dependency.'

'Wise words.' I laughed. 'Hard to follow through on, though.'

'I get by.' He jerked his head towards the window. 'The blocks around the square look affordable.'

Sure, if run-down and unlived-in was your thing.

'Oh no, you don't want to live there,' Anna said hurriedly. 'The square is forever getting rousted—and a few months back there was a shootout. The bullets sprayed through the windows.' She shuddered.

'See, that's why I'm asking.' Maddock tilted his head. 'You ladies know where's safe, and where to avoid.'

Anna nodded sagely. 'If you don't want to stay in one of the Godfreys' buildings, there's another new dev up on the hill. I think the mayor owns it.'

Maddock nodded his thanks. 'And in town?'

'Speak to Irina,' I said. Maddock raised an eyebrow. 'She owns half the town. Irina Sorokina. Her office is on Prospect Avenue.'

'Irina Sorokina. Got it.'

'She's my landlady,' I explained.

'How fun. We might end up neighbours.' His expression gave away disturbingly little.

If we did, I'd have confirmation that the Iron Fists were interested in Maddock. Irina worked for Sayle, though below board. If Irina agreed to house you, it meant Sayle had his eye on you.

That was the price you paid.

'Her places are safe.' My tone was weighty. 'But you pay for it.'

'I'll bear that in mind.' Maddock picked up his drink, sliding off the stool. Conversation over.

'We do have hot water though, mostly.'

He chuckled. 'Hot water, mostly. What luxury.'

I watched him walk away, frowning. Maddock was staying. It would have been better if he left—he had bad timing, what with things getting tense again, and he was attracting the wrong sort of attention. I didn't care about him one way or another, but that didn't mean I wanted him dead. And dead was what he'd get if he crossed Sayle.

I'd need to ask Savannah what she thought of him when she saw him at the clinic. As Maddock had said, we were very different. She might have noticed something I'd missed.

THREE

There was something in the air.

A couple of nights had passed peacefully, without any miscreants in the bar. I always relished the quiet nights, where we were busy but there was no trouble. But tonight I'd been on edge all evening, and I didn't know why.

It was a sticky, humid night, the very end of summer. We were all waiting for the heat to break and autumn to roll in. Maybe that was what I felt: that impending moment where summer would shatter. It was like a frisson of tension in the air that built with every passing day.

'No Maddock tonight.' Anna pouted as I slipped behind the bar to offload a tray of empty glasses.

'He's probably fighting again.' I rolled my eyes. Once they started fighting, it was like an addiction.

'You think?' Anna frowned. 'I wish you'd never put him onto the fights. It ruins all the men.'

'I didn't put him on—he asked. And I can't help it if men want to get themselves ruined, Anna.'

'I know.' She sighed gustily. 'Hey, next week—'

The window shattered inwards, a gunshot echoing around the room.

Someone screamed. Half the room was springing to their feet, the other half diving under tables. I jumped to attention, meeting Anna's panicked gaze.

'Get Tom!'

'I can't! He's not in tonight—'

'ANNA! Get Tom!'

She stiffened, then nodded sharply, sprinting for the backroom. Out in the lobby, someone yelped. Heavy boots clattered on the floor. I glanced towards the window, where Ellery and his team were sitting, praying the Iron Fists would get involved—but he met my gaze with a guilty expression on his face and sat back in his chair. No help there.

The doors exploded open, and seven men poured in, all dressed in heavy black combat gear, with balaclavas covering their faces.

'YOU OWE US MONEY!'

One of the guests screamed. A few stood around awkwardly, others were still sitting, but no one dared try to run now.

'WHERE'S THE OWNER?' The leader snatched a glass of whiskey from in front of an elderly gentleman, downed the liquid, then hurled the glass against the wall. It shattered noisily. 'GET THE OWNER!'

'Oi, you can't do that,' the elderly man protested, springing to his feet. 'I paid for—'

One of the intruders grabbed him and threw him bodily aside. Another pulled his gun and shot into the ceiling.

Someone screamed.

'Anyone else want a piece?'

Every instinct in me cried out to run—but I couldn't, or all hell would break loose. The men fanned out around the room, stealing drinks and throwing people out of their seats. One man stayed by the door, his rifle trained on the bar.

Two men scrambled over the bar. The first grabbed a bottle of whiskey, the second shoved me against the counter. 'You, waitress. Where's the owner?'

'My colleague's gone to get him.'

'Really?' He drove me harder into the splintery wood. My abdomen was going to bruise. 'I think you're lying. Call him down.'

'He's not here. She has to fetch him.'

It was impossible to be calm with a gun pointed at you, but I'd learnt to pretend. This wasn't my first rousting. All I had to do was make sure they didn't shoot anyone. Everything else was just material goods.

'Hurry it up. We want our money.'

I swallowed, my mouth dry. 'Let me get you a drink whilst we wait.'

The leader had approached enough that I could make out his face. He had tanned skin that crinkled around his eyes, all that was visible between his balaclava and his hood. He pulled his handgun from the holster on his belt and cocked it at the nearest table. 'All of you, up.'

The men around the table scrambled out of their seats, backing away from the gun. Three of his men sat, including the guy who had held me down, scraping their chairs and almost knocking the table over. The leader remained standing, his gun on me again.

'Pour us drinks.'

'Yes sir.' Luckily, I could serve drinks in my sleep, because my heart was thudding against my ribcage like a bird trying to escape, and my teeth were chattering. My hands were steady, though. I carried my tray over to their table. With every step closer to the loaded gun, my body felt heavier, my throat tighter.

I set the tray down, lined up the glasses, and poured the first one. Somehow, my hand was steady. I managed two before the leader snatched the bottle.

'Give me that.'

He shoved me back. I staggered, my ankle buckling, and then someone's arms went around me, and a gun was right in front of my face, pointing at the rousters.

'That's enough,' Ellery said coolly.

Why the fuck did we even hire someone to check for weapons?

I straightened up, testing my ankle. It held my weight.

'Easy, pretty boy.' The lead rouster lifted the bottle of whiskey, taking a long pull, before tossing it to his mate. 'You wanna start something? She's just some cheap slut.'

'I think we all need to calm down.'

Cute words, considering Ellery had a gun in the guy's face and his Iron Fist tattoo in full view on his right biceps. I stepped hastily away from him, straightening my apron.

'Maybe we could put the guns away. Tom will be here shortly—'

'Maybe you don't understand what's going on here, little girl.' The leader grabbed me, dragging me against his body. He shoved the gun to my head, warm metal against my temple, and every muscle in my body turned to ice. I couldn't move... couldn't think... couldn't breathe. The world faded to a single point, Ellery's wide brown eyes, his hands trembling on his gun.

Fuck, fuck, fuck.

The man's free hand groped over my chest, his touch callous. 'Maybe I should put that mouth of yours to use—'

Tom burst into the room, clapping loudly. 'Gentlemen, gentlemen!'

The tension shattered. The gun vanished from my temple, the leader shoving me towards Ellery. He caught me, his hands tight against my shoulders. Tom strode over, smoothing his brown suit down. He was a round, balding man, with a powerful presence: no one managed to run a hotel in the most prominent spot in town, on the communal territory of three gangs, without having some serious gumption.

Tom weaselled his way between Ellery and the other man, straightened his suit, and said, 'How about we take this upstairs? I'm sure we can find a solution that benefits all of us, without...' He glanced at me, his smile becoming strained. '...involving any of my staff. Shall we?'

'Moriarty won't be happy,' the lead rouster grunted. I tensed. Moriarty's gang, the Black Hands, was the worst one in town. My skin crawled at the thought that he'd touched me.

'I'm certain we can come to an agreement,' Tom insisted.

For one tense moment no one moved, and I thought they were just going to say *fuck it* and start shooting. Some of Sayle's men might well have done that. Fortunately, Ellery was one of the smarter ones. He tucked his gun back into his holster and nodded sharply. Then he set me back on my feet.

'Will you be okay?' Ellery asked.

No.

'It's my job.' I brushed his hands off. 'Go do your job. And play nice, boys.'

They all laughed. The leader of the rousting gestured to his men, and they all filed out. Ellery glanced towards his table, where Bas stood, and nodded sharply. Tom gestured for Ellery to go ahead, and the rest of the Iron Fists followed.

'One free drink for everyone,' Tom muttered to me as he walked out.

I nodded.

By the time I had cleared the glass off the floor, Anna was back at the bar, her skin stretched taut over a worried expression. She clutched my shoulders. 'I sent Benny to fetch Brenda. Are you okay?'

'Fine.' I nudged her away. 'Free drink for everyone. Announce it or something. I'm going to clean up.'

'Alright.' Anna's concerned gaze followed me out the door.

Brenda arrived half an hour later. Anna and I had managed to calm down the room, and I was looking for something to cover the window. Things were a fucking mess—I was just waiting for Tom to get back. We'd get hell—not that it was our fault. It was just the way things were.

'Benny told me there was a rousting.' Brenda had found me half in the store cupboard, rooting through boxes. 'It's been ages since we had one.'

'We were overdue. Have we got a tarp?' I straightened up.

'I'll find it. You go home, love. You look shook.'

'I'm fine. I just…' Words failed me. I took a deep breath, then another. 'Let me help you with the window.'

'I'll get one of the market boys to do it. I saw a few of them hanging out on my way in. May as well put them to work.'

I rolled my eyes. 'We'll have to pay them. Tom won't like it.'

'Fuck Tom. We clean up his messes all the time.'

'Tom won't like that, either.'

'Harley, go home.' Brenda held her arms out, and I stepped into her hug, leaning my head against her shoulder and breathing in her perfume. It reminded me of my mum. 'Go, sleep it off. Take tomorrow off.'

'I can't.' Not if I wanted to make rent this week.

'At least go get some sleep.' Brenda released me, smoothing her hands down my arms. 'You're shaking.'

'I'm fine.' Maybe if I kept repeating it, it would become true. 'Okay, okay. Let me grab my things.'

Brenda shadowed me out to the bar. I shucked my apron and pulled my heavy coat on. It wasn't coat weather, but I always wore it, summer and winter. It discouraged wandering eyes and was another layer of fabric between me and anyone who got handsy. A piece of my armour.

There was a storm brewing when I got outside. I could feel it in the air. It would rain any day now—though our storms sometimes built for days before they broke.

I rounded the side of the hotel to find the square silent and deserted. Even the hookers were gone—most likely the rousting had scared them off. No one stuck around when shots were fired. You never knew if you might become the next target: an unlucky bystander, or worse, killed for seeing the wrong person doing the wrong thing.

Like my daddy had been.

The dead tell no tales and all that.

I kept to the side of the square, prickles running up and down my spine. The adrenaline was making me jumpy. Every shadow seemed to conceal a masked gunman. Every doorway hid a criminal waiting to make me bleed. I almost puked when I heard the roar of a car engine, the clatter of tyres on loose cobblestones.

The car drew level with me and slowed down. I looked—and wished I hadn't. Matte black paint and dark windows. It was a military SUV, the kind that Sayle's men used.

The front passenger window rolled down, revealing Ellery. Bas sat in the driver's seat.

'Hey, kitten.'

I stepped back. 'What do you want?'

Ellery flinched. 'I was hoping to catch you before you left.' His gaze ran up and down me, as though he could see through my coat. I pulled it closer around me. 'Hop in. We'll give you a ride home.'

'I'm fine.'

'Don't be silly. Come on, kitten.'

I wanted to. I wanted bitterly to just climb in, relax, let someone else take care of me for five minutes. I craved it.

But I couldn't.

I knew how Sayle's men worked. Nothing came for free. The price would be small, easy at first. Ellery liked me, and he'd made his intentions obvious. A blowjob in exchange for a lift home, maybe. And the next time, a hand job in exchange for scaring off my lecherous neighbour. A roll in the hay in exchange for making sure Irina didn't put up my rent.

Regular sex in exchange for keeping Savannah safe.

Sex could buy you anything, but it was a slippery slope. Once you started, you never stopped, and before you knew it, you belonged to the gang.

But that protection was as dangerous as it was temporary. I'd lose myself. I'd expose Savannah to the gang. And what happened if Ellery died? The protection didn't carry over. I'd lose everything and be in a worse position than I was in now.

No, it was me or nothing. I looked after myself. I'd been doing it since I was seventeen.

'I can walk home on my own.'

Ellery's expression contorted: irritation, worry, something I didn't want to identify.

'Kitten. Harley. You went through a lot tonight. Let me help you.'

'I go through a lot every night, Ellery.' My voice was cold and brittle. 'I don't need a man to look after me.'

'This once,' he said softly. 'I don't want you to find out the hard way that Moriarty's men are still hanging around town, waiting to make more trouble.'

Moriarty was well-known to be Sayle's number-one enemy. He was particularly hated around town because his gang had made their fortune through trading slaves—the most disgusting practice in our little pocket of civilisation.

'Right,' I drawled sceptically. 'And what are you going to want in return? A handjob? A blowjob? I'm not one of those girls.'

'Nothing.' His gaze was sincere, but I refused to believe him. That wasn't how it worked around here.

'Nothing? Bullshit.'

'Nothing. I see you home safely, we go our separate ways.' His eyes pleaded with me. 'Come on, kitten.'

Suddenly, I was sick of all of it. Kitten this, kitten that, like he already knew I was going to give in to him. Like he knew where this ended: me in his bed, me as his kept woman.

'Harley,' I snapped, my temper bubbling over. 'My name is Harley.'

'Harley.' Ellery's gaze was too intense, too sincere. I had to look away. 'Let us drive you home.'

I was tired. That was my only excuse. 'I'm not sucking your cock. Not now, not next week.'

'I'm not asking for anything in return. I promise.'

A promise from one of Sayle's men was a dangerous and weighty thing. If he meant it. Which he might not. My stomach churned. 'Fine.'

'Hop in, then.'

I hauled the back door open and climbed up behind Ellery. The inside of the car was comfortably messy. A metal case was discarded in the rear footwell, and Ellery's jacket was on the seat next to me. A radio crackled on the dashboard. I shut the door and pressed my back into the seat.

This was a mistake.

Too late now.

'Took you long enough,' Bas muttered.

'Don't,' Ellery said. 'Just drive.'

'Problem?' I asked caustically.

Bas darted an irritated look over his shoulder. 'You could be more grateful for the favour. We're due back at the compound. Marco is making us take a detour for you.'

'Good for you,' I snapped.

'We don't mind,' Ellery said.

Bas made a noise of disbelief. 'Yes, we do.'

'I'm not sucking your cock, either.' I decided then and there that I didn't like Bas at all. His profile was aristocratic in the moonlight, his gaze angry as he twisted around to check behind the car. His shoulders tense. His attitude bad. I hated him.

'I wouldn't let you near it if you paid me.'

'As if I'd pay you for sex.' I made a noise of disgust. 'As if I'd pay *anyone* for sex.'

'As if you've never been paid for sex.'

'Fuck off.' My anger boiled in me like water in a kettle. 'Didn't know Sayle's men came so principled. Shame you apparently forgot those principles whilst Moriarty's lot were smashing up the bar.'

'Were you expecting us to start a war with Moriarty over you, *kitten*?' Bas taunted.

That burnt. 'My name is Harley.'

'No difference between one hooker name and another.'

I snarled under my breath, reaching forwards to prod his shoulder. Ellery grabbed my wrist before I could touch Bas. 'Alright, kitty cat. Let's put those claws away.'

'Harley is my *name*.' I didn't know why I was so upset; this wasn't me usually, but the whole evening had me off-kilter. 'My parents called me that when I was *born*. And it's rich coming from you. What kind of a name is Bas, anyway?'

'My name,' Bas said coolly, turning us onto Prospect Avenue. How did he know where I lived?

'Come on.' Ellery nudged me back into my seat. 'Don't fight, you two. It's been a long night.'

'He insulted my name,' I said sulkily.

'I like your name,' Ellery said. 'It's sexy and spunky. Like you.'

I scowled. 'You're only saying that because you're still hoping I'll crawl up front and suck you off.'

'I mean, I'm not going to lie. I'd love that.' Ellery winked. 'But not tonight.'

I crossed my arms.

'So you are capable of shutting up?' I could hear the smirk in Bas's voice, and it riled me up all over again.

'Piss off. What's your problem, anyway?'

'You are.'

'I never did anything to you.'

'You're just like every other girl, flirting with men to manipulate them. Deep down, all you are is scared—a scared little girl who couldn't deal with the fact that someone had a gun out in her bar.'

I clenched my fists. *Manipulate.* I hated that he put it so plainly. 'Stop the car.'

'And now you're kicking off like a child.'

'Stop the fucking car. I don't need your help, and I certainly don't need you to be a condescending bastard.'

'Big words from a whore.' Bas hit anchors, the car squealing to a halt. We were there, anyway. He'd stopped in front of Irina's building, which was diagonal across from mine.

'I'm not a whore.' I shoved the door open. 'You're just like every other guy. Hiding behind a big ego. You think men don't get scared?'

I jumped down.

'I think we handle it a hell of a lot better.'

'Sure,' I sneered. 'Waving guns around is better. Mind your big head doesn't get stuck going through the gates of Sayle's compound.'

I slammed the door and stalked off, stewing in my own fury. They were all arseholes, the lot of them. Some of them hid it behind nice words like Maddock, others behind flirty smiles like Ellery. But all men were arseholes when you got down to it.

I didn't need any of them. I could look after myself.

The arseholes were still there when I reached the first floor. I peeked out of the window, keeping to the shadows so they wouldn't see me. The truck was idling in front of Irina's office, where I'd left it.

Well, fuck.

FOUR

I WAS BACK EARLY ENOUGH that Savannah was still awake. She was sitting at the table in the poky little kitchenette, and she looked up in alarm when I let myself into our decrepit two-room flat.

'What are you doing back? Your shift isn't over yet.'

'We got rousted.' I dumped my coat on our saggy sofa and stumbled tiredly over to her. 'Tom sent me home.'

'Rousted?' Savannah's eyes went wide. She looked me up and down, searching for damage. 'Are you okay?'

'Fine, nothing bruised but my dignity.' There was a pan of fried vegetables on the stove. I heaped a few spoons onto a plate and collapsed into the seat opposite my sister.

Savannah and I were identical in every way that mattered: same light brown skin, same long, curly brown hair, same hazel eyes. Same height. Same age.

Twins.

Somehow, that lulled people into assuming we'd be exactly the same in personality.

We were not.

Sav was clever and studious, everything that had made our parents proud. I was the opposite. I'd spent my school years with my head in the clouds, dreaming of moving to the city and dancing on the big stage.

Turns out dreams never survive contact with reality.

Instead, it was Sav who'd achieved her dream, training as a doctor. And I… got by. There was no other option. I hadn't finished school, in the end.

I tried not to think about how my parents would feel. I knew they wouldn't be proud, but that was just how things were.

'Was it Moriarty?' Sav asked suddenly. I looked up from my plate.

'That's what I heard. Why?'

'It's the third rousting this month. They hit Doleman's and the clinic.'

'They hit the clinic?' My heart dropped to rest around my ankles. I spent six days a week at the bar, and Savannah and I kept very different hours, but I hadn't realised I was that out of the loop. 'When? Why didn't you tell me?'

'I wasn't there. It was my day off—last week.' She grimaced. 'I didn't want to worry you.'

'You have to tell me this stuff!'

She stared at her plate. 'I am now.'

My stomach churned. I didn't like the idea that Savannah was keeping something this big from me. I hadn't thought our relationship was that strained. 'I should have seen it coming. Things were quiet for ages.'

Savannah fiddled with her fork. I picked at my food—my sister was a terrible cook, but I would never tell her that. Anyway, it was only partly her fault. There were only so many ways to make taproot tasty, and that was more or less all we could afford to eat.

'You should be careful,' Sav said.

'I'm always careful.' I drew a fist into the sauce on my plate, then scraped it away.

'Are you?'

'Of course I am. You know that.'

I looked up. Savannah was watching me closely, a frown marring her brow. 'Nina said her brother was in the bar the other night. He saw you flirting with the Iron Fists.'

I ground my teeth together. 'I flirt with everyone. It gets me tips. Anyway, Joe's a drunk. What would he know?'

'Drunk people have eyes too, you know.'

'And wandering hands.' I rolled my eyes and ate another mouthful. 'Flirting doesn't mean anything.'

'Maybe not to you, but it might to the Iron Fists. And it's getting you a...' She paused, her expression awkward.

'A?'

'No, it's nothing.'

It was something, alright. My temper fraying, I snapped, 'Just tell me, alright? I can take it.'

'Fine! You're getting a reputation. I get men coming into the clinic who tell me about how my sister is loose and easy.' Sav grimaced. 'If you sleep around, people will think—'

'I'm not *sleeping around.*' I gripped the spoon so hard it cut into my palm.

'It doesn't matter if people think you are!' She clutched the edge of the table, leaning forwards. 'And especially if they see you with gang members. That's not safe!'

'I can take care of myself, Sav.' I put my spoon down. Suddenly, I wasn't that hungry anymore.

'You're not doing a very good job of it!'

'I'm doing a fine job of it. I've been doing it for years. And I don't need you talking down to me when you—When I—' *When you're the only reason I'm stuck in this stupid job, anyway.*

Resentment bubbled over like a pot left on the stove too long. Savannah did good work, necessary work, but she barely brought in enough to cover food every week because the clinic was a charity. I paid our rent, laundry, clothes. I did our chores, our mending. I cooked and preserved food. And the only reason I had to do it… the real reason…

After Dad died, someone had to step up. Savannah wanted to become a doctor. I was the less talented, less clever twin. So I stepped in. I became the one who earned the money that kept us afloat, and Savannah in school.

I had sacrificed my dream for her to reach hers.

But all I got for it was a lecture.

I stood up, calmly scraping together the food on my plate. 'I'm not hungry. I'll eat this tomorrow.'

We couldn't afford to waste food.

'You can run away, but that won't change the fact that I'm right,' Savannah warned. 'You're going to get yourself in trouble, messing with the gangs like that.'

'Then I'll get myself in trouble. I'm going to bed.'

'You never listen.'

'I'm *going to bed*, Sav.' I dumped my plate in the sink and stormed angrily through to our bedroom, but even there I couldn't escape her for long. Our flat only had two rooms and a bathroom. Savannah and I shared the bedroom.

At least we had our own bathroom; there were plenty of people in town who didn't. We had two salaries in our family, so we could afford to live here.

Well, and we had the gang's favour.

Savannah lectured, but she didn't listen. She didn't pay attention. Consequently, she didn't know that Irina was in with Sayle—and that we only got to live here because I had worked for Sayle. One day, Irina would raise our rent prohibitively—the easiest way for her to get us out of this flat—and I'd know that we didn't have Sayle's favour anymore. I was waiting for the day.

I was terrified of that day.

I slept uneasily that night. The next morning, after spending extra time on my dance exercises to centre myself, I scraped together the cash to take a taxi-truck to work instead of walking. The taxis were large grey vans with open backs that roved about town. All you had to do was flag one down and pay the driver cash; they'd drop you anywhere inside the town limits. I sat in the back, huddled into my coat, and watched the streets rattle by. People went about their business, shoulders hunched, heads down. Everyone walked that way, making themselves as small as possible.

Except the gangs. They could afford not to.

The air felt thick that day, so thick I could barely breathe.

What I really wanted was to speak to Theo. He'd tell me what was brewing between the gangs. Theo was my best friend, maybe even my only real friend. We'd known each other since school, and although he was also in with the Iron Fists, he didn't feel like a gang member. I'd known him first.

But Theo was off in the city. He worked as a weapons runner for Sayle. It took him out of town for weeks at a time, and I never knew when he'd be back. It could be next week or even next month.

The truck pulled up on the square, and the driver banged on the partition, my signal to hop out. I waved to him in thanks as I climbed the front steps to the hotel.

Benny was sitting on a folding chair just inside. He jumped up when he saw me, an expression of profound guilt on his face. 'Harley! I heard about Jackson and Talbot—I'm sorry—I should have checked properly if they had guns. It won't happen again.'

It took me a moment to realise he wasn't talking about the rousting, but about last week. I snorted darkly.

'Yeah, sure, I believe that.' Feeling reckless, I pulled my knife and jabbed it handle-first into his abdomen. Benny grunted. The colour bled out of his freckly face. I leant in, putting pressure on his stomach, and hissed, 'If I ever, ever, ever get a gun held to my head in this bar when you were on shift ever again, I will slice the tendons in your ankles and wrists and your mama will be spoon-feeding you the rest of your life, got it?'

Not my threat. But I was a good copycat, and I'd spent enough time around Ellery to learn a thing or two. Anyway, Benny was convinced. He nodded anxiously, jumping back.

'I really am sorry.'

'Sure.' I sashayed past him, tucking my knife back into my belt. I didn't believe him for a second. If the right person greased Benny's palms, he'd let them carry their weapons into the bar. I knew it; he knew it; Tom knew it. And, unfortunately, every corrupt sonofabitch in this town knew it, too.

We all had our price.

Kayla was on the bar, a very tall and beautiful black girl who occasionally covered the night shift. Clearly, Anna had taken the offer of a day off.

She arched an eyebrow at me as I approached. 'Wasn't sure if I'd see you today.'

'I just can't stay away, apparently.' I accepted the apron she passed me with a grim smile, handing her my coat to stash. 'Here's to a quiet day with zero fuck-ups.'

Kayla laughed.

The window was boarded up, casting a shadow across the room, but apart from that the bar was operating as normal. Days like this were always eerie: it felt like everything should be different in the wake of a rousting, and yet we put ourselves back together and carried on as normal.

Normal included Maddock, who entered at his usual time and looked askance at the boarded-up window.

'Good evening,' he said when he reached the bar. He offered Kayla a smile. 'I don't believe we've met. I'm James.'

'I know who you are, city boy.' Kayla rolled her eyes. 'I'm Kayla. Whiskey on ice?'

'No ice.' After a glance around, and noticing that the bar was markedly quieter than usual, Maddock hauled himself onto a barstool and leant his elbows on the counter. 'I heard there was trouble last night. Sorry I wasn't here to help out.'

'I'm not.' I slid a water glass in front of him and filled it, condensation streaming off it to wet the worn wood. 'You'd have got yourself killed, Mr Hero.'

'I'm not a hero.' Maddock chuckled. 'But I'm sure you had it handled, Miss Cool-Under-Pressure.'

I smiled despite myself. I was almost starting to like Maddock. I looked forward to seeing him in the evenings and enjoyed talking to him. Partly because it was a game, trying to figure him out, and I liked the challenge. Partly because he was one of the few men who never touched me without permission.

Him and Bas, apparently, but I'd take Maddock over Bas. Bas was an arsehole.

My smile dropped at the thought. Maddock, catching the look, said, 'Is everyone okay, though? You must have been scared.'

'It happens.' I fixed my smile. 'We've been lucky this summer, but clearly it's back to business as usual. There's no use crying over spilt milk.'

'Or bullet holes in the roof,' Kayla added.

It was so quiet that evening that Maddock decided to eat at the bar, keeping Kayla and me company. At one point, Kayla slipped in back to fetch another bottle of whiskey, and I asked Maddock, 'Did you speak to Irina?'

'I did. She promised to keep me in mind.'

I wasn't sure how to read that. Did that mean she was intending on housing him, or was she fobbing him off? 'There's always the mayor's dev.'

'I'm looking into it.' He leant onto his elbows, his shirt sleeves pulling up to show more bruises. I nodded to them.

'Looks like someone's been brawling.'

'Brawling.' Maddock waggled his eyebrows. 'Is that what we're calling it?'

'Men acting like testosterone-fuelled idiots, throwing punches.' I smirked. 'Maybe Kayla should have given you the ice.'

'I'll take ice for the bruises. I just don't like it in the drinks.'

'Why not?'

He met my gaze. 'Never know what's gone in the water.'

'All of our water is filtered. Tom takes the safety of his customers very seriously.'

'Oh, I'm sure he does.' Maddock relaxed. 'I don't mean any offence by it.'

'Of course.'

His words sat strangely with me. Of course, we filtered our water—but something told me he had meant something else. Why would he be worried about poison or drugs?

Maddock wasn't like the careworn businessmen who came through and never lingered. I was starting to wonder whether he was doing business in town at all, or if he'd lied about it.

But who could I ask? If I asked questions, it would only draw attention to me.

I wasn't the only one who had noticed, though.

The next morning, as I was heading to work, I passed Anton Sorokin on the first-floor landing of my apartment building. He was leaning against the wall, watching an open door with an intent gaze. As I approached, he looked up.

'Well, look who it is. Miss Harley.'

'Anton.' I tensed, struggling to keep my face neutral. Anton, Irina Sorokina's only son, was in his late thirties. He had dark hair and brown skin, and was easy on the eyes. The trouble was, he had wandering hands—and an Iron Fist tattoo on his right upper arm. I'd about had it with gangs this week; I was due a break.

'Haven't seen you around lately.' He trailed his fingers over my arm as I passed.

'What are you doing here?'

His smile grew, catlike and smug. 'Overseeing an eviction.'

We both turned to look at the door at the end of the hall. I heard grunting, and a moment later a dour-looking man appeared carrying a table. John Sloane had lived there with his wife for years. He passed us without meeting our gazes. I felt sick. Was this what Irina had meant about keeping Maddock in mind?

'Couldn't make the rent.' Anton clucked his tongue. 'Tragic, really.'

'I'm sure,' I said drily, starting for the stairs.

'You should watch out.' Anton caught my arm, tugging me against his front, and his free hand slid underneath my coat to squeeze my butt. 'I'd hate for Mama to price you out. You know how the market is these days.'

'Your concern is touching.' I stood very still. Anton had a temper—

it was generally smart to let him get the groping out of his system.

'I'd be willing to put in a good word or you,' he slid his hand to the small of my back, his gaze never leaving mine, 'for a price.'

'Thank you for the offer. I'll bear it in mind.'

I stepped neatly away from him, heading for the stairs. Anton watched, unoffended and unsurprised.

'Don't think for too long. Things can change fast around here.'

'I know.'

I turned his words over in my mind as I descended the stairs. The offer was nothing new; he'd tried the same thing at least half a dozen times before. It was his last words that bothered me. Were they a warning or a threat? Or was I reading too much into them? It was hard to tell with Anton. He never took anything seriously—even when he was shooting a guy in the head.

Preoccupied, I exited my building. A hot wind was blowing up rubbish, and a couple of men were boarding up a first-floor window across the street. I'd barely taken three steps when a taxi-truck slowed as it passed and stopped just ahead of me.

'Kitten!'

I jumped. Ellery was sitting in the back, his jacket thrown off, watching me.

'What are you doing here?' My insides writhed and twisted like snakes—we'd left things badly last time. What did I say to him now?

'Get in.' He beckoned. 'I'll drop you at work.'

'Ellery, *no*.' Did he think this was better than picking me up in a car? It was broad daylight. Anyone could see us together, and I didn't have the excuse of work to create a barrier between us.

'I just want to talk. I wanted to see how you were doing.'

'No.' The word slipped off my tongue before I'd really thought about what I wanted to say. 'No, you didn't. We're not doing that. Not today.'

Ellery sighed gustily, as though the weight of the world were on his shoulders. 'Come sit next to me, love.'

'No.'

'The driver won't wait forever.'

I chewed the inside of my lip. Free drive to work. Hear Ellery out. Potentially be seen with him.

'It's important,' he added.

'Fine, but no funny business.'

Ellery nodded solemnly. I climbed in and settled on his other side, which protected me from the wind—and from anyone potentially looking in and seeing me doing business with a gang member.

'Knock on the partition,' Ellery said.

I thumped my fist against the back of the cab, and the driver pulled off. I sat tense and upright as we bounced over the uneven roads.

'Relax, kitten,' Ellery murmured.

I was trying, but it was awful. He was a solid, warm presence beside me, seeming to suck all the air out of the truck.

Ellery smoothed a hand over my thigh. 'Relax, baby girl. I really did want to see how you were doing. You looked all shook up the other night.'

'I wonder why,' I muttered.

'I'm sorry. I hate to see you caught up in those things.'

His hand was as hot and heavy as a furnace on my leg. I couldn't breathe.

'It's my *life*, Ellery.'

'Let me get you another job. A safer job.'

He'd got me my job in the first place, and we both knew why. Sayle wanted eyes in the Kranikovska.

'No more favours.' I put my hand on his, preventing it from crawling any higher. 'Sayle won't be happy, anyway.'

'Sayle can get information from other people, kitten.'

That stung, even though it shouldn't have. There was a part of me, a sick, fucked up part of me, that liked to feel useful. I pushed the feeling away. That way lay nothing but danger.

'I'm happy at Krani's. I just wish you boys wouldn't make trouble quite so often.'

Ellery grimaced.

'And don't think I haven't noticed that it has been often this last week.'

'It has.' He squeezed my leg. 'I'm sorry, kitten.'

Ellery had a way of apologising that made you believe he meant it. I doubted he did. Every word was honeyed with him, dripping off his tongue, trying to seduce me into trusting him. The trouble was, I wanted his apology to be sincere because I was tired. I wanted, just for five minutes, to just rely on someone else. And here Ellery was, offering.

That was the real danger.

Ellery turned his hand over, lacing our fingers together and shifting our hands into his lap. 'I wouldn't ask for anything in return, kitten. Let me help you.'

I ought to pull away. I knew that, and yet I let him hold my hand. 'Help me how?'

'Stay with me.'

'And when you're away? If you get killed?'

'One day at a time. Stay with me, then we can deal with the next problem.' He traced an old scar on the side of my finger. I'd got it picking up broken glass after a bar fight.

'And my sister?'

'Don't worry about that. I can get one of the other guys to—'

The illusion broke. I pulled my hand away. 'I can look after myself, Ellery. I don't need your help.'

'You want it.'

'We don't always want things that are good for us.' Dangerous words. He looked at me, his gaze as solid as his hand had been on my leg. I felt like he could see right through my skin, right through any mask I put on, to the small, scared girl inside. The girl who was still seventeen, recently orphaned, and had suddenly been pitched into the world of men. I stared back at him, my lips trembling.

Ellery stroked my cheek with the back of his hand. 'If you change your mind…'

'I won't.'

'Alright.' He leant back in his seat, glancing out at the street behind us. I followed his gaze. We were almost at the square.

'Anything I need to know?'

'The new boy is moving into your building.' Ellery didn't look at me as he spoke.

'I know. Irina evicted Sloane. That's cruel, Ellery.'

'It can't be helped. Keep an eye on him. He's been climbing the ranks at The Arsonist.'

'So he's good?'

Finally, Ellery met my gaze. 'Too good. Someone will approach him soon. Probably Kade. If he speaks to you, give him a push.'

'You want him in the bunker?' Guilt tightened my chest—I liked Maddock, and I didn't want to betray him, but Ellery had first dibs on my loyalties. 'You're not worried? I don't think he's in town for business like he said he was.'

'Of course he isn't.' Ellery's eyes were solemn. 'I don't want you near him, truth be told. Whoever he is, he's not James Maddock. James Maddock is a dead man.'

I regarded him in shock. 'How do you know?'

'Sayle killed him. Years back. He was just a kid. Now, some guy wearing his name rolls into town and starts asking all the wrong questions. Guy sure knows how to get to the heart of the matter, if you catch my drift.'

'You think he's deliberately trying to catch your attention?' Presented with a new puzzle, my brain kicked into gear. It made sense. 'He knew to talk to me. Someone told him I was ex-bunker.'

'You never mentioned that.' Ellery frowned.

'I didn't think to. Do you know how many people come through that bar wanting in the cage fights? Besides,' I gave him a pointed look, 'how can I know what's important if you never tell me anything?'

'The more I tell you, the more danger you're in.' The van stopped, and the driver pounded on the partition. Ellery frowned, then reached over me to knock back. I tensed as his arm brushed my front. Then he pulled away again. 'Besides, this is gang business. And you told me yourself that you wanted no part of the gang. You know we'd have had you if you wanted in.'

'I wouldn't have been a part of the gang. I'd have been one of your whores.' Annoyed, I shoved Ellery out of the way so I could get up. He stood, too, pulling me into his arms.

'You'll always be one of us, whether you have the tattoo or not.'

'But the tattoo means everything. It means I can look after myself, not that I'm a gang member's pet slut.'

'You don't have to be a kept woman.' I squirmed and Ellery finally let me go. 'You don't.'

'The future you're imagining doesn't exist, Ellery.'

'Doesn't it?'

I didn't have an answer for that—except the one he didn't want to hear: No. I wasn't joining the gang, nor was I going to trade on their murky protection. Instead, I jumped out of the van. 'Goodbye, Ellery.'

Ellery remained silent, but I felt his eyes on me as I climbed the steps to the hotel.

FIVE

I HAD WELL AND TRULY had enough of the gangs, and it was only Friday. Things could always get worse.

Tom had had the workmen in that morning, and the broken windowpane was repaired—a patch job, like everything in this town. Still, the bar was dark. Heavy clouds had rolled in, fat with the first storm of autumn, trapping the heat beneath them so that the town felt like a vat of soup.

The humidity made me snippy. It was a real effort to be nice to the customers, to flirt like usual. Savannah's words kept rattling around in my head, making me feel cheap and worthless. Ellery's smoky promises taunted me.

'You'll always be one of us, whether you have the tattoo or not.'

Tattoos meant everything in our society. They could indicate marriage, gang membership, slave status, and more. Men got their first tattoo the second they could scrape together the money for it. Having a tattoo made you a man. It was a mark of honour.

It was the same for women, except for one crucial difference: having tattoos as a woman sent a message. *I am not owned by men.* Some men took it as a threat, some as a warning, others as an invitation. Tattoos meant you were playing in their world, and none of them would ignore you.

I had gone with Theo to get his first tattoo when he was sixteen. I'd gone with him to get his second, and his third. I'd gone with him to get his gang tattoo when he was nineteen. I'd watched him smile as the needle pierced his skin. I'd envied him.

He'd offered to design a tattoo for me.

I had refused. It wasn't worth the risk.

What would Theo say about Ellery's offer?

There was no use wondering. I'd long since learnt that the more I thought, the deeper I spiralled. My brain was not a happy place; it waited for every opportunity to spring dark thoughts on me. Best not to invite them in.

Maddock arrived just before the evening rush, with his usual smile. He leant against the bar. 'You'll have to do without my company tomorrow night.'

'Oh, really?' I raised an eyebrow.

'I've got a slot at The Arsonist tomorrow, which I'm told is a considerable privilege.'

'A fighting slot on Saturday night.' Anna flicked the cap off a bottle of beer. 'Someone must like you.'

'I hope someone bets good on you,' I said. Fighters got paid according to how people bet on them—an incentive to keep their fights interesting.

'I hope someone notices me.' He caught my eye. 'You wouldn't know who to look for?'

'You mean you haven't spent the last week or so memorising all of Sayle's boys?'

He smiled. 'Not all of Sayle's boys can invite someone to the bunker, can they?'

True. 'Have a seat. I'll bring you your drink.'

'Thanks.'

I made him wait for it, serving three other tables before I got round to his corner of the room. Maddock's lips quirked up on one side when I approached. 'Busy tonight, hey?'

'It's Friday.'

'So it is. I hadn't noticed.'

I rolled my eyes. *Ha-ha, funny.* Avoiding his gaze, I carefully and thoroughly wiped his table down and meticulously set it for dinner. Then I slowly poured his water.

'I'm fighting a guy named Sterk.' Maddock leaned back in his seat, legs splayed, watching me fuss with amusement. I set a coaster down and put his whiskey in front of him, adjusting it so that it was perfectly centred. 'Heard a rumour that he's gunning for a spot with Moriarty's lot.'

'I don't know anything about Moriarty's lot,' I said tersely.

'That would be silly.' He smiled artfully. 'Seeing as knowing is self-preservation. And you strike me as someone who is very good at self-preservation.'

'You have a remarkably high estimation of me. I'm just a waitress.'

'If I were Sayle,' he picked up his whiskey, swirling it slowly, the amber liquid glinting as it caught the light, 'I would want eyes in the most popular bar in town, don't you think?'

'I prefer not to think about what Sayle does and doesn't want, Mr Maddock.'

I picked up my tray, making every movement slow and calm, but inwardly I was panicking. Once again, he'd thrown the rulebook out. New game, new rules. I didn't like this game. It felt personal.

His eyes drifted to my right upper arm, the skin smooth and unmarked. My hands felt sweaty against my tray.

'Irina found me a flat after all,' he said suddenly.

'Did she?' Guilt supplanted my panic, twisting up my insides. I thought of Sloane. Evicted in the service of Sayle wanting information about Maddock.

Information which I might have been able to give if I'd tried just a bit harder.

Oh, I didn't kid myself. Sloane would probably still have been evicted and Maddock moved into my building. This was Sayle's game: like a spider, he wove his web. He wanted Maddock stuck in it, so he could close the trap at his own leisure. Putting him in one of Irina's buildings made him easily accessible day and night. Putting him in the building I lived in… My job was clear. I'd be the honey that lured the fly.

'Looks like it's going to be number fourteen, on Prospect Avenue.'

'My building.' I summoned a smile. 'We'll be neighbours after all. We'll have to have drinks to celebrate.'

'We should.' Maddock glanced around. 'Your shift ends late, though.'

'I can switch. Everyone wants the dinner shift—you get the best tips.' Either Kayla or Dana would switch in a heartbeat. Only Brenda was constrained by familial obligations.

'Let's plan something for next week, then. I'd like to see your sister again, as well. I enjoyed talking to her.'

Savannah would have loved talking to him, too. Maddock had good manners and never objectified women. In all things, he was good friend material.

Just a shame I wasn't looking for good friends.

'I'll speak to her tomorrow, see when she wants to do it.' I hefted my tray. 'Same as usual for dinner?'

'Do they have the chicken like last night?'

'I think so. Let me pop in back and check.'

Having Maddock in my building would be a disaster; I just knew it. I had two distinct lives: the bar and Savannah. Keeping them separate allowed me to maintain an illusion of privacy. I'd have to warn Maddock not to go tattling to Sav about what he'd learnt about me.

The one benefit of it being Friday was that I was too busy to think. I rushed around, serving the workers who all came in to celebrate the end of the week and spend their wages. I felt sorry for their wives, really, because some of them spent *all* their wages.

Dana arrived at eight, taking over half the room from me. She was about five years older than me and had already been married and divorced. Not that divorce or marriage were legally significant round here these days. She'd seen her husband out the door just in time; a few weeks later he'd crossed one of the gangs and ended up face-down in the river. Dana wasn't the least bit sad about it.

As I loaded several bottles of beer onto my tray, I nudged Dana's hip with mine. 'I need to leave early sometime next week.'

Dana eyed me with a hawklike gaze. 'You want to split tips?'

This was our deal to make sure we both managed to make rent at the end of the week: if she took the dinner shift, I got half the tips.

'Probably won't be worth it. I think it'll be Tuesday.' Savannah worked late on Mondays, my only day off, otherwise we could have done it then.

'Fine, I can do Tuesday night.' She glanced at the door and frowned. 'Not them again.'

I looked—and wished I hadn't. Ellery, Bas, Briggs, Kade. Honestly, I couldn't seem to be rid of those guys. Blowing out an angry breath between my teeth, I said, 'Want to switch halves?' The only free tables were in my half.

'Uh, fuck no. Briggsy gets fucking handsy, and I had enough of that with my husband.'

We both snorted drily. I lifted my tray. 'See the guy with the black hair? By the wall? Give him info about the fights and he'll tip you good.'

'You're passing him on to me?' Dana raised an eyebrow. 'Damn, girl.'

I shrugged. 'Name's James. Doesn't like flirting, though.'

Dana glanced at him, then back at me. 'Not at all?'

'Not that I've noticed.'

'Huh. Haven't had a challenge in a while.' She picked up her tray and sashayed off. I followed, heading for Clem's table.

Clem was one of our regulars, an old man who loved alcohol much more than it loved him. He came in at least three times a week and drank his weight in whiskey whilst playing bridge. If I had that much money, I sure as fuck wouldn't spend it on booze.

I served two more tables before Ellery caught me as I walked past, hooking his fingers deftly through my belt loop. I stopped and, without turning, said, 'Impatience is a vice, Ellery.'

'I know.' He pulled me backwards. I overbalanced into his lap. 'I have lots of vices.'

His breath was warm against my neck, making my ponytail flutter. I shivered. 'You know I'm working.'

'I can see that, kitten.'

'You remember that my job is meant to be non-contact.'

'I'm not paying you.' His hands were loose against my hips. 'You can get up any time.'

It felt like a physical effort to drag myself away. Hadn't I been angry with him? But I liked this Ellery too much—flirty and playful, and not at all serious. This Ellery didn't make big, dangerous statements. He just wanted to touch and please.

He was the most dangerous. I was drawn to him like a moth to a flame.

I stood up, setting my empty tray on the table. Ellery slung an arm around my hips. 'Tell me something good, kitten.'

'Good?' I danced my fingers up his arm and tousled his hair. Mistake. It was soft, thick, and luxurious. 'What can I tell you that you don't already know?'

'Try me.'

Bas was scowling at us. I shot him a coy smile, making his annoyance grow.

'A little bird told me the new boy was given a Saturday slot at The Arsonist.' I traced the shell of Ellery's ear, telling myself it was just for the tips. 'Didn't realise he was such a big shot.'

'Seems the boy has some talent, after all,' Ellery said. 'Enough to impress Bert, anyway.'

'Only Bert? Or has someone else been watching?'

'There's always someone watching, kitten. You know that.'

'Of course.' I bit my lip, sliding away from him, slowly, so that his hand dragged across the small of my back. I picked up my tray. 'And if he were to ask me who to look for…'

Ellery toyed with my belt loop. 'You could tell him to buddy up to the winner from slot four.'

'Marco,' Bas said sharply. I glanced at him in surprise. Almost no one called Ellery by his first name.

'Relax.' Ellery leaned back. 'Harley knows what's up. We'll get four whiskeys, yeah?'

I nodded. Catching his hand, I removed it gently but firmly from my hip. 'Paws to yourself, *Marco*.'

The look he gave me sent liquid heat through my veins. My voice was unsteady as I said, 'See you later, gentlemen. Be good for me.'

The men laughed. Except for Bas—he sat like a stone statue, radiating disapproval. I remembered his sour words from the other day, and resolve formed in my chest. I'd crack that guy. Somehow, someway, I'd get him.

Later, on my way past Maddock's table, I slid a note into his hand.

Winner of slot four tomorrow night.

I was midway through wiping down a table when my worst nightmare walked through the door.

Once upon a time, many a winter ago, I had attended school. There weren't too many senior schools in town, and even fewer that allowed you to finish your education at eighteen. My parents had dreamt of Savannah and me doing well at school and getting good jobs—and they'd moved heaven and earth to make it happen, as I'd unfortunately discovered when Dad died. That meant that we'd attended school with people who were better off than we were.

And that included the men who had just entered my bar: Brody Cavanaugh, Diego Bartholomew, and Louis Godfrey. Their families had all gotten rich from the whiskey trade, and they lived like kings amongst us peasants.

They'd been relentlessly nasty to the 'poor girls' when Savannah and I had been at school… and then they'd had the privilege of witnessing my fall from grace. They weren't marked, but I was pretty sure their families were in big with Moriarty's Black Hand gang. Little criminals, the lot of them.

The three men sauntered across the room, Brody landing a solid smack on my arse as he passed. I gritted my teeth and grabbed the edge of the table for balance before straightening up.

'Good evening, gentlemen.'

'Hullo, *kitten*.' Brody smirked. He was tall, blond, and pale, with a weak chin and a nose that made me think of a rat. Pointy, that was the word.

Pointy-nosed Brody the prat.

'It's Harley,' I seethed.

'*Harley*.' He laughed, as though there was something absolutely hysterical about my name. 'Still serving drinks, then? How the mighty have fallen.'

You'd have thought it was news or something.

'Still serving drinks, as you can see. What can I get you?'

Diego and Louis slid into the seats around the table. Brody leant his hip against the edge. 'Why so cold, *Harley*?'

The way he said my name set my teeth on edge.

'I have a room full of customers.' I offered him my most sickly-sweet smile. 'I'd hate to keep anyone waiting.'

'Oh, of course.' He ran a finger up my arm, but there was nothing flirty about the gesture. He was just doing it to prove he could. 'We wouldn't want anyone to complain and get you in trouble, would we?'

His touch made me feel dirty. I jerked away. 'Whiskey or beer, Cavanaugh?'

Brody's gaze sharpened. My unwillingness to even pretend to flirt damaged his fragile ego. *Let me go cry tears of absolute misery in the back room.*

'Whiskey.' He sat, throwing one arm over the back of his seat, and watched me arrogantly as I headed for the bar.

'I'd forgotten how bad the service was here,' Louis stage-whispered to Diego as I passed.

I let it slide. *Fuck them.*

Unfortunately, they were in my half, so it wasn't as though I could avoid them.

Diego leered down my top as I served them, but I kept my mouth shut. Better to just ignore it. As I walked away, Brody swept a leg out, tripping me. My knees hit the floor, two bottles of beer falling and shattering.

Fuck.

'Oops, how clumsy.' He snickered as I stood and dusted myself off. Several other people were laughing. My cheeks burnt as I retrieved my tray. *What a mess.*

Spilt drinks came out of my salary. Brody was an arsehole.

Seething, I headed for the bar. Anna passed me a towel. 'Are you okay?'

'Apart from wanting to kill Brody?'

Anna cringed in sympathy.

Cleaning up the mess was worse. The beer made everything sticky, and I had to get down on my knees in front of the douchebag brigade. As I wiped the floor down, Louis kicked me sharply in the arse.

'Finally learnt your place in life?' Brody jeered.

That little shit.

Fury flooded my veins. I straightened up and sauntered over to him, lifting my boot onto the edge of his seat. He leant back, then realised he was showing fear and immediately crowded towards me.

'Aw, decided you want a piece of me after all?' he cooed mockingly.

'Oh Brody,' I sighed wistfully. I traced a hand—and the dirty towel—up his front, grabbed the back of his seat... and lifted my foot onto his shoulder. His eyes narrowed.

'What the f—'

Locking my leg around his shoulders, I leant in, putting my lips an inch from his ear. 'You couldn't have me even if you paid me.'

I straightened slowly and seductively. Dance was my kingdom: the area where I had total control—of myself and my audience. He watched me, half-furious, half-aroused. I unfolded my leg and dropped my boot between his knees, an inch from his groin. 'Behave yourselves, boys.'

Then I whirled away, head held high, and went back to my cleaning. No one fucked around in my bar.

A while later, Ellery signalled for another round. I filled four glasses of whiskey and headed over. Briggs waved a twenty, so I slid in between him and Bas to put the drinks down.

He tucked it into my bra. 'Looks like you got Brody well in hand.'

'No one has Brody in hand, not even his daddy.' I rolled my eyes.

'Want us to teach him a lesson?' Kade sounded almost eager.

I laughed. Kade's dislike of Brody was pretty well-known. 'Maybe not this time. I'm sure another opportunity will arise.'

'I can think of a few other things that are rising.' Briggs smoothed his hand up my thigh, feigning a pout. 'You've been terribly unfriendly this evening.'

'Sorry, I don't remember it being my job to entertain you boys.' I set the last whiskey down and stepped away from him, my leg brushing Bas's arm. 'Aren't you meant to be down at the bunker tonight?'

'Why? You wanna see us fight?' Briggs grabbed my thigh. 'Reckon I'd win all my slots for you if you came to watch, baby.'

'Aw.' I tried not to shudder at the feeling of his fingers on my leg. 'Much as I'd love to kiss away your tears of misery when you lose I… have… better things to do.'

Briggs snorted. His fingers skimmed over the knife strapped to my hips. 'And here I thought we weren't meant to bring weapons in the bar.'

I caught his wrist, holding it tightly. 'Staff prerogative. Careful. I'd hate for you to lose a finger.'

'You could kiss it better.'

'Mm, nope. I don't like the taste of blood.' I moved his hand. He let me. I stepped back, tracing a finger up Bas's arm.

'Are you fighting tonight?' What kind of fighter was Bas? I couldn't imagine.

He snatched my hand, quick as a snake pouncing. 'You can flirt with the others. I'm not interested.'

'Aw, it's just a bit of fun.'

'I'm not here for fun.' His eyes were narrowed, glaring up at me. I couldn't resist the challenge. I lifted my arm, bringing his hand to my lips, and pressed a cheeky little kiss to his knuckles.

'One for luck.'

Bas snatched his hand away. 'If you want to muck about, do it with Ellery. He'll more than welcome it.'

I flicked a glance at Ellery. He was watching us, eyes sharp and curious. He beckoned me over.

Smiling, I sashayed around the table, tracing a line over Bas's tense back and Ellery's relaxed one. 'See you later, boys.'

As I headed for the bar, I heard Briggs complaining, 'You scared her off. Don't ruin things for the rest of us.'

'She's a cheap slut,' Bas snapped. 'If you want a whore, pick one up from the square on the way back.'

Ouch. Clenching my teeth, I got back to work.

The last hours of my shift passed quickly, though they weren't without aggravation. Brody and his gang of dickheads lingered, dispensing nasty comments the same way Briggs dispensed arse gropes. I had to cut Clem off after he got angry drunk, and a bunch of factory workers decided to start a fight—always my favourite thing to deal with on a Friday night. I smelt of beer and sweat when I finally escaped, frazzled, and with my hair falling out of my ponytail. The hot air hit me in the face as I descended the stairs; I'd taken the front exit, and I immediately regretted it.

Brody was lingering on the steps.

'Hello, kitten.'

'Brody.' I tried to dodge around him, but he stepped in my way. 'It's Harley.'

'Harley, kitten… Who cares? A hooker is a hooker, no matter what they're called.'

I gritted my teeth. 'I'm not a hooker. Get out of my way.'

'You should watch out. I'd hate for your boss to hear how you talk to your customers. What will you do without this job?'

Every muscle in my body tensed. I had no idea whether Brody could lose me my job, but the thought terrified me. I swallowed, my mouth feeling dry as crater dust all of a sudden. 'Don't do this, Brody.'

He stepped closer. 'If I were you, I'd get a lot nicer, *fast.*'

The door behind us swung open.

'Hey, hey, what's going on here?'

It was Ellery. Relief swept through me, making me lightheaded. I turned to look, and Brody dragged me against him.

'Just having a bit of fun. Nothing to see here.'

'Get off!' My voice echoed in the empty square. I writhed, trying to escape.

Ellery reached casually for his weapon. 'You don't want to be doing that.'

'Don't I? Seems everyone else is doing it.' Brody groped over my neck and managed to yank my coat off my right arm. 'No gang mark. She's not one of yours—unless there's something you'd like to tell me?'

Ellery hesitated—and I seized my opportunity. I jammed my foot down onto Brody's. Everyone wore sturdy shoes around here—except for people who could afford not to worry about scorpions, snakes, dirt, and the other nasties that lurked below ankle height. His fragile loafers stood no chance against my steel-toed combat boots. He yowled in pain, shoving me off. I crashed to my knees at Bas's feet.

'You little bitch!' Brody grabbed a handful of my hair and dragged my head back. I tensed, biting my tongue. *Dick move, arsehole.*

'Pulling hair? I thought we were past that—Ngh!' My words dissolved into a grunt of pain as he yanked harder.

'Stupid slut. You think you're funny? You're nothing but a glorified whore.'

Rage twisted like a snake in my chest. 'At least I can take care of myself. If your daddy died, you'd be out on your arse.'

I shifted up on my haunches, already planning my next attack.

'Enough,' Bas said. I looked up at him. His expression was dark. He didn't pull a weapon; the tone of his voice was enough. 'Cavanaugh, leave.'

Brody snorted. 'As if I'd care what Moriarty's ex-whore wanted.'

Bas's expression grew even colder. He stepped past me, and then his hand shot out, grabbing Brody's wrist. With what seemed like no effort at all, he broke Brody's hold on my hair and twisted his arm. Brody stumbled as Bas forced his arm behind his back, jerking him around so he faced down the stairs. 'Leave, or I'll find a much greater height to chuck you off.'

I couldn't see what Bas was doing, but Brody whined in pain. '—right, alright, I'll go.'

'And stop making trouble—unless you want your father's extracurricular activities spread all over town.'

'Alright, alright!'

Bas released him with a shove. Brody stumbled two steps down, then grabbed the railing and fell against it. 'Sonofabitch!'

'Don't you forget it,' Bas said coldly. Brody fled down the stairs and across the square.

Bas turned, his face still set with anger. To my surprise, he held out a hand to me. As he did, his jacket sleeve slid up, baring his left wrist—and the tattoo on it. It was some kind of bird silhouette, but that wasn't what caught my attention. It was the fainter ink amidst the silhouette; old, poor-quality ink, which stood out in the golden light from the hotel lobby.

It was a slave mark.

My eyes slid to Bas's face. He realised where I'd been looking and hastily yanked his sleeve down. 'Get up.'

I grabbed his hand and let him pull me up. 'Thanks. But I didn't need your help.'

'Right,' he said sceptically. 'I'm sure you had a grand plan to get out of that one yourself.'

I scowled. 'I can take care of myself.'

Bas looked me up and down disdainfully, his disbelief evident. 'I'm sure you can. Go home, little girl.'

For a long second, I considered shoving him down the stairs. It wasn't worth the trouble I'd get in, though. Instead, I lifted my chin and stalked past him, not meeting anyone's gaze. I descended the stairs and marched across the square.

Stupid arsehole men.

But it was interesting. Bas had been a slave.

And thanks to Brody, I was pretty sure I knew who had owned him.

SIX

EVERYONE KNEW WHAT HAVING a string of letters and numbers tattooed on your left wrist meant. All slaves were marked when they were taken, and when—if—they got free, the mark remained with them, a reminder for them and a threat for everyone else. Your freedom only lasted as long as you were able to defend it.

Most former slaves got the mark covered up as soon as they could, generally in the same way that Bas had—with another tattoo. But slave marks were cheaply and crudely done, the ink pushed deep under the skin, which made them hard to cover up. Generally, you could pick out the old ink beneath the new.

It wasn't the first time I'd seen it. In fact, for the first nine years of my life, I'd seen a mark just like that every single day on my mother's wrist.

Bas had been a slave. Now he was free, evidently. Had he freed himself? Or had Sayle bought him free? Everyone knew Sayle didn't keep slaves, but he didn't go around freeing them, either. That meant Bas had probably freed himself, via the only tried-and-true method.

Murdering his master.

He was barely older than me. Crikey. At a guess, I'd say he was the same age as Ellery, twenty-seven, maybe twenty-eight. And he'd been a slave, and now was free.

I didn't know what to do with that knowledge.

He wouldn't want my pity. Besides, I still didn't like him. He was a jerk. But now I knew he had a reason to be a jerk. If anything, that just annoyed me, because it meant my own sense of guilt and compassion was going to force me to put up with him being a jerk.

The logical thing would just be to stay away from him. I had enough going on in my life right now.

Yeah, that was what I'd do. The next time I saw him, I'd just… walk on by.

Right. I didn't believe myself. I was incapable of ignoring jerks. It was my ultimate weakness.

Fortunately, I didn't see Bas again that week. I did, however, see Maddock on Sunday evening.

'Last night,' he said, grinning. 'It'll be nice to have my own place again.'

'Where did you live before?' Anna asked.

His brow wrinkled in a brief frown, before smoothing out again. 'I'm from Brackfields.'

'The industrial city?' I asked.

'That's the one.'

'Can't think that this is an improvement.'

'Oh, I don't know.' He glanced around the bar, lit red-gold by the sunset. 'This town is growing on me.'

I suppressed a laugh. 'Sure, we'll see how you feel after the first time someone mugs you.'

Maddock grinned playfully. 'I'm an accomplished cage fighter now. They'll get more than what they bargained for.'

Anna shook her head. 'James, everyone in this town is an accomplished cage fighter.'

'Okay, not quite everyone,' I said.

'Like who?' Anna looked perplexed.

'Brody?'

'Brody doesn't count.' Anna rolled her eyes. 'Brody's a rat. All the real men in this town fight in the cages.'

'Oh, now they're *real* men,' I teased. 'The other day you were telling me off for putting Maddock onto the fights.'

Anna flushed. 'If he's staying, he needs it.' She glanced at him, adding conspiratorially, 'That's why they do it, you know? To keep their skills sharp.'

'Oh, is that how it is?' Maddock interjected. 'Purely self-preservation.'

'Absolutely.' I smirked, sliding his whiskey to him.

'Thanks.' He toasted me with the glass.

'So… seeing as you're moving, we should do those drinks.'

'Oh, yes.' Maddock grinned. 'I'm eager to see the Benoit twins together in the same room—you know, no one ever sees you together. I'm starting to think there's only one of you.'

'And I've mastered the art of being in two places at the same time?'

I rolled my eyes. 'Trust me, there's two of us. Once you've seen us together, you'll never mix us up again.'

'Is there a secret?' He leaned in. 'I don't want to embarrass myself. Tell me the trick.'

I nudged him back. 'If you can't figure it out, all the money in the world won't help you.'

'I'm not sure paying you will help.'

'No, you'll need the money to get brain surgery, because you apparently can't look past the fact that we have the same hair.'

Maddock laughed. Anna leant in and whispered conspiratorially, 'One of them's nicer than the other.'

'Me,' I added.

'It's Savannah, right?' Maddock asked.

'No, it's me. I'm the nice one.'

They both sniggered. People in this town were so rude.

The next day was my day off, not that I spent much of it relaxing. There were always things to be done: laundry, shopping, cooking, mending. We didn't get a lot in the way of new goods this side of Brackfields; the Brackfields mayor had stopped the trains running in our direction because the gangs kept blockading the tracks. That meant our clothes had to be mended and preserved until the merchants' market, which happened once every six months on the square. Savannah and I both knew how to sew and fixed up our clothes from whatever we could find: an old workman's overall became a summer coat, men's jeans could be resized to women's jeans, and bedsheets could be cut up to become shirts. We weren't unique; that was how everyone in town clothed themselves.

Food had to be preserved because you couldn't always rely on the electricity to keep the fridge cold. That was more of a problem in summer, particularly because we were on the top floor. Come winter, we'd have an advantage; we could just lean out the window and put things on the roof to stay cold.

After a lunch of leftovers, I walked down to Irina's office to pay my rent. Anton was lurking in the lobby of her building, and he studied me like an eagle watching its prey as I crossed the tiled floor.

'Nice day, isn't it, *Harley*.'

The way he said my name made me uneasy. It was playful, but not flirtatious, and that made it sound threatening.

'Anton. What are you doing here?'

His lips twisted into a facsimile of a smile. 'Can't I visit my mother?'

'Of course you can.'

You'd think after fifteen years I'd have gotten used to not having a mother, but I felt the jab anyway. It was a dull, faded ache under my ribs, like an old scar. A wound that had never healed properly.

My mum had been sick, which was one of the main killers out in our town, between the dusty air and dirty water. It could happen to anyone. But it hadn't happened to anyone—it had happened to us. And we couldn't afford medical care.

Breathing through the pain, I knocked on Irina's door.

'Enter.'

I hated visiting Irina. Fear was like a vice around my ribcage as I pushed the door open. Would this be the week? Would she raise the rent? She sat behind her desk like a queen on a throne, overseeing her empire. Irina was a comfortable woman, and her body showed it. She was soft where I was hard. Her face was artfully made up, and her clothes were well-kept. She leant back and smiled at me.

'Ah, Harley Benoit.'

I cleared my throat. 'I have my rent.'

'Right on time.' She held out a hand, her rings glinting. I passed her the bundle of notes. Irina separated them, counting them slowly and exaggeratedly.

'Is that all I get?' She raised one painted eyebrow.

My stomach clenched. I had to swallow before I could speak. 'That's what I paid last week, ma'am.'

Irina hummed. 'You know, I believe you're the only ones paying the old rates anymore. I should look into that.'

It took everything in my power not to react. 'Ma'am.'

She studied me, searching for a weakness, an opening. I felt like a mouse which had caught the eye of a cat.

'You're a pretty girl.' She reached out and curled a lock of my hair around one ring-bedecked finger, stroking it. 'If you ever have trouble making rent, you let me know. I'm sure I can find some way for you to… work it off.'

'That's kind of you, ma'am.'

She patted my shoulder. 'Off you go, then.'

I felt Anton's eyes on me as I passed him again on the way out, but this time I walked straight by him, my shoulders stiff, my gaze on the door. I escaped into the warm air and sucked in several deep breaths. My hands were shaking.

Irina ran one of the biggest brothels in town; I knew exactly how she'd put me to use. There was no way I'd agree to that. I'd take Ellery's offer before I resorted to that.

But if she put the rent up, I might not have a choice. My wage and tips barely covered our expenses at the moment, and I was already working as many hours as I could at the Kranikovska.

I shoved my hair back from my face. Irina on one side, Ellery on the other. I felt like I was being circled by lions. The question was, who would I give in to first?

After visiting Irina, I found myself at a loss. I was too restless to do anything around the flat, but I also didn't have any friends I could go and visit, nor any money to do anything. In the end, I donned my boots and sturdy coat and took myself over to the north side of town.

The clinic was exactly three blocks before the end of town: the north side didn't peter out into sparse family residences, then ramshackle lean-tos made of salvaged scrap, then farms like the south and west sides of town. Nor did it become the rundown industrial facilities that spread out to the east, along the road to Crater's Edge. No, the town stopped dead, the blocks of flats ending abruptly at a road. The flats on the other side had collapsed decades ago, maybe even over a century, blown up by some long-forgotten bomb. The townspeople had cleared the rubble, and for decades there had been nothing.

Then Sayle had moved in and claimed the land for himself.

But Sayle's compound didn't count as part of the town, any more than the mayor's gated complex in the west did.

Three blocks before the boundary, I turned into a low building. The clinic was a temporary structure which had become permanent; a makeshift, rickety building surrounded by a wire fence with a weapons check. A large, rusted sign was tacked to the fence.

Bale Rocks Clinic
FREE CARE FOR ALL
North Crater Charity (NCC)

The girl on the gate looked too young and wide-eyed to actually bully gang members into giving up their weapons. I was pretty sure she ought to still be in school.

She recognised me off the bat and waved me in without checking me, a privilege of being an identical twin. 'Sav is in the end cubicle.'

'Thanks.'

The actual clinic was patched together from salvaged materials. The last mayor had had it built in an attempt to clean up the town, not that it had done him much good. Sayle had shot him in the head. I nudged aside a plastic curtain and entered my sister's domain.

As always, the clinic was a mess of nurses and doctors running around, screaming children, bleeding men, pregnant women—the clinic saw everyone who needed emergency care, which was *everyone*, eventually. There was a hospital in the next town, Crater's Edge, but you could only get in there if you had money to pay for the trip over, and none of us did. The floor was loose wooden boards, and medical supplies were stacked haphazardly wherever they fit. The cubicles were separated by more plastic curtains.

I slipped in between people and made my way down the central aisle to the end. Savannah was leaning over a man seated on a plastic chair, cleaning blood off his abdomen.

'Next time you get in a barfight, Mr Hardwick, I suggest you come to me the same night. Don't try and treat it yourself.'

The man grimaced, though he seemed amused. 'I'll remember that, Ms Benoit.'

Savannah laughed. 'I'm sure you will because this is going to hurt.' Grabbing a bottle of alcohol, she tipped a bit onto a cotton pad and pressed it to the cut. He tensed, hissing.

'Ah, you're punishing me, aren't you?'

'Just doing my job, Mr Hardwick.'

She was flirting, as well. I could hear the smile in her voice, and worse: I recognised Mr Hardwick. A tall, somewhat weedy, but handsome man, he had blond hair, cold blue eyes, and the physique of a fighter. I had seen him in the bar before, usually in the company of gang members.

Savannah fished around in a drawer for something, and Evander Hardwick's gaze drifted to me.

'Looks like you have a visitor, Ms Benoit.'

Savannah straightened up and turned to me. Her eyes went wide with concern.

'Harley! What are you doing here? Are you hurt?' She hurried over, grabbing my arm.

I smiled awkwardly. 'No. I just... didn't have anything to do. Thought I'd come visit you.'

'Oh.' Savannah stared at me for several long seconds, before grimacing. 'You can't—I mean, we're busy. This is a medical facility, not some hangout.'

'I'm not—I mean…' I didn't know what I was doing here. What had seemed like a sensible decision earlier suddenly struck me as impulsive and illogical. 'I can help.'

'No, no, go home.' She steered me out of her cubicle, glancing uncomfortably over her shoulder. 'I have a patient.'

'Right. You just want to flirt with him in peace.' It hit even worse after our conversation the other night—so she thought *I* was getting a reputation, but meanwhile *she* was allowed to flirt on the job? *Hypocrite.*

'I wasn't flirting. I try and make my patients feel comfortable.' She shoved me around the curtain. I barely avoided another nurse who was hurrying through.

'Two more from that fight—'

'I got it, thanks,' Savannah said. 'Harley, you have to go.'

'You know it wasn't a barfight, right? Hardwick's in with the gangs. I've seen him with Moriarty's lot.'

'What are you talking about? Mr Hardwick works as security for the mayor, Harley.'

'Sure, right. As if working for the mayor means anything around here.' I rolled my eyes, pulling away from her. 'I bet he's clean as a baby under that shirt. No tattoos on *his* chest.'

'I'm not stripping him naked to check,' Savannah snapped. 'Unlike you, I take people at their word.'

'Sure, everyone except me.'

'Because you spend all your time acting jealous and sour,' Savannah sneered. 'I get it. Life didn't turn out the way you wanted it. If you tried, you could probably get a better job. So stop inflicting your bad attitude on the rest of us. Some of us have work to do.'

Anger rushed through me like a tidal wave, followed by hurt, but Savannah was already turning away. I clenched my fists.

'I just came to tell you I'm having someone over for drinks tomorrow.'

'Next time, leave a note.' She vanished back around her curtain. Amidst the general din of the clinic, I heard Hardwick's voice.

'Family trouble?'

'My sister's just an attention-seeker. Ignore her.'

The words burnt in my chest. I turned and stalked towards the exit. Why had I even come here? I was an idiot. I burst out into the muggy air and headed for the gate.

'Leaving already?' the weapons-check girl asked.

'Apparently so,' I muttered.

'You're Harley, right?'

I paused, turning to her. She was cute, clean-faced, with blonde hair in plaits.

'I am, why?'

'Is it true what your sister said? That there was a rousting at Krani's last week?'

I bit my cheek against the anger that wanted to pour out. It wasn't her fault my sister was a bitch. 'Yeah, it's true. Why?'

'Just worried.' She scuffed a toe in the dirt. 'The gangs are getting worse, right?'

And here she was on the gate, a prime target to get shot. 'If you see them coming, hide,' I said. 'Don't bother trying to take their guns.'

'Oh, I know.' She smiled tentatively. 'Have a good evening.'

'You too.'

I headed out onto the street. In the distance, the crack of thunder sounded.

The storm was finally rolling in.

SEVEN

IT RAINED MONDAY NIGHT and all of Tuesday, which meant we got almost no customers. To add insult to injury, Tuesday was the day I worked the lunch shift. I loathed the lunch shift, which was the quietest time to work. More people came in at two AM wanting a drink than at ten AM, that was for sure. We served a few people lunch, then a few people post-lunch drinks. I left at four, passing my apron to Dana on the way out.

The market was a bedraggled mess, but I managed to get food for dinner and headed home to cook. On the way up the stairs, I knocked on the door of the flat that had once belonged to Sloane.

Footsteps sounded inside, and then Maddock opened the door, peering through the gap.

'Oh, Harley. Just a sec.' He shut the door, then opened it again, this time without the chain. 'What's up?'

I shifted my weight. This felt awkward—I was always uncomfortable seeing people from the bar when I was at home. 'I wanted to let you know that you can come over around eight tonight.'

'Great. Want me to bring anything?' Maddock grinned. He was dressed in shorts and a vest. I thought he might have been working out, going by the sweat beading on his neck and brow.

'It's fine.' I waved my bag. 'I have everything.'

'Alright. Thanks for arranging this. I'm looking forward to it.' Maddock's smile turned gentle. 'It's nice to have friends around town.'

Friends, right. What could I say to that? It was better to keep him close until I figured out what he was in town for—but as soon as I did, I'd be passing the information straight to Ellery. Stomach churning, I bade him goodbye and headed upstairs.

Savannah got there a few hours later, passing me with pursed lips. She was still angry, unsurprisingly. It was another way we were different: my anger burnt hot, then burnt out, usually to be replaced with a wave of despair. Sav held onto her anger, tending it like a banked fire, stoking it when she needed to call on it. She vanished into the bathroom, then emerged a little while later, clean and changed.

'Who's your guest, then?'

'Maddock.'

'Who?'

'The new guy on the first floor. James Maddock.'

'Oh. He came to the clinic once.'

'I know.'

Savannah scowled. She hated it when I knew things before she told me them. She sidled over. 'What're you cooking?'

'Bean and barley soup with sausage.'

'Oh. Is there bread?'

I nodded. 'Yeah, I got it fresh on the way home.'

'When's he coming?'

'Should be about'—someone hammered at the door—'now. I'll get it.'

I slipped past Savannah and pulled the door open. 'Hey.'

'Hi.' Maddock grinned. 'How's it going?'

'Fine, and you? Come in.' I stepped aside, and Maddock entered, examining everything.

'Your flat is nicer than mine,' he remarked.

'More space, worse climate control,' I said. 'It's good enough for us, though.'

'True.' He grinned and waved a handful of bottles at me. 'I brought beer.'

'You didn't have to.'

'Figured it was the least I could do.' He came over to the stove. 'That smells good. I didn't know you cooked.'

'Did you think I starved?' I passed him a bottle opener.

'Guess not.' Maddock deftly flicked open three of the bottles, then stashed the others in the fridge.

'Here.' He passed me a bottle and handed another to Sav. 'Cheers. You're Savannah, right? We met that time at the clinic.'

'Cheers.' Savannah smiled shyly, and as I watched some of her bad mood fell away. *Figures she'd discard it for him, not me.* 'Yes, I'm Savannah.'

'Twins.' Maddock glanced between us, grinning. 'Damn, you're the first set of twins I've met.'

'Wow, we're so fucking special,' I muttered. People treated us as though we were some weird genetic mutation, not normal siblings.

'Harley!' Savannah shot me a look. 'Ignore her, James. She's so moody.'

I ground my teeth together. *Thanks, Sav.*

'Oh, I like it.' Maddock clinked his beer against mine. 'Makes a change from all the women who pretend they're sweet on me.'

'She can do that, too.' Savannah sniffed.

'*She's* right here,' I snapped. 'And cooking your dinner, so shut the fuck up.'

Savannah sniffed again. Maddock laughed. 'Want me to help out?'

'*You* can cook?'

He smirked. 'What, did you think I starved?'

I laughed. 'I walked into that one, didn't I? Don't worry, it's done.'

We pulled the table up to the window to eat because we only had two chairs. I perched on the windowsill, enjoying the hot bread. We didn't usually have fresh bread, because the only way to get it affordably was to make it ourselves, and neither of us had time. I usually brought back leftover bread from Krani's, and it was always already a bit stale.

Whilst we ate, Savannah rattled off question after question, and I listened closely to Maddock's replies, mostly to correlate the information I'd already managed to gather.

'Where are you from?'

'Brackfields.'

'How long have you been here?'

'Two weeks.'

'And you've been staying in the hotel all that time? Isn't that horrible?'

'It's been okay. The staff are great. The food is…' He wrinkled his nose, glancing at me. 'No offence.'

I laughed. 'I wouldn't eat it if you paid me.'

'Such an endorsement.'

I'd never endorse Kranis' food. I knew what the chef put in there when we were short on supplies.

'How long are you planning on staying?' Sav pulled us back on topic.

'I haven't thought about it.' Maddock sipped his beer. 'My contract with Irina is for three months. We'll see how things go with the Godfreys.'

'You work for the Godfreys?'

'For them? No. I'm negotiating a big contract with a building supply company in Brackfields. But the mayor is…' Maddock tilted his head back and forth and grinned cheekily. 'You know how it goes.'

'Not at all,' I said. 'Never had to buy or sell a thing. I didn't know you worked with the mayor.'

'You sell drinks by the dozen.'

'People come into the bar wanting drinks. That's different.'

'True.' Maddock tore off a piece of bread, dunking it in his soup. 'This is great, by the way. Where do you get groceries?'

'Doleman's has the best supply, but I usually shop at the farmer's market, right at the end of the day, before they go home. That's when you get the best prices.'

'You're a fountain of wisdom,' Maddock said.

'Mm-hmm.' I hadn't missed the way he'd dodged my question. 'You work with the mayor?'

He caught my eye, smiling wryly. 'Only insomuch as he wants a say in every new dev in town.'

'Shame he doesn't want a say in fixing the old ones,' Savannah complained. 'The clinic's a mess. We're patching holes in the walls and putting buckets under leaks.'

When the rain came, everyone had to do that. 'Maybe cosy up to Mr Hardwick,' I said. 'He can ask the mayor to buy you a new roof.'

Savannah shot me an angry look. 'I *wasn't* flirting with him.'

'Who's Hardwick?' Maddock asked in a pacifying tone.

'He's on the mayor's security team.' Savannah dunked her bread angrily. 'Harley saw him in the clinic yesterday, and now she's obsessed.'

'Obsessed?' Maddock raised an eyebrow at me.

'I'm not obsessed!'

'She keeps saying he's in Moriarty's gang,' Savannah explained, waving her bread in the air. 'You know, the Black Hands?'

'The ones who rousted the bar last week?'

'Yes. But I never said I was sure.' I shot Savannah a look. 'I've just seen him with them.'

Savannah scowled. Maddock hummed, looking between us

curiously. 'You know everyone in every gang, don't you?'

'She thinks she does,' Savannah snapped. Maddock shuffled uncomfortably in his seat.

'I wouldn't say that,' I said cautiously. 'I just know who people spend their time with. I've worked the bar for eighteen months. You start to see patterns.'

'Patterns,' Maddock echoed thoughtfully. 'That's a good way of saying it. What other patterns have you seen?'

I didn't like how he had turned the questions on me. 'Well, you always sit with your back to the wall.'

Maddock blinked, surprised. 'Huh. So I do. You noticed that?'

I immediately regretted pointing it out. 'I guess. Once is a coincidence. Twice is a habit.'

I'd noticed more than just that, but I changed the subject. 'I got root cake for dessert.'

'Root cake?'

'It's a local speciality. We can make just about anything out of taproot.'

'We have to,' Savannah said sourly. 'Seeing as it's the only thing that grows here consistently.'

'Sounds nice. I'd love to try it.'

I snorted. 'Give it a few months, you'll be sick of it.'

Over dessert, Savannah continued her onslaught of questions. 'Do you have any siblings?'

'Not a one.' Maddock nibbled a corner of the dense cake.

'And your parents? Are they in Brackfields?'

He shook his head, his expression grim. 'Dead. They died when I was four.'

'I'm so sorry.' Savannah bit her lip. 'I didn't mean to bring up bad memories.'

'It's alright. I barely remember them.' Maddock shrugged like a dog shaking off water. 'My father was in law enforcement so, you know, it's not the safest job anyway.'

'Law enforcement?' I repeated dubiously.

'Brackfields still has a police force.' He grinned. 'Keeps the gangs at bay.'

It was the first I'd heard of it. 'Noble.'

'Not sure the police would agree. Not sure the citizens would agree.' He shrugged. 'I guess it depends on what side of the fence you're on.'

'I think it's good work,' Savannah said. 'I wish ours was more effective.'

'So they can get cleaned up by Sayle again?' I asked. When Sayle had taken over, he'd pushed law enforcement out of most of the town. They still patrolled a fair portion of the south side, but they weren't anything I'd have called reliable.

She glowered at me. 'Maybe they wouldn't be. Maybe they could keep Sayle in line.'

I snorted. 'Unlikely.'

'You think?' Maddock asked. 'Our police manages okay.'

'Harley thinks the gangs are all that,' Savannah said. 'You'd think Sayle was the saviour of our society.'

'I have never said that!' No one hated Sayle more than I did. Just because I was capable of disliking someone without demonising them—like Savannah—didn't mean that I secretly worshipped them.

'It's a matter of perspective. In the bar, she only sees one side of them. But we're the ones who patch up the bullet holes when they go shooting people on the streets.' Savannah prodded her cake. 'The gangs are responsible for almost all of the violence in this city.'

'You must see a lot, huh?' Maddock asked.

'Yep. Saturday and Sunday mornings are the worst.'

'Why?'

'Because those are the days after the fights,' Sav confided. 'They spend all night beating each other up, then hop over to us for free healthcare, taking resources away from people who really need it.'

'You don't like the fights?' Maddock raised an eyebrow.

'Who does?'

'Most people I've spoken to don't seem to mind them.' He trailed his fork over his plate. I kicked him under the table, and his gaze jumped to mine.

'No,' I mouthed.

Maddock frowned.

Savannah looked between us. 'Oh, you mean Harley.' She rolled her eyes. 'Harley's biased. She thinks Sayle's our lord and saviour because he gave her a job in his club. Goes there all the time still—you'd think she missed the place.'

Maddock's gaze had turned sharp.

'That's not true! I haven't been there in ages!'

'Oh, pssh.' Savannah rolled her eyes. 'Anyway, I hope you're not planning on getting into that stuff,' she added to Maddock. 'All it ends in is broken bones and empty wallets. I've seen that story a thousand times.'

Maddock leant back, looking slowly between us. I focused on my cake, annoyed at Savannah, but mostly at myself for not having seen this coming. Maybe it had been a mistake to invite him. I'd thought I could get ahead of things, maybe, by establishing some kind of rapport. But I didn't want to sacrifice my privacy for that.

'Oh, I won't,' he said. 'I'm just here for business.'

Sure, and I'm just a waitress in a bar. What a fucking liar he was.

Maddock got tired of the Q&A after that and steered the conversation to other things as we finished our beers. Eventually, he bade us goodnight and left, and I cleared up for bed.

'He seems nice,' Savannah observed, passing me the plates. 'Not like the others.'

'They're all the same, Sav.'

'They're not. Just because you let all men push you around.'

'I don't.' I was too tired to argue. My anger had burnt out. 'I just see the world as it is.'

'Sure you do. You were the same about Hardwick. You just can't believe some people are capable of being good.'

'Good men are liars.'

'Then explain why James was here. You were the one who invited him.'

I shrugged, already regretting involving Savannah in my plans. 'I was curious.'

'And he's not involved in the fights or the gangs.'

'That you know of.'

'Right, because he's a liar.' Savannah laughed derisively. 'Funny how James has to be a liar, but you're quite happy to grind all over every gang member who comes through your bar.'

Changed my mind. I was not too tired to be angry. 'Fuck off, Sav.'

'Oh, there it is.' Her eyes glinted; she was fishing for a fight, and I'd fallen for her trap. 'Resorting to insults and swearing.'

'I don't grind over men.'

'Except you do. People have seen you and told me about it.'

'People,' I echoed.

'Yes, people.'

'Right, and no people ever lied to you.' I looked down at the soapy water and dirty dishes. I had cooked. My sister was lazy, rude, and entitled. 'You know what? I cooked. You can clean. I'm going to bed.'

I turned, wiped my soapy hands on her sleeve, and stalked off to the sound of her shrieking.

I was in a terrible mood for the next few days. Wednesday was a bad day again, the rain not letting up the slightest bit. Thursday, the storm finally broke, bringing with it a chill wind and skies the colour of dirty pennies.

Grey, overcast, with an overlay of brown. That was the wind whipping up the crater dust, making the streets uninviting and cold. The wind stung your face and whipped dirt in your eyes, so everyone walked even more bent over, hidden behind heavy coats.

Still, winter would bring in more customers. Everyone drank more in winter; it tricked you into feeling warm.

On Thursday, the bar was back to its usual buzz. Anton was entertaining a few men from the rival gangs near the door: a red-haired man with freckles and a brown-haired man whose face was surprisingly weathered for his age. I flirted for all I was worth, partially to spite my sister, and partially hoping for tips. Rent was due every week—I couldn't risk not making it.

Not now.

I was crouched behind the bar, looking for spare coasters, when Anna oohed.

'New boy is back. I thought he moved out.'

'What?' I straightened up too fast, smacking my head against the counter. 'Ouch, fuck!'

It was indeed Maddock. He approached the bar with a wry smile. 'Alright there? That looked painful.'

I rubbed my head. 'My week in a nutshell. What are you doing here? Don't tell me you got lonely already.'

'Harley.' Anna prodded me. 'Be polite.'

'It's alright, he doesn't care.' I waved her hand away. 'Whiskey?'
Maddock nodded. Anna pouted but headed to fetch the bottle.

Maddock leant in. 'I was looking for you, actually. I meant to talk to you about this on Tuesday night, but it didn't seem appropriate.'

Curiosity tangled with alarm, raising the hairs on my arms. 'Me?'

'Mm-hmm.' He straightened up as Anna returned. 'I'll grab a table.'

'Cash up front,' I reminded him.

'Oh yeah. Here.' He passed me a twenty. 'Keep the change.'

Then he was gone. Anna stared at the note, wide-eyed. 'He just overpaid a lot.'

'New boy's flush,' I said. 'And he likes to flaunt it.' I tucked the twenty in my apron. I wasn't saying no; it would cover a significant portion of my rent.

'I'm surprised no one has tried to mug him yet,' Anna said.

'Me too.'

I took my tray and navigated over to Maddock. He'd lost out on his usual table and, maybe in defiance of what I'd said on Tuesday, had hunkered down with his back to the door.

'One whiskey.' I set it down in front of him.

'Thank you muchly.' He picked it up, swirling the liquid before taking a sip. I lingered, watching him. 'You're a hard lady to pin down.'

'I'm in the same place every day.'

'That's the point.' He glanced around. 'You're not easy to catch for a private conversation. I thought I could catch you going to work, or maybe coming home… but apparently we keep missing each other.'

'Well, this isn't exactly a nine-to-five job.'

'I know, I realised that.' He rolled his shoulders. Stiff? Had he been at the fights again?

'You lied to my sister.' It had been bothering me since our dinner. Why should I get in trouble instead of him?

'I know. I'm sorry. But she seemed so…' He tilted his head, grimacing. 'There are so few people in our world who still have that optimism, you know?'

I bit my cheek. I knew. Did I ever know.

'Don't let that fool you. Sav can sniff out a liar.'

'I'm sure she can.' Maddock smiled. 'After all, she's your sister.'

Flatterer. Two tables over, Clem hollered for a refill. I shuffled my weight. 'Time's up, and you wasted it on compliments.'

'I'll have to get another drink then.'

I laughed. 'Clem can wait. Spit it out, new boy.'

'How am I still new?' he complained. Leaning forward, he added, 'It seems I have a new friend, one that I might not have been looking for.'

My breath quickened. 'Anyone I'd know?'

'I hope so. Goes by the name of Andrew Kade.'

'Mm-hmm.' So, Sayle's boys had made their move. 'Interesting. I've seen him around the bar. Tall, black skin, shaved head.'

'That's the one.' Maddock caught my eye pointedly. 'Hangs out with Sayle's lot. He thinks seeing as I did well at the fights last weekend, he might be able to get me a late slot in the bunker on Friday.'

I raised an eyebrow. *Fighting tomorrow.* 'Better not have that second drink, then.'

'Maybe not. Any advice?' Maddock lowered his lashes. 'For a newbie?'

'Why would you think I'd be able to advise you on how to fight? I'm just a waitress.'

'Oh, I think we both know you're more knowledgeable than you pretend to be. Come on, for a friend.'

Friend.

'Fine, one piece of advice, because it's your first time.' I picked up my tray, dipping my head as I did, so I could murmur as quietly as possible, 'Fight smart, not hard. If you bet on the fights, bet low.'

'Thanks.' He toyed with his drink. 'Will I see you there?'

'No.'

'Really? That's a shame. It'd be nice to have a friendly face around.'

His gaze was too sharp. I tensed. How could he know that I had been to the bunker to watch in the past? I didn't go often—but if Theo was here we sometimes went together.

'No promises, new boy.'

I left before he could ask anything else.

I was riled up the rest of the night, and it wasn't because of anger. The truth was, I was jealous: why did Maddock get to go to the bunker, but I couldn't? Why did I constantly get judged for my choices? I'd been so good. I'd followed every rule. It wasn't fair.

I was filled with a storm of pent-up emotions that had nowhere to go.

What I wanted to do was dance.

Dancing was my outlet; it always had been. As a child, I had danced frequently and furiously. I had practised hours every day, pouring all of the wild, uncontrollable emotions into the pursuit of complex steps and technical precision.

I really missed it.

Working in the bunker had changed dancing for me. In many ways, that was my biggest regret; not that I'd skated close to becoming a prostitute, nor that I'd worked for a gang that made their money through extortion and drug dealing. I missed the innocence and naivety that had pervaded dance in my early years.

Ellery and Bas arrived an hour before my shift ended. I hadn't seen them since Sunday, and I'd have preferred not to see them this week, especially not now, when I was already in a bad mood. They, of course, could come and go from the bunker as they pleased, and any other club in town, and no one would stop them, judge them, or mistake them for hookers.

'What can I get you?' I greeted, my tone several degrees sourer than usual. Ellery looked surprised.

'Hey, kitten.'

I tried to find the energy for my usual games, but somehow it had vanished. 'Ellery, Bas.'

Ellery slid his arm around my waist. 'What's up, baby?'

'Nothing.' I stepped away. 'But I have tables to serve. What can I get you? Cash upfront.'

'Two beers.' Bas held out a fiver. His gaze was studiously neutral.

I took the money. 'Coming right up.'

Ignoring Ellery's disappointed face, I headed for the bar and passed Anna the money. 'Two beers.'

'You alright?'

'Yes.' *No.* I was in a bad mood. I wanted to fight someone, and Ellery had just presented himself. It was a bad idea, but chances were it would happen anyway. I always fought the wrong people.

Sav.

My parents.

Ellery.

Theo.

'I'm fine.' I forced a smile.

'Alright, then.' She passed me two chilled beers. Reluctantly, I made my way back to Ellery and Bas and set their drinks down in front of them.

'Two beers.'

'Hey.' Ellery put his arm around me again, not flirtatiously, but like a hug. I tensed. 'Heard we were going to be entertaining one of your friends tomorrow night.'

My stomach flip-flopped. 'So I heard. Don't break him.'

'Concerned?' Bas asked.

'My sister might be disappointed.' I shrugged. 'She seems to like him.'

'You could come watch, kitten,' Ellery suggested, his thumb rubbing circles on the patch of bare skin between my jeans and my shirt.

I felt warm in a way I refused to acknowledge. 'No thanks.'

'Why not? You don't have to do anything but watch.' He stroked the waist of my trousers. 'Bas is fighting. You'll like watching him.'

'Men beating each other up to vent their frustrations. Great entertainment.'

'Aw, don't be like that.'

I moved his hand. 'I have other customers. Sorry, Ellery. We can muck about some other night.'

I walked away, feeling both their gazes on my back. My heart was racing, and the room felt small and airless all of a sudden.

I wanted to go.

I just couldn't go with him.

I should have known he wouldn't leave it alone, though. Hours later, when I got off shift, he was waiting for me outside the back.

'Kitten—'

'Don't.' I started to walk past him. 'I'm not in the mood.'

'I can see that.' He followed me. 'What's wrong, kitten? Did something happen?'

Yeah, everyone else gets what they want, and I'm waitressing for drunk idiots because you needed eyes in the Kranikovska.

'It's none of your business.'

'Come on.' He slid his arms around me, pulling my back against his chest. His jacket was open, his body warm and hard against my back. 'Let me help you.'

I stiffened. Ellery's hands cupped my hips, stroking those awful, tantalising circles. 'Leave me alone, Ellery.'

'Really?' His breath was hot against my ear. 'Is that what you want?'

'Yes, I—' He turned me, and I lost my balance, catching myself with a hand against his chest. 'Ellery, stop.'

'Let me persuade you.'

'No.'

'Not as a trade. Just for fun.' Ellery's hands turned gentle on my shoulders, his thumbs massaging gently through my coat.

'No.' Somehow, my voice came out firm. Ellery dropped his hands, disappointment in his eyes.

'If you're sure.'

'I—' A good half of me wanted to change my mind and throw myself into his arms. 'I'm just tired this week.'

'I know.' He brought his hand up, stroking my cheek with his knuckles. 'Come back to my place. I'll make you dinner.'

'Ellery…'

'Just dinner and sleep. Nothing else. I can sleep on the couch.'

I sighed. Whatever I said, he'd have an answer. Ellery was a devil, tempting me in every way: with pretty looks, offers of warmth and safety—and worse, the respect that I didn't seem to get from any of the others. He'd stopped when I asked him to… and I almost wished he hadn't.

Fuck, I needed to go.

I turned away, starting towards the square. Ellery trailed after me. 'Can I at least walk you home?'

'If I get seen with you… People are getting the wrong idea, Ellery.'

'Do you mean people? Or do you mean Maddock and your sister?'

'Why would I care what Maddock thinks?' I snapped.

'You care what everyone thinks, kitten. It's your biggest weakness.'

He was right; he was always right. When had Ellery gotten to know me so well? I rounded the side of the hotel, kicking the cobblestones disconsolately. 'I need space.'

'Tell me to go, then.'

I looked back at him. His eyes were like silver in the moonlight. 'I…'

A car horn cut through the square, and the moment shattered like glass. I stepped back. 'Sorry, Ellery.'

He cast his eyes downwards for a moment before looking back at me and nodding. 'I'll see you soon, kitten.'

'Yeah.'

Ellery stepped past me, heading for his car. Bas was waiting. Bas was the one who had hooted.

Bas had saved me from myself.

EIGHT

I GAVE UP ON SLEEP when Savannah crawled out of bed and dressed. It was still dark, the horizon just getting light outside our curtainless windows. I had been tossing and turning all night, unable to escape the image of Ellery by moonlight, pleading with me to give in.

I'd spent the last few years trying to convince myself that all he wanted was sex — and whilst I didn't doubt that was part of it, last night had begun to unravel the illusion.

But I couldn't give in. I just couldn't.

At six, Savannah bent over me, her lips brushing my forehead, her hair tickling my cheeks. 'Have a good day.'

She slipped away.

I listened to the front door opening and closing, locking again. Once I was sure my sister was gone, I threw my covers off, letting the cool air dispel the last of my sleepiness, and dressed in light clothes.

I needed to dance.

Our flat backed onto The Arsonist's training ground. In summer, if I opened our bedroom window, I could hear the noise of the pub drifting up. Now that autumn had arrived, all of the windows were shut tight. The training ground was damp and abandoned in the early morning light.

I jogged up my street and then back down Busker Street to warm up, before ducking down the pothole-ridden brick road that led to the TA's loading bay and the training yard.

Once upon a time, I'd attended dance classes: they hadn't exactly been state-of-the-art, but I'd taken a taxi-truck to the nice part of town every day, where there was a studio with mirrored walls, barres, and a proper wooden floor. Those days were over. Now, I made use of whatever I had available. The training yard was an open concrete space with a few picnic benches, some ancient gym equipment, and the old octagonal fighting cage.

No one used this cage anymore; they'd long since built a better one in the basement, which had the added advantage that it was out of sight of any of the lawmakers who were trying desperately to shut down the cage fights. But it worked for my purposes. I climbed over the barrier and began working a few stretches, loosening my body.

How long had it been since the last time I'd just danced?

I still did my exercises every single morning before work, with a fervour that bordered on religion, but actual dancing had fallen by the wayside. I didn't have time. I didn't have a safe space. It was tainted by association with dancing in the bunker…

Excuses.

Once I was warmed up, I moved to the middle of the cage and closed my eyes. I didn't have music, but my head easily filled in the familiar notes of one of the songs we played in the bar, and I began to move.

Dancing came naturally to me. When I heard a song, I could picture the right combination of moves to augment the music—here a jeté, there a pirouette. I choreographed dances in my head on the slow days at work. Now, the moves unspooled like a Pre-Crash film, my body moving as though guided by a puppeteer. I poured every ounce of restlessness, frustration, and fear into my dance, pushing my emotions out of my chest until they filled my entire body and flowed out through my feet into the ground. I threw myself from one move to the next until I was exhausted.

Finally, my feet slowed. I faced an invisible audience, bowing slowly, then straightened up, breathing hard. My hair stuck to my neck from sweat and my thighs ached. It was a good ache, though.

A flicker of movement caught my eye, and I reached for my knife— which wasn't there. I'd thrown my coat over the railing. I spun around—and came face-to-face with Bas.

He'd been jogging; he was dressed in combats and a vest, gun at his hip, and covered in sweat. It was the first time I'd seen him with his jacket off. He had a tattoo covering his left upper arm, a twisting design of two dragons fighting. His right arm only had the symbol of the Iron Fists.

I lowered my hand away from my coat. 'What are you doing here?'

Bas curled his lip. 'Training. What does it look like?'

I shrugged and began collecting my things. I was done—but even if I hadn't been, I'd have left. No way I was dancing for him.

'What were you doing?' He hopped the railing with half the effort it had cost me, straightening up. I rarely saw him standing, and I was glad for it. He was probably eight inches taller than me, enough to be imposing.

'Dancing.'

'I thought you stopped dancing.'

'I stopped dancing at the bunker. I still dance for fun.'

He stared at me. 'You're risking your own safety hanging out in a deserted yard for fun?'

'I can look after myself.'

'I stood there for five minutes before you noticed me.'

Oops. Fuck. My cheeks burnt with embarrassment. 'Well, I hope you enjoyed the show.'

'I didn't. I was just waiting for you to leave.'

His words were like knives in my chest. I didn't know what to do with this feeling. When I'd danced at the bunker, every man who saw me had stopped to admire me. I'd never met someone who was so disinterested, and the more he showed it, the more I wanted to force him to admit that he found me sexy. Why? Was I really that messed up?

'Right.' I stepped closer to him. 'There's training facilities in Sayle's compound. Why would you come here, anyway?'

Under the overcast sky, Bas's eyes were like chips of black ice. 'I like privacy. You can go now.'

'I was here first.'

'Now I'm here.'

We were almost chest-to-chest. I glared up at him. 'What the hell is your problem, anyway? I was just dancing.'

'Dance is frivolous. Some of us don't have time to wait around whilst you practice showing off.'

'Showing off?' I parroted in disbelief. 'You think that's showing off? I'd like to see you do any of that!'

'Why would I want to? I have better things to train.'

'Right, like beating people up. A worthy pursuit.' I rolled my eyes.

'Self-defence is a worthy pursuit.' Bas crossed his arms, scowling. 'Not that you'd know anything about that.'

'I'm plenty able to look after myself!'

'You think because you have a knife and you've kneed a few men in the balls you're an expert? You don't know a thing about fighting. When the going gets tough, you call Marco to look after you.'

'I do not!'

'Instead of learning to defend yourself, you make yourself a burden to the people around you.'

My jaw dropped. He couldn't have hurt me worse if he'd actually stabbed me—his words jabbed right into my most vulnerable parts. 'I'm not a burden!'

'Prove it.'

I didn't stop to think about what he might mean by that—I balled my fist up and punched him right in the solar plexus.

The jab landed, hard. My fist exploded in pain—Bas was like a fucking statue. Then he shoved me. I stumbled off balance, and a second later he slammed me against the railing, the metal digging into my hip.

The pain woke me up. What the hell was I doing? I wasn't usually violent with people.

Bas laughed. 'Pathetic.'

I threw my elbow back into his chest and shoved my boot into his knee. He grunted, his grip loosening, and I managed to twist around to face him. His gaze was alive with something—maybe he liked the challenge. He shoved me harder into the railing. 'You can't get away, can you?'

I twisted, trying to escape him, but he was as immoveable as a wall. Well, if he wasn't going to respect me—why should I respect him?

I went up on tiptoes and kissed him.

I barely had a moment to feel how soft his lips were against mine before his entire body went slack. He pulled away so fast you'd have thought I'd threatened to light him on fire. We stood four feet apart, staring at one another, both breathing hard. Bas glared at me.

'Don't do that again.'

'Don't throw your weight around,' I snapped.

'Why not? Nothing I said was wrong.'

He made me so angry I couldn't think straight. 'If it bothers you that much, then teach me how to fight.'

Bas's eyes widened. I'd finally managed to surprise him.

'No,' he said finally.

'Then drop it.'

'No,' he repeated. 'Not as long as you're asking for the wrong reasons.'

I was *furious*. 'How the fuck would you know why I'm asking?'

'You think you can mess with me by pushing my boundaries,' Bas said imperiously. 'You can't. But as long as you're trying, I won't help you.'

I felt as though I'd been slapped. My hip ached from where it had collided with the railing, but it was nothing compared to the burn of humiliation spreading through my chest. 'Maybe if you weren't so determined to hurt me, I wouldn't have tried!'

'I never tried to hurt you.' Bas's eyes bored into mine. 'You want to control men. I have no interest in being controlled. I'm not Marco.'

I gripped the railing, letting the metal cut into my hands to ground me. 'Please.' The more he denied me, the more I wanted it.

'No.'

'I'll—' But what I might have offered, I would never know. Behind me, someone laughed.

'Didn't take you as the sort who pays whores, Bas.'

I'd never seen anyone do an about-face as fast as Bas did. He twisted, his expression darkening with anger.

'Hannover.'

I turned to see that someone had crept up on me—again. This man was about thirty-five, with shoulder-length brown hair and tan skin. There was something vaguely familiar about him, as though I'd met him before in passing, but I wasn't sure if I had seen him around the bar. I generally had a very good facial recall, and he had a distinctive scar cutting through his bottom lip on the left side. I didn't think I'd seen him before—maybe I just recognised his type: hardened, cruel. A gang member.

And Bas hated him.

I shrugged my coat on as he approached, my hand finding the comforting shape of my knife's handle in the inside pocket. Bas had one hand on his gun, watching Hannover without blinking.

'Shall I tell Sayle that Moriarty's lieutenants are infringing on his territory?'

Hannover made a show of looking around. 'I was under the impression The Arsonist was neutral ground.'

'Only during the fights.'

'So generous of Sayle to allow us in for a few hours a day.' Hannover smiled mockingly. 'Shame he sent the errand boy to pass on his message.'

Bas drew his gun.

'Ahhh.' Hannover chuckled. 'How things have changed. Now that you have a gun, you plan to use it every chance you can get. Going to shoot me, *boy*?'

'Get out of here,' Bas sneered.

'Why? I'm not breaking any of the rules—but you will be, if you shoot me.'

I looked uneasily between the two men. Hannover, whoever he was, looked perfectly relaxed. He seemed amused. Bas, on the other hand, was tense and… Dare I say it?

Yes, yes he was.

Bas was afraid.

It was a fear I recognised: a deep-seated helplessness, the knowledge that no matter what you did, you had no real chance of fighting back. So you reached for the biggest weapon you could, determined that if they took you, you wouldn't go easily.

Hannover sauntered the rest of the way to the cage and vaulted over the railing. Bas took a step back, a myriad of emotions flitting over his face. His hand shook as he aimed the gun. 'Leave.'

'Don't think I will.' Hannover stepped closer to me. 'She's a pretty little thing. One of Sayle's? How much to share?'

'I'm not—'

'I don't share,' Bas cut across me. 'Especially not with you.'

'Oh, but I thought you had plenty of experience *sharing*.' Hannover smirked. 'Or did you get tired of it?'

'I'm not sharing her.' Bas tucked his gun away and grabbed my arm, his grip punishing. I tried to pull away, to no avail. His fingers felt like steel around my upper arm. 'Let's go.'

'Where?' I wasn't sure I wanted to leave with Bas.

'Home.' He shoved me to the gate. It was locked with a padlock, so I scrambled over, almost falling to my knees when Bas didn't let go of me in time.

'Running away?' Hannover asked in a silky voice.

'If you want a fight so badly, I'll give you one,' Bas said dismissively, landing beside me with a muted thud. 'Tonight at the bunker. But Harley is not up for grabs.'

Hannover laughed. 'You wouldn't have the guts, boy. You might think you're strong, now that you have Sayle's men at your back. But some things never change. You still don't know how to look us in the eye, do you?'

Bas's hand collided with the middle of my back. 'Go.'

I realised I'd been staring between the two of them. I stumbled into motion, heading for the road. Bas grabbed my arm again and towed me along, calling over his shoulder, 'I don't need to look you in the eye to shoot you, Hannover. Just remember that.'

Hannover stayed where he was, his laughter following us until he was out of sight.

The moment we reached the road, I yanked my arm away. 'Get off me.'

'You're welcome,' Bas snapped.

'You expect me to be grateful?' My voice was high and shrill. 'I don't know how many times I have to explain this to you! *I. Am. Not. A. Whore.*'

'You can be glad that's all he thinks you are,' Bas hissed. 'You think that's the worst possible thing a man can think of you? Hannover keeps a regular cadre of slaves to abuse in his free time—'

'Like you?'

His hands clenched into fists, a look of such fury flickering over his face that I actually took a step back.

'That is none of your business.'

Oh yeah, Bas had been his slave. It was obvious. I swallowed, guilt making my throat close up.

'I didn't mean—'

'You have no idea what you're talking about.'

'I do, actually. My mother was a slave—'

'And I'm sure she told her beloved daughter all the gory details.' Bas pressed closer to me, invading my personal space. My stomach clenched. I backed into the wall of the pub, my hair snagging on the rough brick. 'You need to learn to keep your mouth shut.'

'I'm trying!' Tears sprang into my eyes. 'You don't know what it's like, alright? The only thing men think when they look at me is how much it'll cost them to get me to spread my legs for a night.'

'At least you have the option of saying no,' Bas said coldly. 'And be glad for it.'

I shuddered. 'I know. I know.'

He backed off a step, his expression closing down until his eyes were as empty and reflective as the glassy surface of a lake. 'Don't go dancing alone in public places again.'

'I don't have anywhere else to do it.'

'Then don't do it at *all*,' Bas snapped, visibly exasperated. 'If Hannover had come across you alone, he'd have raped you, then shot you.'

I bit my tongue. I couldn't just stop dancing. The alternative was losing my mind. 'He followed you there, not me.'

Bas jerked his head, maybe a nod, maybe just a shrug. 'That doesn't make your behaviour any less careless. I'm not Marco. Next time you need help, I'll just walk on by.'

'I don't expect your help. I know what Sayle's lot are like. Most of you will just as soon join in as help a woman out.'

Bas flinched. 'Go home.'

I squashed the urge to argue back. 'Fine.'

For a second, neither of us moved. Then Bas flicked his head angrily towards the road. I turned and left.

When I looked back, he was standing there, staring at me, his hand on his gun.

I shivered and broke into a jog. I didn't like having Bas at my back.

By the time I left for work, it was raining again, and I was in a foul mood.

I was short money for rent, and that meant that if I didn't make plenty of tips this weekend, I was screwed. I wore my lowest-cut top, and when Anton pulled me onto his lap, I made sure to grind plenty and move away slowly.

It wasn't helping.

It was the rain, the fucking rain. It killed our business for about a week or two before everyone got used to it, and business went back to normal. But I couldn't afford it, not now.

If Ellery had come into the bar that weekend, I might well have given in. Given him what he wanted. It would be easy, with him, because I liked him.

But Ellery didn't come in.

Instead, twenty minutes before my shift ended on Saturday, fate sent me a different boon.

There was a hullaballoo in the lobby, and then Tom appeared, signalling me over urgently. I abandoned the table I'd been wiping down.

'What's going on?'

'The mayor is here. I need you to—' He glanced around, his gaze frantic. 'We'd better let them upstairs. Go, go.'

It would mean leaving Dana to cover the bar alone. Grimacing, I nodded sharply and hurried to the door. There was a huddle of men drying off in the entrance hall. I sprinted up the stairs and opened one of the rarely used private rooms. Three sofas were arranged around a low table, with a drinks cart in the corner. I wiped everything down at double speed, then fetched a bottle of whiskey and cracked it open as the men filed in.

The mayor was a stout, unimpressive figure: thinning brown hair, gold-rimmed glasses, and an expensive suit. He was accompanied by two men, both of whom I recognised.

Richard Godfrey and Simon Cavanaugh.

Louis and Brody's fathers.

Simon Cavanaugh was a dead ringer for his son—the same blond hair, the same weak chin. Richard Godfrey was tall, with the softness of a man who never had to worry about where his next meal was coming from. He had curly blond hair and tan skin.

I waited for them to sit, before stepping forwards.

'May I serve you drinks, sir?'

'Please,' the mayor said. 'Tom said there was a bottle of the double-aged… Ah, yes, that one.' He nodded at the bottle I was holding, then turned away, dismissing me from his mind. I poured three glasses and set them down before retreating to the shadows. My job was to be invisible until they needed me again.

The mayor swirled his whiskey, before taking a sip. 'Ah, yes. So, tell me, gentlemen.'

Cavanaugh eyed the whiskey as though it were poison. Lacing his gloved fingers together in his lap, he said, 'We should wait for Rochester.'

Mayor Darling waved a hand. 'He'll be along shortly. We should be sure of the, ah, party line, if you catch my drift.'

Everyone in town could have caught that drift. I relaxed into the shadows, trying to make myself as unobtrusive as possible. What were they talking about?

Godfrey sipped his drink. 'Have you spoken to the contact you mentioned last time?'

'As promised.' The mayor sat back smugly. 'Percival has assured me of his support. All that is left is to move the correct players into place.'

'I would not be overconfident at this point,' Cavanaugh drawled, turning his gaze to the window. His eyes swept over me without taking notice. 'We all know how fickle the criminals in this town can be. The limited assurances we've offered them so far will not be enough, going forward.'

'I do not believe—'

'Yes, we could fill a book with the things you do and don't believe,' Cavanaugh sneered. The mayor flushed indignantly.

'Now, see here. I was the one who approached the different parties to negotiate. I've put everything in place—'

'So you say.' Cavanaugh picked up his glass, swirling the liquid slowly. 'Yet you refuse to share the particulars of *what* you've put in place with us.'

'We can't risk this information falling into the wrong hands before we're ready. If the Iron Fists were to get wind of it, everything could fall through.'

I bit my lip hard to stifle a gasp. They were plotting against the Iron Fists? Did that mean Percival and his gang had allied themselves with the mayor?

Why would the mayor even agree to that?

Mayor Darling slammed his hand on the sofa with a dull thwack. I jerked, and immediately stilled again. Occupied with my thoughts, I had missed what he'd said.

'Even so,' Cavanaugh said.

'Yet we can't let the situation remain as it is, and this is a unique opportunity.' Godfrey's tone was ponderous. 'And, after all, we deserve what is rightfully ours.'

'Precisely!' the mayor exclaimed. 'We made our fortunes on the whiskey trade before Sayle was even born. All he's doing is stealing the fruits of our labour.'

Godfrey nodded, and even Cavanaugh looked as though he was considering the words. 'In the end, the risk to us is small. So long as no one links it back—'

'There will be no evidence. We can allow them to wipe one another out, and when the time is right, we sweep in.' The mayor clasped his hands, beaming.

'And what was the agreement?' Godfrey enquired. He seemed wary.

'It's a simple deal. Our manpower in exchange for their support,' Mayor Darling said.

Godfrey's eyebrows rose. 'What are they asking?'

'Seven per month.'

'A small price to pay.' Cavanaugh waved his hand dismissively.

Godfrey shook his head. 'It's too many. People will notice.'

'It can easily be explained away,' the mayor disagreed. 'My contact assured me—'

'We should be wary of believing the promises of men who, after all, have a vested interest in deposing us.' Godfrey frowned. 'Who will take the fall if this is discovered?'

'Everyone will point the finger at Moriarty. It's only natural,' the mayor insisted.

'You can't be certain—'

'Certainty is a crutch.' The mayor sat forward. 'Gentlemen, the time is now. This is our town. It's long past time that we reminded Sayle of that.'

Cavanaugh was nodding, but Godfrey was still unsure. Before they could continue, the door swung inwards. As one, the three men turned, and then the mayor smiled.

'Ah, Rochester. I was beginning to think you wouldn't make it.'

'A small matter with security. I apologise for the delay.' The man who entered was broad-shouldered and strong, with steel grey hair and cold green eyes. He strode briskly over to the sofas, shaking hands with the other three men, before standing back and gesturing to another man who had followed him in. 'You've met my son, Rodney, haven't you?'

'Of course,' the mayor said. 'At the last dinner. Have a seat, please. Girl.' He clicked his fingers at me. 'More whiskey.'

'Yes, sir.' I fetched two more glasses, bringing them to the table and leaning down to fill them. As I slid one in front of Rodney Rochester, I looked up—and froze.

Recognition slammed me in the chest.

People went on and on about how Savannah and I looked the same—as though we hadn't noticed—but in truth, it was fairly rare for siblings to look exactly the same. I wouldn't, for example, have compared Louis Godfrey and his sister and said they were obviously related. This man, however, was so familiar that the relation was undoubtable.

That hair.

That skin tone.

Those bottle-green eyes.

Somehow, these two men were related to Bas.

They had to be.

How?

I darted a glance at the man's wrist, but it was covered. He wore a dress shirt and chinos, his curly hair neatly styled. His gaze was politely curious, drifting over me without taking note. I was just a waitress, after all, and a cheaply dressed one, at that.

I straightened up and recapped the bottle.

'We were just discussing the plans for the new development,' the mayor began, flicking his fingers dismissively at me. I retreated. 'As I was telling Simon, we'll be needing to—'

'Actually,' Rodney cut in suddenly, 'my apologies, Mayor Darling. Waitress?'

I stepped back over to him. 'Sir?'

'Ice,' he said. 'I'd like ice.'

'Oh. Yes, sir. I'll have to go downstairs.'

'Good. Go now.' His eyes bored into me: the same eyes as Bas, with the same ability to see right through me. I edged to the door. His eyes didn't leave me for a second, not until I was out the door and had shut it behind me.

'We meet again.'

I jumped. Leaning against the wall in the darkness of the hall was another man. I focused on him as he stepped into the light. It was Evander Hardwick, the mayor's security detail.

I stiffened my spine. 'Mr Hardwick.'

'Ms Benoit. The dancer, not the doctor.' He smirked. 'Fancy seeing you here.'

'I'm a waitress, actually. I work here.'

'Oh, of course. Forgive me, I should pay closer attention to where Sayle positions his girls.'

My hands felt sweaty all of a sudden, and my heartbeat seemed impossibly loud in the quiet hallway. Music drifted up from the bar downstairs. 'I don't work for Sayle.'

'You mean you won't be reporting to him that we were here, nor what was discussed?'

It hadn't escaped my notice that Rodney had very quickly found an excuse to get me out of the room. The mayor might be stupid—the very reason Sayle allowed him his power—but his friends definitely weren't.

'I don't think I'm the person you're implying I am, Mr Hardwick.' I tried to sidestep him, but he moved smoothly into my path again.

'That's good.' He caught a strand of my hair, rubbing it between my fingers. His lips stretched into a cold smile. 'Because you know what happens to girls who mess around with things that are beyond their understanding. I'd hate for your sister to end up alone.'

My heart was hammering against my ribcage like a fist against a door. 'Stay away from my sister,' I choked.

'Your sister has nothing to fear from me, Ms Benoit.'

But you do. He didn't speak the words, but I heard them anyway. I shuddered. 'I have a job to do. If you'll excuse me…'

'Of course.' He stepped away, a polite smile on his face. I didn't trust the look. The worst men were the ones who could kill with a smile. It meant they were as broken as I was.

Lifting my chin, I marched past him. I could feel his gaze on my back.

'You should be careful working so late, Ms Benoit. You never know who you might meet on the walk back.'

'I'm perfectly capable of taking care of myself, thank you,' I said primly, before hurrying for the stairs.

Men.

I hated them.

'Everything okay?' Chef asked as I ducked into the kitchen. We all called him Chef, although his name was Doug. He was leaning over the stove, stirring a pot of soup.

'I need ice.'

'Heard there was a private group.'

'Uh-huh. Big hush-hush.' I rolled my eyes, scooping ice into a glass. 'I gotta get back up there.'

'Alrighty, then.'

Hardwick was silent when I reached the hallway again, his eyes fixed on me. I avoided his gaze and knocked on the door before poking my head in.

'I have the ice, sir.'

The men were all standing, obviously saying their goodbyes. Rodney stepped up to me.

'It's alright, we were just finished. But thank you.' He held out a hand, a crisp banknote pinched between his index and middle fingers. I took it. Five hundred new pounds.

Holy fuck.

That was my rent for the next two weeks, right there. I stared at him, my face feeling paralysed. I couldn't think of a single thing to say.

'I think you broke her.' Cavanaugh snorted. 'Girl's probably never seen that much money in her life before.'

I stiffened.

'She'll take it and keep her mouth shut if she knows what's good for her,' Rochester Senior sneered, shooting a pointed look at the mayor. 'Come on, Rodney. Let's go.'

I backed away from the door, letting them out. Hardwick's hand touched my shoulder blades—before I could push him away, he'd tucked another note down my top. I was being paid handsomely for my silence.

I kept mum as the men filed past, their miens relaxed now that they'd concluded their business. Once they were all gone, I entered the room and started clearing up. My shift had long since ended. The sooner I was done, the sooner I could leave.

I should have gone straight to the drop point to leave a note for Ellery, but it was still raining, and I'd finished my shift late. I was tired. I didn't want to roam around the streets alone when there wasn't even the moon to shed its light.

It wasn't sensible.

So I went straight home.

NINE

GUILT PLAGUED ME ALL OF SUNDAY, every hour that went by without me putting a note in the drop. The mayor was here. He met with Cavanaugh and Godfrey. They were discussing overthrowing the Iron Fists.

Does Bas have a brother?

They paid me 600 NP to keep quiet.

The money hung over me like a threat. I hated having to pass Ellery information, but I didn't want to play rich men's games either. That was a game I didn't know the rules of, and I was sure no matter what I did, I'd lose.

I hadn't decided what to say yet, and I was putting it off, but I couldn't get it out of my head. It didn't help that the bar was quiet; even Clem had been scared off by the rain. I distracted myself from the circling thoughts by doing every last task around the bar: I repaired chair legs, sanded away splinters, cleaned the windows, and scraped the stubborn rubber marks off the floor. I was redrawing the chalkboard behind the bar when a voice said, 'Well, isn't this a sight for sore eyes.'

I almost dropped the chalk. Anna squealed. 'Mr Tam!'

It was a privilege of working at the Kranikovska that we got to see almost everyone in town, but I definitely liked some of them better than others. Turning, I offered a smile to our newcomer.

'Hullo, Mr Tam.'

It was weird being formal with one of the Iron Fists, seeing as all of them had seen me dancing in my underwear at some point or another, but Gabriel Tam invited it. There was a sort of high-class glamour in the way he dressed and acted that set him apart from the rest of us.

'Miss Anna, Miss Harley.' He smiled. 'How are my favourite ladies?'

'Great.' Anna beamed at him. She had a crush a mile wide, a sort of hero worship which only seemed to grow with each one of Gabriel

Tam's long absences. 'How was Crater's Edge?'

'Very good, thank you.' Gabriel slid into a seat at the bar. He was a slight man, barely taller than I was, with thick black hair and a serious face that matched his formal demeanour. He gave me a careful smile, and I nodded back. I liked Gabriel well enough, but he was always careful around me; he knew very well that I was an informant for Ellery.

'We've missed you.' Anna set a whiskey in front of him. 'You were gone longer than usual this time.'

'It does seem like a long time, doesn't it?' He sipped his whiskey and smiled. 'Ah, you're spoiling me, Miss Anna. I didn't pay for top shelf.'

'It's on me.' She patted his hand. I turned back to the chalkboard, shading in a curlicue in the corner, my ears perked for potential gossip.

'What were you working on this time?' Anna asked.

'The same as usual. We have such trouble with the supply routes — every time I turn my back, Tango Sierra are blockading again. Everyone wants what the Iron Fists have.'

'Well, of course they do. We make the best whiskey in the West Rim.'

Gabriel laughed. 'That we do. And how have you been, Miss Anna? No trouble here, I hope?'

Anna's voice dipped, and I imagined her leaning in to impart her gossip. 'The Black Hands rousted us a few weeks back.'

'Goodness me. I hope everyone's alright.'

'Oh yes, we were fine. I fetched Uncle Tom, and he smoothed things over. They shot out one of the windows, though.'

Of course Anna had been fine — I'd sent her out of the room before they got there. I was the one who'd had a gun held to my head. I pressed too hard against the board, and my chalk snapped. One half skidded down my leg and hit the counter, leaving a streak of white.

Damnit.

I brushed my leg off and scrambled down from the stool.

'Were you there, Miss Harley?' Tam asked.

'I was, but I can handle roustings.' I shrugged. 'They're just throwing their weight around to prove they can.'

'Harley's cool as a cucumber. You know that.' Anna giggled.

Yeah, I was cool. I gnashed my teeth together, shifting the stool to the opposite end of the bar. These days, I didn't feel cool at all.

'I'm sure she was,' Gabriel agreed.

Our first customers of the evening entered, taking a table by the wall. I grabbed my tray and let myself out from behind the bar. 'I'll be right back.'

'Of course. I wouldn't want to keep you from your job,' Gabriel replied.

It wasn't much of a job tonight. I'd hoped I wouldn't have to use the money Rodney had given me, but it didn't look like I was going to have a choice unless things picked up fast. I'd barely made two NP in tips all day.

I put my best smile on and sashayed over to the table... and the smile melted off my face like ice on a hot day. Hardwick lounged in one of the seats, watching me with a smug grin. His comrade was studying one of the spots where I'd patched the paint on the wall with some interest. He looked up with a smirk. 'This place is looking mighty spick and span tonight.'

It was Hannover, the guy who had interrupted Bas and me on The Arsonist's training ground. My stomach lurched. The Black Hands almost never came into the bar—outside of the roustings—because their territory was outside of the town limits.

'Good evening gentlemen,' I choked.

'Harley Benoit,' Hardwick said. 'We meet again.'

'I work here every day, Mr Hardwick. I don't know why you're so surprised.' I bit my tongue after saying it. Why did I do that? Why cheek the guy who probably worked for one of the gangs? *Harley, you idiot.*

'Oh, so *that's* her name.' Hannover looked me up and down, a slow look, obviously undressing me with his eyes. I suppressed a shudder. *'Harley.'*

'What...' I cleared my throat. 'What can I get you, gentlemen?'

'Why so unfriendly?' Hannover wrapped a hand around my leg, sending shivers down my spine. 'You weren't that cold to Sebastian.'

Sebastian? Did he mean Bas?

I schooled my expression. 'I'm sorry, Mr Hannover. I think you have the wrong impression about me and Bas.'

'Really? Because the way he told it, you're quite... close.' Hannover smirked. I didn't like the look in his eyes—there was a blankness there that unsettled me. I stepped away.

'I hardly know him.'

'You don't have to know a man to suck his cock, darling.'

I cleared my throat again. 'I'm not a whore. Especially not for the Iron Fists.'

Hannover's eyes roved over my torso again. 'If it's free, all the better.'

Gag. I clenched my fingers around my tray. 'What can I get you?' This time, my voice was firm.

'Two whiskeys.' Hardwick's eyes danced in amusement as he tucked a few coins into my apron. He patted my wrist. 'Off you go.'

Biting my tongue, I turned and walked off. I kept my chin high and my shoulders stiff—but I could feel their gazes burning my back.

What were they doing here?

Better question: how could I get rid of them ASAP?

Gabriel and Anna watched me worriedly as I approached. I schooled my expression, signalling for Anna to pour two whiskeys.

'Everything alright, Miss Harley?' Gabriel asked.

I forced a smile. 'Perfectly alright, thanks.'

Gabriel's gaze slid past me, settling on the two men as his brow creased in a frown. Anna passed me the two whiskeys. I wrapped my hands more firmly around my tray, took a fortifying breath, and made my way back into hell.

Hannover's grin was as smug as a cat that had got in the cream. He watched me approaching, arms crossed, legs stretched out, so I had to dodge around them to set the drinks down.

'So, if you and Sebastian don't have an arrangement, what were you doing with him on the training ground?'

'We met by coincidence.' I put a whiskey in front of him. 'Enjoy your drinks. If you need anything else'—*shove the request up your arse*—'let me know.'

'Running away so soon?' Hardwick asked.

'She doesn't seem to be in the mood to entertain,' Hannover drawled.

'If you require entertainment, I'm happy to turn the music up.'

'Oh, come now.' Hannover dragged a finger up my side. I flinched away, and he laughed. 'You know that's not what we mean. It's not as though you have anything better to do, is it?'

'My job does not consist solely of putting drinks on tables.' The moment I said the words, I regretted them. 'I have other things to do—behind the bar.'

'Such as reporting on us to Gabriel Tam?' Hannover smirked. 'Look at him, so eager to leap to your protection. Maybe we should give him a reason—'

I cleared my throat, drowning out his words, and stepped back.

'I think you're scaring the lady, Dean,' Hardwick said.

Scaring? My gaze snapped to his, my irritation boiling over. I refused to be scared of them, not on my territory. 'Doesn't the mayor need security on Sundays, Mr Hardwick?'

Hardwick laughed. 'Occasionally, I am permitted a day off. As are you, I presume.'

'I keep to myself on my days off.'

Hardwick's smile only grew. Hannover stroked my hip again. 'You be careful, love. That mouth is going to get you in trouble.'

My heart was racing, but I plunged ahead anyway, trying to claw back control of the situation. 'Really? I find most people appreciate my sense of humour.'

His gaze was as cold and dark as the ocean—at least, how I imagined the ocean to be. I'd never seen it. His lips twisted into a cruel smile. 'Oh, I could think of better uses for that mouth.'

Recognition cut through me like a fog lifting. The constant itch of déjà vu suddenly made sense—I knew where I had seen Hannover before. The first time I'd met him, he'd put a gun to my head.

'It was you,' I said in sudden realisation. 'At the rousting.' As soon as I said it, I wished I hadn't. *Idiot, idiot, idiot.* The last thing I needed was to paint a target on my back.

Hannover leant back, smirking. 'Surprise.'

'Not really.'

Our gazes clashed. This time, I refused to look away.

'Not really, indeed.' He smirked, his hand ghosting over his side, where I guessed his firearm was concealed. Benny was on the door again, the little worm. 'Would you like a replay? Last time we were interrupted at such an… *interesting* moment.'

Footsteps thudded against the tiles in the lobby a moment before finally, finally, more customers arrived. My smile was thin on my face.

'I'm afraid I'll have to ask for a rain-check, Mr Hannover, as delightful as your offer is.' My words dripped with sarcasm. Hannover, far from being offended, roared with laughter.

'I can see why Sayle's brats like you. You seem like a smart girl.' His fingers slid through my belt loops, yanking me to a halt as I tried to step away. At once, my heart rate kicked up, panic seeping in. I tried to sidestep, but he held fast. 'You be careful, pretty girl. Sebastian isn't the man you think he is.'

'But he's twice the man I think you are.'

Hannover's eyes narrowed. I was shocked at my own recklessness—but if there was one thing I couldn't abide, it was a slave owner. The thought of what kind of atrocities this man had wrought on Bas made a fist clench around my chest. No wonder Bas was so tense all the time—no wonder he'd looked so scared when he saw Hannover. That look haunted me. Anything that scared a man as strong as Bas had to be terrifying indeed, and I wanted no part of it.

'You be careful,' Hannover repeated. He drew his hand away slowly. My skin crawled everywhere he touched. 'Off you go, pet.'

He patted my butt. I almost puked. I hurried away from them and didn't look back, but the feeling of his fingers on my hip stayed with me for the rest of the night.

I left with a great deal of caution that evening, halfway afraid that Hardwick and Hannover would linger to make another attempt. Being shared by those two in a back alley was not high on my to-do list. I was alert to every noise and movement, but I saw no sign of them. The only people I passed were two men haggling with one of the streetwalkers.

'One at a time,' she insisted.

'But we're paying.'

'I told you, if you want to share, it costs extra, not less...'

I hurried away before they saw me and thought I was one of her co-workers.

My route home was circuitous, and not just because I was avoiding troublesome spots. I had to go via the drop. Having people like Hannover in the bar was bad news; we'd had an awful number of Moriarty's men around recently. Their compound was a good way out of town, and they had their own watering holes—no need for them to encroach on my bar... unless they were planning something. I reached the drop point and paused to check the note, penned on the back of an order form in my messy handwriting.

We need to talk. Mayor had meeting with Rochester/Cavanaugh/Godfrey. Hannover & Hardwick in bar tonight. H

I slipped the note into the box and headed home.

The lights were on when I entered. I shrugged my coat off and moved beyond the entrance to find Maddock and Savannah sitting on the sofa, having what looked like a rather intimate heart-to-heart.

'Oh, you're back.' Savannah waved with her beer. 'You're late.'

'This is when I always get home,' I muttered tersely. I unlaced my boots, nodding to Maddock as I bent down. 'I didn't know you were having company.'

'It was a spontaneous thing. I bumped into him in the hall.' Savannah was tipsy, I could tell by her cheesy smile and the way she enunciated her words very carefully.

'You're welcome to join us if you want,' Maddock added.

I glanced between them, the way they were turned to one another on the sofa, the two beer bottles already discarded on the floor, their happy smiles. Jealousy, hot and irrational, surged through me.

'No thanks. I'm tired.'

'You sure?' Maddock asked. 'I have more beer downstairs.'

'I'm sure. Enjoy your evening.' I skulked into the bedroom and shut the door, listening to the two of them giggling as I got changed.

It was my own fault for introducing them... though Savannah would have met Maddock eventually, I supposed. Had he told her he had joined the fights yet? How had he done in the bunker? Was he going back?

The questions burnt on the tip of my tongue, but I resisted the urge to go back out and ask. Not with Savannah there.

I showered the feeling of Hannover's hands off and went to bed instead.

The next morning, in defiance of Bas's warning about dancing alone, I went to the training ground again. The town was starting to look like a sorry mess; there were black streaks running down the sides of the buildings where the rain was washing the coal dust away, and parts of the roads were underwater where the drains were blocked up. I passed a couple of men and women trying to unblock one—the water had flooded over the sidewalk and was washing up against the basement windows of one of the older buildings on the street.

The training yard was soggy and deserted. In the next few weeks, weeds would sprout through every crack in the paving. Within the month, the dusty brown rock would be replaced with scraggly greenery as far as the eye could see: our whole landscape transformed. By midwinter, it would be brown again.

I found a broken broom to one side and used it to push the water out of the cage before starting my warmup. I had a lot of thoughts competing for my attention—Hannover and Hardwick, the mayor, my note to Ellery, Savannah and Maddock—but when I danced, those thoughts grew quiet. Today's dance was a gritty number, with lots of leaps. I felt as though I was fighting the air, or maybe fighting myself.

Then I slammed into something and stumbled.

It was Bas—and he looked furious.

'Are you completely fucking stupid?' he snarled.

I caught my balance, panting from the exertion. 'You're lucky you crashed into me when you did. My next step would have taken your eye out.'

'As *if* you could take my eye out,' he sneered.

Fury flooded my veins. I was already warmed up, full of restless energy, so I lifted my right leg in a perfect leg extension, pivoting until my boot hit his shoulder.

'Like so.'

Bas grabbed my ankle. 'And now?'

I shifted so he was holding my weight and I could lower my upper body and touch the floor with my hands.

'What will you do if I let go?'

'Try it and see,' I sneered, my voice strained from hanging upside down.

Bas's hand slipped away, and I pivoted into an illusion, my dance teacher's voice echoing in my head… *'Point your feet, Harley—and keep that leg straight!'* I stepped out and landed on two feet, facing him.

Bas pressed his lips together.

'You could at least pretend to be a little impressed,' I complained.

'Why? I don't find it impressive.'

'I don't see you doing anything half as difficult!' I didn't think there was anyone in this town who made me as mad as Bas did; I'd never experienced anything like it.

'You don't know anything about me. It's not my fault you're blind to everyone but Ellery.'

I snorted. 'I don't know what you think is going on between me and Ellery, *Sebastian*, but there's nothing between us.'

Bas's expression turned frigid. 'What did you call me?'

'Oh, isn't that your name? That's what Hannover called you.'

He took a step towards me, gravel skittering under his boots, and I jerked back.

'When did he tell you that?' Bas hissed, his lips barely moving.

I lifted my chin, glaring at him. 'I had Hardwick and Hannover in the bar last night. Now all of Moriarty's lads think I'm available for hire, thanks to you.'

'You think I care about that?' Bas reached for me—I thought he was going to choke me, but he dropped his hand a few inches short and dug his fingers into his thigh instead. 'You fucking—Don't ever call me that again.'

'Why? It's a nice name.'

'It's *not my name.*'

'Okay, okay.' I shuddered. There was a wildness in his gaze that made me think he was on the very edge of control. I had done that to him—and it scared me. I'd made him plenty mad in the past, but I'd never had this effect on him before. 'I'm sorry, Bas.'

Bas relaxed in increments, first his shoulders, then his fists, and finally his face. He breathed deep, once, then again. 'Don't repeat that name. And why are you cosying up to Hannover, anyway?'

'Um, I serve drinks in a bar. Why is everyone continually surprised that I talk to gang members? I can't exactly tell them to fuck off.'

Bas shook his head, flexing his fingers. 'Who did you say Hannover was with?'

'Evander Hardwick.'

'Who's that?'

I blinked. 'You don't know him? I thought he was one of Moriarty's lot.'

'He's not.'

'Oh.' I frowned. 'He works security for the mayor. I always thought he was a plant from Moriarty. Though I guess he makes it kind of obvious if he is.'

'He could be a plant for the mayor.' Bas rolled his eyes, as though the suggestion was hilarious. Frankly, it was. I didn't think the mayor had the brains to spy on the gangs, and even if he did try, someone would probably have him killed and replaced.

'The mayor doesn't need a plant with Moriarty, anyway. He's big in with the Cavanaughs, Godfreys, and Rochesters.'

Bas's expression shut down instantly—proof, if I'd needed it. 'You saw Rochester?'

'They met on Saturday night in the bar. You have a brother, don't you?'

'No.'

'I saw him. Rodney.'

'Drop it,' he said flatly.

I pressed my lips together. 'Why?'

'It's none of your business. I don't owe you anything.'

He was right, and I was being a nosy bitch. I scuffed my toe against the ground. 'Fine, sorry.' That was the second time I'd apologised to him in the space of one morning. I really wasn't on form today.

'Did you tell Ellery?' Bas asked suddenly.

'I dropped a note last night telling him to contact me.'

Bas seemed to weigh his words for a long time. 'Next time you need to report something about the Rochesters, come directly to me.'

'I don't have any way to contact you.'

Bas pursed his lips. 'I'm here every morning.'

'Why?'

'Because I don't like training with the others.'

'I meant why should I tell you about the Rochesters, rather than Ellery.'

'Because.'

'Because…' I raised an eyebrow. 'I won't do it if you don't give me a reason. I'm not stupid enough to cross Sayle for a guy I hardly know.'

Bas scowled. 'You're not crossing Sayle. I'm one of the Iron Fists. Do you always ask this many questions?'

'No, because usually I don't have to.'

'Right, I forgot. Your fancy dance moves and amateur flirtation loosen everyone's tongues.' He couldn't have packed more disdain into his voice if he tried; his words were dripping with it. I crossed my arms.

'Amateur?'

'Yes, amateur.'

'At least people like me. You couldn't manipulate someone into doing what you wanted if you tried.'

'Couldn't I?' Bas stepped closer. I backed up, and my back hit the railing. I was on the edge of the cage. When had that happened? Bas took another step, his legs touching mine. He radiated heat, despite the cool morning.

He ghosted a finger up my front, before tucking it under my chin and lifting my face so I was looking at him. We were so close I could feel his breath on my face. We were so close, I could have gone up on tiptoes and kissed him. My heartrate kicked up a notch.

'Next time you see Rochester, come straight to me.'

'No,' I said stubbornly.

Bas's eyelids lowered. His gaze was pure heat, and I wanted to lean into him. 'Yes.'

'No,' I repeated, though my voice sounded weaker this time.

He tangled a hand into my hair, tilting my head sideways, and put his mouth by my ear. 'I'll make it worth your while.'

I shuddered, helplessness washing over me. My body wanted him, but my heart was thudding against my ribcage, a panicked rhythm that made my fingers tingle. I needed space, and fast.

'Get off me,' I choked.

Bas pulled back, surprise in his gaze. He studied me searchingly for a moment, then released my hair and stepped back.

'I'll do it, just don't touch me,' I said.

'What? You only like it when you're in control?' he asked in disgust.

'Something like that,' I panted. It was better that he thought that than that he learnt the truth. 'Will you still come here in the middle of winter?'

'If it gets too cold, I'll contact you with alternate arrangements.' Bas was still looking me up and down, as though he could peel my skin back and see what lay beneath. I shivered.

'Fine. I'm going now.' I grabbed my coat and scrambled inelegantly over the railing. Bas watched me doing it.

'Harley,' he called. I turned back reluctantly. 'It would be better if you stayed away from the Rochesters. You won't like what they do to their enemies.'

I didn't like any of the men in this town, but there was no point in telling him that. I turned away without a word and headed home.

TEN

ONCE AGAIN, MY DAY OFF was spent doing chores, but for once I didn't mind. Keeping myself busy was the best way to keep my mind occupied. The moment I was idle, I started remembering Bas's hands on me.

I shuddered.

I hadn't felt that way with anyone in a long time, except maybe Ellery, but the sick, cloying fear hadn't changed. The feeling of helplessness haunted me. I hated myself for being that weak.

Most of all, I wished Bas hadn't been the one to see me like that. I could have handled it if it was someone else, but not him. He already seemed to think I was pathetic.

I busied myself with all sorts of menial tasks, before finally making my way across the road to Irina's office. I'd split the five hundred in the register at Krani's in secret, even though I still didn't like the idea of using the money at all.

But rent had to be paid.

Anton was in the office when Irina bade me enter. He stood from the seat he was slouched in, moving towards the door.

'This is a good thing, Mama. You'll see.'

'Never trust a woman, Anton. I raised you better than that.'

Anton laughed. 'You were the best example, Mama. Hello, Harley.' He fixed a sharklike smile on me.

'Good afternoon, Anton, Madame Irina.' I swallowed against a lump of fear in my throat, stepping aside so Anton could exit.

'Harley, my dear. Come in, come in.' Irina was all smiles as she ushered me over. 'How are you? Do you have good news for me?'

'I have my rent, ma'am.'

'Excellent, excellent.' By her face, she was actually disappointed. Sometimes, I thought Irina lived for the moments when she told people they were being evicted. It was the same terrible instinct that plagued all of us: taking pleasure in watching someone else being miserable for a change.

I handed her the bundle of notes. She counted them slowly, before tucking them in the top drawer of her desk. 'How are things, my dear?'

'Alright, thank you, ma'am.'

'Good?' She raised an eyebrow. 'Business at the hotel is going well?'

I shrugged awkwardly. 'I couldn't say, ma'am. I just do my job.'

'But surely you must have some idea,' she prodded. 'Based on how many people are coming in.'

'There's always a lull when it rains, ma'am, but I don't know how that affects the business. Tom handles those things.'

'Of course, of course.' She smiled, and my stomach clenched in terror. 'Well, unfortunately, times have been hard for some of us. I'm afraid that as of next month I'm going to have to raise your rent by ten percent.'

My throat closed up. I couldn't breathe. 'Y-yes, Ma'am,' I choked out.

'You understand?'

'Y-yes.'

'Excellent. Then from the week after next, I'll be expecting one sixty-five from you.'

'O-okay.' My voice was barely a whisper.

'Good girl.' She smiled benevolently. 'Don't look so worried, dear. You and your sister are good tenants. Remember, if you ever have trouble making the rent, you can come to me, hmm?'

'Yes, ma'am.' I was going to be sick.

'Alright. Off you go.'

'Thank you, ma'am.' It took every ounce of control I had to just walk out of there. I burst out of the lobby into the rain, a sob exploding out of my throat.

Fifteen new pounds extra didn't sound like a lot, but it was the difference between eating three meals a day and… not. Savannah's wage was a pittance, and mine barely covered rent and food. I couldn't afford the increase. Not now.

Not when I was already so close to the edge.

I felt like the walls of the surrounding buildings were pressing in on me, like everyone in town was staring at me—even though the streets were empty, the pounding rain forcing even the most hardened of citizens inside. Even the weekend market had been cancelled this week; everyone was waiting to see what the rain did.

Last year, it had petered out, replaced by months of frigid wind.

The year before, it had rained and rained and rained, until the streets turned into rivers and everything that wasn't bolted down washed away.

I returned to my flat. The ceiling was leaking, water falling in a steady drip-drip-drip from three different spots in the kitchen. At least we could collect it and filter it for drinking. The sofa sagged pathetically, and when I flicked the light switch, nothing happened. The electricity had probably been switched off until the rain ended.

One sixty-five was daylight robbery for this place, but what could I do? It was central, it was safe… There wasn't anything better, or at least there wasn't anything better that was also affordable and safe for two unmarried women.

I sank onto the sofa and covered my face. If I rationed the money Rodney Rochester had given me, then it could probably tide me over for a couple of lean weeks in the bar. But that depended on the rain letting up. The longer it rained, the worse business got. People would be saving money for the inevitable repairs. And The Arsonist undercut us at times like this; they cut their whiskey with water and sold it for half the price.

If the rain didn't let up…

I couldn't think about that right now.

Sighing, I got up and fetched my mending. I had to do it now, before it got to the darkest months when there wouldn't be enough hours of daylight to work in.

I had just finished darning a hole in a thick knitted scarf which my mother had made for me before she died when there was a knock on the door. Setting my work aside, I padded over, sliding my knife out of my coat on the way. I took no chances, especially when I was at home alone. I opened the door with the chain still on.

Maddock stood in the hallway, the grey light casting odd shadows over his face. 'Hey.'

'Sav's not here.'

Maddock shifted his weight. 'I wanted to talk to you, actually.'

'Me?' I asked blankly. 'Don't you have work?'

'Have you seen the roads on the south side? Even my truck can't get through there.'

I hadn't—I never had any reason to go to the south side, and I definitely wasn't crossing the river today—not when there was a decent chance of the bridges washing away. Two years ago, three of the bridges had been destroyed in the floods. But I could fully believe that the Godfrey dev had been badly affected; everyone knew there was a reason why that land had been fallow for this long.

'Uh, okay. Hold on a sec.'

I shut the door to take the chain off, then shuffled back to let him in. Immediately, I was hyperaware of everything: Maddock's precise position behind me, the sound of his breathing, how small the room was. I hadn't been alone in my flat with a man before, ever. I felt vulnerable.

I hated it.

To distract myself, I headed for the kitchen. We had leftover chicory root coffee from that morning, so I put the pot back on the stove to heat up and rinsed two mugs. 'What's up, then?'

'I saw you heading in.' Maddock leant against the counter, watching me. 'Thought it would be nice to catch up. I hardly see you anymore.'

'I've been busy at work.'

'I know.'

We stood in awkward silence as I pretended to focus all of my attention on the pan I was heating. The mood was a far cry from Savannah and Maddock's easy laughter last night; he and I seemed to have almost nothing to discuss. I chewed the shredded skin on the inside of my lip, and as soon as the coffee started to boil, I tipped it into the two mugs.

'Want to sit?'

'Yeah.'

We sat on opposite ends of the sofa. My knife was digging into my hip, so I eased it out of my belt and put it on the floor. Maddock leant down and grabbed it.

'This is nice.'

'It's not mine.'

'Really? You use it a lot, considering.'

I shrugged. 'I have it on loan, I guess.'

'From…?'

I shrugged again. The silence stretched awkwardly.

'Alright, then.' Maddock put the knife down. 'Sorry, I don't mean to make you uncomfortable. I thought it would be fun to hang out.'

'I'm not really a fun person.'

'I see that.' His words had no bite to them, but they still hurt. 'You never seem to have trouble chatting with people in the bar.'

'That's different. That's work.'

'Okay.' He fiddled with his coffee. I found myself once again with the urge to apologise, as though I were the one intruding on his day, instead of the other way around. Instead, I bit my tongue and pulled my knees up to my chest, hugging them.

'You alright?' Maddock asked softly.

'Yeah. Sorry, I'm not good company today.'

'That's okay.' He brushed his hair out of his eyes. 'You want me to take a look at those leaks for you?'

I followed his gaze to the kitchen and shrugged. 'They just come back a few weeks later. There's no point. Hopefully the rain will stop soon.'

'I didn't realise it rained this much here.'

'We don't do anything by halves.'

Maddock laughed, and I cracked a cautious smile. He kicked his boots off and prodded my knee with a toe. 'That's better. You shouldn't get so down on yourself.'

I shrugged again and sipped my coffee. 'I'm not really the person you see at work.'

'None of us are.'

'I've never seen you at work.'

Maddock laughed. 'You'd find me very boring. It's all financials this, building materials that. I can talk for hours about the difference between red sand and yellow in making concrete.'

I wrinkled my nose. 'Sounds awful.'

'Well, one makes more sturdy buildings than the other. So it's not so awful for the inhabitants, I guess.'

'Providing the building is made from the right one.'

Maddock grinned wryly. 'Which it isn't always, I'm afraid. We have crater dust in plentiful supply. Every second day someone asks me why we can't just use that instead of bringing in the more expensive stuff by train. Sorry, I'm boring you, aren't I?'

'Not really. You don't talk much about your work.'

Maddock was silent, and for a moment, the rain pattering continuously on the roof was the only noise in the flat.

'I suppose not.' He sipped his coffee. I fiddled with a loose thread on my jeans.

Maddock cleared his throat. 'So… I wanted to talk to you about the bunker.'

I looked up. 'What about it?'

'You used to dance there, didn't you?'

I squirmed. 'Haven't we had this conversation before?'

'I guess. But you got out.' Maddock studied me. 'Not a lot of people who managed to quit, are there?'

'The bunker isn't a drug.'

'Yeah, but gangs aren't usually good about letting people go.'

My palms felt clammy all of a sudden. 'I don't know. I wouldn't know anything about that.'

'Why did you dance there in the first place?'

I couldn't seem to escape his gaze, his green eyes scrutinising me. My tone came out short and sharp. 'My family had a debt to Sayle. Someone had to pay it.'

Maddock raised an eyebrow. 'It occurs to me that Sayle could make better use of a doctor than a dancer.'

Anger and regret twisted up my insides. 'Sav wasn't qualified yet.'

'And you were?'

'Are you asking for a demonstration?'

My voice came out more aggressive than I'd intended, but it did the trick. Maddock grimaced. 'No, sorry.'

'Because I can give you one. I trained professionally. I—' was being stupid. I bit my tongue. 'Look, dancing was an easy way to make money. That's all.'

For a few moments, the only sound was the rain drumming against the windowpanes. I stared at my hands, wrapped around my mug.

'Sorry,' I muttered at length.

'Sorry,' Maddock repeated. 'I'm making you uncomfortable. Should I go?'

I shrugged. He started to rise, and I changed my mind. The only thing waiting for me was my own thoughts.

'You can stay.'

Maddock was perched on the edge of the sofa, lacing up his boots. 'You sure?'

'Yeah, why not? I have nothing else to do. Except…' I glanced around. 'Cooking. Mending. The usual stuff.'

Maddock smiled. His smile was slightly lopsided; he only had a dimple in his left cheek. I'd never noticed before, but it made him look younger. 'All the stuff I'm meant to be doing, too.'

'S'not as though it won't be waiting for me tomorrow.'

'True, that.' He leant back, picking up his mug. I nodded to it.

'Want me to make more?'

'It's alright. I drink too much of the stuff, as is.'

'Sav loves it. I find it bitter.'

'You like sweet things?'

For some reason, that made me giggle. I put my mug down so I didn't spill. 'Don't tell. It's my secret.'

'Next you'll tell me you hate whiskey.'

'I actually don't drink that much.'

'No!' Maddock laughed. 'Godfrey gave me a bottle of the Maker's Choice. We should try it sometime.'

'I'm not sure I want to drink anything that was even briefly owned by Godfrey.'

Maddock wrinkled his nose. 'When you put it that way... But then, I imagine he'd hate the idea of me sharing it with you, so...'

'That's true.' I bit my lip to hide a smile.

'I didn't know you knew Godfrey.'

I shook my head. Better not to mention that I'd seen him recently. 'I know his kids. Louis and Lucille. I went to school with them.'

'Really? I don't think I've met them.'

'You wouldn't have met Lucille. Her parents are quite protective of her. Louis goes to the bunker, though. You might have seen him around.' I gestured with a hand. 'Tall, blond, hangs out with Brody Cavanaugh and Diego Bartholomew.

Maddock shrugged. 'I've only been to the bunker twice.'

'Really?'

'Andy suggested I take it slow. He's probably right. I find it a bit overwhelming, to be honest.'

It took me a moment to realise he was talking about Kade; I usually only heard him referred to by his last name. 'You're getting along with Kade, then?'

'Shouldn't I?'

I felt my cheeks heating up. 'Kade's nice. They haven't corrupted him yet.'

Maddock laughed. 'I guess we can both be corrupted together, then.'

'I wouldn't be so blasé if I were you,' I muttered tersely. 'They get to everyone eventually.'

'But not you?'

Was I uncorrupted? I didn't feel that way. 'I'm not a gang member.'

'Despite that, you know a lot about the Iron Fists and the bunker.' His gaze had turned searching, and entirely too intense. I found myself looking away, studying the threadbare sofa, the pattern almost invisible.

'What are you really saying?' I muttered.

Maddock cleared his throat. 'Have you ever thought about using what you know for good?'

His words fell between us like stones dropped into a pond: utterly irrevocable, creating ripples that would change everything. I swallowed.

'What does that mean?'

'You know what it means.'

'Spell it out for me.'

The silence stretched between us, taut and filled with danger. If he said nothing, we could go our separate ways and never speak of this again. If he answered… that path led nowhere good, and I wanted no part of it.

Maddock rubbed his temples, then fixed his gaze on me. 'The gangs in this town are out of control. People live in fear…'

'You've barely been here a month. How can you know what we are or aren't scared of?'

'Aren't you scared?' His tone was provocative.

I bit my cheek, unwilling to lie. 'Being in a gang isn't what makes men dangerous.'

'Of course. All people are capable of being dangerous. But gangs invite a certain type of behaviour.' Maddock's expression was open and sincere, encouraging me to believe he was the good guy.

But was he? He definitely sounded naïve and idealistic right now. But good? I barely knew him.

'So you're one of them? Like the mayor and his band? Who want to enforce law and order?'

He frowned. 'I'm not working with the mayor.'

'But you do work with the mayor—you said so yourself.'

'I sell building supplies—'

'I'm not a fool, Maddock.'

'James.'

I glared.

Maddock shifted, sighing. 'I really do sell building supplies, but you're right—that's not all I do.'

'If you think there's anyone in this town who hasn't figured that out...'

'No, listen.' He leant forward, his mien intent. 'I do sell building supplies. Specifically, the company I contract with sells building supplies for military purposes; high budget, secret contracts which have to be fulfilled discretely. You get what I mean?'

'You shouldn't be telling me this.' I put my coffee aside. It was cold, anyway, and my stomach was curling in on itself like a hedgehog.

'Not really, but I'm willing to take a risk on this one,' Maddock replied. 'The mayor brought us out here for a specific purpose, a contract they want to build on the down-low. Can you guess?'

'The mayor wants to take back the whiskey distillery.' I didn't need to guess; it made sense after the conversation I'd overheard at Krani's.

'More or less,' Maddock said. 'It's bigger than that—he's hoping to provoke a war and let the gangs wipe themselves out. But the resulting fighting… It'll be disastrous for Bale Rocks. It's the people like you and your sister… ordinary civilians… who will suffer. The mayor doesn't care about protecting the people.'

'So…'

'So my people have a vested interest in protecting the citizens of Bale Rocks. There are other ways to fix the problems here than starting a war. But for that I need information. Someone who has seen the inner workings of the different gangs—who knows who can be trusted, who works for which gang, where the information is flowing. Someone like you.'

I shook my head. Every muscle in my body was tense, as though it was trying to physically fight off his words. 'I'm just a waitress.'

'Are you? Sayle's men trust you.'

'No,' I said.

'No? I've seen you with Marco Ellery. He walks you home.'

There was a huge difference between 'walking someone home' and what Ellery did, which was basically a form of stalking. But explaining my relationship with Ellery to Maddock would mean explaining it to myself—something which I'd been avoiding doing for years. I certainly wasn't breaking that resolve for Maddock.

'There's nothing between Ellery and me. He's just a guy I flirt with. Like every other arsehole in the bar.'

The look in Maddock's eyes said I wasn't fooling him, but I didn't care.

'Do you really want to live this way for the rest of your life?'

'Of course not, but that doesn't mean I'm tying myself to *you* to get ahead! I barely know you!'

Maddock flinched. 'I'm your friend, Harley.'

'I don't have friends.'

'Everyone needs friends.'

I pressed my lips together. I didn't need friends. I'd tried back at school—and quickly realised that most people were only your friend when they needed you, not when you needed them. My only real friend these days was Theo, and that was only because I knew Theo would never ever ask me for anything—and I wouldn't ask him for anything. No favours, no help, no owing each other.

That was the rule.

'Not me.'

'What about Savannah?'

'She's my sister.' A dangerous thought occurred to me. 'Did you make this offer to her?'

Maddock shook his head, his gaze sliding away from my face.

'You better not be lying to me. I will kill you,' I warned.

'I'm not your enemy, Harley.'

'I wasn't born yesterday, *Maddock*.'

His whole face seemed to draw together as he grimaced. He didn't like being called by his last name. Why? Before I could push for answers, he said, 'I know that. I know more than you think I do.'

'Oh yeah? Like what?'

'I get it.' His tone was gentle. 'What it's like for people to look at you and see someone else.'

No one understood that. They looked at Savannah and me and saw the same person. 'Do you?'

Maddock leant in. 'My father—people say I look like him. What they really mean is they want me to be him.'

I gnawed on one of my knuckles, taking that in.

'But you're not.'

'But I'm not.' He smiled carefully, a guarded expression. 'I know you're not like your sister. I know you're more than just a waitress. You're capable of more. They put you there, didn't they? The Iron Fists? But that doesn't mean you have to stay. You can be more than what they want you to be.'

'That's not… I don't…' My thoughts were racing, too fast for me to form coherent words. 'I'm perfectly capable of deciding what I want in life. I don't need you to tell me that.'

'Of course not. But I can give you options. Options that Marco Ellery could give you—but we both know he never will.'

Ellery had offered me a lot, more than Maddock probably realised. But still, Maddock wasn't wrong. Ellery couldn't give me freedom. And yet, I doubted Maddock could give me freedom, either. All I'd do was trade one master for another.

'I'm not taking that risk,' I said firmly. 'I think you should leave.'

Maddock stared at me for several long seconds, before nodding. 'I understand.'

I crossed my arms. 'I don't think you do.'

He hadn't grown up in our town. He didn't know what it was like to constantly be walking a tightrope between three different gangs, to fight a fire on one side of town, only to have a new one flare up somewhere else.

'I do. I know what it's like to be scared and feel trapped.'

Maddock would never, *could never*, know how I felt. 'Just go.'

'Alright.'

He shoved his feet in his boots, picking up his mug as he stood. I took it from him, setting it aside, and followed him to the door. Maddock's gaze was like a physical weight between my shoulder blades as I unlocked and opened the door.

'Thanks for the coffee,' he said.

'You're welcome.'

He stepped out and headed for the stairs. Then he paused and turned to me.

'If you change your mind, the offer will stay open.'

'Goodbye, James.' I shut the door.

ELEVEN

THE BAR THRUMMED WITH ACTIVITY. It was Thursday; things were heating up for the weekend, and for the last two days it hadn't rained, although dark clouds threatened to burst at any moment.

I was making the most of it. We'd turned the music up, I'd tucked my shirt up to bare my midriff, and I was dancing in between the tables, entertaining the groups of men and women who had braved the waterlogged streets to get their alcohol fix. The mood was jovial. Anna had even cajoled the chef into making fried cheese balls to give to the customers.

If only I was enjoying it as much as they were.

In my head, I had composed dozens of different notes to Ellery, trying to explain what I knew and how, but yet, I hadn't committed any of them to paper. I told myself that I didn't know enough to share with him yet—but the truth was that I knew what the repercussions would be, and I wasn't ready for them.

I wouldn't support Maddock, but I didn't want Ellery to put a bullet in his head, either.

And Ellery would if he found out that Maddock was trying to take on the gangs. Sayle never allowed a threat to go unchecked.

Despite the thoughts churning in my head, I kept a smile on my face and flirted like a pro. I needed those tips like no tomorrow—I was determined that I wouldn't depend on Rochester's largesse this week.

Even if it meant going without coffee. Savannah would kill me, but there were worse fates.

Towards the end of the dinner rush, I danced my way back to the bar to refill my jug of water. Anna emerged from the back, lugging a bucket of ice, and paused.

'Oooh, is that who I think it is?'

I turned around—and almost dropped the jug.

Rodney Rochester was standing in the doorway to the bar.

'What about him?' I asked, feigning nonchalance as I set the jug down on the tray. 'That's that Rochester guy, isn't it?'

'Rodney Rochester.' Anna gave me a pointed look. 'He's rich, Harley.'

'I know.'

'Oh, come on.' She waggled her brows. 'Rich and hot. Don't tell me you haven't considered it at least once?'

'I haven't.' I'd never marry a guy for his money.

'You're lying.'

'I'm not.'

'Yes, you are. You're blushing.'

'I'm not.'

Anna elbowed me. I shot her a glare. 'Anna, cut it out!'

Anna giggled. Over by the door, Rochester finished surveying the room and, evidently finding it to his satisfaction, strolled inside. Another man followed him: tall, blond, pale, aristocratic.

Oh no.

There was only one thing worse than having Brody Cavanaugh in the bar, and that was having his cousin here. Dorian Cavanaugh or, as Dana called him, Dorian of the Wandering Hands, was a jerk in the worst way. Everyone knew he was the reason you didn't want to work for the Cavanaughs—their female staff had a tendency of disappearing. This was a small town; small enough that rumours spread, even if you got rid of everyone who knew the truth. Dorian Cavanaugh had gotten too friendly with his staff more than once.

Cavanaugh and Rochester took seats by the window. Anna prodded me in the arm.

'Go take their order.'

'Yeah.' My feet felt glued to the ground. I had to force them to move. I approached the table, clutching my tray like a shield, trepidation making my stomach tie itself in knots. Pausing outside of reaching distance, I said, 'Good evening, gentlemen. What can I get you?'

Cavanaugh flicked me a dismissive glance before looking away again.

'Two whiskeys,' he said. 'Top shelf.'

'Yes, sir.'

I backed off again, relieved that that seemed to be it. Rochester's gaze followed me: back to the bar, collecting the order from Anna, and across the room again. He never looked away for a second. Irritated, I leant forward, letting my shirt fall open as I set the drinks down. He averted his eyes immediately.

I suppressed a smirk.

'Can I get you gents anything else?' I asked in a breathy voice.

'That's all,' Cavanaugh said tersely.

'You sure? Water is on the house.' I winked at him.

Cavanaugh's eyes drifted to the front of my top. 'You don't have anything we're interested in. Scram.'

Rude. Brushing my hair back from my face, I sauntered off, putting an extra sway into my hips.

'Rochester is watching you,' Anna hissed as I rounded the bar again.

'With an attitude like that, he can learn to keep his eyes to himself.' I put my tray down. 'Ignore them. They'll get bored in an hour.'

Fuck Cavanaugh. I didn't want him slobbering over me, anyway. It'd be a cold day in hell before I climbed into his bed.

Unfortunately, it didn't end there. Cavanaugh and Rochester lingered for a good two hours, drinking slowly, Rochester watching me all the while. I didn't know what I'd done to catch his attention, but I was sure nothing good would come of it. His eyes never left me as I moved between the tables and flirted with the other customers. The back of my neck itched from the pressure.

What did he want?

Whatever it was, he didn't find it that Thursday night. I avoided him studiously, pretending I hadn't noticed his staring. I went to their table only when Cavanaugh waved for me, and it was only Cavanaugh who spoke to me, demanding drinks.

'He is rude, isn't he?' Anna asked once they had finally left. 'I can't believe he clicked his fingers at you. What does he think you are?'

'A dog.'

Anna snorted. 'That's not even funny. Did he tip?'

'Nope.'

'Rich pricks.'

'Exactly.'

'I'd still marry one of them, though.' She sighed wistfully.

'Does your uncle know you have such low standards?'

Anna swatted my arm. 'Not as though they'd ever look at me. Rochester looked at you plenty, though. Why didn't you talk to him?'

'I don't need that complication in my life.' I grabbed a cloth to go wipe down their table. 'Got enough already.'

'I'd do that complication.' Anna waggled her brows. I shook my head.

The next day, Rodney Rochester came back.

My heart sank when he walked through the door. *Not again.*

It was drizzling, not enough to deter the Friday night crowd, but enough that they were miserly and not in the mood for tipping. I was squeezing them for every penny they had; I didn't need someone watching me and putting me off my act.

Another man followed him in, someone I didn't know, and he had a scantily clad woman draped over his arm.

'Ah,' Anna blurted.

For fuck's sake. We even had a sign by the door warning that customers couldn't bring prostitutes into the bar.

'I'll handle it.'

'You sure? I can get Tom.'

'No, it's fine. I'll handle it.' I picked up my tray and heaved a deep sigh. Time to test Rodney Rochester's mysterious interest in me.

I walked purposefully over to their table. The woman was certainly attracting plenty of attention—but then, why wouldn't she? She was wearing a top so small it could barely be called lingerie and heels so high I was surprised she could walk at all. She was also sitting on Rochester's friend's lap, stroking his chest and cooing at him.

It was a good act; to know she wasn't enjoying it, you'd have to know who she was. Her name was Mia, and she was a regular on the square. I passed her almost every night on my way home from work.

When she saw me, her face contorted. 'Please,' she mouthed.

'I'm sorry,' I mouthed back. I was going to have to kick her out, and that would cost her a nice rich client. It wasn't that I wanted her to lose out—but if I didn't kick her out, I could lose my job.

And I knew exactly which one was more important to me.

I stopped by the table, avoiding Mia's gaze, and cleared my throat.

'Gentlemen, good evening. I'm afraid it's against our policy to allow escorts in the bar.'

'You going to take her place?' Rochester's friend was weak-faced, with small, cruel eyes. The sort of man who put others down to feel better about his own inadequacies.

'I'm just doing my job, sir. If you want to sit there, I'm afraid Ms Mia needs to leave.'

Mia started to stand, but the man grabbed her hips, dragging her backwards. 'I'm paying. You're not going anywhere.'

'She can stay as long as she gets dressed and sits in her own seat,' I said evenly, offering Mia an apologetic look. 'And she'll need her own drink.'

'Yeah, or you could go get your manager down here, and we'll see about docking her fee from your pay.'

Forcing the irritation out of my voice, I said, 'I'm happy to fetch the manager, but he's only going to say the same thing, sir.' I took a step towards the door, as though I was going right now. Mia shook her head.

'I'll leave.' She wormed her way off the pig's lap. He sat forward, his eyes fixed on me.

'Well then maybe I'll leave, too. How's that for a solution?'

'That would be an acceptable solution, sir,' I replied.

'Don't see that you're dressed much different to her, though.' He looked me up and down pointedly. 'Maybe you made this policy up to get rid of your competition.'

I gritted my teeth. 'There's a sign on the front door, sir. Right when you come in. You can't miss it.'

Rochester snorted. Mr Piggy narrowed his eyes. 'Are you saying I can't read?'

Come to think of it... 'Would you like me to fetch Mr Tom?'

'Just get rid of her, Bradley,' Rochester said. It was the first time he'd spoken in my presence in the bar—not that he looked at me. 'She isn't going to serve us otherwise.'

'Then let's go somewhere else!'

'We're here now.' He slid a couple of folded bills into Mia's hand, which she tucked into her bra. 'That should cover it. Off you go.'

'Thank you.' Head down, Mia scarpered through the door. I watched her guiltily. Pigman clicked his fingers in front of my face.

'Get on with it, girl. We don't have all day.'

I gnashed my teeth together. Sadly, I wasn't allowed to kick him out—or smack him over the head with my tray. It was tempting, though.

'What can I get you, sir?'

'Two whiskeys,' Rochester said. He looked at me now, his green gaze intense. My smile felt painted on; if I moved my lips, it would crack.

'That'll be ten new pounds.'

'Pricey for the swill you serve,' Bradley sneered.

I pressed my lips together harder, waiting expectantly. Rochester peeled off another note and handed it to me without looking.

'Thank you,' I muttered, hurrying off to take shelter behind the bar. Anna was watching me with something like sympathy.

'Dana will be here soon,' she said.

'I don't suppose I can hide in the back until then?' I served ice into two glasses and passed them to her before I gave in to the urge to spit in them.

'And have me serve the tables?' Anna shuddered.

'Why not? They'll probably like you.'

'I always forget the orders.' Anna screwed up her face. 'Besides, I don't think I could take them groping me. You're so calm about it.'

'Practice,' I muttered, grabbing the order for table two. 'You know, you could suggest to Tom that we seat customers, instead of letting them seat themselves.'

'Why?'

'So I can put all the arseholes in Dana's half.'

She sniggered as I departed for Clem's table. Damned if I wasn't going to make Rochester and the pig wait for their drinks.

And then on Saturday Rochester came in again.

'Is he stalking you?' Anna asked.

'Maybe.' I glanced around the room and caught Dana's eye. A second later, she sauntered over.

'Problem?'

'I need a favour.'

She followed my gaze. 'Thought you wouldn't mind the rich boy.'

'This rich boy has been in three nights running.'

'He's crushing on her,' Anna said.

'He is not!' I hissed.

'He so is! Why else would he come here every night?'

I opened my mouth—and realised I didn't have an answer to that.

'You see?' Anna crowed.

'Maybe he just enjoys making my life miserable? Or maybe it's you he's crushing on.'

'He doesn't stare at me.'

'One of us needs to serve him, you realise that, right?' Dana smirked.

'You go,' I said.

'Alright. But don't blame me when I get your tips.'

'He doesn't tip, anyway.'

'Rats. What's the point of a rich guy who doesn't tip?' Dana rolled her eyes, fluffed her hair, and headed off. I watched tiredly as she flirted with Rochester.

'But really,' Anna said, already reaching for a bottle of whiskey, 'he likes you.'

'I doubt it.'

She shot me a look. I pretended to be checking on my tables.

'Whatever you say, then.'

'I do say,' I muttered, grabbing my tray to hit up table seven. Rochester was a problem, one that I was going to have to deal with. Unfortunately, the one way I had to deal with it involved putting myself in Bas's path—and I'd successfully avoided dealing with any of the Iron Fists this week. If I saw Bas, chances were I'd see Ellery, and if I saw Ellery… chances were I'd end up telling him my rent had been hiked.

Not a good idea.

To add insult to injury, Rochester tipped Dana a hundred percent. Fucking dick.

Sunday morning, I was up before Savannah. It was her day off, and she always slept in whenever she could. I dressed and crept outside into the rain.

Within five minutes, I was drenched. The things I did for Bas, honestly. I carried on, though, because damned if I was going another night of work with Rochester hanging out in the bar.

It was too wet to dance, and anyway, I wanted to see what Bas did when I wasn't on the training ground, so I tucked myself under the overhanging roof at the back of the pub to wait. I was there for about fifteen minutes before the soft sound of footsteps reached me through the rain.

Bas jogged into view.

He was wet to the bone, his dark hair plastered to his forehead and his tight vest sticking to the ridges and planes of his defined muscles. Instead of his usual scowl, his face was relaxed.

Bas was a very attractive man.

Somehow, I hadn't noticed before. I'd never actually had a chance to just observe him when no one else was around. Usually, he was tense, glaring, alert, like a wolf waiting to attack. When he was alone, some of his intensity fell away.

He jogged to the cage and paused there, catching his breath for a moment, before vaulting over the railing and dropping to do a set of push-ups. His muscles bunched and flexed, every movement visible under the wet vest. His tattoos seemed to shift and writhe as he worked. If I listened hard, I could hear the soft puffs of his breaths. Every move he made was a demonstration of strength and discipline.

I was mesmerised.

What would it be like to be that strong and capable? Dance required discipline, but that was where I'd always fallen short: I was too impulsive, too brash. My movements were always just a little wild, and I never stuck to the choreography.

Besides that, dance had always focused on being lithe and graceful, not being strong. You didn't openly display your strength.

I wanted what he had.

He stood, stretched his shoulders, and left the cage to move to the pull-up bar. I edged a little out of my hiding place to watch him—and Bas dropped down, spinning to face me, his hand on the knife strapped to his thigh.

'Who's there?'

Fuck, his instincts were good—I didn't think I had made a sound. I stepped out, wincing as the cold rain soaked through my hair and ran down the back of my neck.

'It's Harley.'

Bas's hand slid away from his knife, though it was still close enough that he could grab it if he needed to. He strode over, wiping his hair back from his face with one hand.

'What are you doing here?'

I padded closer, shivering. 'You asked me to tell you anything I learnt about the Rochesters.'

Bas frowned as he halted in front of me, his eyes sweeping over me. 'And?'

'Rodney Rochester has been into the bar with his friends the last three nights.'

A dozen emotions played over his face. His eyes were dark in the grey light. 'Why are you only telling me this now?'

I crossed my arms. 'Because it would have been a bit suspicious if you had pitched up in the bar the day after he did. You remember the part where my job as an informant only works if no one knows I'm an informant?'

'Everyone knows you're an informant.'

I scowled. I was more subtle than he gave me credit for. 'Do they? Is that why they all come into the bar to flaunt their business?'

Bas pressed his lips together, his eyes taking me in from head to toe again. After a moment, he caught my shoulder and nudged me back under the overhang. 'It wasn't raining yesterday morning.'

'Yesterday morning Rodney hadn't been in the bar three nights running.' I pulled away from him, hugging my arms around myself.

'And you think he'll be there again tonight?'

I shrugged. 'I have no idea. You wanted a report. I'm reporting.'

If anything, Bas looked even more irritated. 'Do you know why he's been there?'

'No.'

'Do you know anything?'

The more he pushed, the less I wanted to answer. 'No. I don't draw conclusions. I just tell people what I saw.'

'It didn't occur to you to ask?'

'No, actually.' Suddenly, I was annoyed with everything. Why had I thought he'd be grateful for me telling him? Clearly, that had been a fundamental lapse in judgement. 'I've told you what I know. Can I go now?'

Bas gestured dismissively. 'I never forced you to come here today.'

Oh for the love of all that is holy. This guy was the most hypocritical arsehole in town. 'Should I have dropped a note to Ellery instead, then?'

'Would you really have dropped a note to him over this?'

'Of course!'

Bas turned away, but not before I caught a scowl twisting his lips. He stared out across the damp training yard, as though it might hold the answers to his questions.

'If you want more information, you need to find someone else. I don't do that,' I said. I reported what I saw and heard only.

'Too much danger for Harley Benoit?'

His mocking tone pissed me off more than anything else. 'Sorry, I didn't realise I was supposed to risk life and limb for every arsehole who crosses my path. I thought I was just some whore who was conveniently positioned to tell you what you wanted to know—or isn't that what you said?'

'I never called you a whore.'

"No difference between one hooker name and another," I quoted angrily. 'Yes you did, that night in your truck.'

Bas flinched. He'd obviously forgotten, and that hurt even more than his words did. I was that unimportant to him—and meanwhile, everything he said seemed to cut me to the core.

'I'm done,' I snapped. 'I'm going. Like fuck I want to hang out in the rain for your sake. You get what you get, and if you want more than that, then get your own fucking arse to Krani's and ask Rodney why he's hanging out there.'

'You couldn't handle having both of us in there at once.' Bas's eye glittered angrily. I'd pissed him off. *Well, good.*

'You seem to be under the mistaken impression that I care what you do.' I scuffed my boot angrily against the floor. 'You're nothing to me. I told you that as a favour and nothing else. Next time will cost you.'

'Is that how it is?' There was a silky undertone to his words, dangerous and seductive. I took a step back, quailing under the intensity of his gaze.

'That's how it is.'

'And what price will you demand?' Bas pressed closer; he never touched me, but I felt his presence acutely all the same. 'My body in exchange for information?'

'No, I—' That wasn't what I'd meant at all!

'How nice it must be for you to turn the tables on the men you disdain so much.'

His gaze seared me, and shame and anger heated my cheeks. I put both hands on his chest, shoving him back—or trying to, anyway. 'Get away from me!'

Mistake—it was a terrible mistake. Bas radiated heat, his muscles as hard as rock under his wet clothes. I could feel everything, and my thoughts scattered in a thousand different directions, half terror at his closeness, half desire. *I could pull him closer—*

My back hit the wall, my breathing the only sound aside from the rain. I'd pushed myself away instead; Bas was unmoved, and he stared at me as though I was a ridiculous child throwing a tantrum.

'Don't do that again,' Bas said coolly.

'Get away from me!' My breath was coming too quickly; I couldn't seem to get enough oxygen, and I was starting to feel lightheaded. 'Back off!'

Bas stepped back. Clarity rushed in again. I had to go. I edged away from him, keeping my back to the wall.

'I'll tell you what I see and hear in the bar, and nothing more,' I said shakily. 'That's all I do for Ellery, and that's all I'll do for you.'

'Don't threaten me unless you're willing to make good on it.'

Clearly, gratitude was a foreign concept to this guy.

'I said I'd do what you wanted. *Goodbye*, Bas.' I finally turned my back on him and hurried away.

TWELVE

Fact: I could not trust myself around Bas.

Fact: Bas was dangerous for my health.

Conclusion: I needed to avoid him at all costs.

I returned to my flat soaked through and permeated by a deep sense of shame, both for the way I behaved around him and for the reactions he managed to draw out of me. What was it that made us keep trying to provoke each other? Okay, I could admit that I toyed with people. I knew that. I messed with them, found threads I could tug at. But I never did it like this; I was never digging for weaknesses. I tried to make people feel good—because people who felt good tipped good. Bas and I were doing the opposite.

It was like he had a knack for finding my raw edges and rubbing up against them. But worse, I was doing the same to him. Consciously, when I was alone, I knew I had to stop. But the second I was in his presence, it became my only defence mechanism.

Why?

What the hell was going on?

The real question was why I'd even agreed to his stupid deal—and why I hadn't backed out the second he'd started getting pushy. With Ellery, the answer was obvious. I owed him a certain amount for helping me get the job at Krani's. Thanks to him, I had relative financial stability and some modicum of independence. What had Bas offered me?

Nasty epithets, insults, slurs.

In short, Bas had been a total jerk… but I was still playing his game. He just seemed to have some sort of power over me.

My self-respect was clearly at an all-time low. What had happened to the woman who'd vowed she'd never let men jerk her around again? Where the fuck was she hiding?

I moped up the steps, trailing water droplets across the dirty floor. From now on, I was going to kick whatever messed-up habit I was forming with Bas. Right this second. If he came into the bar tonight, I would act like he wasn't even there.

A door swung open, spilling golden light across the dirty hall. I drew up a hairsbreadth before I crashed into Maddock.

'Whoa, sorry!' He jerked back, then looked me up and down. 'Harley! What happened?'

'Fucking rain,' I grumbled, shoving my wet hair out of my eyes.

'Really? I thought it looked like it was letting up.'

I caught his eye. As one, we burst out laughing.

'Guess not, then.' Maddock grimaced. 'Ah, fuck it. I can spend another day indoors. Where were you?'

'Dancing.' It was a ready lie—one no one who knew me would question. I danced. And yes, I was mad enough to dance in a storm.

'In the rain?' Maddock quirked a grin.

I shrugged. 'It helps me think.'

'Oh.' His face fell. Suddenly, an aura of sheepishness crept around him: he scuffed his foot, fiddling with a loose splinter in his doorframe. 'Ah… I…' He cleared his throat.

'You?' I asked, confused.

'I ambushed you in the hall for a reason.' Maddock met my gaze through his hair. 'I thought I should apologise for the other day.'

Oh, for fuck's sake.

'And you thought you should do that in the hall, where everyone could overhear?'

He jerked a thumb over his shoulder. 'I'd invite you in, but I didn't think you'd be interested.'

I looked down at myself; the longer I stood still, the bigger my puddle got. 'Maybe not right now.'

'Well then. I'm sorry if I overstepped my boundaries the other day. I respect that—'

Damnit.

I grabbed his arm, steering him into his flat. 'Not in the hall!'

I couldn't get the door shut fast enough, afraid that he'd use the time it took to launch a few more apologies into the void. Where everyone could hear. Didn't he realise that Irina had spies everywhere?

'Sorry, sorry.' Maddock grinned. 'Not in the hall, I got it.'

'You realise your neighbour is the bartender in Sayle's compound, right?'

Maddock blinked. 'Uh, how do you know that?'

I shot him a look. 'Look, I don't need any apologies. You said your bit. I said mine. We're good.'

'We didn't really feel good. I mean, I didn't feel good about it. I get that you're scared. I shouldn't have tried to take advantage of that.'

'Is that what you were doing?' I glared into his eyes, refusing to let him look away. 'I think you were being a fucking idiot. For all you know, I could have gone straight to Sayle and told him what you said.'

'Did you?' Maddock asked warily.

'No, but that doesn't change the fact that I could have.' I prodded him in the shoulder. 'Did it ever occur to you that I could trade the information you gave me in for protection? You think I like living in a dumpy flat with broken heating and a leaky roof?'

Maddock grimaced. 'Okay. Fair. Gotcha. So... offer something better next time?'

I snorted.

'I didn't turn you in. I don't involve myself in any of that shit. And I'm perfectly capable of looking out for myself. I don't need men offering me *better deals*, got it?'

Maddock nodded hastily. 'Got it. Loud and clear.'

'Good.' I patted him on the chest. 'Don't go out. It's miserable out there.'

Maddock laughed. He caught my eye, and then I was laughing, too. I leant against the wall, giggling furiously, and finally some of the bad mood Bas had provoked fell away. After a few seconds, I collected myself.

'I needed that.'

Maddock grinned. 'Me too. I'm starting to see why Tom likes you working on weekends.'

'Because I'm hot?'

'Because you know how to keep the lads in line.'

I snorted. If only he knew. 'Brenda's much fiercer than I am.' I patted his arm again. 'Anyway, I want to dry off. See you around?'

'Yeah, see you.'

I left Maddock with muddy footprints on his floor and a grin on his face and headed upstairs to shower.

The rain persisted for the rest of the day, leaving me drenched by the time I got to work—I'd had to wait ten minutes for a taxi-truck to come by. Business was poor, and I halfway anticipated that I'd gone to Bas for nothing; Rodney wouldn't come in at all.

I was wrong.

'Again?' Anna asked when he stepped through the door, looking like he'd gone for a comfortable evening stroll rather than braved the rain-drenched streets. 'He must seriously like you.'

'He's an ass.'

'You don't like any men.' Anna rolled her eyes. 'Nina Sallinger is quite pretty. You should talk to her.'

'Who? Oh, I don't like women, either.'

'So, what, you're going to just grow old alone?'

'Why not?' I grabbed my tray. 'Better than marrying someone who uses me as a punching bag whenever he gets drunk.'

'Bloke would have to get drunk to handle you, lovey,' Clem called from the table beside the bar.

'Is that why you come around so often?' I asked sweetly. The old men broke into a chorus of hoots. I smiled fondly. Clem was an arsehole, too, but I preferred his brand of arsehole to Rodney Rochester's, that was for sure.

I made my way over to Rochester, who was sitting alone against the wall, surveying the room. His green eyes settled on me as I approached. I met his gaze—I'd already decided I wasn't going to give him an inch tonight.

I raised an eyebrow. 'Alone tonight? Guess you'll have to lower yourself to actually speaking to the staff.'

'I could point and grunt. It wouldn't be much different from your usual clientele.'

'Sorry, the sign on the door says no pets.'

Rochester's expression creased in disdain. 'Do you talk to all of your customers that way, or have I uniquely earned your displeasure?'

'Which answer would annoy you more?'

'I already know the answer.'

'Then why waste my time?'

I wouldn't have been this bold, normally, but the guy had been here four nights running now. He clearly didn't care about the quality of the service.

'I'm paying for your time.' He slid a five onto the table. 'Whiskey, please.'

'Technically, you're only paying for the drinks. My time is not for sale.' I smiled thinly, snatched the note, and tucked it very ostentatiously into my bra. Rochester offered me a look of supreme disgust. Clearly, someone didn't like to dirty himself with the commoners.

So why come here at all?

I puzzled over it as I moved around the room, checking on a table of women—all of them security from one of the casinos—and refilling Clem's water. By the time I made it back to the bar, I'd reached a conclusion.

Rochester wanted something from me.

But what?

Was he trying to make sure I'd kept quiet about the mayor's meeting? If that was it, what did he hope to gain from lurking in the bar? He didn't really think I was so unsubtle as to pass information to my customers, did he?

'And so?' Anna asked. 'Looked like you were getting along with him after all.'

'I called him a dog, actually.'

'*Harley!* You didn't!'

'Not in as many words.' I passed her the money. 'Glass of the barrel-aged. Put ice in it.'

'He doesn't usually take ice.'

'I'll do it, then.'

Anna scowled, but before she could protest, Ellery's team swung into the room, laughing buoyantly. Well, Kade and Briggs were laughing. Bas's gaze swept the room, all traces of humour vanishing when it landed on Rodney. Ellery caught sight of me, and uncertainty crept into his gaze.

What?

He'd never looked at me like that before.

I cast back for what I might have done—was this because I'd refused his offer of staying the night? Or was it because of the note I'd left, the one he'd never replied to?

I couldn't ask him now, though. Too many people listening in.

Screwing my courage to the sticking point, I headed over to Ellery's table. Rochester watched me from one side, Bas from the other. My skin prickled. I felt like there was a spotlight on me.

Don't trip, I told myself with grim amusement. I reached their table and traced a finger playfully over Ellery's tense shoulders.

'Evening, boys. Didn't think I'd see you out to play on a night like this.'

'Aw, we just couldn't stay away from you, baby.' Briggs leered at my chest. I brushed the back of my nail up his cheek, then took hold of a damp curl of brown hair and tugged it firmly.

'Behave.' I met Bas's gaze over the table. He watched me like he was trying to burn me with his eyes. Was my flirting that offensive? I let my smile grow and spoke directly to him, leaning forwards slightly so my shirt fell open. 'What can I get you tonight?'

Bas's eyes narrowed as he looked me *slowly* up and down before catching my eyes again. Was that interest? Really? I was dressed differently tonight; I'd foregone my usual skimpy tops and was wearing an old men's dress shirt, unbuttoned low and belted over a pair of skin-tight trousers. You could hardly see any of my skin—but for the first time, Bas had looked.

And it sent a thrill down my spine that I'd never felt before. More than just a sense of victory. I felt warm all of a sudden, and I nearly missed what Ellery had said.

'We'll have whiskeys for the table.'

'Coming right up.' Releasing Briggs, I turned to Ellery, toying with the collar of his jacket. 'You've been a stranger this last week. Hope I didn't scare you off.'

'Just busy.' He looked up at me, his brown eyes opaque; I couldn't read what he was thinking, where usually he was an open book. 'Did you miss me?'

'You know I missed you.' I flicked my fingers against a freckle on his left cheek. 'You should come by more often. Wouldn't want you to forget about me.'

Ellery caught my fingers, squeezing them. 'As if we could forget you.'

'Mm, well I'd hate to run the risk.' I winked at him as I pulled away, slowly, so that his fingers brushed over my palm. 'Pay up, boys.'

Ellery snapped to attention, the spell broken. He fished in his pocket and pulled out a twenty. 'Keep the change.'

'Good boy.' I patted him on the shoulder and backed away. 'Be right back.'

Briggs slapped my butt as I walked away.

Rochester was my next stop. I set his whiskey—sans ice—on his table with a thud. He tipped his head back, his curls falling across his forehead. 'What, no witty commentary?'

No, I save my witticisms for the people who tip.

'Just doing my job, Mr Rochester.'

'I see. And were you just doing your job when you were rubbing yourself all over the Iron Fists, too?'

Ooh, he was asking to wear that whiskey.

'I don't discuss customers with other customers.' I smiled tightly. 'Enjoy your drink.'

I didn't enjoy the way his eyes followed me across the room.

I couldn't remember the bar ever being this tense, except maybe during the last rousting. All we needed was for one of the other gangs to arrive, and I was sure the tensions would spill over into a full-on fight. Even Clem noticed, and he was deep in his cups already.

'Looks like the boys are spoiling for it, eh?' he asked when I came by with another round.

'They'll behave if they know what's good for them,' I said tersely. I could feel Ellery's eyes burning the back of my neck, but I was determined not to look at him. One of us had to stay professional tonight, and it was going to be me.

I never should have told Bas that Rochester was coming round. I'd made everything ten times worse.

'You tell 'em, Harley,' said Bill, one of Clem's friends, with a gap-toothed grin.

I winked at him. The men all tittered.

Despite my significant apprehension, tensions remained at a simmer. I was behind the bar, about an hour before the end of my shift, when Anna's eyes went wide.

'What?'

She nodded over my shoulder. I turned to find Ellery leaning against the bar.

'Hey.' I frowned at him. Ellery never came up to me in the bar. He'd always let me approach him in the past.

Ellery tapped his fingers restlessly against the wood. 'We have to go. Will you be okay?'

'Okay?'

'With Rochester. Bas said you were concerned about him.'

Bas had said that? I shifted uneasily. 'I'm not concerned about him. He just puts off the other customers.'

Ellery's brow creased. His gaze drifted to Anna, and I sensed that he was picking his words carefully because we weren't alone. 'If there's any trouble, you know where to find me.'

I bit the corner of my lip. *Bold, Ellery.* 'I don't like trouble.' I wanted to ask him what he was doing about the mayor—but I didn't dare with Anna right there. 'I'll be fine. I can handle Rochester.'

Ellery nodded sharply. 'See you around, then.'

'Bye.'

He turned and stalked off, joining the others by the door. Bas was watching me closely, and I felt like my dissatisfaction was written across my face. Sometimes I wished Ellery and I could speak openly about our relationship—but what would we say? I wasn't sure I knew him anymore. He seemed to be running hot and cold these days, and I didn't know why.

'What was *that*?' Anna asked.

'I… have no idea.' What could I say? That was strange, even by Ellery's standards.

When I got in on Tuesday, Anna reported, 'Rodney Rochester wasn't there last night. I think he really is coming here for you.'

'How would he know I wasn't going to be here last night?'

'Huh.' She frowned, considering it. 'Your day off is the same most weeks. Maybe he asked?'

'Tom doesn't give out info about our shifts.'

Anna pouted. 'You are so unromantic, you know that?'

I rolled my eyes. 'Well, we'll soon see if he's here tonight.'

'He will be,' Anna predicted.

'He won't.'

'Pfft,' Anna muttered, flicking her wet fingers at me, before reaching for a towel. 'Seriously, you have no sense of romance. I pity the guy who tries to win you over.'

'There won't be one.'

But Bas's expression from Sunday night popped into my head. I bit my lip, turning away hurriedly before Anna could notice that my cheeks were warm. Why? Bas was nothing to me.

'You say that now,' Anna sang, passing over my tray and apron. 'But when Rochester comes in —'

'*If.*'

'—when Rochester comes in, we'll see what you do then.'

Clucking my tongue, I pushed my way out from behind the bar and went to wipe down tables.

I proved right that evening: Rochester didn't show his face — to my immense relief and Anna's considerable disappointment. My unromantic notions went unchallenged, though unfortunately, so did my struggle to make rent. Business was poor, tips were poorer.

Outside, it rained on.

At a quarter past eleven, Tom stuck his head in to find Anna and me lurking in the bar alone.

'Close up and go home,' he suggested. 'No one's going to come by now.'

'But...' Anna trailed off, evidently unable to think of a compelling reason to stick around.

'It's fine.' Tom waved towards the back door. 'You can clean up and go.'

There was no point in hanging out, so I gave the tables a last wipe-down before waving to Anna. 'See you!'

'Yep.' She grinned saucily. 'Maybe Rochester got held up by the weather and he'll be back tomorrow.'

'Anna,' I groaned.

Outside turned out to be every bit as miserable as I was anticipating. The cobblestones on the square were slippery, and the fountain was turning into a swimming pool. Even the streetwalkers weren't out tonight.

What an awful night.

I scuffed my feet through the puddles, my coat pulled high to stop the rain from going down the back of my neck. This time of year always sucked. I ought to be used to it... but instead, it smacked me in the face again every year.

Sighing, I pulled my coat tighter around me, hurrying my steps. The sooner I got home, the sooner I could get to bed.

I heard the whisper of tyres on damp asphalt a moment before a sleek black car pulled up beside me. I looked up sharply, all of my nerves firing off a warning at once.

The front door slid open, revealing a bulky man who was silhouetted against the dark, rainy night.

'Miss Benoit?'

I trusted my instincts better than an unknown driver of a fancy car. I turned and sprinted away.

Loud footsteps thundered after me. I barely made it five yards before someone grabbed my coat, hauling me back.

'LET ME GO!'

'We just want to talk.'

'FUCK YOU!' I slammed my foot down on the man's boot, but he didn't even grunt. Damn him and his steel-toed boots. I squirmed like a cat in a bath, elbowing and scratching at everything I could reach, but he lifted me effortlessly, carrying me back to the car.

'STOP! STOP!'

Someone laughed. 'Quite the squirmer, isn't she?'

'Open the boot,' my captor grunted. To me, he added, 'If you had behaved, you could have ridden in the back.'

'FUCK YOU!'

I braced my feet against the back of the car, pushing back with all my might. They weren't getting me in there. They were… not… getting me… in there!

The second man jabbed the handle of a knife into my thigh, and a pain, almost like an electric shock jolted up my nerves. Instantly, my leg went weak. I lost my leverage against the edge of the car, and they shoved me in.

A moment later, the boot lid was shut, plunging me into darkness.

THIRTEEN

I DUG MY FINGERS INTO MY THIGHS, my lungs aching from holding my breath as I tried to get my panic under control.

The car boot was tiny and cramped, and I felt every hole in the road, every stone we drove over, every corner the driver took too fast. My head was tucked into my chest to stop it from hitting the side of my prison.

An interminable amount of time later, the car drew to a halt.

Although it had looked shiny from the outside, the car was a clunker; the engine made unhealthy growls, and water had leaked through the seal around the boot, wetting my clothes in several places. My arms and legs ached as I struggled to breathe through the panic that made my chest tight.

I had to be ready when the boot opened.

Footsteps rounded the car, heavy boots crunching on gravel. A moment later they paused, and in the lull, I heard a lighter tread as someone else came near.

Two people.

I'd go for the knees. They would probably expect me to go for the groin—and there was always the risk that one of them would be a woman. No, the knees were best. I braced myself, ready to spring into movement.

'Did you get her?'

'Yes, sir.'

Two men. One of the voices was peripherally familiar.

The boot lid began to lift.

I palmed my knife.

Orange artificial light filtered in, blinding me. A hand grabbed my arm, hauling me up, and the next second I was thrown to the ground. My hands and knees hit gravel and little jolts of pain shot up my limbs.

Footsteps crunched. I twisted sideways, lashing out with the knife.

A boot landed hard in my middle. I sprawled onto a concrete floor.

My knife slipped out of my grip and skittered across the ground.

'Oof!' I grunted. *Fuck, ow, that hurt.*

Someone crouched down and picked up the knife. 'Are you going to behave now?'

Again the mild tone. Recognition tugged at me.

I forced myself up to my hands and knees. Someone's hand appeared in front of me, but I ignored the offer and hauled myself up to my feet on my own strength. I was standing on the edge of a dirt lot surrounded by industrial buildings. Twisting, I looked at my assailant.

It was Rodney Rochester.

The tall, broad-shouldered man stared down at me, disdain colouring his handsome features. He turned my knife over slowly in his fingers.

'That was not very clever.'

'Fuck you. What the hell do you want?'

'I want to talk.' He smiled. Disbelief washed through me.

'And it didn't occur to you to just ask me in the bar?'

'Naturally that was out of the question,' he said evenly. 'To meet in public? Undoubtedly, my enemies would hear within the hour.'

Yeah, from me, I thought darkly. He could fucking bet I was going straight to Bas to tell him that his piece of shit brother had had me kidnapped.

Rochester turned the knife over again. 'This is a very nice piece of hardware.'

'Yeah, and it's not yours.' I held out a hand imperiously. 'Give it back.'

'All in good time.' Rochester tucked his hands behind his back. 'I think you'll listen better without it.'

'You fucking piece of shit!'

'You are terribly rude. I would have thought Tom would hold his waitresses to higher standards.' Every word he said was clipped and perfectly enunciated. He was everything I had hated in boys like Brody and Louis. It made me itch to wipe the smile off his perfect face.

'Tom pays me to keep men in line.'

'A job you do excellently, I must say.'

'Compliment not accepted.'

Rochester chuckled. 'Ah, I'm starting to see how it is. You must drive my brother crazy.'

My mouth opened… and closed again without me saying a word. Bas, he was talking about Bas. *Holy fucking shit.*

Wrongfooted, I turned to look around at our surroundings, trying to buy myself time. We were under an overhang, the rain drumming loudly on the sheet metal roof above us. A single orange light illuminated the back door of some kind of industrial office. The plaque beside it read RocCo. Industries.

Beyond the pool of light, I saw almost nothing. Between the heavy darkness and the thick rain clouds, the night was as black as peat.

'Where are we?'

'An industrial site not far from town.'

It had been hard to judge distances from the boot of the car. I crossed my arms. 'I'd like a bit more detail, thanks.'

Rochester raised an eyebrow. 'Do you speak to everyone like that?'

'No, only rich arseholes who think they can push people around according to their whims.'

Rochester laughed. 'Gracious, you are bold. I could shoot you out here and no one would ever know.'

I swept my gaze over him: light suit jacket, slacks, dress shoes. 'You don't have a gun.'

'Jack over there does.'

I glanced at the driver, the one who'd dragged me into the car. Burly and obviously packing, a typical security type. I squinted at his face, taking in the old break in his nose, the way his eyebrows drew together in the centre, and the snick in his left ear.

'Looks like someone's gone a few too many rounds at the TA. He still able to aim straight?'

Rochester's lips quirked up. He'd smiled before, but this one was real. A sliver of humour, a crack in his armour. 'I assure you, his aim is perfectly adequate. However, I didn't bring you here to shoot you. As long as you behave, we will both leave this place… much improved for our impromptu meeting.'

'That's one way to say 'attempted kidnapping,'' I scoffed.

'I believe the kidnapping was successful.'

'Uh, I hate to break it to you, but you failed when you let me out the car. If you think *Jack* is getting his hands on me again—'

'Jack, leave us,' Rochester said suddenly.

Jack flicked a glance in our direction, nodded sharply, climbed in the car, and drove away. Just like that. I eyed Rochester up and down sceptically. Did he really think he could take me if I kicked off? If I got my knife back, we'd be having a *very* different conversation.

'I hope he's going to circle round and pick you up,' I said.

'My car is parked around the side of the building.' Rochester leant against the rough brickwork and folded his arms over his chest. I eyed my knife, held loosely in his grip. Maybe if he was distracted... 'May we talk now? Or do you have any other aggressions to get off your chest?'

'Well, seeing as you asked...' I watched his brow quirk in irritation. 'You know what, never mind. What did you bring me here for?'

'As I said, I want to talk.' Rochester adjusted his stance. 'About my brother.'

'What brother?'

A slight frown flitted over his face before he masked it. 'You know my brother. You recognised me the first time we met—therefore you know him. And I'm guessing you were the one who brought him into the bar the other night.'

I lifted my chin obstinately. No way I was confirming that accusation. 'I don't know anything about your family. You're going to have to spell it out for me.'

'Playing innocent is not in your best interests, Miss Benoit.'

'Really?'

He looked me over, his gaze sweeping me from my damp curls, which were slowly frizzing out from the humidity, all the way down to my well-worn steel-toed boots. 'I can't imagine a waitress makes a great deal of money.'

'I imagine my wage would look very small to a man who can afford to walk around in bespoke suits and hire ex-military security staff,' I snarked.

'I won't do you the disservice of denying that,' Rochester said mildly. 'Objectively speaking, I imagine it's quite hard to support yourself on your wage, especially when security is such a concern for a woman living alone.'

'You assume I live alone.'

'Initially, I assumed you were living with my brother or one of his... comrades. But that appears not to be the case.'

Oof, that was not a kind accusation. 'I'm not a whore.'

'I imagine you would be more accommodating if you were.'

Bastard.

'Cut to the chase,' I snapped. 'I don't like men who hide behind pretty words.'

'Very well.' Rochester suppressed another frown. 'I have a brother. You know him by the name of Bas. It's short for Sebastian.'

I kept quiet, pinching my lips together. I might not like Bas, but I'd sure choose him over Rochester. Rochester assessed me before continuing, 'For various reasons, he and I have fallen out of contact in recent years.'

Yeah, I thought, bitter with anger on Bas's behalf, *because whilst you've been living snug and secure in your gated mansion, he's been suffering unimaginable hardships as a slave.*

'What's that got to do with me?'

'I want to rekindle contact. I'll pay you—handsomely—if you help facilitate that.'

I couldn't help it; I laughed. It burst out of me like the bark of a dog. 'Are you crazy? Have you met Bas? I don't want to get stabbed!'

'I have, in fact, met him,' Rochester said, utterly serious. 'I assure you, I have thought this through extensively. I was able to observe the two of you amply in the bar the other night. I believe he feels some… affection for you.'

'You're insane.' I shook my head. 'I think we're done here. You wanna talk to your brother? Start by apologising to him. You have no idea what he's been through—'

'But he's told you?' Rochester asked eagerly. He took a step towards me, clenching his hands into fists.

'Of course not. I've known other ex-slaves in my life.' I glared up at him. 'He won't talk to you. I can promise you that right now.'

'Two hundred new pounds every time you bring me information,' Rochester said. 'And a thousand when you arrange the meeting.'

'No deal. I'm not getting involved in your family shit. Talk to him yourself.' No way I needed that hassle in my life—especially when he was offering that much money. Anyone willing to pay that much was lying about the dangers of the job.

'I *can't.*' His tone was fraught with frustration, but I still just wanted to laugh. Did he even hear himself? He was so afraid of his own brother that he wanted me to pass messages like we were thirteen-year-olds in school.

'I'm not helping.'

'Three hundred NP. Each time. That has to be more than what you earn per week at the bar.'

It was—significantly more. I shook my head. 'Rochester, all the money in the world isn't going to convince me to wade into this one. I don't know jack about Bas, but you know what I do know?'

Rochester shook his head, creeping despair in his eyes.

'I know that he's been to hell and back. He deserves dignity. If he wants to talk to you, let him come to you.'

'He won't.'

Exactly, I thought. Why the fuck would he want to? Rodney Rochester had everything that should have been Bas's. Which begged the question: how had one son grown up in luxury, the other as a slave?

What had Bas said?

'You won't like what they do to their enemies.'

I was willing to bet that there was foul play involved here. Either Rodney was guilty… or his father.

'Then leave him be,' I said.

'Five hundred,' Rochester pressed, his eyes wide and his expression wild. 'Not to pass messages. Just keep me informed that he's alright.'

Shit, that was a lot of money. Rochester was all kinds of desperate. It actually hurt me to respond.

'No.'

'Miss Benoit…'

'No. I'm not for sale.'

'You wouldn't have to worry about money. You could move out of that dump you live in.'

It sent a shiver down my spine to learn that he knew where I lived, but I pushed that away to think about later. 'No. I can look after myself.'

Rochester pressed his lips together, then heaved a sigh. 'I'm convinced that you would be able to put in a good word for me with him.'

'I'm convinced you're insane.'

'But,' he continued as though I hadn't spoken, 'I can see that you're not willing to negotiate. I will keep the offer on the table for the next few weeks. Should you reconsider, I know Jack takes drinks occasionally at the Kranikovska. He can pass me a message from you.'

Why the fuck couldn't he have just done that in the first place? I bit my tongue, shaking my head.

'I'm unlikely to reconsider.'

'Times are hard, Miss Benoit. I'm offering a lot of money. You never know what could come up.'

I knew exactly what was coming up—my rent. But there was no way *he* could know about that. I gritted my teeth and nodded. 'May I have my knife back now?'

'So long as you promise not to attempt to use it on me again.'

My ribs still ached from where Jack had kicked me. 'So long as you don't try to bundle me into the boot of a car again.'

'Very well.' He held the knife out, handle first. 'Did Bas give you that?'

'No.'

'Hmm.' What he read into my answer, I couldn't tell. 'Do you want a lift back?'

'I'll pass, thanks.'

'Are you sure? It will take you half an hour to walk. And it's raining.'

Sense warred with pride. Pride won. 'I'm good, thanks.'

Rochester chuckled. 'Suit yourself.'

He sauntered around the corner. A moment later, I heard a car door slam, and another sleek black car drove past, gravel skittering under its tires. It turned right onto the road and vanished, leaving me alone.

I was an idiot.

Heaving a sigh, I started walking.

FOURTEEN

NEXT TIME PRIDE TRIED TO get a look into my decisions, I was going to tell it to fuck right off.

My legs ached, and I had a blister developing on my right foot. It throbbed with every step I took. To make matters worse, I was completely drenched. At least I hadn't gotten lost; it had been a fairly straightforward walk along the main road back into town, and I'd managed to pick up a taxi-truck about five minutes after hitting the residential area.

I had cursed Rochester with every step.

Rich men thought they could play God, and the rest of us would align neatly to their whims like the pawns in my dad's old chess set.

I refused to be like that.

I'd never empathised with Bas quite this much, but the way I felt right now, I sure as heck wasn't going to be betraying him.

Rodney Rochester could go hang.

Even if he'd offered me a fucking fortune.

He'd laid his trap well, though, because now I was curious. So curious it ached.

How had Bas ended up a slave? What had gone wrong? Who had betrayed him?

The questions burnt on the tip of my tongue. I could go tomorrow morning, tell him about Rochester's offer, and ask.

But the money stopped me. I'd have liked to say I couldn't be bought, but I still remembered the gut-wrenching fear of not having enough money to make rent. And my rent was going up this week. One sixty-five. The words hammered away in my skull like the beat of a drum.

One sixty-five.

One sixty-five.

One hundred and sixty-five new pounds.

The difference between me and homelessness.

With Rochester's money, I wouldn't have to worry. With Rochester's money, I could finally get someone in to fix the leaky ceiling. With Rochester's money, I might be able to save up for a better place.

One sixty-five.

I let myself into my building.

One sixty-five.

I climbed the stairs.

One sixty-five.

I unlocked my front door and slipped in, turning back to bolt the deadlock.

'Harley?'

I spun around, my heart jumping into my throat. Savannah stood silhouetted in the doorway to the bedroom, a dressing gown wrapped around her shoulders.

'Why are you back so late?'

'Sav?' I croaked. 'God, Sav, you scared the crap out of me!'

'You think?' She padded closer, but I still couldn't make out her face. 'Where have you been? I woke up and you weren't here! I was worried.'

I shifted uncomfortably. Savannah was the last person I wanted to share the details with. 'I… it's… stuff happened at work, and…'

'You were at the bunker, weren't you?'

Anger bubbled up in my stomach at her accusing tone. I clenched my fists. 'So what if I was?'

'You always go back to that place! When will enough be enough?'

The injustice of it was like a knife in my stomach. How dare she be so fucking judgemental all the time? What had she done to help us out of the depths of poverty? Pissed off, I shoved away from the door and began shucking my wet coat. It stuck to me; I was wet through and chilled to the bone. 'It's none of your business what I do.'

'It's my business if you're going to a place that's bad for you.' Savannah flicked on the light. 'And you're all wet. Don't drip on the floor. Who's going to clean that up?'

'I am. You never clean.' I bit my tongue. I hated being nasty to Savannah; she worked harder than I did. 'Sorry—'

'I clean plenty. Just because you never notice—'

'I do notice, okay? I shouldn't have said that.'

'You're always so self-centred.'

'I said sorry!' I kicked one boot off and began work on the other. 'I said I'd clean it up.'

'Forget it. I'll do it.'

'No, no.' My tone dripped with sarcasm. 'I know you have to be up early tomorrow. Let me get it.'

Savannah swore under her breath, just loud enough for me to make out. 'Honestly, I don't know why you go back to that place. It's like you want men to degrade you—'

'I do not!'

'Then stop giving them the opportunity to!'

I gritted my teeth, resisting the urge to throw my boot at the wall. I hadn't even been at the bunker, but if I told her that now, she'd want to know where I had been instead. The last thing I wanted was to involve Savannah with someone like Rodney Rochester; he'd chew her up and spit her out. Yet, what else could I tell her? I was exhausted; I couldn't think of another explanation.

'Am I not allowed to have fun every once in a while?'

'There are more important things in life than having fun.'

'Yeah,' I mumbled bitterly, 'especially for me.'

'Oh, woe is you,' Savannah scoffed, turning back to the bedroom. 'You're so hard done by, Harley. I don't know how you cope.'

I didn't know either.

Savannah slammed the door behind her, and I slumped onto the sofa, staring blankly into the darkness. This was so fucked up; I didn't know what to do. Bas or Rodney? It seemed like it didn't matter what I chose, things just got worse and worse… and I was exhausted. Trying to fix things, trying to keep things normal for Savannah… I had no energy anymore. Life had just taken so much out of me.

Tiredness washed over me all at once. *Fuck cleaning.* I turned sideways on the sofa, resting my head on the armrest, and was asleep within seconds.

I woke up shivering. Someone—Savannah—had covered me with the blanket from my bed, but it didn't help much when I was wearing wet clothes. My head pounded, and my eyesight was blurry.

Shit. I needed a hot shower. We'd be screwed if I got sick now.

I staggered to my feet. Savannah had cleaned the floor and turned my boots upside-down to dry. I stumbled into the bathroom. My reflection was an ugly mess in our cracked mirror. My eyes were puffy, my hair frizzy.

I switched on the shower. It sputtered out a meagre trickle with tell-tale reluctance.

'No, no, no, not today!' I swore viciously under my breath. Fucking old building with its fucking shitty hot water system and witch of a landlady who never repaired anything.

I stuck my hand under the spray, willing it warm, but it remained icy cold. 'No, come on, come on, please.'

I sagged against the wall, sobbing futilely. No hot water. Today, of all days.

Okay, think… think.

I felt foul; my legs ached, and my throat was parched. I started in the kitchen with a hot cup of coffee. That, at least, warmed me up.

We were low on food, but I managed to scrounge together enough to make a sort of bready broth with a hunk of stale bread I had from Krani's. After eating it, I felt more or less human; I'd go by Brenda's place and ask if I could use her shower. We did favours for each other all the time. I could probably offer to do some of her mending in return.

And once I was clean and warm, I could figure out what to do about… Rodney.

And Bas.

But mostly Rodney.

Brenda lived southeast of the square, in the basement flat of an older apartment block. They'd stuffed foam around the windows to stop them from leaking, but the flooding didn't seem to have reached them yet. I followed Brenda down a flight of rickety steps and emerged into the cramped living room of their rabbit-warren-like flat. The room was stuffed to the brim with furniture, the floor littered with discarded toys.

'You're in luck; we do have hot water. I managed to get both boys through the bath this morning.'

'Did you?' I caught sight of the two boys, who both looked distinctly sulky. 'Oh, hello there.'

'HARLEY!' Cal shot up from the sofa, a grin blossoming on his face. 'VROOM-VROOM!'

'Vroom-vroom, that's right.' I grinned, catching Cal as he hurtled at me and scooping him off the ground. I felt warmer already, just being out of my flat and around people. Cal was five, and an absolute darling.

His older brother, Ty, lurked near their saggy sofa, clutching a tiny ball of fluff and watching me suspiciously. Ty was eleven and took being the man of the family *very* seriously.

'Hey, Ty.' I set Cal down so I could wave. 'How's school?'

'I'm down to four days,' he said.

'Uh-huh? Whatcha doing the other day?'

'Apprenticing with the Mackenzies.'

'They run the granary. He's learning all about storing and milling grain,' Brenda said proudly.

'That's fantastic. And what have you got there?' I nodded to his bundle. The bundle yapped, and Ty hugged it tighter.

'Nothing.'

'It can't stay,' Brenda said sternly. 'Dobbs will kick us out.'

'I'm gonna take it to the Mackenzies.' The dog squirmed, and Ty clutched it to his chest. 'Jim said he'd look out for it.'

It yapped again. I approached with some caution. Ty loosened his grip, and a tiny little head with huge eyes peeped out at me. A puppy.

'He's pretty.'

'He is, and super smart.' Ty jerked his chin up. 'He stopped Cal from getting run over by a taxi-truck yesterday.'

'Mm-hmm. That is smart.'

'Promise you won't tell.'

'I won't, pinkie swear.' I held my hand out. Ty shook pinkies solemnly and finally released the dog from captivity. It was small and malnourished, but otherwise in reasonable condition. Maybe Ty would get lucky and one of the farms would find a home for it. I scratched it behind the ears before glancing at Brenda.

'Let me make you tea,' she said.

'No, no, I just came to use the shower. I don't want to be a burden.'

'Nonsense.' Brenda shook her head. 'You look flushed. Take a tea and a hot shower. And a bit of porridge, too, if you want.'

I shook my head. It all sounded very tempting, but I knew Brenda was just as stretched as Savannah and I were—and she had two extra mouths to feed. 'I'll be as quick as I can.'

'Alright.' She patted my arm.

The hot shower was the best thing I'd felt in months—much hotter than our water got. I dried myself and dressed in warm clothes. There'd be no looking sexy in the bar today, not that I was in the mood for that.

I wrung as much water out of my hair as possible, then left it loose to dry and went to find Brenda again. She was by the door, speaking to a harried-looking woman who had a little girl by the hand.

'...and Ty is going with Jim Mackenzie after school, so no need to bring him back. Oh, and let Cal's teacher know that I can do the meeting on Wednesday next week; I've managed to push my shifts around. Thanks, Dianne.'

'No problem,' the other woman said. She caught Cal's hand. 'Come on, then, boys. To school.'

'Ugh!' they both groaned in unison.

I managed to wave bye to them, and they piled out the door, leaving Brenda, me, and the dog. Brenda pushed a steaming mug into my hands.

'I said it was alright.'

'And I said I didn't mind.' She smiled, pushing a pin that had worked its way out of her pineapple bun back in. 'There are biscuits, too, if you won't take porridge.'

'Maybe one,' I said, and before I knew it, she had set me up with a bowl of porridge, a refill of the bitter herbal tea, and two biscuits. I ate them with mixed feelings—they were hands down the best thing I'd tasted all week, but I always felt weird accepting food from people who were as hard up as me.

'So,' Brenda said, heaving herself into the seat opposite me. Brenda was a big woman, strong, with russet skin and a striking face. 'Tell me what happened.'

'Nothing happened.'

'That's not a nothing face, love. That's a 'I've done something I shouldn't have' face. Is there a boy involved?'

'Boy? Brenda, I'm twenty-four!'

'Boy, man, they're all the same.' Brenda waved dismissively, before taking a generous sip of her tea. 'Who is he?'

'No one.'

'Oh, love.'

I scowled, turning my focus to my porridge. 'Brenda, it's not like that.'

She leant over and patted my hand. 'Tell me something else, then.'

Behind me, the dog yipped. Brenda scowled. 'Hush, you. You'll bring the landlord down on us.'

I sprinkled a few crumbs in front of it, which it happily devoured.

'I don't know what to tell. It's raining. Business is bad. Irina put my rent up.'

Brenda huffed. 'That woman is a shrew.'

'I know.' I pushed the oats around my plate with my spoon. 'But she's my landlady. And it's safe there.'

'And, of course, you're not in the basement,' Brenda added, gesturing around her flat.

'Yeah.' I forced myself to take a bite, then a second one. Food was food, even if I felt bad taking Brenda's food.

'This man of yours…'

'There is no man, Brenda.'

'Harley, love, I wasn't born yesterday. Let's pretend we're both on the same page, hmm?'

I sighed.

Ignoring me, Brenda continued, 'This man wouldn't happen to be, ah, *affiliated* with the boys up on the north side, would he?'

She meant the Iron Fists, of course. I pressed my lips together, knowing my reaction was giving me away.

'Harley…'

'I know, I know, but—I haven't actually done anything. He just… exists.' I wasn't even sure which *he* I was talking about. Historically, that would always have meant Ellery—Ellery was the only man I had ever let close. So why had Bas's face popped into my head when Brenda started probing? Bas was no one. I barely knew him.

'Men love to exist, don't they? They get all up in your private life and personal space, and exist so loudly you just can't ignore them.'

'Yes!' I said enthusiastically. 'That's exactly it. And then—and then…'

'Then they get you to fall for them, get bored, and wander off to get into someone else's personal space,' Brenda said. 'Don't go falling, Harley. Cut those feelings off before they get you hurt.'

'I know.' I stabbed my spoon into my porridge, wishing it was something more visceral than soggy oats. 'I know.'

'I know you do. But the heart doesn't listen, does it?'

'Ugh, you make it sound like I'm soppy over some guy. I'm not Anna.'

Brenda laughed. 'No, you're not. But Anna doesn't give as much of herself. Her crushes are just passing fancies. When you fall, you'll give all of yourself. That's who you are, Harley.'

'An idiot?'

'It's not stupid to fall in love. Just don't lose yourself in it.' Brenda offered me a wry smile.

I covered my eyes with one hand, sighing, and used the other to scrape my porridge together so I could eat it properly. 'I'm not going to.'

'That's the spirit.' Brenda grabbed the teapot to top up her mug. 'I'm thinking of teaching Ty to drive.'

'You don't have a car.'

'Manny found one for cheap. He thinks it's a good deal—so it probably isn't—but I was thinking I could ask Clem's buddy to look at it. You know, the one who owns the car shop?'

'Rocky.'

'That's the one. You think he'd do it?'

I sipped my tea. 'Don't see why not. It might cost you, though.'

'Oh, that one has a girl he goes to on the regular. He'll probably ask for a few drinks on the house, or maybe to do his mending. But if Ty could drive, he could learn to drive the tractors on the farms. It'd see him good when he finishes school.'

'He could drive to pick you up from work,' I said.

'Nah, that'd be a waste of gas. It's not such a bad walk.'

We both looked at the windows, then exchanged glances.

'I'll put a feeler out about cars, if you want,' I said. 'I might be able to find someone with a better deal.'

'As long as it's not one of Sayle's boys.'

I wrinkled my nose. 'Brenda, I don't mix business with friends.'

Brenda laughed.

I felt better for having talked to Brenda—the closest person I had to a mother. She was no replacement for my own mother, who had been gentle, kind, and oh-so creative. But then, I'd never had to look my mother in the eye as an adult. Brenda's pragmatism probably suited me better.

I pushed those thoughts away before my mood could take a turn for the worse, and headed to work. Kayla was on the bar, fiddling with a disassembled beer tap.

'No Anna?'

'Anna's off with some gentleman or the other.'

It was alright for people like Anna—she could miss a day, or switch shifts, and not feel the repercussions for the rest of the week. Then again, she had a secure home with Tom.

'Anyone I know?'

Kayla shrugged, passing me a pair of screws to hold. 'Tam.'

Oh fuck.

'But he's…'

'I know.' Kayla tucked the screwdriver between her teeth and reached up to shove her braids back. 'But it's her business, right?' she said around the screwdriver.

'Right. Do you need help there?'

Kayla worked the screwdriver out of her mouth and put it back to work. 'No. I've been asking Tom to fix this fucking thing for weeks. Tom don't do nothing I ask. You know what he's like.'

I did. Tom was a pretty hands-off owner.

'By the way,' she said suddenly, 'my boss at the casino is looking for people to work a few shifts. One of his girls has gone and got herself pregnant. He wants smart girls, you know, who don't pop off to the backroom to rub a guy off for extra tips.'

I snorted. 'What's the pay?'

'Seven an hour plus tips.'

That wasn't bad. I took the screw Kayla held out. 'I'll think about it. Who's your boss?'

She slanted me a glance. 'That'd be Rollins. But he's just the manager.'

I could guess who the owner was—if not Percival, then someone loyal to him who didn't mind his business being a front for gang activities. Percival's gang had a finger in most of the casinos in town. Kayla gestured for me to hold a pipe out of her way. As I leant in to help, I slotted the face and name together. Rollins: tall, bald, tattoos over his head, and a moustache.

'Can't imagine Rollins in a suit.'

'He pulls it off okay, actually.' Kayla waggled her brows. 'Let's say the customers don't ask to see the manager too often.'

I smirked. 'Sounds good.'

But I wasn't going to take the offer, tempting as it was, because the last thing I needed was another gang breathing down my neck. Sayle and Moriarty were giving me enough to deal with already.

After work that night, I walked back to Brenda's to pick up her mending, as I'd promised. When she opened the door, she yanked me in.

'Gracious, girl, I didn't expect you to come by tonight. You got a death wish?'

'No, why?'

Brenda jerked her chin towards the door, as though we could see through it. 'The place across the road is teeming with Moriarty's lot.'

'What?' I opened the door again, ignoring her as she hissed my name. Across the road was a battered apartment building. The bottom floor was a weapons shop. Above, a tacky sign proclaimed that the first floor had been converted into the office of the North Crater Charitable Organisation. 'The weapons shop?'

'The charity, love. Get in here.' Brenda tugged me away from the door and slammed it shut. 'They started showing up there about three weeks back. Not sure what happened to the old charity workers.'

'Huh.' I glanced at the stairs. 'Can I go up there?'

'*Harley!*'

'Five minutes, and then I'll pick up your mending and you can pretend I was having tea at your place.'

Brenda pursed her lips. 'I'm coming up there with you. Wait one minute.'

She hurried downstairs before I could protest. I heard her whispering to the boys, and then she reappeared and dropped a scarf over my head. 'Last thing you want is them looking up and seeing your pretty face in the window.'

I smiled, wrapping the scarf around me to cover my face and hair. 'Let's go, then.'

We crept up the stairs. The first-floor windows were boarded up, but on the second floor we could see out, down into the first floor of the building opposite. One side was dark, but on the other side of the stairwell, the flat was brightly lit. Two bedrooms, plus the main room, were visible.

'Is that what I think it is?' Brenda asked.

I squinted at the furthest bedroom, my heart clenching in my chest. There were five… no, six people in the room, squashed together in a sort of pen that was separated from the rest of the room by metal bars.

All were hunched over, clutching at one another, and their clothes looked dingy. The dim lights glinted off metal on their wrists, either shackles or cuffs. At least one of the people was small enough to still be a child.

I let my gaze slide across the other visible windows; the second bedroom was empty, and I could only see slivers of the main room. At that moment, someone appeared who had obviously just entered from the stairwell, sauntering from window to window, over to a desk. He stopped, leant over to press a kiss to the lips of the woman behind the desk, then threw his heavy coat and hood off.

My heart sank.

It was Hannover.

Hannover was trading slaves in our town.

FIFTEEN

I ELICITED NO LESS THAN four promises from Brenda to be careful and keep the boys indoors before finally leaving out the back. I headed straight for the drop point—I couldn't not tell Ellery about this. I had to do something, and what was the alternative? No way could I let them take slaves from our town. We had never tolerated slavers operating within the town limits.

If Ellery didn't get back to me, I was probably going to do something stupid. But that was for Harley of tomorrow to worry about.

Harley of tonight slipped soundlessly through the small cobblestoned streets around the square, moving from shadow to shadow. I'd walked this path so many times now that I could do it in my sleep; I knew where all the good hiding spots were, and where to avoid so I didn't disturb either the hookers or the homeless. I turned onto Kirk Street, passing the ramshackle church with its DIY steeple, which ran the soup kitchen. I'd never really glanced twice at their sign—but now the logo jumped out at me.

Printed in the corner of the SOUP FOR ALL poster was an overlapping NCC. North Crater Charity.

A shiver ran down my spine, and suddenly I fervently wished I was back home in my bed. Home was safe. There were no slavers lurking there. I turned onto the unnamed back street where the drop was and froze.

Two figures, little more than silhouettes in the weak moonlight, stood in a doorway. I drew back, heart in my mouth, pressing my hand to my lips to muffle my breathing.

'…warning you, it won't go the way you think.'

'…the mayor's backing…'

That voice was familiar. I swallowed hard.

'As if the mayor has that kind of power.'

'Money is power.'

'If you keep thinking that…'

'Look, can you do it or not?' The man's voice rose in a sharp, angry snap, and suddenly recognition hit me. Hardwick. That was Evander Hardwick. But who was he talking to?

Tense and poised to run, I manoeuvred so I could look down the street. The two men had shifted; I could see both of them in profile now. Hardwick was a tall, slender figure. He was talking to someone considerably shorter than him, slight, and dressed in sleek clothing.

'I'm doing my best,' the shorter man murmured. 'But these things have to be done slowly.'

'We don't have much time left. If we want to stay ahead of Moriarty—'

'That's your problem, not mine.'

A tense silence fell between them. I could hear my heartbeat, impossibly loud.

'I can't guarantee anything for at least two weeks,' said the shorter man. 'You'll just have to work out a new timeline.'

He turned to leave, and shock jolted through me.

It was Gabriel Tam. Gabriel Tam was meeting with Evander Hardwick.

Was Tam a traitor to the Iron Fists?

Tam was looking right at me.

'Who—'

I turned and sprinted. Forget the drop, I had to get out of here. I turned haphazardly down one street and then another, my boots slapping the cobblestones. I could hear a second set of footsteps in pursuit—but only one. Tam or Hardwick? Could I outrun him? Where had the other man gone? What would they do if they got me?

I had to get home.

No, not home. I'd lead them straight to Savannah. I had to hide— but where?

Panic closed in on me. I continued to run, turning left, right, left, right—I had no idea where I was anymore—and no clue where to go— but I did know that my pursuer was gaining on me. I could hear his frenzied footsteps echoing off the walls—

I couldn't let him grab me—

I burst onto the main road abruptly, almost falling off the edge of the pavement. Main Street had a high curb, over a foot. I drew up short, stopping for one dangerous second. *Shit, that would have been a bad fall.*

Footsteps behind me. I turned left, north, and sprinted.

And slammed into someone. A hand clamped over my mouth, cutting off my scream, and strong hands dragged me towards the road. I bit down.

'Get off—get—' My back slammed into something hard.

'Girl, girl,' someone hissed. 'Stop fighting—Fuck!' I'd kneed him in the balls, but he didn't release me. 'You fucking stupid girl.' He slammed me back, my head whacking against the metal—a car. Pain exploded through me, and in that moment he wrestled me into the car. I landed sprawled in the rear footwell, and for a moment I couldn't seem to get a grip on anything. The door slammed shut as I grabbed the back of the front seat and pulled myself up.

'No!' I snarled, throwing myself at the door, but it locked before I could get it open, and then the man climbed in the driver's seat. I lunged at him, wrapping my hands around his neck. He laughed.

'Girl, I am your only hope of living to the morning. That is a very bad idea.'

Recognition cut through my panic—I knew that voice. It was Hardwick.

'You're kidnapping me!'

'I'm saving you. You want Tam to shoot you in the head? Because he will, and no one will ever find your body. Men like him can make little girls like you disappear easily enough.'

I struggled to get a grip on his neck. The headrest dug into my chest. Hardwick grabbed one of my hands and squeezed, much stronger than I was capable of.

'Even if you get rid of me, what are you going to do?' His voice was strained. 'Can you drive?'

I let my hands fall away, scowling. 'That doesn't mean I trust you to help me.'

'Sit down.' Hardwick rubbed his neck. 'A rabid stray would be more grateful than you are.'

'Fuck you.' I dug my nails into my knees to ground myself. Hardwick pulled the car away from the kerb onto the silent street. I stared outside, trying to find Tam, but he seemed to have vanished.

'Where are you taking me?'

'Northside.'

'To Sayle's compound?' I croaked.

'That was the plan.'

'Why?'

'Why not?' Hardwick turned the wheel. He was a smooth driver, for the speed we were going. 'You are in very far over your head. I hope you're as good friends with Sebastian Rochester as you seem to be.'

The name had an odd effect on me. It was the first time I'd heard Bas called by what I could only presume was his full name. I couldn't quite reconcile Sebastian Rochester with the sullen, glowering man who had insisted that his name was Bas.

'How do you know I'm friends with Bas?'

'Hannover has a big mouth. It wasn't hard to extrapolate—Sebastian rarely does things without reason. Therefore, I deduced that your meeting was more than just a negotiation on sexual services. All I had to do was post someone to watch the training ground, to see if you came back.'

Fuck.

Fuckity fuck fuck fuck.

I was so screwed.

'I'm not involved with Bas.'

'Not in the way Hannover thinks you are, that's for certain.' Hardwick turned us down another street, and suddenly I could see the clinic just ahead of us. He really was taking me to the north side.

I braved another question.

'What's your business with Gabriel Tam?'

'That is for me to know, and you to be a good girl and keep your pretty mouth shut about.'

'Fuck you.'

'Ah, yes, a sensible sentiment considering that I could just turn around and shoot you.'

'Then why don't you?'

Hardwick turned just enough that he could see me. His gaze was hard, a stark contrast to his mild tone. 'Because now you owe me. And, like Marco Ellery, I understand the benefit of being owed a favour by the pretty waitress at the Kranikovska. When I ask, which I will, you're going to pay that favour back.'

'I'm not informing for you.'

'We shall see, Harley Benoit.' He stopped the car and nodded down the street. 'I trust you can see yourself the last few hundred yards?'

'Yes,' I said sullenly.

'Good girl. Off you go, then.' He pressed a button, and the locks popped open. 'Send Sebastian my regards.'

'Arsehole.'

'Always, Miss Benoit, always.'

I climbed out. No sooner had I shut the door than Hardwick pulled off, his car vanishing soundlessly into the darkness. I pressed my hand against my chest, breathing hard. Holy shit, that had been…

I didn't even know what that meant.

Why had he helped me? Why drop me here?

What had the conversation I'd overheard been about?

I needed to speak to Ellery—I couldn't think what else to do. Hardwick was right, I was in way over my head. This was above my pay grade. I'd do what I always did: pass the information to Ellery and let him solve the problems.

Stomach churning, I headed for the front gate of Sayle's compound. The closer I got, the brighter the floodlights seemed. I squinted against them as I approached the gate. A guard appeared, dressed head to toe in black combats, and trained his rifle on me. I froze.

'State your name,' he snapped gruffly. *Fuck, of all the luck.* I had to get a guard who didn't know me.

'Uh, Harley. Harley Benoit.'

'What are you doing here?'

My mouth felt dry, and I struggled to get the words out. 'I need to speak to Marco Ellery.'

'What for?'

'It's… personal.'

The rifle barrel lowered a few inches. My heart was beating so hard I thought it might burst right out of my chest. I felt dizzy. 'Ellery's busy.'

'It's important!' I stepped closer, and the guard swung the rifle up to point at my face again. I stopped dead, raising my hands above my head. 'I have to see him, please!'

'Look, girl.' The guard dropped his rifle and shook his head. I squinted, trying to pick out his features, but I didn't recognise him. 'Ellery's got business. He ain't got time tonight, and even so, he knows he's not meant to be bringing his whores back here.'

'I'm not a whore. My name is Harley Benoit. Look, just tell him I'm here, he'll explain—'

'Get lost, girl. You can suck his dick some other night.'

Footsteps crunched behind him as another man walked into view. This person I did recognise—it was Briggs. *Damnit.* Why couldn't it have been Ellery, or even Kade? But Briggs was better than no one.

'Briggs!'

Briggs turned. Catching sight of me, he jogged over to the gate. 'Ello, baby. Whatcha doing here?' Turning to the guard, he added, 'It's alright, I got this.'

The guard nodded sharply and retreated.

'Ellery, I need to see Ellery.' I tried to pour urgency into my voice.

Briggs turned back to me, frowning. 'Ellery's busy, baby. Want me to fill the gap? I can take care of your needs.' He waggled his brows suggestively.

'I'm not here for sex, Briggs!' I clenched my fists. Honestly, was that really all they thought about when they saw me? 'I need to speak to him right now!'

'He's otherwise engaged. It's me or nothing, baby.'

I gnashed my teeth together. Of all the luck. What I wouldn't have given for Kade or Bas to walk by.

Bas.

'Is Bas around?'

'Aw, for real? You'd pick Bas over me, baby?' Briggs slapped a hand against his chest. 'That hurts.'

'Briggs, this is serious.'

He laughed. Leering down at me, he said, 'Everything's bloody serious with you, innit? Tell you what. I can get a message to Ellery… for a price.'

Motherfucker.

'I'll kiss you,' I said. I was that fucking desperate. 'If you'll just tell Ellery to come find me—'

'I was thinking something a bit more, well, *more,*' Briggs suggested. 'Come on. You know I'll make it good for you.'

I wanted to puke. 'A kiss or nothing.'

'A handjob.'

'Here? Briggs, that's fucking—'

'You wanna say you're too good for it? But you're not too good to spread your legs for Marco, huh?' Briggs leered at me. 'You've got an attitude that you don't deserve, Harley Benoit. Marco spoils you.'

My mind raced. I couldn't believe I was about to agree to this—but I didn't know what else to do. I couldn't drop a note, not when Tam and Hardwick had met right there. Did they know that was where the drop was? I couldn't meet Bas tomorrow morning either. Everywhere was compromised.

'Fine, a handjob.'

'That's the spirit.' Briggs nudged the gate open. 'In you come, babygirl.'

Swallowing against the bile in my throat, I slipped through the gap. Briggs caught my hand, tugging me into an alleyway and down the side of a large truck. 'We'll be private here. I'm so glad you saw things my way.'

'How could I not?' I choked.

'Kiss me.'

I went up on tiptoes and pressed my lips against his. How quickly could I get this over with? My head swam, but somehow I managed to get his belt and trousers open. He was already hard. His tongue tangled with mine, and I let him kiss me, tasting beer and cigarette smoke because it was easier than looking at him whilst I did this. I wrapped my hand around his cock, using my thumb to spread his precum, and began to jerk him slow and steady.

Briggs broke the kiss. 'That's it, babygirl. Like that.'

He shoved me back against the wall, kissing me again. His tongue plundered my mouth hungrily. I sped up the movements of my hand, squeezing, willing him to hurry up. He grunted.

'Fuck, you're so good. I missed this. Tell me you missed it, too.'

Speech was beyond me. I faked a moan, drawing him in for another kiss, and added a little twist to my wrist. Briggs grunted again and pressed me harder into the wall, his hips jerking erratically. 'Fuck, you're gonna make me cum. You like that? Tell me you like that.'

But I didn't need to say anything. I jerked him twice more and felt him stiffen before he ejaculated sticky liquid over my hand. He groaned long and low, before pulling back. 'Come back to my room with me.'

'No. You have to get the message to Ellery. That was our deal.'

Briggs's face shifted from mellow to furious in an instant. 'You manipulative slut.'

'That was the deal.' I wiped my hand on the bricks. 'Go fetch him.'

'Like fuck!' Briggs's hand cracked against my cheek. My head thudded against the bricks. I gasped in pain, bringing a hand up to cover my cheek. The skin burnt. 'You think I'm gonna go get him so you can suck his cock next, you stupid whore?'

'You promised!'

Briggs laughed. Taking a breath, he spat in my face. I flinched.

'Get lost, slut. You weren't that good anyway.'

He turned and stalked off, doing his pants up as he left. I stared after him, burning with humiliation.

I was such a fucking idiot.

Nausea churning in my gut, I turned and walked home. The worst part was that I couldn't even take a hot shower when I got there, to wash the feeling of Briggs's hands off me.

SIXTEEN

The upstairs lounge was filled with shouts and laughter. I stood behind the bar, my head throbbing in protest as I poured drinks and avoided the gazes of seventeen spoilt brats.

You'd think by our age, people would have done a bit of growing up, but clearly only poor people were expected to grow up around here. The rich of the town got to stay immature and spoilt, never touched by life's hardships.

Those were the people I was performing for today because today was Lucy Godfrey's birthday.

As I was reminded every time someone spoke to me, because it was, in fact, my birthday, too.

Lucy was two years younger than me, the sister of Louis Godfrey, who was also somewhere in the fray tonight. She considered it a personal insult that she had to share her birthday with Savannah and me and had made a point to be awful to me during our school years and at our shared dance classes.

Not much had changed.

It was Saturday; it had been three days since I'd seen Tam and Hardwick at their midnight rendezvous, and there was no word from Ellery. At some point soon, I was going to have to face the fact that Briggs had not passed on the message and figure out what the hell I was going to do. With the drop compromised, and Sayle barring outsiders from his compound, I had no way of contacting Ellery. For the last three days, however, I had hidden. I'd gone to work, done Brenda's mending, talked to people, stayed away from the training yard, and otherwise behaved perfectly normal. I was as normal as normal could be. Nothing to see here.

Nothing at all.

If only I could get the thought of the slave pen out of my head.

'Oi, kitten, get me another one of those mixers!'

Diego appeared out of the hubbub, sauntering over to the bar and bracing his hands against it. He leant over to leer down my top.

'It's Harley,' I muttered.

'Harley,' he purred, sending a shiver down my spine. Diego was objectively handsome, with brown skin, straight brown hair, and a cheeky smile. I'd had a crush on him, once. Fifteen-year-old Harley had had very poor taste. 'How's it going, *Harley*?'

'Fine thanks, and you, *Diego*?'

Diego smirked. 'You know who I haven't heard from in a while?'

I passed up three drinks onto the bar counter for a group of girls, then turned to scribble their prices in my book. They were on tab, and it was my job to cut them off when they hit their limit.

'Harley,' Diego whined.

'How am I supposed to know which whores you're banging at the moment, Diego?'

Diego laughed. 'Oh, kitten, you always did have a great sense of humour. But I was talking about your boy Theo. Where's he at these days?'

I bit my lip, keeping my back to him as I added the drink I was about to make him to the tally. 'How should I know? I don't keep tabs on him.'

'Because it has been a *while* since I saw him last. Hate to think he'd gone and snuffed it before I could rematch him in the cage.'

A chill ran down my spine. I pushed the feeling away. 'I'm sure Theo is fine. He's in the city, that's all.'

'I sure hope so, for your sake.' I turned back in time to see Diego's sharklike smirk. 'You're looking mighty lonely these days.'

'Is that so?'

He dragged his eyes up and down my body. 'That is so.' He leant in further. 'I could keep you company.'

I had to press my lips together to stop myself from laughing. 'You're looking in the wrong direction.'

'Pardon?' Diego's brow furrowed in confusion.

'Lucy Godfrey is over there.'

Annoyance flickered in his gaze. 'I'm talking to you.'

'Oh, really?' I made a staticky noise. 'You're breaking up. I can't hear you.'

'Piss off, Benoit.'

'Gladly.' I set a glass on the counter and poured a shot of whiskey.

'Except I can't go far. I have to serve the drinks.'

Diego shook his head. 'You know, you could do worse than me. At least I look after my toys.'

'Mm-hmm, yeah.' I pushed his drink over to him. 'But I am not a toy.'

'Better to belong to me than to the Cavanaughs.'

'Yeah, the Cavanaughs aren't getting anywhere near me, I can promise you that.'

Diego snorted. 'Sure, that's what you say now. But I know girls like you. A couple of hard weeks and you'll be out on your arses. You really going to pick the brothels over me? That's crazy.'

'I'm crazy. You can fuck off now. You've made your case.' I smiled at him, just to drive the point home. 'And I'm not buying.'

Diego shrugged. 'Thought I'd offer. Shit's coming that won't go well for you and yours.'

He sauntered off.

'What does that mean? Diego!' But he was gone. I ground my teeth together, gripping the edge of the bar counter. For fuck's sake. More cryptic comments, more men talking shit. My life in a nutshell.

Sometimes I just wanted to walk away from this dump and never look back.

But where in the world was better? At least in Bale Rocks I knew the lay of the land, even if the land was pretty fucking rocky.

Snorting at my own poor humour, I rechecked the tab. I could have paid three weeks' rent with this tab, and they had blown through it in a couple of hours. Laughter bubbled up behind me, and when I looked Brody and Lucy were approaching, his arm slung comfortably around her back.

'Oi, Benoit. Ice,' he said.

I reached for the scoop and a glass.

'No, no, we need the whole bucket,' Brody insisted. He was listing ever so slightly to the side, but I preferred him when he was drunk. Drunk, he became an uncoordinated mess, and he wouldn't be able to grab me.

'There's not much in the bucket.' I heaved the half-melted ice bucket up onto the counter. Lucy peered over it, her long brown hair brushing the edge of the metal.

'We need more,' she decided. 'Go get it.'

Please.

'I have to wait for Dana to come back.' I'd sent her to get another bottle of whiskey about five minutes ago.

'We need it now,' Brody snapped.

'I'm not allowed to leave the bar unattended.'

Brody scowled, swiping clumsily at my shoulder. Lucy said sharply, 'Excuse me, aren't I paying you?'

Technically, her daddy was paying me. 'That's true.'

'If I say go get ice, then go fucking get it.'

I pressed my lips together. 'I can't leave the bar unattended.'

'What do you think we're going to do?' Brody slurred. 'We're not barbarians.'

Actually, barbarians was a damned good description. 'If I leave the bar, I could lose my job.'

'If you don't leave the bar,' Lucy leant in, her blue eyes glittering dangerously, 'I will *make sure* you lose your job.'

Trapped. Fuck. The Godfreys owned the Kranikovska's building, and I didn't want to find out just how far their influence on Tom extended.

Gripping the ice bucket, I muttered through gritted teeth, 'I'll be right back.'

There was a small cupboard-like room behind the bar. I shoved the ice bucket into the dumbwaiter, then headed out from behind the bar and hurried to the door. The hall outside was empty. Where the fuck was Dana? I almost tripped on the stairs and swung into the main bar.

'Anna—where's Dana?'

Anna looked up from the shots she was pouring. 'Dana went home.'

'What the fuck?' I suppressed a groan. 'Why'd no one tell me?'

'She had to run. Family emergency with her mother. Harley, who's upstairs?'

I shook my head. 'Fucking rich kids wanted ice. Can you—'

'There's no one upstairs?'

'No, and I have to get back up there. The bucket is in the dumbwaiter.'

'Alright, I'll refill it.' Anna shooed me off. I sprinted back into the lobby and collided with a brick wall in human form.

'Oof!'

I staggered back. Bas caught my shoulder, steadying me. I'd run, as per my usual luck, into him and Ellery.

'Harley.' Ellery's tone was distinctly cool. Not something I could worry about right now. I dodged around them to the stairs. 'Where are you going?'

'Upstairs. I'm working a private event.'

'We need to talk.' Ellery hurried after me.

'We can't talk now. I'm working. You have to come back later.'

'Oh, is that how it is?' Ellery's voice was cold, so cold. I paused in front of the double doors to the upstairs bar and turned back to him.

'Ellery? What's going on?'

'Well, apparently you were so desperate to see me the other night and now, what, you've changed your mind?'

Fury rushed through me. 'Briggs did tell you!'

'Oh yeah.' Ellery stepped forwards, towering over me. 'He told me *everything.*'

Fuck. What did that mean? I wiped my suddenly sweaty palms on my jeans. 'Look, Ellery—I can't do this now—You have to come—'

'So, go on then. What was so urgent?'

'If you knew it was bloody urgent, why'd you take two days to come and see me?' Hot rage made my skin prickle. We glared at each other, Ellery unmoving. Behind him, Bas was frowning lightly.

Damnit, why did he have to do this? We needed to have a calm conversation about what was going on—but right now, I wanted to slap him.

'I'm done,' I snapped, turning away. 'I have work to do. If you're just here to be a prick, go be a prick to someone else.'

'Not as though it matters what I say to you, does it?'

I twisted back. 'What's that supposed to mean?'

'Well, if you're gonna act like a cheap whore...'

My palm itched with the desire to slap him. He deserved it, but I wasn't picking a fight with him. I'd lose. 'Go to hell. Where were you the other night then? Shagging some slut? Why are you allowed to sleep around, but I get judged for it?'

By Ellery's flinch, I knew I'd guessed right. 'Well, you certainly did a good fucking job of it, by the sounds of things.'

When I saw Briggs, I was going to wring his fucking neck. 'Excuse me for being desperate. Not like I'd just been chased through the fucking streets by an arsehole with a gun or anything.'

Ellery reeled back. 'What?'

'Not that you seem to care.'

'Why didn't you say so?'

'Because I spent twenty bloody minutes trying to get into that stupid compound to talk to you!' I sucked in a breath, trying to calm myself down, to no avail. 'It's all very well offering your help, but if I can't bloody reach you—'

'You could have dropped a note—I checked yesterday.'

'The drop is compromised. Everything is compromised.' I clenched my fists. 'I saw Hardwick and Tam having a secret meeting right there, talking shop—you have a traitor, and he saw me.'

Ellery frowned. 'Tam's been investigating Hardwick on our instructions.'

'That's not what it sounded like to me!'

'That's what it is, though.'

'Then explain why he chased me through the streets!'

Bas and Ellery exchanged looks. 'I think you're confused, Harley,' Ellery said slowly.

'I'm not confused!' All the fear and panic came rushing back. Truth be told, it had never left. I'd just suppressed it under a blanket of normalcy. Now, it exploded out, taking me over, until I felt like I was vibrating with it. I hadn't imagined what I'd seen and heard. I'd certainly never considered that Ellery might not believe me.

'You're not taking me seriously,' I snapped.

'It's not that,' Ellery said in far too calm a voice. 'There's just more going on than what you realise, and—'

'You were scared,' Bas said, his tone a warning.

I was used to my fear being used as a weapon against me, but not like this. Not to invalidate what I'd gone through.

'Fuck you,' I hissed. 'If you're not going to listen to me then maybe I should take my information to someone else.'

Ellery snorted. 'Sure, I bet Briggs would love to have it—and you apparently like him better than me. Shall I set it up for you?'

Ouch.

An almighty crash sounded from behind me, and all of us jumped. I'd completely forgotten where I was meant to be.

'I have to go. We're done here.'

'Harley, don't—'

I threw the doors open.

'MANAGER!' Brody howled, his face a smug, pale omen of doom. 'MANAGER!'

I took the wreckage in with horrified eyes. Louis held the hose of one of the beer taps and was dispensing beer directly into Diego's mouth. Lucy and her posse were digging through the fridge behind the bar. The crash appeared to have resulted from a group of men wrestling and knocking one of the tables over. I felt sick. Marching over to Brody, I snatched his collar.

'What the fuck did you do!' I hissed.

'MANAGER! SHE'S ASSAULTING ME!'

I balled up my fists, but someone grabbed me, towing me backwards.

'Lemme go!'

'He's not worth it, Harley. He's just a stupid child,' Bas said calmly. 'Don't lose your job over him.'

'That *child* is older than me.' Tears stung my eyes. I'd probably already lost my job. I had never hated my life more than I did in that moment. 'Let me go!'

Bas's grip loosened. He was almost hugging me, his hands loosely around my wrists, his arms draped over my shoulders, but for the first time, I didn't feel like pulling away. Bas had a certain calm confidence that made me feel as though I could lean on him and he'd just… make my problems go away.

If only.

I was so fucking stupid.

'MANAGER!' Brody howled again. Tom barrelled through the door.

'What's going on here?'

He took in the scene and looked straight at me. I stepped away from Bas, who dropped his hands from my shoulder. For some reason, I missed his warmth immediately.

'I went downstairs to look for Dana—' I could barely get the words out. My throat felt tight.

'It's our fault,' Bas said. 'We distracted her.'

Tom's eyes narrowed. 'I'll be right back. Tidy this up.'

He marched out of the room. Feeling sick, I stepped away from Bas. I pointed at Brody and hissed, 'If you even think about lying, you little worm—'

Brody smirked. 'It's not my fault you can't do your job, *kitten*.'

I ground my fingernails into my palms and stalked past him to the bar. 'OUT,' I snarled. Lucy jumped a mile, her friends giggling wildly.

'Yeah, I mean you.'

'We're not doing anything. Just helping ourselves. I paid for it.' Lucy picked up an ice cube and flicked it at me, sending her gaggle of idiots into peals of laughter. The ice cube bounced off my arm. I scowled.

'No, you did not. Get out of here.'

'C'mon, Lou.' Diego chose that moment to grow a conscience. 'Let's leave the whore to clean up her mess.' Or not.

'I paid for this,' Lucy insisted.

'We can go back to mine and open a bottle of *real* whiskey.' Diego smirked at her. 'C'mon, the whore's hardly worth it.'

Lucy giggled. 'Oh, fine then.'

I watched stonily as the immature idiots filed out of the bar. As Diego passed me, I pointed to the table. 'Pick it up, Diego.'

'I didn't do it.'

'Do I look like I care?'

Diego snorted and sauntered off. So much for that. I snatched a dustpan and brush and started sweeping up broken glass. My shoulders were so tense they might have been made of steel, and I was biting my tongue so hard I tasted blood. I wouldn't cry—I couldn't cry—

'Harley.'

I jumped. Ellery had followed me to the bar.

Standing up, I dumped a panful of glass in the bin. 'Fuck off, Ellery.'

'No, listen—'

'No, you listen.' I glared right into his eyes. 'You just talk. You never listen. I am not your pet. I am not some toy you can fool around with and then put on a shelf. You have no right to get upset when someone else pays attention to me. I needed you the other night, and you weren't there. You are *never* there when I need you, only when it's convenient to you.'

'Harley, I—'

'We're done, Ellery. I'm my own person. I look after myself. I can take care of my own problems. You want some woman who'll look pretty and only talk when you want her to?' I gestured to the square. 'Go buy one.'

Ellery opened his mouth, but no words emerged. I turned my back on him, getting back to sweeping up glass.

When I looked again, he was gone.

Tom reappeared a moment later, Anna in tow. She looked at everything with wide eyes as she slipped behind the bar. Tom beckoned me ominously.

'I told him you didn't know Dana was gone,' Anna hissed.

'Thanks.'

'I won't let him fire you.'

'It's okay, Anna. Thanks.' I patted her arm and headed for the door, my heart sinking lower with every step. When I reached Tom, he was shaking Brody's hand, assuring him that reparations would be taken care of. He turned to me, his expression cold.

'Outside.'

'Yes, sir,' I mumbled.

Tom followed me out, shutting the door firmly behind him. Then he sighed. 'I like you, Harley. I really do. But you cannot leave the bar unattended.'

'They wanted ice, and Dana hadn't come back.'

'But according to Brody Cavanaugh, you were gone more than five minutes.'

I couldn't tell him that Bas and Ellery had waylaid me. 'That was my mistake.'

'It was.' Tom shook his head. 'Usually you handle things better than this.'

I hunched my shoulders. 'I'm sorry, really.'

He sighed again, raking his fingers through his thinning hair. 'Brody is asking that I fire you. But you're one of my best. I can't let you go. So... I'm going to have to take the cost of the lost goods out of your salary. I'm sorry.'

He was sorry? I wanted to laugh hysterically. Fuck Brody. This was his fucking fault—I hadn't missed that he'd been drunk when I left the room and sober when I came back. Little shit had set that up. I shook my head sharply.

'Of course, I understand.'

'I'm glad.' Tom patted my shoulder. 'You can head downstairs and finish your shift there.'

'Thank you, sir.'

'I'll let you know how much you owe.'

Whatever it was, I already knew I couldn't afford it. 'Yes, sir.'

I pulled away and stumbled downstairs, my boots feeling like they were weighed down with lead. This on top of everything. Brody was such a shit. I clenched my fists. *Ooh, I could break his nose for this. Fucking little poncy prince.*

I seethed for the entire rest of my shift. My temper was so bad that even Kayla didn't want to talk to me, and she usually had the thickest skin of all of us. When I finally got off, I went straight home, not even bothering with the detour I'd been taking the last few nights in case I was followed.

I didn't care—I was itching for a fight.

The light was still on when I got home. Savannah was sitting on the sofa, her face grim. My heart, already residing somewhere around my boots, sank even further.

'Hey.'

'Harley.' Savannah scuffed her toes against the floor. 'How was work?'

'Crap on toast with added crap sauce. Why?'

'We ran out of coffee.'

'Uh-huh.'

'Look, if you don't have time to do the groceries before work, then just tell me. I'll work something out.'

I gritted my teeth, feeling suddenly, irrationally upset.

'I did do the groceries. Coffee is expensive, Sav.'

'So? We've never had a problem affording it before. I invited James over, and we didn't have any—'

My throat ached. I had to work to get the words out. 'Well, we have a problem now. Irina put our rent up.'

Savannah's mouth dropped open. 'When?'

'As of this week.'

'I... But... Why didn't you tell me?' she demanded.

I groaned, wishing I hadn't brought it up. Did we really have to do this *right* now? All I wanted was to shower and go to bed.

'When has there been the time? I barely see you, Sav.'

Savannah crossed her arms. 'You mean you didn't want me to know.'

I gestured in what might have been agreement. What was I supposed to say? 'You have enough on your plate.'

Savannah stared at me, her expression unreadable. She looked me slowly up and down, taking in the stains on my jeans, my sweat-soaked top, my frizzy hair. It had been a bad day. I was tired. I wanted to sink into bed and sleep for a year.

'Are we short on rent this week?' she asked.

I could have laughed. We were short on rent every week. This week was a fucking disaster. I nodded. 'Yes.'

'Alright.' Savannah stood, smoothing her hands down her legs. 'I'm going to fix this, Har. Don't worry.'

'You? Wait, what? You can't—'

Savannah shook her head. 'Go to bed, Harley.'

She crossed to the door, shoving her feet into her boots. 'I'll be back in a bit. Don't worry.'

I took a jerky step towards her, but it was too late. She cast one last angry look at me and slipped out the door, shutting it firmly behind her. I heard the lock thunk from outside. Savannah was gone.

I slumped back on the sofa and buried my face in my hands with a groan.

Happy fucking birthday to me.

SEVENTEEN

I CONSIDERED MY OPTIONS MULTIPLE TIMES during work the next day.

With the exception of Brenda, I was currently the only person in town who knew what Moriarty was up to. I burnt with the need to tell someone, and I didn't know who. I couldn't burden any of the other women at the bar, and Tom wouldn't care about it unless it affected his business. If I told Savannah, she'd go rushing into action trying to help and probably get herself caught.

That left two alternatives:

Ellery and Bas—but that would mean talking to them, which I had no interest in doing after what Ellery had said to me.

Or Maddock.

I had considered that option multiple times since finding out about the slaves, but each time something had stayed my tongue. Maddock seemed to have a good awareness of what was going on in the world and a finely developed sense of justice. He fought for things grander than his own survival, which was more than I could say for myself.

Still, I didn't trust him. I knew too little about him to be sure.

That left me with the dangerous and terrifying third option: come up with a plan to handle it myself.

But how? I'd never had to deal with anything near this magnitude before. I didn't even know where to start.

That, of course, brought me back to options one and two.

Tell someone.

There was always Bas, but he hadn't believed me yesterday either. What was to say today would be any different? Besides, I had a feeling that we wouldn't be on speaking terms for much longer, if we even still *were*.

I reached my building without making up my mind. Maddock's light was on, his shape silhouetted against the window. What did he even do in there all the time?

Had he meant it about helping our town?

Could it hurt?

Following my gut instinct hadn't helped me one bit so far—so I decided to do the opposite. I headed upstairs to my flat, slipped my boots off so I could walk silently, and grabbed a sheet of paper, scribbling three words across it.

NORTH CRATER CHARITY

Then I crept back downstairs and crouched down in front of his door. There was a narrow gap between the door and the floor, and with a bit of effort, I managed to wiggle the paper into it. I stood and took a deep breath. I could feel my pulse racing in my throat, and my palms had started to sweat. Was this a mistake?

This was a mistake.

I looked down, but the paper was fully under the door. I couldn't get it back now.

I was committed.

Fuck it.

I knocked three times firmly on the door, then turned and fled silently up the stairs. One floor up, I heard Maddock opening his door. I stood as still as a statue, listening for any hint as to what he was doing, but there was only silence.

The door shut again.

My whole body seemed to come alive, as though every part of it was rebelling all at once. My heart pounded like a jackhammer, my stomach was twisted into knots, and my lungs ached from holding my breath. I gasped pitifully and sagged against the wall.

It was done—I'd told someone.

But would it be enough?

Would he understand?

Hopefully, he'd at least investigate if he really did want to do good in our town.

My hands shook as I climbed the stairs, let myself into my flat, and prepared for bed.

I wiped my hands down on my legs, trying to rid myself of the clammy feeling. Unfortunately, there was no way to wipe away guilt.

Why did I feel guilty?

I didn't owe Bas anything.

I just couldn't shake the feeling that I was selling my soul to the Devil.

The Devil's car pulled up. The passenger door slid open, and I climbed in, shutting it again so that I was hidden behind the blacked-out windows.

'Interesting spot for a pick-up,' Rodney Rochester commented in his usual mild tone.

'Better to be seen picking up a whore than an informant, Rochester.' I leant forwards, switching on the radio. Static buzzed out of the speakers. After a bit of tuning, I found Theo's favourite station, Crater FM, which played mostly loud, screamy Pre-Crash tunes. Not the sort of music I imagined Rochester choosing, though he weathered it with an unamused smile.

'I don't typically pick up whores, as a matter of fact.'

'Well, tough,' I said, glancing out the window as the Hustle Highway slid by. That wasn't the road's actual name, but it was an almost ubiquitous nickname for the main road that ran from the square due east to the casino strip. This was where most of the streetwalkers worked.

I had dressed accordingly, in a small top and skirt, and no less than three Johns had eyed me up before Rochester had arrived.

I shrugged my coat off and put it over my legs. Rochester turned the heating up. *What a gentleman*, I thought bitterly.

'What changed your mind?' he asked.

'That's absolutely none of your business.'

Rochester chuckled. 'Just trying to make conversation. Would you prefer we get right down to it?'

'Yes, actually.' The quicker we got this over with, the quicker I could go home to nurse my wounds.

'Fine, what have you got for me?'

My stomach seemed to have snarled itself up into knots, and I had to work to get the words out. 'Cash up front.'

Rochester was silent for a moment, tapping his fingers against the steering wheel. Had I misjudged? He'd seemed so desperate before. Would he back out now? Had I missed my chance to push for a good deal?

'Half and half,' he said finally.

I swallowed a sigh of relief. 'Okay.' I nodded to an alleyway. 'Park there.'

'Why?'

'Because it'll look like we're parking there to have sex.'

Rochester's expression told me exactly what he thought of that notion.

'What, is Rodney Rochester too good for common whores?' I rolled my eyes.

'I don't pay for sex.'

'Well, that's one thing you and your brother have in common.'

He absorbed that tidbit hungrily, his hands clenching on the steering wheel, before releasing so he could put the handbrake on. 'Did he tell you that?'

'Cash first.'

Rochester pressed his lips together. He didn't like the transactional nature of our arrangement, but I refused to let him forget it. This was business only. I wasn't getting dragged into his relationship with his brother.

'Here.' He took an envelope from the centre console, flipped through the contents, and pulled out a crisp two-hundred note. 'Will that suffice?'

'Depends on what you want to know.' I leant back, stretching my legs out so that the coat fell to the side a little. Rochester's gaze was drawn to my legs; he blinked and looked away again.

'You're not quite as principled as your brother. He never looks.'

'He looked plenty when you were flirting with his friends in the bar.'

'Did he?' I raised an eyebrow, tucking the cash into my bra. Rochester followed that movement as well.

'Why didn't you flirt with him? I thought you liked my brother.'

'He doesn't like it when I touch him, and I don't force myself on people.'

'Or you thought it would annoy him more if you flirted with everyone but him.'

Rochester was more perceptive than he let on. I shrugged.

'Everything I do annoys Bas. What's the point in trying to avoid it?'

'Annoys him how?'

The more he relaxed, the more Rochester gave himself away. Despite his high-handed declarations, he was attracted to me. His eyes would drift, then he'd catch himself again. And he was desperate for the slightest bit of information about Bas—things that he could have found out just by approaching the man himself.

So why hadn't he?

I filed that question away to ponder later.

'Annoys him as in he doesn't like it? I don't know. He thinks I'm stupid.' I said the words without inflection, but they sent a pang of hurt through me. It didn't feel fair that Bas hated me so much.

Well, I suppose I'm earning his hate right now.

Guilt crawled up my throat again, robbing me of words.

'What does he say?'

'To me?' My tone was sharper than I intended. 'That I'm pathetic, that I'm a whore. Is that what you want to know?'

Rochester cleared his throat. 'Sorry, I meant what do you talk about?'

'Uhhh.' That was a trickier question. What did we talk about? 'We mostly just argue.'

'Argue? What about?'

'Everything?'

He frowned. 'You're not really trying here.'

'I don't know what you want me to say! I really don't know that much about it him,' I protested.

'If you want the rest of the money, you're going to have to do better than that,' Rochester said levelly, adjusting the cuffs of his jacket.

'You're the one who asked to meet.' I crossed my arms. 'Why would you think I know things, anyway? Just because I recognised you one day in the bar?'

'I saw you with him,' Rochester insisted. 'If you knew you didn't have enough information, why did you agree to the meeting? Or was your plan to scam me of money?' His eyes narrowed. 'I'm no fool, Harley Benoit.'

Money made fools of all of us, whether we had it in abundance or whether we had none at all.

Especially me.

'He goes running every morning,' I blurted before I could think the better of it. 'To the training ground at The Arsonist. If you want to see him, go there, early in the morning. Just don't expect him to be happy you're there.'

'You see?' he said mockingly. 'You do know things.'

My temper spiked. 'That's it. Hand over the money, or the deal's off.'

Rochester laughed. 'You are cheeky.'

He tossed the envelope into my lap. 'Off you go, then.'

I had served my purpose, and now I was dismissed. Furious, I threw the door open.

'I'll be in contact,' Rochester promised. 'And next time I expect better results.'

I ground my teeth together. 'You'll get what you get. I'm not prying into Bas's private life.'

'Then you'll get paid for what I get.'

I slammed the door and stalked off. What an arsehole.

My heart thumped erratically in my chest as I hurried down the street. I hated what I'd just done, but the simple truth was I'd had no choice. If it was me or Bas, I had to pick myself. I didn't know what Savannah thought she could do to get the money—she'd been gone for half an hour on Friday night and come back to simply say that it was sorted—but whatever she had planned, I couldn't let her do it. Not Savannah. It had to be me.

So I'd gone straight to Rodney's henchman last night at the bar and passed him a note.

Tonight, 2 am, Hustler Highway.

It meant sacrificing sleep, but the sooner I got it done, the better.

That didn't mean it felt good. In many ways, Bas was innocent in this whole thing. And I felt like a total bitch. He'd made a choice to stay away from his brother, and I had no right to undermine that.

I closed my eyes and took a deep breath.

'You sellin', girl?'

I twisted to the side. A bloke was lounging on a doorstep about three yards into an alleyway, the side door of a bar. When he caught my eye, he jerked his hips suggestively.

'No,' I snapped.

'Aw, can't a guy get a good time around here?'

I hurried away.

The next morning, I left a note for Savannah—*Got the rent money for this week. Don't worry. Har x*—and went to The Arsonist's training ground. The rain seemed to have more or less abated, and I couldn't wait to dance. I was desperate to clear my head.

And if Bas pitched up…

I almost hoped he didn't.

I hopped the railing into the cage and stretched slowly, luxuriating in every movement of my body. Strong. Disciplined. I could be those things without people like Ellery. I didn't need him. Somehow, some way, I'd make my own way in life. Somehow.

Once I was warm, I set my coat aside and took up position, lifting my arms and humming the opening notes.

But the steps didn't come.

Instead, I danced a routine I knew like the back of my hand. My body went through the motions, but my mind was scattered. Clarity didn't arise. I felt like a puppet on a string.

At length, I slowed. This had been a mistake. I couldn't dance like this. It felt tainted.

I gripped the railing, letting the cold metal dig in, and stared down into a dirty puddle. A couple of tears trickled down my face.

'Fuck.'

Never mind this; I'd just leave. At least I hadn't run into Bas. That would just have made everything worse.

And then I heard footsteps.

He was here.

Damnit. It was too late to hide. I pulled my coat on, scrubbed my fingers over my face to get rid of the tears, and climbed out of the cage. Bas stopped in front of me, frowning.

'What are you doing here?'

'It's none of your business.' I tried to step around him, but he moved fluidly into my path.

'I thought you were done with us.'

'I was dancing, okay? It has nothing to do with you.'

'I told you to stop doing that.'

My temper reared its ugly head. 'You don't get to tell me what to do.'

'Someone needs to get it through your head that you're playing with fire when you come out here alone.'

'What I do with my life is my business.' I crossed my arms, trying to hide my unease. He was suddenly too close for comfort. 'Stop sticking your nose in it.'

'Stop putting it in my path.'

'Or what? You don't own this town.'

Bas stepped closer. 'And you think you do?'

'I think I care a lot more about the people in this town than you do.' I clenched my fists, fighting the urge to shove him away. 'You lot, up in your cosy compound, with all the comforts you could want. We're just sheep to you.' I stepped out of his way. 'Just stay away from me.'

'Tell me what you wanted to tell Ellery.'

'You didn't believe me the other day; why would you now?'

'It wasn't the way you think it was. Briggs only told us you'd been by on Saturday. Ellery came as soon as he knew.'

I stopped walking. 'I don't care.'

'Don't you?'

'No. I'm done with the Iron Firsts. You bring nothing but trouble.'

'You'd rather blame us than take responsibility for your bad decisions,' Bas mocked.

'Bad decisions?' I whirled back to face him. 'I was desperate to speak to him, and all I got was Briggs trying to take advantage.'

'That's not how it sounded to me.'

'Oh yeah, I'm sure Briggs spun a mighty tale. He always does.'

Bas's gaze narrowed. 'And how would you know that?'

All of a sudden, my heart was in my throat. 'I—That—that's none of your business.'

'You see? Your bad decisions, your problem.'

'You have no idea what you're talking about.' Tears pricked at my eyes. I swiped my fingers over them, but it was too late. A couple escaped anyway. 'You have no right to talk to me like that.'

Bas stared stonily down at me, like I was a cockroach, and he was considering how best to squash me. And suddenly I was so done with it.

'I came here to clear my mind so I could figure out what to do.' I laughed bitterly. 'But you don't care about ordinary people's problems, so I guess I'll just go.'

I spun on my heel, stalking down the access road.

'Wait!' he called.

I kept walking.

'Harley!'

Bas sprinted after me. I resisted the urge to run; he'd only catch me. I kept walking, my steps even, as he fell in beside me. 'What's going on?'

'What do you care?'

Bas ground his teeth together. 'Harley, this isn't a game.'

'This may come as a shock, but I'm not playing games. I'm trying to survive. Maybe you've forgotten what that feels like.' I glared up at him. 'Maybe it's so comfortable with the Iron Fists that you've forgotten what it's like when every day is a fight for survival.'

Bas's lips twisted. 'I haven't forgotten.'

'You just think my methods are stupid.' I turned up Busker Street. 'But they're the only ones I've got.'

'If you came here for a reason, why didn't you just say so?'

'I did tell you: I came here to dance. Has it ever occurred to you that for me dancing is the same as you going for a jog or, I don't know, climbing in the cage and beating someone up?'

'Shockingly, I don't regularly climb into the cage and beat people up just to clear my head.'

I glanced at him and snorted derisively. 'You all do that.'

'Not me.'

'Wow, you're so special.'

Bas rolled his eyes. 'You are such a brat, you know that?'

'Says the guy who judges me every time I go dancing. Maybe I'm just sick of you making the same nasty comment every time you see me.'

'Because you're being stupid.'

'But what do you *care*?' My voice came out loud and angry, cutting through the morning stillness.

Bas locked his jaw, marching next to me in silence. I glanced around, suddenly on edge. I felt bizarrely exposed, walking next to Bas on the street. His presence should have had the opposite effect; he was clearly much more capable of handling danger than I was. But alone, I felt like less of a target. Small animals could hide easier in long grass, and I was a very small animal compared to him.

A kitten, where he was a wolf.

Ellery's pet name for me suddenly took on a new and rather unflattering meaning. Was that why he called me that? I'd always liked it because it made me feel special. But suddenly it wasn't special. It was demeaning.

We were in full view of the entire street; anyone could see me walking with him, and Bas's gang mark was on display. Hardwick's words came back to me. Should I warn Bas that Hardwick knew he came here every morning? Was Hardwick a threat? Had Tam really been investigating him on Sayle's orders?

It was a distinct possibility: I couldn't shake the feeling that I'd misunderstood everything. But then why had Tam chased me, if not to keep me from revealing his meeting with Hardwick? Was Ellery right? Or was I just manufacturing doubts?

'Why didn't you ask for me the other night at the compound?' Bas asked quietly.

I glanced at him again. His expression, as usual, was a closed book. I got nothing from his ice-chip eyes, his sharp jaw. He was clean-shaven, his hair damp with sweat. I was struck by the difference between Bas and Rodney. Bas was a well-honed weapon, ready to spring into action at any moment. Rodney had no understanding of the world beyond his gated mansion, of the things that motivated ordinary people.

'Why would I?'

'You could have.' Bas shrugged. 'I was available.'

What difference would it have made? Briggs would still have asked for the same thing. But I couldn't tell him that; the words stuck on my tongue. 'I didn't know you were in the habit of doing favours.'

'Well, now you do.'

'Now, I'm not asking.' I stopped walking. There was an itch under my skin, making me restless. It was what had driven me to dance this morning, and it was still there, making me clench and unclench my fists. I felt an acute sense of powerlessness, the same I'd felt standing at the compound gate on Wednesday night: I was no one, I was an outsider. 'It's easy for you to just stand there and tell me what I should have done. You weren't the one at the gate, being called a whore and an attention-seeker.'

'Why didn't you tell them who you were?'

'I did!' I took a deep breath, trying to calm myself. 'I told the guy, but... no one listens to me. Men with big guns don't have to listen to women, do they?'

Bas's expression said he thought that was stupid, but what did he know? Despite the overlap in our experiences, he wasn't a woman, and he never would be. He'd never know what it felt like for men to dismiss you with a single glance. He had no idea how I had felt when Ellery had treated me like a hysterical kid.

I'd never, *never* forget Ellery's words. '*If you're gonna act like a cheap whore…*' I swallowed. Relying on Ellery had got me to where I was today. I had always thought this was an improvement.

But what if it wasn't?

What if things had got worse without me realising?

I'd got in trouble and run for Ellery. Briggs had taken advantage of that and used it to drive a wedge between me and Ellery. Well, fine. From now on, I'd solve my own problems.

'You know what? It doesn't matter. I won't make that mistake again.'

'Shutting us out isn't going to help you.'

I scowled. 'Letting you in didn't help me either, Sebastian.'

Anger flickered in Bas's gaze. 'Don't call me that.'

'Then don't tell me what to do.'

Our gazes clashed—stalemate. He stared down at me, as though he could glare me into submission, but suddenly, I didn't care. Not what he thought, not what Ellery thought. I'd come here trying to figure out what to do, and this was it. I was done with the Iron Fists. I'd take Rochester's money, and Savannah and I could find somewhere new to live. Somewhere not controlled by Irina and her affiliation with Sayle.

We could rise above our circumstances. I had to believe that.

Bas looked away. 'Look, if you're going to run around like a reckless idiot, at least let me teach you how to defend yourself. That's what you wanted before, right?'

The offer was like a punch to the gut—my resolve wavered, and I hated myself for it. Now he offered? *Now?* It felt like far too little, far too late.

Like he was just doing it to hurt me. The same as he'd accused me of.

'No thanks,' I said. 'I'm good.'

'You're good?' Bas asked incredulously.

'Sure. Theo's offered before. When he gets back to town, I'll get him to teach me.'

'That could be weeks or months from now.'

'Then it is. In the meantime, I can look after myself. I've been doing it for years. I can do it for a few more weeks.'

Bas stared at me, his brow creased with frustration. He opened his mouth to speak, but maybe he could read my decision on my face. I was done listening to him. I was done taking anything from the Iron Fists. He shut his mouth again.

'From now on, you're on your own with Rodney,' I said. 'I'm not interested in your family drama, either.'

'That's not a problem,' Bas said tersely, 'seeing as there is no drama.'

'Good for you.'

We'd reached my turnoff. I stepped into the alleyway, then turned back. 'I won't bother you on the training ground again. But you should know that I'm not the only person who knows you use it. So I hope you know who your enemies are.'

Bas's gaze was inscrutable. I walked away, feeling his eyes on my back until I turned the corner and was out of his sight.

Well, fuck.

But I felt better, lighter, for having said my piece. I was done with the gang, and that was right. That was the best thing for Savannah and me, and I knew it was what my parents would have wanted for us, too. They had never intended for me to get wrapped up with these sorts of dangerous men. They'd wanted better things for us.

Just too bad they had died before they'd managed to achieve that.

My mood was so much improved that day at work that even Tom poked his head in to remark on it.

'You seem to be doing better.'

'I guess. I—I've been doing favours for people to try and get up the money quicker.'

An expression of guilt flitted across his weathered face. He scratched the back of his head and sighed. 'You know if it could have gone any other way…'

'I know.'

It wasn't fair, but it was true. The Cavanaughs and the Godfreys were worth a lot of money to Tom, and I was just a waitress.

Tom patted my hand. 'It's just a blip. They'll have forgotten about it soon enough.'

Yeah, they'd move on to their next trick.

But even thinking about Brody Cavanaugh and the evil Godfrey siblings couldn't dampen my new resolve. I had laboured under the threat of the gangs in this town for too long. It was time to start planning my way to freedom.

I spent that week plotting and making subtle enquiries. Finding a place to live was a complicated endeavour; it wasn't enough to just go look at a place and decide you liked it. We didn't have the money to afford that luxury, and besides, there were safety considerations. We had to live in the town centre or the northwest. Definitely not in the southeast, which was the most dangerous. We also needed to be in an area that didn't regularly get rousted or see shootouts. And I didn't want to be on the ground floor or in the basement, because they were most prone to flooding and break-ins.

No small order.

On Wednesday, I took Brenda her mending before work. She looked surprised to see me when she opened the door.

'Is your hot water out again?'

'No, I brought you your stuff.' I passed her the canvas bag. She blinked in shock.

'Gracious. Please tell me you didn't stay up all night to finish this.'

'Not exactly.'

Brenda frowned, tugging me into the hall. The carpet squelched under my boots. 'Harley, it could have waited a week or two.'

'It's alright. I couldn't sleep the other night, so I did it then.'

It was a problem that cropped up on and off. It had nothing to do with how tired I was and everything to do with my mental state. Usually, I coped with it by dancing, but I'd cut myself off from the training ground now, and I hadn't thought of an alternative yet.

Brenda shook her head. 'Love…' She sighed. 'Come get a tea. You look cold.'

'If you don't mind.' I trailed her downstairs. The boys had evidently already left for school, but the dog was still there. It yipped at me and came over to sniff my boots.

'Still got the fluffball?'

Brenda groaned. 'They've named her Sally. Honestly, sometimes I don't know what to do with those boys.'

'At least she's cute.' I scratched the dog's neck.

'Cute and *hungry*.'

We exchanged the wry grimaces of people who understood what it was like to struggle to put food on the table. Brenda gestured me over to the sofa and chattered to me as she boiled water on the stove.

'We didn't get the car in the end; Manny's deal fell through. But I spoke to Rocky, and he might know someone else who's selling cheap. Looks like it's in slightly better nick.'

'That's good.'

'Mm-hmm. He's also looking for someone to manage his accounts for him. What do you reckon? I could be an accountant.'

'You could.' I sat forwards. 'Would you quit Krani's?'

'Maybe. I don't think Tom would miss me—I'm not as pretty as you kids.'

'Rubbish. You're gorgeous and you keep the drunks in line.'

Brenda offered me a lopsided smile. 'They can't perv on me, though.'

'I'll bet they do anyway. I've seen you in a skirt.' We grinned at each other. Brenda came over, passed me a mug, and settled beside me. 'Speaking of jobs, Kayla mentioned that the Lucky was looking for people. You could ask her about that.'

'I'd need a car to get out there. I'll blow half my wage on taxi-trucks every day.' Brenda frowned. 'The casino… That's gang territory, isn't it?'

'I think so.'

'I couldn't risk it. Not with the boys.'

'Yeah.' I blew on my tea, making my hair flutter and tickle my cheeks.

'You seem different.'

I glanced up, frowning. 'Different how?'

'Happier? More tired, for sure.'

I laughed. 'I always need more sleep than I get this time of year. But I am happy, I guess. I'm looking for a new flat.'

'You are?' Brenda raised an eyebrow. 'Your place is so safe.'

'You know why, though.'

Brenda sighed heavily. 'You want to cut yourself loose? I admire your bravery.'

She was right; even if I was done with the Iron Fists, living in a building that was protected by them was worth its weight in gold.

'Irina's trying to push us out anyway. She hiked our rent.' I sipped the tea, grimacing at the bitterness. 'I'm just trying to stay ahead of the next catastrophe.'

'If you ever need a sofa to sleep on, you know… I know Manny isn't the best of flatmates, but you can come here any time.'

'I couldn't intrude like that.'

'Harley…'

'No, Brenda.' I shook my head. 'It's really kind of you to offer, but we're not desperate yet. And we won't be if I find something before Irina puts us on the street.'

'Okay.' Brenda squeezed my knee. 'But you let me know.'

'I will.' *Not.*

Brenda gulped her tea, before glancing at me slyly. 'What about your man? Where's he at, then?'

At her words, my treacherous brain immediately jumped to Bas and Ellery. I'd been avoiding thinking about them all week, but that was like trying to avoid looking at the wart on Clem's nose: the harder you tried, the more it sucked you in.

'Ugh.'

Brenda laughed. 'Good ugh or bad ugh?'

'Bad! Did you hear about Cavanaugh and the Godfreys?'

'I heard they smashed up the upstairs bar when you were on duty.' Brenda raised an eyebrow. 'That's not like you, love. You're always on their tails.'

'I got distracted.' I scrunched my nose up.

'Distracted by a certain one of Sayle's enforcers?' Her forehead crinkled. 'Harley, love…'

'I can't help it! They make me so angry.' I shook my head. Brenda laughed.

'Gosh, for a minute I thought you meant you were sexing them up.' She covered her mouth with one hand. 'Should have known better.'

'I'd never do that.'

'You're such an innocent thing. I don't know where we found you.' Brenda grinned. 'You flirt like a pro, but you can't fool me.'

'Shut up!' My cheeks were burning. I rubbed them one-handed. 'I don't want to talk about men. Men are stupid.'

'Oh, there's no doubt about that.'

We both giggled.

Finally, I straightened up. 'I thought about what you said. About feelings. And I'm done with Sayle's boys. I'm tired of them yanking me around like a puppet.'

Brenda blinked owlishly at me. 'What do they think about that?'

'It doesn't matter, does it? It's my choice.'

'Mm-hmm. They're not best known for letting people go.'

'They'll have to get used to it,' I said firmly.

'I suppose…' Her sceptical tone was a bit insulting, honestly.

'You don't think I can do it?'

'No… I don't doubt you.' Brenda looked grave. 'But Marco Ellery doesn't seem the type to just let you slip away.'

'Well, you're wrong about that. He pretty much already told me he wants nothing to do with me.'

Brenda raised an eyebrow. 'I see.'

On the way out, I managed to convince her to let me nip upstairs. 'They won't see me, I promise.'

'Just be careful. I know you mean well, but the next thing you know, they snatch you.'

'I know. I will be.' Especially now. Before last week I'd have said Ellery would move heaven and earth to get me away from Moriarty if I got caught by his gang. Now… I wasn't too sure.

I slipped up to the second floor and peered out the window, keeping to the side so I was mostly hidden. In the day, it was harder to see across. The light cast reflections on the windows. Still, after a bit of squinting, I could make out what was going on in the charity office.

The slave pen was empty.

So, they had moved the slaves out… and not collected more. Yet. Would they? I couldn't believe they had snatched those people opportunistically, not when the office was set up to hold them. It seemed too well planned.

But how were they managing to move slaves through the town? The mayor had always strictly legislated against slavery, and law enforcement—what little of it we had—would not have stood for it. Nor did I think the other gangs would; they'd have leapt on the excuse to push Moriarty out of town. No, this smacked of a coverup. Somehow, they were getting away with this in plain sight, and no one seemed to have realised.

That meant it was probably a fairly new operation—not enough people had disappeared yet to arouse suspicion. It also meant there was probably someone, or several someones, helping cover it up.

Did Moriarty have spies in the other gangs?

Hardwick was a possibility. After all, I didn't know for sure who he truly worked for. Whoever it was, it definitely wasn't the mayor—even if he was ostensibly on the mayor's payroll. Probably, he was high up in one of the gangs.

Was he powerful enough to hide this from the mayor?

Or was someone else involved? Someone powerful?

A sudden, terrifying thought occurred to me. When the mayor had met with Cavanaugh and Godfrey, he'd mentioned securing Moriarty's support. What if he'd agreed to turn a blind eye in exchange for Moriarty's help?

He wouldn't do that, would he?

An odd sense of fear crept up on me. I'd never felt anything quite like it before. This wasn't the immediate fear of danger, nor the fear of becoming homeless that I lived with every day. This was something deeper, something primal and existential.

Things were changing.

The stable, organised world I'd built for myself in the last two years was collapsing.

And I didn't know what to do about it.

EIGHTEEN

ON SATURDAY, I RETURNED TO Hustler Highway. I leant up against the boarded-up front of an electronics shop, waiting for Rodney Rochester.

A car crawled to a halt in front of me. I kept my head down, avoiding eye contact. A moment later, it moved on.

I hated this.

Two men hovered by the entrance to an alleyway, smoking, both dressed in skin-tight jeans and clingy tops. Across the road, a woman in white thigh-high boots eyed me as though I was infringing on her territory. I tapped my fingers agitatedly against the plyboard behind me.

Come on, come on.

Finally, Rochester's shiny car came into view. He slowed in front of me. I hurried over and scrambled into the passenger seat, slamming the door.

'Miss Benoit.'

'Mr Rochester.' It was a relief to be behind the dark glass, where no one could see me.

Rochester manoeuvred the car off Hustler Highway, and down a side street, where he parked up. Then he dropped an envelope in my lap.

'This time I'll ask questions.'

I sat back, cradling the envelope. My stomach churned with an acidic combination of relief and self-disgust. The money would help Savannah and me. The price was so small.

I still hated myself for paying it.

Pushing away thoughts of what Bas would do if he found out, I focused on Rochester. 'What do you want to know?'

'Who does he spend time with?'

I swallowed. 'The enforcers are in teams. I can tell you who's on his team.'

Rochester nodded.

'Marco Ellery, Duncan Briggs, and Andrew Kade.'

'Ellery?' Rochester seemed surprised. I frowned.

'You know him?'

He shook his head too quickly. A lie. 'I thought the Ellerys were farmers.'

I had to shrug. Ellery had been one of Sayle's men since I had started dancing in the bunker, more or less. He was twenty-eight now, which meant he'd have been at least twenty-one when he joined, assuming he'd joined around the same time I had started dancing for Sayle. Most people started working younger than that.

'He could have been, but he definitely isn't now.'

'You don't know?' Rochester's green eyes glittered in the light of a passing car.

'I don't really have deep conversations with them, you know? Generally, we don't touch private stuff.'

'Yet you know Sebastian was a slave.' Rochester's expression was unreadable.

I grimaced. 'I recognised the mark on his arm.'

'Ah.' Rochester's gaze dropped to his lap, where his hands were twisted together. He seemed… regretful? I wasn't precisely sure. He was almost as hard to read as his brother, sometimes.

'How'd he end up a slave, but you didn't?' I asked.

He looked up sharply. 'That's none of your business.'

'I answer all your questions.'

'I'm paying you,' Rochester said coolly. 'I'm not here to give you private information concerning my family.'

'Wow, touchy.'

That earned me a glare. 'For someone who claims she doesn't have private conversations, you certainly do take a lot of liberties.'

I shrugged. 'For someone who's violating his brother's boundaries, you sure are protective of your own.'

Rochester glowered. 'How do you know he goes running every morning?'

Back on track, then.

'My flat overlooks the training ground. I've seen him there.'

'I doubt that. The way you spoke last time, it sounded as though you've met him there.'

Damnit. Rochester was more observant than I'd expected.

'I have, once or twice.' I shifted in my seat.

'What were you doing there?'

'Training.'

He looked me up and down disdainfully. 'You don't fight.'

'Uh, now who's taking liberties?' I gave him a pointed look. 'We're here to discuss Bas, not me.'

'Women don't fight in the cage,' he said decisively.

'Okay, one, that's not true,' I said haughtily. 'There are a few women who fight, and they do very well at it, I might add. Two, who the fuck do you think you are? There are more reasons why a person might train than because they enjoy gratuitous violence.'

'Big word for a waitress.' His lips curled in a sneer.

The look I gave him could have sliced through glass. 'I'll leave.'

'You won't get the rest of the cash.'

Rochester was getting too bold. I reached for the door handle. 'You won't get the rest of the information. What do you suppose would happen if I told Bas that we'd had this little chat?'

Fear flickered in his gaze. 'You wouldn't do that. He'd be furious with you.'

'You think I care about that? You know me terribly well for someone who only met me a couple of weeks back.'

Now he definitely looked afraid. 'If you tell him, you'll ruin everything I've been working towards.'

'That is really not my problem.' I leant my shoulder against the door and watched him smugly. 'No personal questions, no accusations or insinuations, and definitely no threats not to pay me. Don't think I won't tell Bas, because I absolutely would.'

'You'd pass up the money just to harm me?' Rochester asked incredulously.

The trouble with rich people was they really didn't understand desperation. I would drag him down with me if I had to, and I'd do it gladly. I let him read that in my face, and I knew he got the message.

'I agree to your terms,' he said reluctantly. 'When did you first meet him?'

'The end of summer.'

He nodded solemnly.

'Have you seen where he lives?'

'Uh, no! Who do you take me for?'

The slow look Rochester gave me said it all.

'I don't go into their compound,' I said tersely.

'Never?'

I'd been in to visit Theo's flat, but I just shrugged. Rochester decided to move on.

'Have you asked him about me?'

'Yes.'

'And?' He leant forwards. 'What did he say?'

"I don't have a brother."

Disappointment played over Rochester's face. 'That's it?'

'What were you expecting?'

Rochester cast his gaze down to his hands again. He looked absolutely crushed. 'Nothing, of course.'

'He didn't deny it after the first time.' Why was I telling him that? Maybe because he looked so bloody miserable. I was going soft, wasn't I?

'Really?' Rochester looked up hopefully.

'He didn't confirm it, but he didn't deny it. He told me to stay away from your family.'

Rochester's eyes roved over me, though this time it wasn't sexual. My skin crawled anyway. 'He's not wrong. Father would like you.'

Charming. If there was one thing I didn't need in my life, it was being liked by Rochester senior. I still remembered the dismissive way he'd spoken to me. I shuddered.

'Then I'll trust that you're going to keep these meetings very quiet,' I said flatly.

'You have my word.'

Ugh, so noble. I rolled my eyes. 'Anything else? I kind of want to sleep sometime tonight.'

'I thought you regularly kept late hours.'

I shot him a look.

'No private questions,' he said. 'Fine. You call my brother Bas?'

'That's what he asked to be called.'

Rodney frowned in confusion. His expression turned distant, as though he was seeing something beyond the fancy trimmings of his luxury car.

'Why?' I added.

I didn't really expect him to answer, so I was surprised when he said quietly, 'That's what they called him.'

They?

As though realising what he'd just said, Rochester straightened up. 'That's it for tonight. I'll pick you up at the same time and the same place next week?'

'Three blocks down,' I said, reaching for the door. 'Never the same place.'

Rochester nodded sharply. I climbed out of the car and started for home, thoughts swirling around my brain.

'That's what they called him.'

Who were *they*?

Moriarty's men?

Why? I didn't understand Bas at all.

By Sunday, it was raining again, a light but persistent drizzle that somehow managed to wet everything. The bar still thrummed with activity: we had a group of rangers in who'd come back from the wastelands to the north, and Clem and his friends were playing bridge, arguing good-naturedly back and forth. Below the murmur from the bar and the croon of the music, I could hear a steady drip-drip-drip from the back hall. Even the Kranikovska's roof was finally giving in to the never-ending rain.

I stepped behind the bar again, carrying a tray full of empty glasses.

'Can you run it straight in back?' Anna asked. 'We seem to have a shortage of glasses tonight.'

'I'll check with them.' I pushed my way through the back door and into the kitchen. There were three people back there: the chef, the dishwasher, and Bella, who cleaned the rooms upstairs. As soon as she saw me, she straightened up, feigning disinterest.

'Wasn't doing nothin'.'

I smiled. Bella thought none of us had realised she was sleeping with the dishwasher. I set my tray in front of the two of them. 'I won't tell. Lynn, Anna says we need more glasses.'

'I'll have a load out to you in two ticks,' Lynn replied.

'Thanks.'

I waved to them and ducked back out—and froze.

Ellery and his team of enforcers had just entered the bar.

Briggs was with them.

Oh God, I was going to puke.

I stepped back towards the kitchen door, and then Ellery's gaze found mine, his expression so cold I felt like my blood had frozen in my veins. Every breath seemed to scratch my throat like rusty nails, and my head swam.

What were they doing here?

No.

It didn't matter.

I took a deep breath and grabbed my tray. They were here for business. I was at work. And I was resolved to stay away from them. I could be professional.

Keeping my head held high, I marched over to them. 'Good evening, gentlemen. What can I get you?'

'*Kitten,*' Briggs drawled smugly. I raised an eyebrow and tapped my foot impatiently.

'It's Harley, if you don't mind.'

I was so sick of that nickname being used against me like a weapon. If they wouldn't listen to me when I told them not to use it… I'd find a way to make them.

I surveyed them evenly before settling my gaze on Kade, the safest person to look at. 'Drinks?' I prompted.

'Four whiskeys.' Bas held out the money. For a second, my eyes met his. My stomach swooped, familiar guilt making my chest ache.

I looked away, tucking the money into my apron. 'I'll be right back.'

My heart raced as I walked back to the bar, but it wasn't fear—it was excitement. I had survived. I had looked them in the eye as an independent woman, and not let them put me down. It was a tiny victory, but a victory nonetheless. The first step to surviving without Ellery in my life.

'Is that your sister?'

Anna's question stopped me in my tracks. I spun around and stared.

Savannah was standing in the doorway.

Oh my God.

I watched in silent horror as my sister turned back to speak to someone, laughing, before she entered the room. A man followed her in. I'd seen him around the bar before, though I had never spoken to him. He had red hair, pale, freckly skin, and a gangly build like a jumper that had got stretched in the wash.

'What is she doing here?' Anna hissed. 'And who's she with?'

'No freaking clue.' Savannah never came to the bar. I wasn't even sure when was the last time she'd been out with friends. I ducked my head, seriously considering hiding in the back room for the next hour, but the two of them had already sat down. I shook myself and started towards their table. What was Savannah doing here? Why here? Who was the redhead?

I'd seen him before; I was sure of it. But who was he affiliated with?

I swept my gaze over them, searching for clues. The redhead wore sturdy combat boots, cargo pants, and a fitted jacket. Savannah had borrowed my jeans and top, and every time I looked at her I did a little double-take. My sister usually wore practical clothes, not skin-tight jeans and crop tops.

I reached them and took a deep breath.

'Sav,' I blurted out, 'what are you doing here?'

Okay, that had come out wrong. But it was too late to take it back. Savannah's gaze cut towards me, her chin lifted defiantly. 'What, are you the only person allowed to go out on their day off?'

'Did you have to come *here*?'

'Where else would I go? This is a bar. I want a drink.'

Savannah almost never drank.

'I work here.'

'So? Does that mean I'm banned from the premises?'

My mouth dropped open. The redhead snorted, and I turned on him. 'Who are you?'

'Why?' His lips twisted into a mocking smile. 'Afraid I won't be good enough for your precious sister?'

'Greg.' Savannah put a warning hand on his shoulder. 'Harley, this is Greg Talbot. You remember him—we went to primary school together.'

I did know him, but not because of school. I knew him from the bunker, and the second I met his blue eyes, I knew that he remembered, too. A dirty grin spread over his face.

'You're the sister who used to dance for the Iron Fists, right?'

I lifted my chin. 'So what if I did?'

'No reason.' He slouched back arrogantly. 'Just trying to figure out where I know you from. You getting us drinks or what?'

I ground my teeth together, feeling the beginnings of a headache. So much for my good mood.

'What can I get you?'

'I'll have a whiskey. Neat.'

I nodded to him and caught Sav's eye.

'Same,' she said.

'You sure? We have mixers and—'

'I can drink whiskey, Harley. I'm not five.'

I bit my tongue. 'That'll be six NP. Cash upfront.'

Talbot rolled his eyes exaggeratedly, sliding a tenner onto the table. 'You'd think the staff would have more trust for their regulars.'

'I'm just doing my job,' I said through gritted teeth. I tucked the note into my apron. 'I'll be right back.'

Savannah nodded, an unyielding expression on her face. She was angry with me. Again. *Great.*

I headed back to the bar, trying my best not to hyperventilate. My sister was in the bar. My sister. Savannah, who worked as a doctor, who disdained the sort of men that hung around this bar. Savannah was here.

With Greg Talbot.

Who was one of Percival's Aces.

Fuck.

I couldn't take my eyes off Savannah as Anna poured the drinks. She was looking very friendly with Talbot, touching him casually and laughing at whatever he said. My chest felt tight. Savannah wasn't stupid enough to get involved with the Aces, was she?

No, she hated the gangs.

Maybe she didn't know who he was?

I ducked below the counter, pretending to look for a fresh bottle of whiskey. I just needed a second to centre myself. Two deep breaths did it. I stood again, taking the tray Anna had just filled.

'You alright?'

'Of course. Why wouldn't I be?'

Anna smiled carefully. 'That's for table twelve.'

Table twelve, Ellery's table. Fixing a neutral expression on my face, I made my way over.

'Whiskeys.' I set the tray down with a thud, resisting the urge to glance at Savannah. *Don't look, don't look, don't show them any weakness…*

'Am I seeing double?' Briggs drawled.

'What, have you never seen twins before?' My voice was terse and sharp.

Ellery leant in, a dark look on his face that I didn't like at all. 'Your sister is making *trouble*, kitten.'

'She's a big girl. She can take care of herself, *Ellery*.'

He laughed derisively. 'Really? Doesn't look like she's doing too good of a job over there. Cosying up to Percival's boy? Not a wise idea.'

I put the last drink down with a bang, almost spilling it. 'Sorry, I forgot you thought you had a monopoly on my family.'

Our gazes clashed. Ellery's brows drew together. 'Kitten, I—'

'I have work to do. See you later, boys.'

I turned and stalked off before he could try anything stupid. Like apologising. That would be stupid indeed. It might even persuade me to forgive him—and I couldn't allow myself to do that.

No way.

I wove between the tables, doing my job with unrivalled ferocity. As long as I was busy, I didn't have to pay attention to Ellery—or Bas, who was watching me with narrowed eyes. Were they here on business? Did it have something to do with Talbot being here? Would it be arrogant to presume that this had something to do with me?

When I made my way back around to Savannah's table, Talbot said, 'You could join us when your shift ends.'

He shot me a mocking smile. I narrowed my eyes. He better not be entertaining any funny fantasies about *twins*.

'No thanks.' I mechanically swapped their empty glasses for full ones. 'I'm pretty tired. I think I'll just go straight to bed.'

'You sure? I'll make it worth your while.'

My eyes found Savannah. I wished they hadn't. Hurt was written across her face, and when I met her gaze she scowled at me. I knew exactly what she was thinking—but what could I say? It wasn't my fault Talbot was being a prick and flirting with me.

'I don't think that's a good idea,' I said tersely. I couldn't resist a glance over my shoulder. Ellery and co were watching me closely. I wet my lips nervously.

'Hate for you to get in trouble with your boys there.' Talbot smirked.

'They're not my boys, and I don't care what they do. I just don't want them up in my business,' I said coolly. 'If you'll excuse me, some of us have to work in the evenings.'

I stalked off.

It rankled: there were other bars in town. Savannah could have gone to other places. It wasn't that I wanted her to—I was glad she was here so I could keep an eye on her. But why did she have to parade around with Talbot? She'd gone and made my life infinitely harder.

'Harley!' Clem waved.

Groaning, I headed over to him, already prepared to tell him he'd had enough for the night.

The evening seemed to go on forever. Both the Iron Fists and Savannah's table lingered, as though they were each waiting for the other to leave. I pretended not to notice them, and finally, my shift drew to a close. I dumped my apron in the wash basket and draped my coat over my shoulders.

'I'll see you on Tuesday,' I murmured to Anna.

'Not me. Kayla will be on.' She smiled, her cheeks turning pink.

I studied her suspiciously. 'How come?'

'I might have a date.'

Oh boy…

'Who with?'

Her blush deepened. 'Gabriel Tam—I know what you're going to say, but he's a total gentleman. Stop looking at me like that, Harley!'

'Like what?'

'I *know* he's with the Iron Fists.'

He was more than that. I frowned. 'They're all the same, Anna. You can't trust them. I've seen Tam with members of other gangs—'

'You're one to talk,' Anna snapped. 'I've seen you climbing all over them.'

Oh, ouch. That really stung. I zipped my coat up, turning to leave. 'Alright, well, enjoy your date.'

If she didn't want to listen, I couldn't make her.

'Harley, I didn't mean it like that.' Anna bit her lip.

'I know.' I forced a smile. 'Goodnight, Anna.'

She'd meant exactly that. People thought I was a slut. I'd carved out a reputation for myself, and now I was going to have to live with it.

Scowling, I stalked across the bar to the front entrance. Savannah tried to catch my eye, but I kept walking determinedly. I didn't want to speak to her—I knew she thought the same of me as Anna did. I crossed the lobby and stopped at the front doors, scanning the rain-drenched square for a taxi-truck. There were none. *Damnit.* Just when I wanted one. I really didn't feel like walking all the way home in the rain.

I vacillated for a few moments, hoping one would come along.

'Leaving already, Harley?'

Briggs.

My mood soured further.

I turned back to the lobby, with its checkerboard floor and dark wood-panelled walls. Ellery, Bas, Briggs, and Kade spilt out of the bar. Crossing my arms, I watched them approach.

'What?'

'Aw, don't be so unfriendly.' Briggs cupped my cheek. I stepped deliberately away from him, rain wetting my back as I moved into the open doorway.

'Don't touch me.'

Briggs laughed, a braying, awful laugh like a donkey.

'Why so cold, baby?'

I had a sudden, chilling realisation: without Ellery's favour, I was just as exposed to the shenanigans of the Iron Fists as any other woman. The thought made me feel colder than the rain could.

'Leave me alone,' I said, fighting for calm. I could feel my lips twisting into a grimace, and I bit my tongue to keep my face neutral. I worked here. They wouldn't try anything here, would they?

Against my will, my gaze slid to Bas. He had one hand in his pocket, the other toying with his car key. His gaze met mine, eyes uncaring. Of course, I'd made it clear I wanted nothing to do with him anymore... so he'd washed his hands of me, too.

I hadn't expected it to hurt. It was like a sucker punch straight to the stomach, winding me.

Briggs advanced another step, but this time I refused to stand down. He ended up right in my personal space, staring malevolently down at me. 'You weren't so unfriendly last time.'

I steeled myself. 'Back off, Briggs. Last time was a mistake.'

Now I'd done it. Fury crept over Briggs's face, dark and wicked. 'Not sure I'm on board with that, *kitten.*'

'My name is *Harley.*' Fear clenched its fist around my heart, cutting off my breath. I stepped back, and rain washed over me. Automatically, my eyes found Ellery.

He stared back, his expression apathetic.

I was alone.

I put my hand on my belt as Briggs grabbed my shoulder. 'Seems to me you could do with an attitude adjustment.'

Did I dare pull a knife on a member of the Iron Fists? My hand clenched around the handle so hard the ridges dug into my palm. My heart pounded in terror. All I could see was Briggs's smug expression.

'Harley?'

Briggs wheeled around. I leant sideways and caught sight of Savannah.

No. No, no, no, no, no.

'Sav,' I choked. 'You're leaving?' *Please go back into the bar. Now.*

'What's going on?' Savannah strode up, fearless as always. Her eyes landed on Briggs, who squeezed my shoulder in warning. 'Harley?'

'Nothing. I was just waiting for a taxi-truck.' The tremble in my voice betrayed me. Savannah frowned. I looked uneasily at Ellery, then back to her. Greg Talbot strode into the lobby, shrugging his coat on, and I felt the shift. It was a subtle change, but the atmosphere felt fraught all of a sudden.

'What's this, then?' Talbot's hand grazed his gun belt. Did no one check their fucking weapons around here?

'Nothing for you to concern yourself with,' Briggs sneered. 'Run along, kiddies.'

Talbot stepped towards him, his chin raised haughtily, his hand obviously on his gun. 'Don't think I will, actually.'

'Greg!' Savannah hissed anxiously, grabbing his arm. 'Don't get involved.'

Her eyes darted to me. I met her gaze steadily, anger ballooning in my chest.

Talbot shook Savannah's arm off. Briggs laughed. 'Got yourself a keeper, Talbot? Can't say I blame you. The Benoit twins are quite something, aren't they?'

'Fuck. Off,' I mumbled under my breath, but it came out too loud.

Ellery's gaze jumped to me. 'Something to say, Harley?' he snapped.

I met his eyes. 'Not to you.'

'Lover's tiff, Ellery?' Talbot crowed.

Ellery's gaze never left mine, his face as impassive as a statue. 'Don't see that it's any of your business, Talbot.'

Talbot snorted. 'The Iron Fists really have gone downhill if they can't even keep their whores under control anymore.'

'Greg!' Savannah cried. I took two sharp steps forward and stopped dead when Ellery swung around, his gun in hand and pointed right at Talbot's face.

'Care to repeat that?'

'You heard me.' Talbot's eyes glittered like beetles.

Panic blew through me like an icy wind. I couldn't look at anything except Savannah. Her face was bleached with fear, her eyes as round as dinner plates. We were seconds away from all-out violence. I had to get her away from here.

'You want me to blow your teeth out, Talbot?' Ellery's voice was as deep and dark as a freshly dug grave. 'I'd be happy to oblige.'

'Dunno. Seems like your aim is a bit off these days.'

'You want to bet on that?'

Ellery flicked the safety off. I grabbed a handful of his jacket, yanking to get his attention. 'Ellery! Stop!'

Ellery turned his gaze on me, his eyes cold as ice. 'Get out the way, Harley.'

My heart was pounding like a jackhammer. What was I doing? 'No. You're mad at me, so be mad at me.'

'You want me to shoot you?' he asked coldly. I couldn't tell if he meant it or not.

'NO! But I don't want you to start a fucking war because I gave Briggs a handjob!'

My words dropped into the space between us like a hand grenade: explosion imminent. I winced, but I refused to take my eyes off of Ellery. He snorted.

'Like I give a shit about that.'

'You're sure acting like you care.'

With jerky movements, Ellery flicked the safety back on his gun and shook off my grip. At least he wasn't going to shoot me, not today. 'As I recall, you were the one who washed your hands of us.'

'You haven't been such a great friend lately either,' I snapped. 'Get off your high horse. Go home, Ellery.'

'Or what?' His eyes were dark with anger.

'Or I'll bar you from the hotel for carrying weapons.'

I didn't actually have the power to do that, but I was tired: tired of

Ellery acting like a dick, tired of Briggs being a pig, tired of them throwing their weight around. 'Just leave.'

Talbot snorted. 'That's right, Ellery, listen to your whore.'

Ellery twisted and fired a shot, quick as a flash, and then Talbot crumpled. The noise reached me belatedly, the gunshot making my ears ring. I staggered backwards in shock, grabbing the railing so I didn't fall down the stairs. *Oh shit. Oh shit.*

Talbot snarled, a wordless expression of pain and fury. With one hand on his bleeding leg, he pulled his gun and pointed it not at Ellery, but at me.

My brain went blank, my grip on the railing the only thing keeping me upright as my legs grew weak and my vision tunnelled. I opened my mouth, but I couldn't remember how to speak.

Stop. Make him stop. Please.

'Greg—' Savannah's voice reached me through the sound of my pulse thudding in my ears. I tried to find her with blurry eyes, but instead, I found Bas, who pulled his own gun and put it to Talbot's head.

Talbot croaked wordlessly.

'Drop it,' Bas said tersely.

Talbot's gun dropped to point at the floor. The world came back to me, too fast, too vivid. I swayed.

'Here's what's going to happen.' Bas's voice was as unyielding as stone. 'You're going to walk out of that door, get in your car, and drive away. If you hesitate'—Bas cleared his throat sharply—'or try to shoot one of us, I will find out how much of this clip I can empty into your body without killing you. My bets are on all of it.'

'You've got to be joking,' Talbot said shrilly. He was listing sharply to one side, his face bleached of colour and his expression frozen; the only part of him that moved was his eyes. 'Percival won't stand for this.'

'I doubt Percival cares about your wellbeing nearly as much as you're imagining.'

'You think he'd listen to you?' Talbot's eyes swivelled wildly, as though he was searching for allies. Savannah stood with her back pressed to the wall, her eyes so wide I could see the whites all around the irises. Talbot looked at me instead. 'You're no better than *she* is.'

'Do you really think I care what you think of me?' Bas sneered.

'I don't have to listen to a trumped-up whore—' Bas kicked Talbot's injured leg, and the redhead sagged to the ground, yowling. Pitilessly, Bas stared down at him. 'Leave, whilst you can still walk to do it.'

Talbot swallowed hard. 'Fucking nutjob.' He clawed at the ground, struggling to get up. Savannah darted in and grabbed his arm, throwing it over her shoulders.

'Come on, let's go,' she hissed urgently.

'Fuckin cunts,' Talbot slurred, stumbling like a drunk. Savannah hauled him to his feet and steered him towards the door. Ellery grabbed my coat, yanking me out of their way.

For a second that seemed to last forever, Savannah was in front of me, staring at me. *Come with us*, her eyes pleaded. My voice seemed to have vanished. I opened my mouth, then closed it again. Helplessly, I watched as Savannah dragged Talbot outside and down the stairs, leaving me with the Iron Fists. Bas lowered his gun, his expression foreboding. Behind him, I caught sight of Tom. When our eyes met, he mouthed, 'Okay?'

I nodded. Tom vanished back into the bar and shut the doors. I was on my own.

Bas tucked his gun away. Ellery released me with a scowl.

'You're welcome.'

Fury rushed through me, obliterating my fear. 'You expect me to be grateful? That was your fault!'

'If we hadn't been here—'

'If you hadn't been here, I wouldn't be here!' My voice was too shrill, too afraid, but I couldn't figure out how to dial it back. 'You arseholes are the only reason I was still here, or have you forgotten already?'

Ellery gave me a stony look. 'Mind yourself, Harley. None of us has any obligation to you.'

Bas coughed softly, almost quiet enough that I'd have ignored him—but not quite. My gaze swung to him. He met my eyes head-on. 'Go home,' he said.

'Don't order me about.'

'You want to stay?' Bas shrugged, zipping up his jacket with sharp motions. 'Suit yourself, then. I'm done.'

He stalked to the door, coming so close that I stumbled back into the doorframe. Bas stared down at me, his eyes speaking louder than words: *You're pathetic.*

'So much for looking after yourself.'

I tipped my head back, refusing to be cowed. 'There's no shame in being good at running away. At least people don't get hurt around me.'

For a moment, Bas tensed, and I thought I'd finally pushed him too far. Then he suddenly whirled around, grabbed Briggs by the shoulder, and hauled him out into the rain. 'Sort your shit out, Ellery. I'll bring the car around.'

'Oi,' Briggs grunted. 'I wasn't done.'

'Yes, you were.' Bas stalked down the stairs. Briggs shot one last angry look my way, before following him. The two of them splashed down the stairs and out of sight. Kade lingered in the doorway, looking uneasily between Ellery and me.

'Alright, Miss Harley?'

'I'll be fine.' I favoured him with an awkward smile. Kade nodded and followed Bas and Briggs. That left Ellery and me, staring one another down. The three feet between us might as well have been a chasm a mile wide.

'Look, Ellery,' I started, although I wasn't sure what I wanted to say.

Ellery jerked as though breaking himself out of a stupor. 'You can't belong to me and Briggs, Harley.'

'I don't belong to anyone.'

Ellery shook his head. 'I can't do this. We can't—You're either gang business, or you're my business, but you can't be both.'

What the fuck did that mean? 'I don't want anything to do with the Iron Fists.'

'I'm one of the Iron Fists,' Ellery snapped. 'You can't separate it.'

What was he on about? I felt like I was losing the plot. 'If this is about Briggs—'

'Of course it's about Briggs!' Ellery clenched his fists, vibrating with anger. 'What's he got that I haven't?'

'Nothing! I don't want to sleep with either of you!'

Ellery reeled back as though he'd been slapped. 'Then we're done here.'

Of course. 'That's all you ever cared about?' I grasped the door to steady myself. 'Fucking typical.'

Ellery's face had gone blank, his eyes glassy. 'I won't come to you for information again. I won't bother you in the bar.'

'That suits me fine,' I replied coolly.

We stared at one another.
A car hooted outside. Bas.
'Goodbye, Harley.'
Ellery turned and stalked out into the rain.

NINETEEN

I FELT SICK THE WHOLE NEXT DAY, the feeling not helped at all by Irina's leering smile as I paid her the one sixty-five rent. I couldn't shake the sense that I'd made an irrevocable mistake, though neither could I figure out what the mistake had been. I was better off without Ellery—but his expression haunted me every time I closed my eyes.

My usual chores could barely hold my attention. I was tired, but too wired up to sleep. I wandered around the flat restlessly.

The lights went off with a snap.

Damnit.

Now I was cursing my inability to focus. We'd probably have no electricity until morning, and it would be dark soon.

I sank onto the sofa, staring gloomily at the wall. What to do with myself?

I couldn't just sit here.

Fuck it, I'd go see Savannah. She'd know what had happened to Talbot, at least. And I wanted to see her face—reassure myself that she was fine. I hadn't seen her since last night. We were clearly long overdue a conversation, too. I'd let things fester between us for too long.

I set off.

It felt dark outside, even though it was still light. The thick clouds lent everything a gloomy air. Not that our town needed help with that—it managed to look gloomy quite well on its own. I caught a taxi-truck up to the north side and hopped out by the clinic. They had swapped their weapons-check lady for a bulky-looking man, whose jacket bore the logo of a local security company on it. Was this the mayor finally taking action to protect his town?

Probably not.

The clinic was an election campaign asset—maybe he was anticipating trouble.

The conversation I'd overheard weeks ago popped into my head again, for the first time in a while. I had never managed to tell Ellery about it, and I felt a sudden spur of guilt. It had, after all, been important…

But then, Ellery had told me himself that the Iron Fists had other ways of getting information.

So let them find out another way. They could manage without me.

Steeling myself, I let the mayor's guard frisk me and confiscate my knife, then headed inside. At least he was fastidious.

The clinic was in its usual state of chaos when I entered. A mother was trying to corral a herd of children, whilst several nurses were sorting out a few wooden crates of stock. Savannah was in her usual cubicle at the end. I followed the sound of her voice, but when I got close, another voice jumped out at me.

'…asking to be shot in the head, honestly.'

'I don't condone violence, Greg,' Savannah said with an air of patient exasperation.

'Would you rather they continue to run amok?'

I paused in the entrance to the cubicle. Greg Talbot was sitting on a plastic chair with his leg up on a second chair, whilst Savannah tended to another man, who had wicked-looking scratches up his calf.

'I'd rather none of you made my job harder.'

I stepped out of sight, my heart thumping in my chest. What was Talbot doing here?

'You can't have it both ways,' Talbot said. 'We're either dealing with the threat, or we're leaving it alone, and both routes involve violence.'

'Everything involves violence in this town.' Savannah sighed. 'I can't give you a rabies shot, Luke. We haven't got any on hand. You'll need to go to Crater's Edge for that.'

'Will I be fine without it?' asked a gruff voice.

'Probably not,' Savannah said brusquely. 'I'll give you the antibiotics that I can give you now.'

'I haven't got time to go to Crater's Edge—'

'Well, if you can convince Mr Moriarty to stop blockading the supply routes from Brackfields, then we will be able to stock a greater variety of medical supplies again.' Savannah cut herself off with the crinkling of a foil wrapper, then the sound of water running. 'Drink and swallow.'

Someone—Talbot, I thought—laughed. 'That's right, Luke. Swallow.'

'Crude,' Savannah snapped.

'Come on, you liked me a lot better last night.'

'Don't think because I took your side once that means I'll do it every time,' Savannah said coolly. 'Especially not if you involve my sister in your games.'

'Your sister involved herself. Everyone knows she's sleeping with Ellery—it's not my fault she's tarting around with the Iron Fists.'

An icy fist seemed to clench around my chest. I held my breath. *Deny it, Sav. Please.*

Savannah was silent for a long moment. Finally, she said, 'I'm not debating this topic with you.'

'Because you know it's true.'

'I—' Silence. 'I don't want to talk about last night.'

I backed away slowly. An odd feeling was growing in my gut. I couldn't name it. I didn't want to name it. Suddenly, coming here seemed like a mistake.

I walked out, passing everyone in a daze. I almost left without retrieving my knife, but the guard called to me, 'Miss, your weapon!'

'Thanks,' I mumbled, tucking it into my coat.

There were no taxi-trucks around, so I walked. My thoughts churned in my head like dust blown up by the wind, but no single one stood out. I probably shouldn't have been as hurt as I was—it wasn't as though I hadn't known what Savannah thought of me—but it was still a blow to actually hear it.

And when had everyone decided that I was Ellery's woman?

Ellery and I had never even kissed.

What the fuck was going on?

'Where you going, baby?'

The voice snapped me out of my thoughts. I looked up, suddenly struck by the unfamiliarity of the buildings around me. Where was I?

I'd been walking on autopilot. *Stupid, stupid, stupid.* How could I be so careless?

A man stood from where he'd been sitting in a doorway. The street I had turned down was small and dark, not the sort of place where I should have been walking this close to nightfall.

I took a step back.

'Don't run off, baby. You just got here.'

The man was tall, roughly dressed in tattered overalls, and his face was in shadow. He took several steps toward me, and I saw something glinting in his hand—a bottle.

'I—I don't want any trouble.'

'Trouble?' He laughed, an odd, breathy sound. 'Oh no, me neither. Just a bit of friendly conversation.'

Fuck, I was in trouble.

'I think I took a wrong turn. I'll just, um—I'll just head back.'

'Leaving so soon?' He threw the bottle against the wall. It shattered with a crash, the noise rattling through me. I jumped and turned to flee.

The next moment, the guy slammed into my back, knocking me into the wall and pinning me against it.

'GET OFF!'

'You women!' He laughed. 'All the same. So fucking cold.'

'GET OFF ME! GET OFF! LET ME GO!'

I writhed fruitlessly, panic making my vision black. My knees hit the ground, and he kicked my back, knocking me forwards and driving the breath out of me. I wheezed desperately, unable to tell which way was up. A hand grasped my hair, dragging my head around. He spat in my face.

'Fucking keep still!'

'Let me go!' I croaked.

'Damn bitch.' He knelt over me, his knee digging into my thigh and forcing my legs apart. I struggled to get away, shoving at his arms and shoulders, his face, his eyes—whatever I could reach. His grip on my hair turned painful as he kept me in place. With his other hand, he fished a knife out of his belt and sliced at the front of my coat.

I brought my other leg up, trying to shove my boot into his stomach. He grunted, and then the knife was against my neck.

'Fucking keep still, or I'll cut your throat open, girl.'

A sob wrenched out of my chest. *No, no, no...*

'Please,' I begged in a pitiful voice. 'Please, don't do this.'

'Shut your slut mouth.'

He released my hair to scrabble at my top and jeans, pushing the top up so my stomach was bare to the cold air. Then he got my button open and yanked at the tight jeans.

'Damnit. What is this shit?' He took the knife away from my throat so he could saw at the thick denim—and I lurched up, slamming my forehead against his nose.

He howled in rage. 'You little bitch!' He slapped me. My head cracked against the paving making my ears ring.

'For that, I'll cut your tongue out. Or maybe I'll fuck you with the knife.' He laughed. 'Yeah, that'd be fucking fun, wouldn't it?'

He managed to pull my jeans aside and put the knife back to my neck. I lay there, fear turning my body to ice. I couldn't move. I couldn't even swallow, though I tasted blood in my mouth. I'd bitten my tongue.

He was going to rape me.

He pulled his trousers down clumsily, shoving his hands down the front. His eyes fluttered shut as he grunted, jerking himself off. 'Yeah, this is gonna be so fucking good. You think you can deny me?'

A few tears trickled down my face. *Sav… I'm sorry.*

The knife went slack against my neck.

My heart skipped a beat.

His eyes were still closed, but at any second they could open. I didn't have time to reconsider.

I grabbed his hand and yanked it towards me, wrenching my head up so I could bite him *hard*.

He dropped the knife. In that second, I brought my leg up again, jamming my boot into his groin. The man collapsed onto me, snarling. One of his hands went to my neck, whilst the other scrabbled for the knife. 'That's it, you little bitch! I'm gonna—'

My hand closed around the knife. I slashed wildly, but he knocked my arm away. For a moment, his weight shifted—I could move. I lurched up, and he shoved me down again, my head thunking against the ground. Pain exploded through me. I squirmed, slashing the knife again and again into empty air—it connected with something and he grunted in pain—

BANG!

For several seconds I was deaf. The world seemed to fade out.

When it came back, the man had slumped sideways, unmoving, and I was looking at the profile of another man, gun in hand.

I pressed my back into the ground, holding out the knife as though that would actually protect me. Then the man tucked the gun back into his jacket and looked at me.

It was Bas.

Bas had shot my would-be rapist.

And now he was going to… My brain ground to a halt, unable to come up with a logical conclusion to that sentence. I watched in terror as Bas strode closer and crouched down, studying me.

'Are you okay?'

My mouth opened, but no words emerged.

'Harley...' He looked me up and down, then took my hand, carefully prying the knife away out of my grip. 'Come on.'

He helped me up, not that I did much to aid the process. My legs didn't want to support my weight. Bas propped me against the wall, then helped me out of my ruined coat and shrugged his own jacket off, wrapping it around my shoulders.

'Did he hurt you?' A pause. He licked his lips. 'I mean, do you have any injuries that need tending?'

I worked my mouth, trying to find my voice. 'I... don't think so.'

'You have blood on your neck.'

I touched my neck and felt a sting of pain. *Oh.* 'He must have cut me. The knife...'

Bas used the edge of his sleeve to wipe the blood away. 'It's just a scratch. Let's get you home.'

With firm, gentle hands, he helped me put my arms in his jacket and zipped up the front. Then he offered me the knife again. I shook my head.

'It's not mine. Mine's in my coat.'

Bas picked up the coat and dug through it, finding the hunting knife I'd taken from Ellery. He put it in my hand, wrapping my fingers firmly around it. 'Come on.'

He rested a hand on my shoulder, steering me out of the alleyway. I tried to look back, but Bas dragged me unerringly onwards. I had no idea where we were, but he seemed to know, and a moment later we were passing a familiar building with boarded-up windows and a sign reading *Olde Phoenix Theatre—Oldest Building in Town!* I'd only strayed about two or three streets off my path.

As we walked silently through the darkening streets, shame began to creep up on me. I was such an idiot. That situation had been entirely preventable if I'd just been paying attention. If Bas hadn't come by then...

'Th-thank you,' I whispered.

Bas glanced down at me. 'Think nothing of it.'

'You must think I'm such an idiot.'

He frowned. 'What were you doing there?'

'I'd been at the clinic. I just… took a wrong turn.'

Bas sighed. 'Why were you at the clinic? You weren't hurt last night.'

'No… I just wanted to see my sister.'

His expression spoke volumes about what he thought of that notion. 'Don't you live with her?'

I shrugged. Bas shook his head and tugged me down the street. 'Come on.'

'Where are you taking me?'

'Home. Where else?'

'Oh.' I hadn't really thought about it, but now that I did, a horrifying possibility took root in my mind. 'I… I owe you, don't I?'

Bas glanced sharply down at me, as though he could read where my thoughts had gone. 'I told you, don't worry about it.'

'I—I—' My teeth had started chattering, despite the warmth of Bas's jacket, and I couldn't get them to stop. 'I can't really repay you. I don't have any money.'

'Harley…'

'I don't… I can't…' I clutched at the knife. There was only one thing men wanted from me, in my experience, and the thought made my stomach curl in on itself. Would Bas do that? Save me just so he could get a piece of me himself? He'd never shown any interest before, but that didn't mean he wouldn't take it if it was owed.

Oh God.

'You don't owe me anything,' Bas said sternly. 'Except a promise that you'll stop wandering around after dark. It's too dangerous at the moment.'

I shook my head. He said that now, but what if he changed his mind tomorrow, in the light of day? Terror made me lightheaded. I wanted to run away, but the fear of being alone kept me stumbling along beside Bas.

'Wh-what were you doing there, anyway?'

'Patrolling. And you're fucking lucky I was.'

'I took his knife. I was looking after myself.' My lips felt numb. Bas looked at me, a strange expression on his face. Almost like admiration, but it couldn't be that.

'You did,' he said slowly. 'But could you have killed him?'

I shrugged.

Bas sighed.

We walked the rest of the way in silence until we turned onto Prospect Avenue, and there my flat was. I was home.

No sense of relief came. I felt numb.

When we reached the door, I took my coat from Bas and dug through the pockets until I found the key. I twisted it in the lock but paused with the door open a crack. 'I… I'll be fine from here.'

Bas glanced down at me, his expression dismissive. 'I'll walk you to your door.'

I wanted that, and at the same time I didn't. Partly because of the tiny, lingering fear that if I let him upstairs, he would suddenly change his mind and demand repayment from me—my body in exchange for my life. Mostly, it was just shame. I'd been inside Sayle's compound. It was military and uniform, not at all luxurious, but everything was clean, new, and functional. My flat was emphatically the opposite, and Bas had never held back with his judgements. He would certainly have strong opinions about my living arrangements.

But the thought of being alone, even in my own stairwell, made my skin crawl. I nodded without looking at him, pushing the door open properly. Bas followed me, a silent and foreboding presence as I climbed the stairs to the top floor. I unlocked my flat with shaking fingers and opened the door. The flat was as silent as I had left it. I flicked the light switch, but it remained dark.

'Our electricity went off after lunch.' My voice was barely a whisper. 'I have candles.'

'Is there hot water?' I couldn't discern Bas's tone of voice, and that scared me.

'Yeah, the water's heated by gas.'

'Fine. Go shower. I'll wait.'

He was waiting? Why? What for? For me to be clean, so he could—

My stomach turned, and just like that, I knew I was going to puke. I fled to the bathroom, feeling my way in the dark, collapsed to my knees in front of the toilet, and brought up the contents of my stomach. *Oh fuck. Oh fuck.*

I vomited until there was nothing left and then sat there, shaking, waiting for my stomach to settle. My heart was galloping in my chest, and my skin was damp with cold sweat. Finally, I caught my breath and managed to wash up in the dark, splashing icy cold water on my face to calm down.

Bas would have heard through the walls.

Humiliation burnt in my chest as I stepped out of the bathroom again. On the plus side, he probably wouldn't want to sleep with me if he thought I was sick. But now he had yet another excuse to think I was a pathetic waste of space.

The lounge area was empty. Had he left? But no—after a moment, I found him standing over the stove in the kitchen. He'd lit it and was boiling water. I scuffed my feet against the ground, and he looked over.

'I told you to shower.'

'I'm not… I mean… I need a torch.' I edged closer, wary of being in his personal space, and fingered open the top drawer. Bas watched my every move, but he didn't speak. Maybe he was disgusted. Maybe he was waiting for me to speak. I wasn't going to. I certainly wouldn't bring my moment of weakness up if he didn't.

Palming the torch, I backed away again. 'I'll be right back.'

Bas nodded and went back to mincing the chicory root for coffee. I took shelter in the bathroom and climbed into the shower. The water sputtered cold, hot, cold a few times, before settling on a shade above lukewarm. *Good enough.* I turned my face into the spray, letting it wet me down, and choked out a sob.

Fuck.

I was such an idiot.

Fuck.

That had been really fucking close.

Fuck.

The tears came thick and fast, my sobs violent enough to make my whole body shudder. My hands were shaking so badly I could barely hold the soap—but I forced myself to. I had to get the feeling of his hands off my body. I scrubbed myself until the tears abated, and then a few more times, until my skin felt raw, and the water had run cold. Then I climbed out of the shower and dried myself off.

I was going to have to face Bas again. I was going to have to look him in the eye.

So much for being stronger without the Iron Fists.

I put my oldest, ugliest clothes on as a possible deterrent and crept out to face my saviour.

Bas was sitting at the kitchen table, a mug of coffee in front of him. He'd rested his head against the wall, and at first, I thought he was asleep. His eyes were closed, his breathing even.

I got about a metre away before his eyes snapped open. I froze, caught in his gaze, and we stared at each other.

'You're… you're still here.'

'Did you expect me to leave?' he asked gruffly.

'No,' I mumbled. I reached up, gathering my damp hair into a loose ponytail, baring my neck. His gaze didn't waver from my eyes. I felt about two feet tall. 'So… um…'

'You should drink something. It'll help.'

'Help…?'

'With the shaking.'

I dropped my hands so I could see them. They were shaking. A shiver washed over me, then another, and suddenly it became uncontrollable. I clenched my fists, my teeth chattering.

'I—I'll sleep it off. I'm fine.'

'Are you?' Bas stood. I skittered backwards, my hip smacking the edge of the counter. He watched me as though I'd proven a point, but I didn't care about that. Standing, he seemed to fill the room. This flat wasn't designed to have big, tall men in it; with him here, it felt like there was no space left over for me.

He moved over to the stove and poured a second mug of coffee, holding it out to me. 'Drink. Do you have a blanket?'

'What for?'

'For you. You're cold.'

'I—But—' My brain felt sluggish; I couldn't figure out what he wanted, and part of me wanted to scream, *Can we just skip to the sex part now?* That, at least, would have made sense.

Him making me coffee and asking for blankets did not make sense.

I pointed to the bedroom. 'My bed is the one on the right.'

'I really don't care where your bed is.'

'That's where the blankets are.'

His brow wrinkled in a frown. Setting the coffee down beside me, he departed for the bedroom. I waited until he was out of sight before picking it up and taking a big sip. It scalded my mouth and sent a burst of painful clarity through me. The hazy edges of the room sharpened back into focus. My body shook harder. I needed to sit, or better yet, to sleep. The best thing would be to put off repaying Bas until another day. Likely, he had reached the same conclusion. I'd make a poor bedfellow today.

I nodded to myself and moved to the sofa, my legs shaking so hard that I couldn't walk straight. I made it and sagged onto the less lumpy side, pulling my knees to my chest.

Okay. I could do this. I took a smaller sip of the coffee. I had been here before, and I had survived. I could do it again.

Bas came back with an armful of blankets, dropping them beside me. 'Wrap those around you.'

I complied. He was right, it was better. Between that and the coffee, warmth began to creep into my body again, enough that I was confident in studying my saviour. He leant against the windowsill, sipping his coffee, his gaze distant.

Then his eyes jumped to mine. 'What?'

'I owe you,' I whispered.

Bas frowned. 'Not this again. What do I have to tell you to convince you that you don't owe me?'

'It's not fine.' It couldn't be, because he'd helped me, and I couldn't bear the thought of that loose end lingering, waiting to trip me up. 'You wouldn't be here unless you were after *something*. Tell me what you want.'

'Nothing.'

'Then why did you help me?'

'Would you rather I'd left you to your fate?'

I scowled. 'People don't do good deeds just for the sake of it.'

'Harley, I'm trying to look after you —'

'Look after me?' I laughed derisively.

Bas tipped his head back, groaning. 'You're impossible.'

'I just want to know what you want from me.'

'I don't want anything!'

'Everyone wants something!' I was angry without warning, without control. I jumped up, spilling blankets onto the floor, and put my hands on my hips. 'Just tell me. You want me to suck your cock? Or give you a handjob, like I did for Briggs? Or maybe that's not *enough* for you?'

Bas's gaze sharpened. 'I don't do that.'

'Do what?'

'I only have sex with people who consent to it.'

'I am consenting!'

'No,' he said flatly. 'You're not.'

'How? I literally said I didn't mind.'

'You're scared and traumatised. What you say and what you *want* are not the same thing.'

'I'm not traumatised!'

'Aren't you?' Bas made a sudden move towards me. I jerked back. 'Yes,' he said darkly, 'you are.'

'I just don't like having you in my flat—'

'Why? Because you're scared of me, too?'

The words made me shudder. 'No,' I lied. 'I'm just not used to having guests over.'

Bas's look said he wasn't fooled at all. 'Even if you were capable of consenting right now—which you are not—I have no intention of having sex with you, and certainly not as repayment for helping you.'

His clipped, rushed tone made my head spin. I didn't believe him for a second. 'Sure, you and every other guy in this town.'

'I am not *every other guy.*'

'Wow, yeah, you're such a special snowflake.'

Bas clenched his fists, then took a deep breath, visibly forcing himself to relax. 'That has nothing to do with it. I don't mix sex with anything. Not business, not money, certainly in exchange for saving you.'

'Then what *do* you mix it with?' The words were out before I could stop them, or remind myself that I actually didn't want to know anything about Bas and his sex life. There was no reason to even ask, and I scrambled to think of a way to take them back.

'Nothing. Sex is for pleasure and pleasure only.'

'Except if you don't mix it with money, you can't exactly pay a whore.'

'Shockingly, it is possible to have sex with a woman—or man—who is not paid to be there.' Bas scowled. 'Maybe that's not the way you do it, but I do.'

'I'm not stupid. I know that.'

'Then what's your point?'

'I don't know!' A sob worked its way up my throat, defying my efforts to suppress it. Another shudder wracked my shoulders. 'It's not like I've ever—'

I snapped my mouth shut far too late. Bas's expression had shifted to one of realisation and surprise. I ducked my head, feeling like my face was on fire, waiting for his condemnation.

'You're a virgin?' He sounded faintly surprised.

'No… That's not what I was going to say.' My cheeks felt about to explode.

'Then…' The atmosphere between us felt heavy suddenly, as though the air was too thick to breathe. 'Has this happened before?'

'No… not exactly. It's stupid. You'll think it's stupid.'

'I don't think you're stupid, Harley.'

'You will.' I felt stupid. I turned away from him, picking up my blankets. Bas appeared beside me suddenly, startling me. He took the blankets and laid a hand against my shoulder.

'Come on, I'm putting you to bed.'

I twisted, pulling away.

'To sleep!' Bas tipped his head back and groaned in frustration. 'Honestly, you're so skittish, I don't know how Briggs even convinced you to do anything.'

'That was business.'

'Sex should never be *business*. If you mix the two, you end up losing sight of what matters.'

'What matters?'

Bas shot me a dark look. 'Go to bed, Harley.'

I glared at him. I felt patronised, and that made me angry. Thrusting my words at him like knives, I said, 'Do you know how I ended up dancing in the bunker?'

Bas shrugged one shoulder uncaringly. 'Is it relevant?'

'Maybe not to you,' I snapped. I wanted to hurt him. He was so unflappable, and I wanted to see him crack. 'When my father died, he owed Sayle money. Quite a lot of money, actually.'

Bas raised an eyebrow.

'So you paid it off by dancing.'

'Not exactly.'

From one second to the next, all of the hurt came rushing back. It might have been seven years since then, but it hadn't diminished in the slightest. I'd never forget those days—I'd never forget Jackson appearing at the house with the news: your father is dead.

Now Sayle owns you.

'My father had borrowed money to put Sav and me through school,' I explained. 'He knew that without it, Sav would never get into medical training. He was trying to pay it off, but then he died. And that left Sav and me. We didn't own our house, so the only thing I had to sell was… Well, Sayle said he'd write off part of the debt if I did him a small favour. It's not much, right? Just go where he tells me, sleep with this guy who has a *fancy* for virgins.' I shuddered.

'Harley…' Bas's voice trailed off into nothing.

I soldiered on. 'Briggs was the one who was supposed to take me and collect me. He was the one who saw me immediately after.' Crying, bleeding. 'And I suppose he decided he wanted in on things… or maybe he just likes sloppy seconds—' A sob wrenched out of my throat. So much for being strong.

Bas shifted, sliding his arms around me. I pressed my face into his chest. He smelt of sweat, soap, and something smoky. It was nice. Comforting. 'You don't have to tell me.'

'Even you don't want to hear.'

'Not like this. Not if it upsets you to tell me.'

'But that's the world we live in. You, Briggs, Ellery… the only thing any of you want from me is sex.'

Bas rubbed my back in slow, soothing circles, letting me cry into his chest. He was warm and so very solid, and the longer I spent there, the less I wanted to move. I almost believed him when he whispered, 'That's not true.'

Finally, he stroked his hand over my hair, before gently pulling away. 'Will you sleep now?'

I nodded. I was exhausted. My throat ached from crying, my nose was running, and I could feel my hair sticking to my face. I must have looked like a total mess, but Bas withheld comment and guided me to the bedroom.

'Are you leaving now?' I sat on the edge of the bed, torn between reluctance and hope. As much as I wanted him gone, I also wanted him to stay.

'I need to report in at the compound before someone discovers the body. It'll be better if Sayle hears what happened directly from me.'

'Oh.'

'I won't mention you.' Bas's expression was inscrutable. He tossed my blankets back on the bed, studying the room as he did. It wasn't much: two beds, a chest of drawers, the window looking out on The Arsonist's training yard. We'd stuffed a towel against the bottom of the window because it didn't seal.

'Right. Thanks,' I muttered unenthusiastically.

Bas's eyes slid back to me, assessing my face. 'Do you want me to stay?'

I shrugged.

'I can stay until you fall asleep.'

'I need to lock the door behind you.'

'Or I can come back tomorrow and give you that self-defence lesson you turned down before,' he said pointedly.

A compelling offer.

'I have work tomorrow.'

This time, his face was perfectly readable: *You're going to work tomorrow? Are you serious?*

I grimaced.

Bas sighed. 'The offer remains open, in any case. You know where to find me if you want to take me up on it.'

'Thanks,' I whispered.

'Alright.' He started for the door. I got up and trailed after him, watching as he found his jacket and shrugged it on again, checking for his gun. Then he opened the door and stepped out.

'Harley?' He paused on the threshold, looking back at me. 'You did good.'

His eyes met mine, as solid and unyielding as usual. Then he turned and left without another word.

TWENTY

THERE WAS NO MARKED IMPROVEMENT in the following days. It didn't
rain; the bar was fairly quiet, and I continued with my life. The truth
was that, although everything felt different, nothing had changed. My
personal experiences were irrelevant in the grand scheme of things, a
tiny blip on the radar: I was still on the outs with the Iron Fists, there
was no evidence that Maddock had done anything with my tip about
the North Crater Charity, and none of the gangs had made any major
moves that I could discern.

On Wednesday, Anna was back, all smiles after her date. I let her
prattle on about it but didn't engage. I was afraid if I opened my mouth,
my suspicions about Tam would come pouring out.

On Friday, I shared my shift with Brenda.

'We still have the dog,' she lamented during a lull.

'You'll never be rid of it.'

'Manny complains constantly, but I just don't have the heart to tell
the boys—The farm won't take it, it's too small—' She shook her head.
'The silly things we do in life, hey? Anyway, how have you been? You
seem tired.'

For reasons unknown to me, lying felt harder than it had last week.
'…Okay, I guess.'

'Okay, you guess?'

'Uh…' I pretended to be busy refilling my jug of water. 'Things have
been a little… stressful. And… I'm worried about Anna.'

'Anna? Why?'

I bit my lip. I'd mentioned it as a distraction from my own problems,
but truth be told, I was worried. 'You know she's got friendly with
someone?'

'Mm-hmm.' Brenda leant against the bar, watching me. 'One of
Sayle's boys, right?'

'Gabriel Tam.' My courage ran out. I couldn't tell Brenda my
suspicions. It wasn't right to involve her in anything dangerous, not

when she had two children to care for. I finished, somewhat underwhelmingly, 'It just worries me.'

'I'm sure Anna will be fine. She's fairly sensible when it comes to safety.'

'Yeah, but… the Iron Fists.'

We exchanged a glance. Brenda frowned. 'Well, I wouldn't. But what do I know? I got Manny.'

Manny was many things, in my opinion: an alcoholic, an arsehole. But he wasn't a murderer. Then again, Bas was a member of the Iron Fists, and he'd helped me. I swallowed, forcing down the anxiety that threatened to overwhelm me at that thought.

'Yeah.'

Brenda squinted at my face. 'What's going on?'

'I don't know. Have you noticed things are… tense around town?'

'Well…' Brenda surveyed the empty room through critical eyes. 'Did I tell you about my cousin?'

'No.'

'About two weeks ago, she was heading home from work—she's a cleaner in one of the Godfrey buildings, the one down on Broad Street. Anyway, she was walking down Kilter Passage—you know that little street where the tattoo shop is?'

Everyone knew the Kilter Street tattoo parlour. Three years ago, a few of Moriarty's men had raided the place, dragged the owner out, and shot him. Turned out, he'd been helping slaves escape north. For some reason, no one had touched the empty shop since then; it stood boarded up, like some kind of memorial.

'What happened?'

'There was a shootout. Three or four guys. She thought it was some kind of drug deal gone bad. She didn't stick around to find out—when the guns came out, she got the hell out of there.'

'That's terrifying.'

'Yeah.' Brenda looked grim. 'But they never used to trade in that area. It's always been safe 'round Broad Street and Main.'

I bit the inside of my cheek. Broad Street ran directly east-west, ending with the mayor's office, a glamorous, white-washed building surrounded by tall walls. It was one of the few areas in town where there was a reliable—if not honest—police presence. 'You know who they were?'

'Lila said Moriarty.'

Moriarty again. Those guys were getting all over town these days—and the Iron Fists didn't seem to be doing anything about it. Or maybe they couldn't anymore? Some people said Sayle had gotten too used to being in power. Maybe he'd gotten too comfortable, as well. Maybe he wasn't driving threats out anymore.

'That's not good.'

'I know.'

A group of men sauntered through the door, all of them in fatigues, and my heart seized up in my chest. Was it—? But no, no it wasn't. Not Ellery, not Bas. These men were younger, and more relaxed. They looked like new army recruits, on leave from the base halfway between Bale Rocks and Crater's Edge.

'They're a long way from home,' Brenda whispered.

'Yeah.' I grabbed my tray, an uneasy feeling in my chest. Things were changing; the power landscape in town was shifting, and I didn't like it at all. When things changed, people got hurt. People suffered.

The gangs would wage war, but it was the rest of us who would die.

Except… I might have a way to rise above that fate.

If I was brave enough to take Bas up on his offer.

I was being a coward, but the truth was that I felt guilty. It had been easy to hate Bas when he'd been just another enforcer for the Iron Fists. But he'd saved me and—so far—not asked for anything in return. That had humanised him in a way I hadn't wanted.

It was more than just the feeling that I owed him. Annoying and argumentative as he was, he'd actually been kind. That meant something. I couldn't, in good conscience, continue spying on him for Rodney. Not now.

The trouble was, I was betting Rodney wouldn't look kindly on me backing out—which only left me one option. I was going to have to tell Bas what I'd done.

It was not a pleasant thought.

Bas would be furious. I'd be annihilating what little goodwill he might have harboured towards me.

So I'd been delaying. I knew I had to tell him, but that didn't mean I wanted to.

I made it to Saturday. My next meeting with Rodney loomed ahead of me, and guilt kept me up half the night. In the morning, I dressed quietly and snuck out.

The streets were cold and damp. The weather was turning again; the wind had changed direction, bringing a chill from the northeast, and colouring the horizon red with crater dust.

It was going to be a long, cold winter this year. It always was when we had red skies in autumn.

On the training ground, I found myself looking around anxiously. Both Rodney and Hardwick knew that Bas came here in the mornings, and I didn't want either of them to see me with Bas. But although I checked everywhere I could think of, I didn't see any spies. I took cover under the overhang, waiting for Bas to arrive.

It didn't take long before he jogged up, as focused as usual. He was wearing long sleeves today, his only concession to the cool weather.

Bas drew up in surprise when I stepped out from under the overhang.

'Harley.'

'Hi,' I mumbled self-consciously.

Bas frowned. 'I didn't think you were going to come.'

'Yeah, I…' *Just tell him!* But the words froze on my tongue. 'I needed a few days.'

'Of course.' Bas contemplated a moment, then jerked his chin towards the cage. 'Climb in.'

He managed it in a single elegant leap; I scrambled over the railing and dropped heavily onto my heels. Bas watched my every move with judgemental eyes.

'Do you have any experience with self-defence?'

'Uh…' I shifted my weight uncomfortably. The moment to tell him the truth seemed to have passed, and I felt even worse for having missed it. 'Theo taught me a little.'

'Theo Dunne?'

'Yeah, him.' It surprised me that Bas knew Theo, because Theo had been out of town for at least three months now, and I'd only met Bas after he had left. But I wasn't sure how to ask, so I kept quiet.

'Fine,' Bas said. He hummed thoughtfully. 'Take your coat off. Have you warmed up?'

'I jogged over.'

His gaze was critical, but whatever he was thinking, he withheld it. 'I'm not going to teach you to fight immediately. You need to build your fitness and learn to run away first.'

'I know how to run away.'

His face said he didn't believe me. 'There's always room for improvement. Do you know how to do push-ups?'

I levelled a glare at him, before lowering myself to the hard, dirty concrete. Yuck. At least it was wet, which diminished the risk of creepy crawlies. I found a reasonably clean spot and set to work, slow and steady.

One… two… three…

'Fifteen,' he said abruptly.

'Fifteen push-ups?' I sat up, panting. Dance, as it turned out, had not prepared me at all for what Bas considered to be fitness training. 'I don't think I can do fifteen in a row.'

'That's how many bullets are in the magazine of my gun,' he corrected. 'If you're cornered, that's one of the most important things to remember.'

'Why?' I croaked, rubbing my palms. Push-ups on the gritty ground were quite painful on the hands.

'Because most of the gangs in this area are using either stolen military-issue handguns or rifles. If it's the former, they'll have fifteen shots to kill you before they have to reload. Hide, and then strike.' He met my gaze. 'Reloading is when they're the most vulnerable.'

'Some people carry two guns.'

'Also true. That's why you need to know your enemy.'

'I'm pretty sure most of my enemies don't carry guns. I'm more likely to run into trouble with homeless guys.'

Bas tilted his head, considering. 'I was thinking of Hannover. Homeless people will only have knives. Or broken glass.'

'And desperation,' I muttered. Desperation was a powerful weapon. The less you had, the harder you fought to keep it.

'Are you desperate, Harley?'

I nodded.

'Don't be.' Bas met my eyes. 'Desperation clouds your judgement.'

I scowled. 'Bit hard not to be desperate when you have a gun pointed at you.'

He inclined his head in what might have been a nod. 'That's why you have to learn to run away.'

For the next twenty minutes, Bas put me through my paces: squats and lunges, pull-ups and crunches. I was sweating within minutes. He stood over me, a look of patient disinterest on his face. I felt very small; the gap between us seemed to widen with every move I made. Bas made the same exercises look easy.

At length, he said, 'That's enough.'

I leant against the railing, wishing for a drink of water. 'What next?'

'Next you come back tomorrow.'

'What?'

Bas raised an eyebrow. 'You're exhausted. And you look like you haven't slept.'

I hadn't. Pouting, I said, 'What does that matter?'

'If you overwork yourself, you'll get injured.'

'You manage.'

He gave me a don't-be-stupid look. 'I train every day. Come back tomorrow, do the same thing.'

'But I need to know how to fight—' I started desperately. Fear clawed at my chest, that ever-present, all-encompassing feeling of helplessness.

'You do know how to fight.' Bas's gaze and voice softened. 'Harley, you know how to fight. You fought that guy off the other day. What you need is to be strong and fast.'

An odd emotion filled me then, one I'd not felt in years. It was something I'd experienced whenever my parents told me they were proud of me... something I thought I'd never manage to reclaim.

I swallowed hard, suddenly feeling like I might cry. That would be embarrassing.

'Uh... okay then.'

'Okay.' The way Bas caught my eye, I realised he knew what his praise meant to me. How awkward. 'I'll see you tomorrow.'

'Yeah,' I mumbled.

I felt sicker than ever that evening when I met Rodney. I had lied to Bas, and now I was going to lie to his brother. My principles lay shattered into a million shards at my feet, and the only person I had to blame was myself.

I twisted my fingers into the hem of my coat as I provided pro forma answers to Rodney's questions. Yes, I had seen Bas this week. Yes, it was true that he'd been there when someone was shot in the lobby of the Kranikovska. No, he hadn't been kicked out. He'd left on his own, and anyway, Tom almost never permanently banned people. Yes, I had been there. No, it had nothing to do with me or Bas. It was just ordinary gang violence.

It was a relief to escape the car again, money tucked into my coat. Rodney was getting more demanding by the week… and I hated myself more with every hour that went by.

I had to tell Bas.

But the words stuck on my tongue the next morning, and the next. Instead, Bas put me through a fitness routine designed—in my opinion—to make me too exhausted to think. I stumbled through Sunday, and after training on Monday morning I went straight home and back to bed. I couldn't keep this up, but I also couldn't let anything drop.

Voices woke me from a surprisingly deep sleep. I jerked up. The bedroom was dark—what time was it? My memories of the day came back slowly… I'd gone to take Irina my rent and pick up groceries, and then… fallen back into bed. Again.

Oops.

I stumbled out of bed, kicking over my boots, and grappled around for a jumper. It sounded like Savannah was home, with… someone. A man? Uneasily, I peeked out of the bedroom.

It. Was. Greg. Talbot.

He and Savannah were in the kitchen together, both turned to face each other. The space between them seemed awfully small.

I threw the bedroom door open so viciously that it hit the wall. Savannah jerked up.

'Harley!'

'What is he doing here?'

'Harley, don't,' she hissed.

'Get him out!'

'Oh, like you've never had people over!' Savannah was standing over the stove in the kitchen, Talbot leaning against the window. Bas had stood there just a few days ago, and… I wasn't going to think about that night.

'I tell you beforehand!'

'Do you?' Savannah scowled, stirring the pot on the stove with a little too much force.

'Of course!' Talbot was smirking at me, and I felt sick to my stomach.

'Like you've never had someone round here and not—You know what?' Savannah shook her head. 'I don't even know what your problem is. He's my friend.'

'He's—' But every argument I could think of sounded stupid. 'Never mind. I'm going back to bed.'

'It's seven PM.'

'So? I'm tired.'

I retreated to my room. The electricity was on, so I had light to do my mending by, at least. I could hear Savannah and Talbot's voices, though the door muffled their words so I couldn't make out what they were talking about. Did it matter? Did anything matter anymore? I felt like everything had slipped so far out of my control that it would take a miracle to claw it back.

About an hour later, Savannah knocked on the door and peeked her head around. 'I made dinner.' She seemed in a milder mood. I tossed my mending aside and followed her through to the main room. Talbot was absent, to my relief.

'I don't like random people coming into the flat,' I grumbled.

'He's not a random person.' Savannah scowled. 'He's my friend.'

'He's also a gang member.'

Her face darkened. 'You're friends with gang members.'

'I'm actually not. Besides—' I felt like I'd swallowed rocks, but I said it anyway. '—I don't let them in the flat.'

'He's my friend.' Savannah grabbed a plate, turning her back to me as she served herself. 'He's not going to hurt me, or you.'

Are you sure about that?

'Not in the flat, Sav. This flat has to be safe, or what do we have left?'

Savannah's hair had fallen forwards to cover her face, hiding her expression. 'What if we could have better?'

Ice filled my veins. I gripped the edge of the counter. 'The Aces can't give us that.'

'How do you know?'

'None of the gangs make anything better. You said it yourself to Maddock—James—that they just make violence and—'

'Just because the gangs do, doesn't mean Greg does. He's better than that.'

'You saw him at the Kranikovska!' I cried.

'He was provoked! That wasn't *his* fault.' Savannah glared at me.

My fingers were clenched so tight that the counter edge dug into my skin. 'Isn't that a bit hypocritical? You don't hear me assuring you that Ellery is going to change things for us.'

Savannah rolled her eyes. 'I don't see you avoiding him, either.'

'I don't speak to him that often,' I murmured. 'Actually, we barely speak at all anymore.'

'Uh-huh.' Savannah snorted.

'Sure, you never believe anything I say,' I snapped bitterly.

'Because you always lie!'

'That's not true!' My anger surged abruptly. 'I don't lie to you. And I definitely don't do anything that would put you in danger!'

'I haven't put you in danger!' Savannah screeched. 'Greg's not dangerous! He's my friend!'

'That's fucking rich coming from the person who spent the last two years criticising me for being *friends* with Ellery!'

'Ellery's a thug!' Savannah's eyes were wide, her face wild. She set her plate aside and turned to face me fully. 'Greg's different!'

'How do you know?'

'I just do!' she snarled.

I laughed.

'I DO! I know because I'm dating him, alright?'

My jaw dropped. I stared at her in shock—she honestly couldn't have surprised me more if she'd told me she was running away to join the circus. 'You're what?'

'I'm dating him.' Savannah stuck her chin in the air. 'I'm an adult woman. You don't get a say in my life choices.'

'Funny, because you've never held back from criticising *my* life choices.'

Savannah whipped around, snatching her plate. 'I should have known better than to expect you to support me.'

She stomped off to the bedroom, leaving me gaping after her.

What a fucking hypocrite.

Shaking my head, I helped myself to the food and ate it bite for bite, even though I wasn't the least bit hungry.

There was no sense in wasting food.

TWENTY-ONE

THE NEXT FEW DAYS WERE lonely but peaceful.

Bas turned out to be a harsh taskmaster: sparing with praise, free with criticism, and absolutely unbending in his demands. But I got fitter, even if he still hadn't let me try to punch him.

I still hadn't worked up the courage to tell him the truth. I told myself it was because I was afraid he'd quit giving me lessons. But the crux of the matter was that apart from work, he was my only social interaction at the moment. Savannah hadn't spoken to me since our argument, and my relationship with Anna had been strained since I'd criticised her relationship with Gabriel Tam.

I'd done an excellent job of pushing people away, that was for sure.

Before I knew it, another Saturday had rolled around, and with it, another meeting with Rodney. I sat in his car, shivering in the crisp, wintery air. My hands were pressed against one of the heating vents.

'You're really not trying,' Rodney grouched. He was frowning at my hands. I smoothed them against my thighs.

'We've been through this before. I'm doing my best.'

'You haven't actually done anything. You're supposed to be developing a relationship with Sebastian.'

'That was never the deal! The deal was information only.'

Rodney shook his head. 'You haven't given me anything I can work with. You won't even talk to him.'

I talk to him plenty, just not about anything I want to share with you.

I crossed my arms. 'What's next? Going to ask me to sleep with him and tell you what it's like?'

Rodney jerked back, a disgusted expression crossing his face. 'That's not—'

'Did you go to the training ground?' I snapped. 'That was useful information.'

'Yes, but he wasn't there.'

'Well, maybe you went at the wrong time?' Or Bas was smart

enough to have avoided him. He hadn't mentioned it, though.

'I followed your instructions.' Rodney raised an eyebrow. 'Maybe you gave me bad information.'

'I did not!' I said hotly. 'I've been totally honest with you!'

'I doubt it,' he sneered.

Fucking prick. 'Well, if you can't trust my information, maybe we should discontinue our arrangement.'

Rodney frowned. 'I thought you needed the money.'

'Not at the cost of my integrity.'

'What integrity? You're an informant, not a nun.'

Oh, ouch. His words sent a burn of humiliation through me. My worth, denigrated in one sentence. I was an informant.

I was a traitor.

I gnashed my teeth, trying to control myself. *Fuck this. Fuck him.* I grabbed the door handle.

'I think it's time for me to leave.'

'Without your money?' Rodney raised an eyebrow imperiously. I snapped.

'I don't need your money that badly.' The lie burnt my throat. With the way things were, I needed it sorely. But no way in hell would I let Rodney know that.

'I think you do.'

'You know nothing about me.' I was grasping the door so hard my knuckles had gone white. 'Don't ever think you know anything about who I am or what I need.'

I opened the door.

'I can make you regret this,' Rodney threatened.

'Going to turn me over to the slavers like you did your brother?' It was a wild guess, but Rodney went as white as a sheet.

'I—That's—I didn't—Did he tell you—'

'If you want to know, go ask him,' I sneered, slamming the door.

My temper lasted until I got home. I stood just inside my door, practically hyperventilating as I realised what I'd done. Oh, that was stupid, so stupid. Rodney might have been a prick, but he was paying for something that didn't involve sex. Without that… At least I had a bit saved up. Enough to pay rent for the next couple of months, assuming nothing went wrong.

But what then?

Fuck.

How could I do that? Why couldn't I control my temper better?

Okay, okay. There would be an answer. I paced to the bedroom, kicking my boots off on the way. I'd find a solution. I always did. There were other ways of making money in this town.

I'd be fine.

We'd be fine.

I slept badly that night. I wasn't at all prepared to face Bas the next morning, and the situation was made worse by the fact that he was in a foul mood when I arrived.

'You're late,' he snapped when I climbed into the cage.

'Sorry, I overslept.'

His gaze darkened. 'I can't hang out here waiting for you, you know. I do have things to do.'

Could have fooled me.

'Then why bother volunteering?' I snapped.

Bas stared at me, fury written across his face. After a moment, he turned away with a scowl. 'For fuck's sake. I'm trying to help you. Do you have to be so contrary all the time?'

'I'm not contrary—I just—' Words failed me. He was right—I fought everything he said. But I couldn't figure out how to stop.

'You just don't trust me,' Bas filled in.

'I do,' I insisted miserably. He'd helped me. He hadn't asked anything in return. Maybe we'd gotten off to a poor start—maybe Bas was the most antagonistic jerk on the planet—but if I ignored his dickish comments, he actually seemed to be almost… kind.

'No, you don't. You're holding back.' Bas turned back to me. 'Do you really still think I'm going to demand sex as payment for helping you out?'

His words startled me. The thought hadn't even crossed my mind for a few days, and I suddenly couldn't remember when I'd abandoned the notion.

'No, that's not it.'

'Then what?'

I stared at him, uncertainty warring within me. I had to tell him the truth. I didn't want to, but I had to.

'Your brother approached me a while back and offered to pay me for information about you,' I blurted out.

The words hung between us in the still air. Terror washed over me as I studied Bas, waiting for his reaction.

A range of emotions cascaded over his face, before they all vanished, locked down behind a blank façade. 'I see.'

'I said yes.'

'I know,' he said flatly.

'You… know?' I parroted, confused.

'It makes sense. I've seen where you live. You can't make that much as a waitress. Money must be tight. You wouldn't be the first person Rodney's tried to get information out of.'

The logical, unemotional assessment hurt me more than angry words would have. Everything he said was so true, and yet none of it made me feel better.

'I've stopped.' I shuffled my weight. Should I leave? 'I did do it for a while, but I told him last night that I wouldn't anymore, and, well, I thought I should come clean to you, because…' *You've been nice.*

'Don't you still need the money?'

I squirmed under Bas's cold gaze. Shrugging, I mustered a light tone. 'I can find other ways of getting it.'

'Right.'

'So… I'll understand if you don't want to train me anymore.' His face was so blank, I couldn't tell if he was angry. His body wasn't tense at all… but there was no way he wasn't.

'Why wouldn't I?'

'Uh…' Was he for real? 'Because I betrayed you? I mean, it's been ages, and I didn't really tell him much, but…' *Shut up, Harley.* 'But I'd understand, anyway.'

Bas's eyes bored into mine. 'I don't make promises lightly. I said I'd train you, so if you still want me to, then I will.'

'Oh.' His expression was unreadable, but a muscle ticked in his jaw from the strain of holding his reaction back. Yep, he was furious.

I should have said no and walked away. A clean break between us. I had cleared the air, and that should have been it. But if recent events had taught me anything, it was that my meagre self-defence skills were not enough, and I couldn't afford to wait. I knew it was selfish, but I would have to force my presence on him until I found someone else to teach me.

My stomach roiled with guilt. 'Alright. Please teach me.'

Bas nodded. 'You can start your warmup, then.'

I had to admire his ability to compartmentalise. You wouldn't have thought that I'd just told him something so awful, not the way he behaved. He maintained the same cool, brisk demeanour that he'd always had.

And yet… I could feel the difference.

There was less feeling in his praise, less care when he asked how I was feeling. Whatever little trust had been developing between Bas and me, I'd shattered it. I had ruined the last good thing left in my life.

What a star.

All that was left was work, and I spent the rest of the day in a state of hyper-alertness, afraid that I'd fight with someone, or make some other stupid mistake. Today would be the day I'd get fired, wouldn't it?

Still, I made it through half of my shift with no drama. Kayla appeared at six-thirty, dressed in biker denims, with her braids twisted together down her back. She popped her helmet behind the bar.

'What are you doing here?' I asked, passing her an apron.

Kayla nodded to Anna. 'Missy there is going on a date.'

I caught Anna's eye. She went pink. 'Gabe's taking me out.'

'Tam, again?' I groaned. '*Anna.*'

'Don't be like that! I think he's really serious!'

'Men like that only want one thing.' I glanced at Kayla for support, but she just shrugged.

'People can change,' she said. 'Maybe he really does like Anna.'

'Maybe,' I muttered sourly. *Didn't stop him from chasing one of her friends through the streets, did it?*

Anna rolled her eyes. 'Harley doesn't believe in romance.'

I gnashed my teeth.

'Can't wait for the day some guy blows you off your feet.' Kayla laughed.

'I'm taking my break,' I muttered, scowling at both of them.

'I'll walk you out,' Anna said cheerfully, tossing her apron under the counter.

That didn't suit my desire to be alone at all, but I nodded grudgingly. We traipsed out into the back hallway and doubled around towards the staff stairs at the back of the lobby.

'You know, if you got to know Gabe, you'd see he's really sweet,' Anna said.

I scuffed my feet against the ground. 'I'm sure he is.'

'Not all the men in this town are gorillas waving guns about.'

I snorted. 'I'd rather they were; gorillas probably wouldn't be able to figure out where to shoot.'

Anna shot me a look. We paused just inside the hallway. 'Come on, Harley. What's nagging at you? You've been moody for ages.'

Everything. 'Nothing.'

Anna raised both eyebrows. 'Not sure I believe that.'

I huffed. 'Fine, look—Tam. I've just seen him around town, doing some shady stuff. Talking to people he shouldn't. So… just be careful, okay?'

Anna frowned. 'People he shouldn't?'

'Evander Hardwick, for one.'

At that, her face compressed into one of disbelief. 'Doesn't Hardwick work for the mayor? He's hardly what I'd call dangerous.'

'Does he? Are you sure about that?' I crossed my arms, leaning against the wall. 'The point is—how much does Tam actually tell you about what he's involved in?'

'Nothing. I don't want to hear about that violent stuff.'

'But then, how can you know he's not involved in anything dangerous? I don't want you getting roped into something and getting killed!' My voice had shot up at the end. I took several deep breaths.

'I trust him, Harley. He doesn't need to tell me every little thing he does.'

'How can you trust him if he doesn't tell you?'

Anna shook her head angrily. 'That's the trouble with you, Harley. You don't trust anyone.'

Her words were like a knife between my ribs. 'I trust you!'

'But do you tell me anything?' Her gaze was hot. 'How are you any different than Tam, then?'

Ouch. 'I'm not doing anything that could get you killed.'

'Neither is he!'

We stood staring at one another, both of us panting as though we'd exerted ourselves physically. I was beyond furious, hurt jabbing into me like thousands of little needles. Before I could think to retaliate, a head popped around the wall, followed by a person, dressed in black casual clothes.

'Evening, ladies,' Tam said with a smooth smile. He took in our aggressive stances, and the smile slipped. 'Everything alright here?'

I jerked in shock. *Fuck, did he hear?*

'Yes,' Anna said primly. She wrapped her hand around his elbow. 'Let's get out of here.'

Over her shoulder, she shot me a dirty look. I stayed where I was, arms crossed, hip leant against the wall, glaring after them until they were out of sight. Then I sagged.

Fuck.

I didn't want to fight with Anna, but sometimes it seemed like fighting with people was all I was good at.

I made a concerted effort to keep my mouth shut for the rest of my shift. At least with Kayla that wasn't too hard. She wasn't nearly as talkative as Anna—though she did shoot me amused glances every so often, so I knew she'd picked up that I was being deliberately reticent.

I halfway anticipated that Bas wouldn't show up the next morning, but there he was, waiting for me as usual, and he oversaw my training with the same surly silence he'd subjected me to the previous day. By the end of the session, I felt like my stomach had knotted itself so badly I'd never get it loose. After training, I jogged back, my mind already on my shower, and then bed. Sleep seemed like a welcome escape right now.

I drew up short at my front door. Benny was leaning against the wall, one leg kicked up against the brickwork, smoking.

'Harley.'

'Benny.' I frowned. The only reason he'd be here was if something had happened at the Kranikovska. 'What's up?'

'Tom wants to know if you can work today.'

It was on the tip of my tongue to say no. I was exhausted. I didn't want to work an eight-hour shift today. Even if I did need the money.

'Why?' I asked cautiously.

'He didn't say.' Benny shrugged, dropping his cigarette and scuffing it out with his boot. 'You in? He said he'd pay twenty percent extra on top of your wage. And I really can't be arsed to go over to Kayla's.'

I sighed. 'Fine.'

Benny grinned, his teeth white against his brown face. 'Excellent. See you at twelve.'

'Yeah,' I mumbled, already calculating if I could get a nap in before then. Prognosis: probably not.

When I rolled up into the bar at midday, Tom was wiping down the counter. The room was silent: no music, no people. Just Tom, looking as exhausted as I felt.

I frowned, approaching slowly.

'Thanks for coming in,' he said.

'Sure.' I paused, looking around. 'No Anna?'

'No.' Tom's brow was creased with worry. 'I've called Brenda in for the evening shift. Anna didn't come home last night.'

Unease crawled in my belly. I gripped the counter to steady myself. 'You haven't seen her?'

'No. She left straight from work yesterday; I haven't seen her since about midway through her shift.' He squinted at me. 'You were on with her, right?'

'Yeah.' I thought of our argument and felt suddenly breathless.

'She wasn't behaving oddly?'

I shook my head. 'She went off with Gabriel Tam. On a date.'

Tom's face contorted oddly. 'I know.' He sighed. 'Dana should be here shortly. Can you two hold down the fort while I go look for Anna? I'm sure she just stayed over with her beau, but...'

But people going missing was never a good thing in this town.

'Of course,' I promised. 'If there's anything else I can do...'

'I'll ask.' Tom nodded firmly. 'You're a good kid, Harley. Thanks for your help. You can take tomorrow off, okay?'

'Okay. Thanks.'

He headed out. I settled behind the bar, my stomach squirming like it was filled with worms. Anna. Missing. Anna missing. I couldn't quite get the words to fit together in my head. Anna couldn't be missing, because Anna was my friend, and she was sweet, and no one should want to hurt her.

And I had a sinking feeling that I'd been right.

Tam was fucking bad news.

Was there anything I could do? Could I get a note to Ellery? It stung my pride, but... Anna was worth it. Would Ellery help Anna? Most of our regulars had a soft spot for her—I didn't know if that would be enough, but I had to hope.

I nodded to myself.

I could suck up my pride for my friend.

Dana swung behind the bar. 'Wasn't expecting you. What are you doing here?'

'Anna's missing.'

'Oh, woah.' Her eyes went wide. 'Missing? How? When?'

'Since last night. She went on a date.' As I spoke, I began untying my apron. 'Listen, Dana, I need a huge favour. I might know someone who can help, but I need to go now.'

'Go? But you're on shift.'

'Right, 'cause it's heaving in here.'

Dana looked around the room and snorted. 'How long will you be gone?'

'Half an hour, max.' I grabbed an old order form and a pen, scribbling my note. I didn't have time to go all the way across town, not now, so I'd try the drop. If there was no word from Ellery by the end of my shift, I would go to Sayle's compound.

'Fine, but be quick.' Dana took her apron. 'And if Tom asks, I'm not lying for you.'

'Tell him I'm trying to help.'

I practically sprinted through town to the drop point. My thoughts seemed to sound in time with my footsteps. *Must-help-Anna. Please-let-her-be-alright.* Over and over again, like a drumbeat. Finally, I reached the little backstreet. I bent over, panting for breath. Too fast.

Once I'd recovered, I moved to the defunct post box, crouched down, and slotted my knife into the latch. It turned obediently, the door swinging out.

Inside was a note.

HB

If you want to see your friend again, come to the bottling plant tonight, 1AM, alone.

My heart sank.

Oh, fuck.

TWENTY-TWO

THE BOTTLING PLANT WAS A dark shape against the moonlit sky, like some hulking beast waiting to swallow me up. As quietly as I was trying to walk, my footsteps still sounded impossibly loud as I passed the abandoned guard post and entered the forecourt.

This had been part of Sayle's empire, one of the entry points to the tunnels that ran under the north side of town, but after Moriarty had blown one of the buildings sky-high a year ago, they had abandoned it. Still, I thought there ought to be at least one guard here. Sayle wouldn't leave a potential entryway unguarded, would he?

Some creature skittered across the floor, and I jumped. Shit, this place was a nightmare made real.

No, I couldn't go down that path. *Think, Harley, think.* Where would Anna be? How could I get her out of here safely?

This was my fault, I didn't doubt it. This was because I had overheard Tam's conversation with Hardwick. He was trying up loose ends. So it was on me to make sure that Anna survived.

I reached the entrance. My feet slowed without my permission. The doors had long since broken off their hinges, leaving a darkened doorway like a gaping maw.

I swallowed. *Get on with it.*

The moment my boot hit the floor inside, the lights flared. I froze in shock, blinking spots out of my eyes. *Shit.*

'Hello, Harley.'

I was looking into the barrel of a gun. My mind went blank.

'I wasn't sure you would come,' Tam said. He jerked his head towards a flight of stairs. When I didn't move, he did it again, more insistently, and I realised I was supposed to climb it. I did so with wooden movements, more like a puppet than a human being.

'Where's Anna?' My voice sounded entirely foreign to my ears.

'At home by now, I'd warrant.'

'Wh—what?'

'She was never part of the plan; only you.' Tam followed me up the stairs, his boots clanging against the metal. 'I was hoping you would care enough to come after her—you're a little difficult to get a read on, honestly. I thought you cared about Marco Ellery, but you haven't spoken to him in weeks. Then there's your sister, but I couldn't get close to her. She spends too much time with Gregory Talbot.'

You're telling me.

I reached the top of the stairs and shuffled out of his way. Tam climbed up beside me and gestured down the catwalk with his gun. I moved along until I reached a section where the metal railing had broken.

'Stop here.'

I stopped and turned to face him. My palms were clammy, and I wiped them on my jeans. Beside us was nothing but a twenty-foot drop. Did he mean for me to jump?

'I never told anyone.'

'But you could.' The worst part was that Tam was smiling. He looked friendly and kind, the man who came into the bar occasionally and was always so nice to the staff. Not a criminal. Not a murderer.

How could he be doing this?

'I am sorry,' he said. 'I like you, Harley. I really do. You're a smart girl. But I can't just let you compromise my operation.'

'I—I'm a woman,' I croaked. The words surprised me. I wouldn't have been brave enough to say them under any other circumstances, but… I was about to die.

'Pardon?'

'I'm not a girl. I'm a woman.'

Tam smiled. 'Of course, forgive me. You're a smart woman. Too smart, in fact, for your own good. I wish you hadn't seen anything… but it's too late for wishes, now.'

'Why now?'

'I beg your pardon?' His gun was perfectly steady, aimed at my face.

'Why wait this long?' I was growing in confidence the more I spoke. 'I could have told any number of people by now.'

'I wasn't sure it was you, in the beginning.' He tilted his head, his expression turning thoughtful. 'Then you overplayed your hand—first with Ellery, and then with Anna. A shame, really. People listen to you far more than is healthy.'

I swallowed. It sure didn't feel like anyone listened to me. Did that mean Ellery had looked into it? Or had Anna mentioned something?

'Surely there are other ways to silence me.' My voice was shaky and pleading. 'I could be useful to you. I could help you.'

'The same way you've been playing the Rochester brothers off against one another? I think not.'

He knew about that? How?

Tam read the question off my face. 'Yes, Harley. I know all about your sordid little affair with the Rochester brothers. I've been watching you very closely. How clever to get what you need from each of them... but then you went and ruined it. That's what I don't understand. Why not keep playing both of them? You had what you wanted.'

'I had what I needed.'

'I don't see the distinction.'

'No, you wouldn't.' If he could have seen the difference, he wouldn't be about to kill me. 'Please, just let me go.'

Useless, but I had to try.

'No.' Tam inched closer. 'I must say, you did me quite the favour. I don't know how you managed to break faith with Ellery, but you couldn't have timed it better.'

I took a step back. My foot hit something, metal skittering against metal. I looked down. A hammer.

'What's that got to do with anything?'

'Oh, nothing. I just didn't want him coming running to the rescue when I eliminated his girlfriend. It would have been awkward— keeping my cover.' He smiled. It was a completely incongruous expression. How dare he advance on me with a smile on his face? Did I mean so little?

Yes, that was it.

I meant so little to this world that my death would be fleeting; a tiny effort, a few tears shed by family and friends, and then... forgotten.

I wasn't going down that way. I refused. Harley Benoit would not be pushed aside that easily.

'You assume I need Ellery to save me.'

'Oh, there's no chance of you saving yourself. You're just a girl and you are in *very* far over your head.'

It was my fate to be dismissed by men who thought they were better than me. But they forgot one important thing: I was used to being the underdog. And I would fight to the bitter end.

I took another step, my boot hitting the hammer again. It clanged against one of the support posts on the railing, then fell between the gaps to the ground below, landing with an almighty thud. Tam and I both jumped.

'What are you going to tell Ellery?' I kept moving backwards, grasping the railing for support, even as rust flakes scratched my fingers. 'When I'm gone?'

'Why tell him anything? There's no way he'll link it to me.' Tam advanced, unhurriedly, as though he had all the time in the world. 'You should have told him everything when you had the chance.'

I had told him everything. He just hadn't believed me. Would he care? If I disappeared, would he wonder if that one awful fight had something to do with it? Would he look into what I'd said?

It would be too late.

'It doesn't matter. I don't care about him.' My hand found the end of the railing. Empty air. The stairs at the other end of the catwalk.

'That's a shame, because he cared about you.' Tam's smile looked overstretched. 'You could have made something together. A nice life. Isn't that what all you girls want? A strong man to care for you, a nice home to come back to?'

'What an antiquated notion,' I sneered. 'Who says I can't look after myself?'

'You don't seem to have done too well so far.' Tam raised his gun a little.

'That's what you think.' I dived for the stairs. The gun went off, the bullet missing high, the noise impossibly loud as it echoed off the cavernous walls and abandoned machinery. My boots thudded as I leapt down the stairs; two-thirds of the way down, I jumped over the railing. The gun fired behind me again. I hit the ground and rolled out. *Thank you, twelve years of dance classes.* My gaze zeroed in on the hammer, my mind running back to what Bas had told me.

They'll have fifteen shots to kill you before they have to reload. Reloading is when they're the most vulnerable.

Fifteen, and two shots already fired. I had to avoid thirteen more.

Or I had to get the gun away from him.

The hammer lay on the ground a few feet away. It would do as a weapon in a pinch. I snatched it up and plunged between the machinery, trying to find something solid to hide behind.

Where was the exit?

But even as I thought it, I discarded that idea. The bottling plant was surrounded by several hundred feet of empty land—no cover. Tam would pick me off easily.

No, I had to hide here.

'Come out, Harley. You can't hide forever.'

There was another way out.

The tunnels that crisscrossed everywhere under the north side of town. If I could get through the evacuation hatch… I knew the tunnels pretty well. I might be able to lose Tam, or even run into someone friendly.

Something clattered, far too close to me. I froze. Was that Tam? He spoke again.

'Harley… don't make this harder than it has to be.'

What the fuck did he think I was going to do? Walk up to him and let him kill me?

I shuffled sideways, trying to get a vantage of the doorway. The manhole covering the tunnels was in the next hall. Would it be accessible? Only one way to find out—I had to get there.

My gaze fell on one of the pieces of rubble littering the floor. I scooped it up and hurled it in the opposite direction. Then I darted from my hiding place across three yards of exposed space and leapt behind the skeleton of an old conveyor belt.

BANG!

Every shot of the gun sounded like a detonation. My ears rang, my heart beating so furiously I thought it might burst right out of my chest.

'That was foolish.'

He'd seen—and now he was coming towards me. *Fuck.*

I lunged behind another machine, and then I was beside the wall and a door.

I yanked it open and hurtled through.

Suddenly, I was in the bowels of the plant. A narrow corridor stretched in either direction, lined with doors to old offices and storerooms. My footsteps pounded against the floor as I ran, trying to figure out where I was on the fly. The opposite side to the main entrance, but I might find a side exit. And if I took a right here—*BANG!*

Pain exploded in my left arm. I launched myself around the corner, gasping, and through another door. The second hall. The manhole…

…had been covered with concrete.

There hadn't been a guard on the front gate.

Suddenly, I understood. This access route to the tunnels had been permanently sealed off. There was no way in.

BANG!

I tripped, my ankle giving out beneath me. Crawling, I hauled myself behind another piece of machinery. I was trapped. How many times had he fired? Four? Five? I couldn't remember. I'd lost count already, and suddenly all I could think of was Bas. What he'd say—how I'd failed at staying calm. I'd forgotten everything he was trying to teach me.

Would he miss me?

Would he care if I didn't pitch up to training tomorrow?

A few tears escaped my eyes.

No, he wouldn't. And that was on me—I was the one who'd betrayed his trust.

I was an idiot, and now I was paying for it. Alone.

Boots crunched on the rubble. I scrambled to my feet, wincing as I put my weight on my ankle. *Ouch.*

But I had no time to lose. I sprinted for the next hulking machine. My only chance was to keep running—*BANG!*

The next bullet whistled by so close that my hair rustled in the breeze. I stumbled against a metal wall, my left arm throbbing as it slammed into the uneven surface. *Shit!*

'You can't run forever, Harley.' I couldn't tell where Tam was, but he sounded close. His voice echoed strangely in the huge hall. 'Is this really the way you want things to go?'

You're going to kill me anyway.

I slid along the wall, trying to breathe as silently as possible, and peered around it. There he was, about five yards away. I plotted a route between me and him.

Had I gone crazy?

He was right. This wasn't how I wanted things to go. I didn't want to leave things bad between me and Bas, or me and Ellery. I didn't want to leave Savannah alone. I wanted better.

A sense of calm filled me. Resolved, I crouched down and took my boots off.

On bare feet, I could move silently. It was one of the first things you learnt as a dancer: how to be light on your feet. Graceful. Delicate. Maybe I would never be a fighter like Bas, but I'd bet he couldn't move as quietly as I could. I slipped soundlessly through the shadows to a tall machine that seemed to have broken in half and crouched so I could use the broken arm as cover to get behind another conveyor belt. Then I went down on my stomach and crawled beneath the metal supports. My abs and arms strained, but I forced myself to take it slow.

Something scraped above me. I froze, my arms shaking with the effort of keeping myself inches off the ground. I couldn't see Tam, so I had to listen for his footsteps. He didn't seem to be moving.

Sighing softly, I continued on my way. I hauled myself out from under the conveyor and took shelter behind some kind of small vehicle with two prongs that extended from the front to lift things. The cab stood open, the steering wheel rusted off. I edged around it and found myself level with Tam.

I counted to ten in my head. He was aiming his gun where he thought I was, waiting for my next move.

I redoubled my grip around the hammer and lunged.

Tam swung around—*BANG!*

The next bullet ricocheted off the wall, and I slammed the hammer against his kneecap.

Tam dropped the gun, howling in pain.

'YOU BITCH!'

I went for his other kneecap. He grabbed at my neck, and I struck the soft side of his calf. Damnit. His injured knee drove into my stomach as he collapsed on top of me. I wheezed as he groaned in pain.

'That was really unnecessary.'

'I *don't want* to die.'

'But you will.' I could see it in his eyes: he was deadly serious. Maybe he'd hesitated in the beginning. Maybe if I'd been smarter, I could have talked him out of it. But now that chance was gone. He was going to kill me.

I swung the hammer wildly at his head.

His hands closed around my neck, squeezing hard. Panicking, I dropped the hammer and snatched at his hands, scratching them with blunt nails as I tried to pull them away. I couldn't breathe! He felt impossibly heavy over me, and the world was fading in and out like a bad signal on the radio.

No!

I let one of my hands drop to my side, where my trusty knife was tucked into my coat. Tam's hands tightened on my neck. Black spots were growing on the edges of my vision, and my lungs screamed for air.

I reached for my last vestiges of strength. This *had* to work.

I jerked my arm up and slashed him in the face.

Tam fell back—*BANG!*

The gun went off, deafening me, but I wasn't wasting a second.

But could you have killed him? Bas had asked me when he'd saved me from being raped.

Here was the answer.

I drove my knife into Gabriel Tam's neck.

His eyes went wide. The gun dropped to the floor as he lifted his hand to his neck. I stared at him, my heart racing. My hand was slick and wet and warm with blood, and suddenly he felt like a block of lead on top of me.

He fell sideways, dislodging the knife. More blood welled up, more and more and more. I pulled the knife out, hugging it to my chest, watching powerlessly as he sagged sideways and just...

Died.

He was dead.

I'd killed him.

Oh fuck, I'd killed him.

I'd killed a man.

I'd killed a member of the Iron Fists.

Fuck, fuck, fuck.

I turned sideways and puked. Tears were streaming down my face, and my stomach heaved over and over again. I was out of control. I scrambled backwards, hauling my legs out from under Tam's body.

His dead body.

I had to get out of here.

No, wait. I had to hide the evidence. Or they would know it was me and come after me. They wouldn't care that it was self-defence. Or would they? Would they even know it was me? People died all the time. I hadn't told anyone I was coming here... and he wouldn't have told anyone, right? Or they might link him to my disappearance. So... no one knew.

Leave. I had to leave. If they linked Tam's death to me, Sayle would put a bullet in my head. You didn't survive crossing the Iron Fists.

I forced myself up.

The ground was cold under my feet. *Right, my boots.* I hurried over to where I'd left them, shoving my feet in without doing the laces up. Then I headed for the door.

I had to get out of here.

Outside was dark. The moon seemed to have vanished. The air was cold against my hot cheeks. My breathing and footsteps sounded impossibly loud as I sprinted across the forecourt. I reached the gate and skidded to a halt. There was a car waiting on the road, headlights off, just a glint of moonlight against black metal. The headlights flicked on, and the door popped open.

I backed away slowly as a tall man climbed out, but he approached me with confident footsteps. Could I run? Where would I go? Not inside—I'd only trap myself.

'Well, aren't you a sight for sore eyes?'

I drew to a halt, my throat closing up with fear. It was Hardwick.

'What… what are you doing here?' I gasped.

Hardwick smiled. 'Cleaning up the mess, one way or another. I take it Tam is dead.'

'How do you know…' *Cleaning up the mess. Cleaning up my body. Oh my God.*

I stepped back.

Hardwick laughed.

'None of that, now, Miss Benoit. I did say cleaning it up one way or another. I don't care which of you lives or dies… but I suspect you're going to care very soon.'

'Wh—why?'

'Because now my spy is dead. And unless you want me to tell Sayle what you did… I'm going to expect you to take his place.'

TWENTY-THREE

THE LUCKY 2089 WAS ONE of a series of casinos in Bale Rocks, the majority of which were located in the northwest of town. It wasn't an area I ever went to; you followed Hustler Highway straight to the end, where it eventually became Casino Way. The road continued out of town, linking to the two main roads that headed north into the wasteland, or west to Boughton—though that road was considered impassable these days. I'd rarely had a reason to get out there before— why would I? It was Percival's territory.

I had the taxi-truck drop me at Crimson House, one of Irina's brothels. Better that no one knew where I was really going. With my scarf and hood drawn up to hide my face, I walked the last half mile to Casino Way.

The dilapidated glory of the street was visible from a fair distance: large, brightly painted signs, advertising the casinos, strippers, and deals. Strings of lights covered pretty much everything, though today they weren't working. I moved through puddles of light from the streetlamps, passing the few police officers who usually hung around here looking for drunk idiots to fine.

I crossed the parking lot to the ornate four-storey building that housed the Lucky 2089, but when I tried to walk around the side, a man stepped out of the shadows to block my path.

'The visitor's entrance is round the front.'

I looked him up and down slowly: shaven head, pierced nose, grimly-set mouth. He was built like a bull and looked like he could throw me halfway across the parking lot without batting an eyelash.

Not a man to make trouble with.

I lowered my hood.

'Evander Hardwick is expecting me.'

'Name?'

'Harley Benoit.'

He unclipped a radio from his belt, hitting the call button.

'Hardwick in? He has a guest.' I got an appraising look. 'Pretty little lass.'

The radio crackled. 'Send her in.'

The bull nodded, clipping the radio back onto his belt. 'Straight ahead, second door. Someone will let you in.'

'Thank you.'

My footsteps sounded loud in the quiet night. The sky threatened rain again; the clouds hadn't burst yet, but it seemed to be enough to keep the majority of people in for the night. I was alone.

I knocked on the second door. It slid open, casting a sliver of light over the rubbish-strewn ground. A rat scampered away.

'Harley Benoit?' The man who held the door was younger than I was, a wide-eyed kid. Probably a new recruit; he certainly looked fresh-faced. Had he ever killed a man? I doubted it.

'That's me.'

'Come in.'

He led me down a corridor, through a door, and up a flight of stairs. Where downstairs had only had functional décor and whitewashed walls, upstairs was a study in luxury. We passed several doors, each with a brass name plaque on it.

Manager

Chief of Operations

Owner

Head of Security

That was where we stopped. The boy gestured for me to knock, before vanishing back down the hall. I sucked up my courage and rapped my knuckles against the door.

'Enter.'

I nudged it open, finding an office beyond. The curtains were drawn, an exposed lightbulb casting yellow light over a heavy wooden desk. Hardwick leant against the desk, and a second man sat on a sofa under the window. He was a short, muscular figure, with a thatch of brown hair and cold eyes behind round-rimmed glasses. He wore a suit and watched me with interested eyes.

'Harley.' Hardwick smiled, though there was no warmth in the expression. 'This is Percival.'

Ice flooded my veins.

I had seen Sayle a few times, from across the room. He would often make an appearance at the bunker, but he'd never had time for any of the dancers. To have a private audience with Percival? One of the three men who ran this town?

I was shaking in my boots.

I cleared my throat, aiming for a disaffected tone. 'Sir.'

'Harley Benoit, I take it.' He gestured me in. 'Shut the door. Please.'

I complied, using the moment to collect myself. His gaze seemed to burn right into me, as though he could see through my clothes, my skin. Despite the cold temperature, I suddenly felt sweaty.

'Have a seat.' Hardwick gestured to a wooden chair. 'We'll get right down to business, shall we?' He cast a glance at Percival, before looking back to me. 'As we are all aware, we have recently suffered the unfortunate loss of Gabriel Tam, who had been informing us of the Iron Fists' activities. Seeing as Harley was responsible for his fate, I propose a simple switch. Harley can replace Tam as our spy.'

It was hardly my fault, considering that Tam had tried to empty his gun into my head. I bit my tongue against a retort.

Percival looked me up and down. 'She doesn't look like much of a spy.'

'Ah,' Hardwick said with a smirk, 'but you see, that's where you're wrong. Harley is quite close to several members of the Iron Fists. And I think you'll find her... quite motivated, indeed.'

'Is that so?' Percival raised one bushy eyebrow.

They weren't up-to-date on their information. I wasn't close to the Iron Fists anymore. But my survival depended on them believing that I was, so I was hardly going to disabuse them of the notion.

'I'm a waitress at the Kranikovska. I've been using the position to pass information to Marco Ellery.' My voice broke on Ellery's name. I coughed to cover it.

'She also used to be a dancer in the bunker,' Hardwick added.

Percival reappraised me, his lips pursed. 'Now that, I can use.'

Uh-oh.

'Sir?' I asked nervously.

Percival smiled. 'I often say women can go where men cannot, don't you agree, Harley? Backstage at strip clubs... on laps during private conversations... into men's hearts. You have access to all their most vulnerable places.'

'I—I guess.' I didn't like what he was getting at.

'Oh, you'll be doing more than guessing. That's where you'll be going for me. On their laps, in their beds.' He nodded to Hardwick. 'Yes, I think this will work excellently.'

Hardwick smiled.

'I'm not a whore!'

'So principled,' Percival said dismissively. 'No, you're a spy. And that means you'll be... and *do* exactly what I tell you to.'

'But—' My throat closed up. I watched in disbelief as he stood, murmured something to Hardwick, and left. The door shut behind him with an ominously final-sounding click.

I turned to Hardwick. 'You can't do that. I promised you information, not my body!'

'And how else do you imagine you'll get the information?' Hardwick leant back, clasping his hands in front of his stomach. 'You aren't exactly swimming in usable skills, are you?'

I gaped at him in fury. For a second, I contemplated pulling my knife and stabbing him. Kill him, run, catch the first taxi-truck I saw up to Sayle's compound... and tell Ellery everything. If I came clean, maybe he'd believe me. Then reality set in again. For sure, Hardwick had anticipated that possibility and planned for it. He probably had a messenger poised to go running straight to Sayle—or worse. I could think of any number of ways they might silence me. Hardwick was friends with Hannover and the Black Hands, too.

No, I was trapped.

I glared at him. 'I won't whore myself out for you. I'd sooner stab myself.'

Hardwick smiled. 'Well, there is always the alternative.'

'Alternative?' That sounded even worse.

'I'm quite close to your sister. If you aren't amenable, I dare say she will be.'

Stark, cold terror suffused my body. Not Savannah. I'd sacrifice anyone else, but not my sister. 'No! No, I'll do it. Just... stay away from my sister.'

'I thought you'd see it my way.'

He held out his hand, and I shook it, feeling sick to my stomach. This was it. I had damned myself. I was once again bound to one of the gangs—not through debt, but through blackmail. Through my own stupid mistakes.

And there was nothing I could do about it.

It started raining on my way back, but I was beyond caring. I trudged through the rain and arrived home to my blessedly empty flat. I had no idea where Savannah was.

But I was glad she wasn't here to see me.

Leaving my damp coat and boats by the door, I entered my bedroom and knelt by the bed. I shoved my bed covers back and fished under the bed until my fingers found the box I'd tucked there years ago. Out of sight, out of mind… or something like that.

For the first time in almost two years, I slid it out. The top was taped down; I slit the tape with my knife and lifted the flaps. A haphazard tangle of leather and lace looked out at me, a collection of outfits that I'd begged, bought, inherited, or even just made myself from scraps. The clothes I'd danced in.

I rested my head against the edge of the bed, wrestling with the choice I was about to make.

But there wasn't a choice, not really.

Me or Savannah.

Savannah or me.

It always had to be me. I couldn't let Savannah's dream wither and die.

Swallowing hard, I pushed the box back where I'd found it and stood.

Half an hour later, I was standing in front of the gates of Sayle's compound. I'd taken a taxi-truck, but the driver had insisted on dropping me two streets short of the no-drive zone. I was wet through after walking the last two blocks. I walked up to the guardhouse and waited.

Someone hopped down, their boots thudding against the ground, and rounded the gate post.

'Miss Harley?'

It was Kade.

'Hi, Kade.' I shuffled my weight. 'Is Ellery here? I need to speak to him.'

'Sure.' Kade shoved the gate a touch open, enough for me to squeeze through. 'You're soaked! Stand under the overhang whilst I radio someone to fetch him. Did you walk all the way?'

I shook my head, tucking myself against the side of the guardhouse.

'The taxi-truck driver wouldn't get any closer. I had to walk the last bit. He still charged me the full price, though.'

Kade grimaced. 'Yeah, we get that all the time. Here.' He shrugged his jacket off, wrapping it over my shoulders, and ducked back into the guardhouse. I heard him speaking. '...Kade here. Can someone send Ellery to the gate? ...Thanks. Over.'

He stepped out again. 'You want to climb up here? You look freezing.'

'It's okay. I'll get water everywhere.'

'Come on.' Kade offered me a hand, a kindness I didn't deserve right now. I let him pull me up into the cramped hut, and he passed me a thermos. 'It's a bit cold now, but help yourself.'

'How'd you get gate duty?' I asked, trying to find a spot that was safe to drip.

'Donnell is sick. I said I'd take his shift.'

'That was nice.'

Kade shrugged, looking a little sheepish. 'We all have to do it. The quicker I get it done, the longer I get to wait before my turn comes around again.'

'Sound logic.' I poured myself a bit of chicory coffee and took a careful sip. Lukewarm—but still warmer than I was. 'Thanks for this.'

'No prob. Ellery will be here in a minute.' Kade squinted at me, his dark brow creasing in concern. 'Are you alright?'

I turned my head away slightly. 'Fine.'

'Are you sure? If you need anything...'

I swallowed. 'It's okay. I know Ellery will help.'

'Well, alright, then.' Kade frowned but let it slide.

Looking at him, I realised Kade was actually kind enough to do me a favour and not ask anything in return. Shame I hadn't tried speaking to him before. Unfortunately for the both of us, right now I needed someone who wouldn't be kind. It would be easier to take advantage of Ellery than Kade.

Heavy footsteps reached us a second before Ellery jogged up. 'Crikey, the weather's shit today—Holy—Harley?'

He was up in an instant, bracing himself in the doorway so he could look me in the eye. 'What are you doing here?'

'I—I need...' Tears pricked at my eyes. I drew in a shaky breath. 'Can we talk at your place?'

Ellery frowned, looking me up and down a few times. 'Alright, I guess.'

I handed the thermos and jacket back to Kade. 'Thank you… Sorry I dripped all over the floor.'

'No problem.' Kade grinned. 'I get off shift in ten minutes. It can be someone else's problem.'

I smiled reluctantly. 'See you around.'

'Sure. If you change your mind about needing help…'

'I'll let you know,' I lied. I turned and followed Ellery out into the rain.

We crossed a large open concrete yard—both a loading bay and a deterrent for anyone who tried to break in. Although I couldn't see them, I was conscious that there were other guards watching us. Beyond that, there were several warehouses where Sayle stored the bulk of the whiskey he'd got rich from. The flats were to one side of the compound, utilitarian metal and concrete buildings with four storeys apiece. I picked out Bas's truck, parked neatly in front of the building we approached. The metal was scraped open down one side of the vehicle.

The front door didn't lock. Inside was dry, but not warm. Ellery glanced at me once we were under the fluorescent lights. 'You don't look too good, kitten.'

'I…'

'Hey.' He caught my hand and squeezed it. 'Come on, let's go upstairs.'

'You don't live with Bas, do you?' That possibility hadn't occurred to me before, but if Bas was there, my whole plan was going to be blown open in an instant.

'Nah, I have my own place.' Ellery pulled me over to the stairs, and we ascended to the second floor. He unlocked the last door. 'This is me.'

'Nice.' I'd only seen Theo's flat before, which was a study in barely contained chaos. Ellery, by comparison, was fairly organised. He had few items of furniture, all of them old but well-maintained, and almost nothing in the way of décor. The main room was open-plan, and I could see through a doorway to the bedroom. Tall windows were uncovered, offering a view of the compound's warehouses.

'Thanks. Do you want a drink?'

I shook my head, then changed my mind and nodded. 'Whiskey?'

'Sure.' Ellery cracked a bottle and poured us each a glass, nodding with his chin to the sofa. 'Have a seat.'

I shrugged my coat off and sat carefully on the edge of the sofa. I was dressed more sexy than functional, and my skimpy top didn't do much to keep me warm. Ellery brought me my whiskey and did a double-take when he saw me.

'Damn, you look good, kitten.'

'Thanks.' I snatched my whiskey and took a big gulp before setting it aside. It was now or never—if I waited, I'd chicken out, and I wouldn't be able to do what I had to do to win back Ellery's favour. With one last slow breath to fortify myself, I stood, put an arm around the back of Ellery's neck, and kissed him.

Ellery responded in an instant. His free hand came up to tangle in my damp hair, tilting my head sideways so he could claim my lips. His mouth was lush and soft against mine. He sucked my bottom lip, his teeth grazing it, sending heat flooding through my body.

I wanted him. How long had I wanted this man for? Longer than I could remember. He'd been my first real crush, the first man I'd actually wanted to spend time with…

My mouth opened on a gasp, and his tongue swept in, tangling with mine, exploring every inch of my mouth. He tasted of mint and something else, something distinctly him, and I pressed closer, wanting more of it.

He broke the kiss suddenly, breathing hard. 'Harley… Fuck, kitten.'

Untangling his fingers from my hair, he took a sip of his whiskey, then set it aside. 'Come here, baby.'

He sat, pulling me onto his lap. I crawled over him, terrified and aroused in equal measures. I'd never felt like this before, never gone this far before. I felt like a freight train hurtling towards a cliff—the only way was forwards, and forwards lay certain destruction.

And I wanted it. In this moment, here and now, I wanted the sweet oblivion I knew Ellery could give me.

I clutched the collar of his T-shirt, leaning in. He captured my lips again, kissing me harder this time. There was a desperation in the way his hands clutched at me, the way his lips moved against mine. Our teeth clashed, his tongue finding every nook and cranny, every sensitive spot as he moved from my lips to my jaw, then my neck. I moaned. Everything felt too good; I was acutely aware of everywhere he touched me, like the world had come into hyperfocus.

It was too much.

It wasn't enough.

I felt about ready to jump out of my own skin.

Ellery's lips found the neckline of my top, following it as it swooped down towards my breasts.

'Is this what you want, kitten?'

'Please...'

'Let me take care of you.' He kissed his way to the curve of my breast. 'How's that sound, kitten?'

'Ellery, I...'

'Marco.'

I shuddered. 'Marco. Please.'

'Mmm.' I felt his hum through my entire body. His hands found the hem of my top, pushing it up. I lifted my arms so he could get it off, letting him see the prize beneath.

'So beautiful.' He bent his head, finding my nipple through my thin bra and sucking it into his mouth. 'So sexy.'

'Marco... Marco.' My mind felt foggy with desire. I ran my fingers through his hair. It was soft against my fingers. I tugged gently, and he groaned.

'That's it, kitten. Just like that. I won't break.'

I pulled harder, relishing the noise of pleasure he made. This was everything I wished my first time had been. I knew Ellery would make it good for both of us—take care of me... The thought twisted and burrowed its way into my chest, and suddenly I felt cold. I couldn't do this. I had to—I had to stop.

I pulled away, almost falling off his lap. Ellery looked up, confused. His lips were swollen, and his pupils dilated with lust. I suddenly understood, painfully well, what Bas had meant about mixing sex with business.

'This was a mistake.'

'What?' Ellery breathed. 'No, kitten. This is...' He struggled for words.

'I didn't come here for... I shouldn't have mixed...' I shuddered. 'I need a favour,' I blurted out.

Understanding dawned on his face. 'And you thought I wouldn't help you unless you slept with me?' Ellery's voice turned cold. He raked his fingers through his hair. 'Fuck.'

I scrambled off his lap, the cool air chilling my heated skin. Ellery stood, his whole body tense. I'd made a terrible mistake.

He strode past me towards the kitchen, snatching up the bottle of whiskey and drinking straight from it. Then he turned and slammed his fist into the wall. 'FUCK!'

I jumped backwards. Ellery sank his face into his hands. The skin over his knuckles was broken and bleeding. I felt sick to the stomach.

'I… I'll go.' I could ask someone else, maybe.

'No.' Ellery looked at me, and there was something so broken in his expression, as though I'd driven a knife into his chest. 'Fuck, I…'

He strode over to me suddenly, his hands crashing down on my shoulders, and then he was kissing me hard—harder even than before, as though he was dying and I was the cure. He engulfed me, holding me to him. I was surrounded by him—too hot, too heavy—and panic rose up in my chest like a wave, dragging me under. I shoved against his chest, my throat tight, black spots on my vision.

'Lemme go, lemme go!'

Ellery released me, and I stumbled back, swaying dizzily. He was breathing hard, a desperation in his gaze like I'd never seen before. I pressed my hand to my chest, willing my heart to slow down.

'I…I…'

'This is my fault,' Ellery groaned. 'I did this. Fuck!'

He looked like he wanted to punch something again, but there were no walls within his reach. He covered his face instead, dragging his fingers through his hair so it stuck out like he'd been electrocuted. 'I'm so sorry.'

'What for?'

'You… you were always so hard to reach, I thought I could… I don't know… But I never wanted you to feel like you owed me anything. I wanted you, kitten, just you. I don't…' He broke off, shaking his head. 'I turned this into business, didn't I? It wasn't meant to be this way.'

'I don't… I don't understand.'

'I never realised. I thought if I got you in my bed, no matter how I did it, I could convince you to stay there.' Ellery sighed. 'I've messed this all up. I'm such an idiot.'

He'd fancied me? All this time? I was stunned.

'I don't… I didn't realise…'

'I know. Damnit.' Ellery shook his head. 'I don't want you to sleep with me because you owe me, Harley. Just tell me what you need.'

I swallowed, my throat aching like I'd been crying. I'd fucked everything up, and the worst thing was that I'd been warned. I just hadn't understood. For all I'd thought I knew about Ellery's world, somehow I'd totally missed the point.

'I'm sorry. I'll go.'

'No.' He picked up my whiskey, pressing it into my hands. 'I want to help you, Harley. Just not like that.'

He glanced around and found my top, passing it to me. 'Whatever you need, just tell me.'

'I...' The lie felt dirty on my lips. 'Irina put up my rent. I... I was wondering if I could get my old job at the bunker back. Or maybe bartending. Whatever is available.'

Ellery sucked in a shaky breath. 'Okay,' he said. 'Okay. I'll ask. You need help making rent this week?'

I shook my head.

'You sure? I can help you. Really.'

I shook my head again. 'I'm okay, I just... I don't want to put the burden on Sav.'

'Of course you don't.' He kissed my forehead, impossibly gentle, and somehow that made everything hurt worse. 'I'll ask around. Stay the night tonight?'

'I shouldn't.'

'Please? I don't want you walking back through town in the rain.' He touched my forehead where he'd kissed. 'I'll take the sofa. I won't touch you, I promise.'

'I...' I was weak. The more I fought the realisation, the more I proved it. 'Okay, I will. Thank you.'

Ellery smiled sadly. 'Think nothing of it.'

TO BE CONTINUED

WHAT'S NEXT?

Dear reader,

Thanks for giving *Rise* a chance! I hope you enjoyed reading about Harley's adventures as much as I enjoyed writing them.

I'd love it if you could take the time to leave a review on my Amazon and Goodreads pages. Reviews are the best reward an author can receive.

If you want more from this world, please join my mailing list. You will receive a free short story, as well as updates about my writing, sneak peeks at new projects, and freebies from other series.

And if you want to explore my other books, check out my website.

You can also follow me on my socials to learn more about me.

See you in the next book!

Freedom comes at a price. When the time comes, will I be able to pay it?

Danger is stirring in Bale Rocks.

Maddock's arrival seems to have triggered something. Light is shining into the cracks of our society, and more skeletons are being exposed than I could possibly have imagined.

Percival and the Aces have spies everywhere.

The mayor seems to be collaborating with notorious slave traders the Black Hands.

The Iron Fists' grip on power is slipping with every day that goes by.

As I battle to keep myself and my sister safe, the mistakes begin piling up. It seems like if I make one wrong move, my whole life will go up in flames. The answer lies in convincing Bas of the secrets I've uncovered, but after what I've put him through, I don't know if he will ever trust me again.

As things come to a head, can I find a path to preserve the peace in my town and keep my family safe, or will the price of my freedom spell disaster for the people I care about?

***

REVOLUTION is book two in a four-book slow burn dark romance series. It cannot be read as a standalone. The series contains mature language, intense sexual situations (including references to non- and dubious consent), and violence in keeping with the post-apocalyptic setting. It is not intended for readers under the age of 18. The series ends with a happy ending.

Hunters are supposed to hate vampires—but everyone will betray their people for a price. Nathan is about to discover his.

Nathan is a vampire hunter on the cusp of graduation. He's been training for this his entire life: the moment he qualifies and joins the rest of his family in their noble calling.

If only it were that simple.

His grades are a mess, his social life is a disaster, and what's worse, his best friend is a witch! Add to that, his vampire uncle is back in town and his crush might just be supernatural too, and you have one big melting pot of potential parental disapproval. Nathan doesn't think he can take much more, and then the dark mages come to town.

As bodies begin piling up in the streets, Nathan finds himself pulled deeper into political intrigue and a deadly plot that will pit him against his own family. When the girl he likes comes under threat, Nathan races against time to solve the mystery... well aware that with every step he takes, he comes closer to his father exposing all his secrets.

ACKNOWLEDGEMENTS

Another book, another acknowledgements page—and the team is expanding.

Starting a new series, and a new genre, is always exciting. So much goes into creating the book you see before you, and I couldn't have made it what it is without the dedicated (and often extremely last-minute) work of the following people.

To Debra, my cheerleader and alpha-reader, thanks for taking a risk on this one!

To Pierre, who, upon hearing I was embarking on a romance novel, quite delightedly provided suggestions for how best to get Bas topless in every second scene (sorry I didn't include any of them, but there's always the next book!).

To my editors, who yanked open every plothole and shone a spotlight in, and also flagged up every single participle construction. If there was ever proof that editing is essential, that was it.

To Josh, who agreed to do a last-minute turnaround on the map, and as usual did a stellar job.

To MIBL, who created the gorgeous cover of my dreams.

To my dad, who has supported me tirelessly through three novels now (and is probably sick of hearing about them).

And lastly and mostly to my mum, who formats and advertises my novels, lets me bounce ideas off of her, and lets me cry on her shoulder when I've had no sleep and I have no clue and everything is going wrong. And who beta-read the book for me, even though she's a self-proclaimed lover of feel-good novels. Sorry, and I promise one day I'll write a happy one for you.

P.S. Lastly, to my own brain, which kept me up at four AM creating evermore convoluted and contradictory plotlines, please stop. Just stop. Some of us want to keep normal hours! 😊 But thank you anyway for grabbing hold of this idea and refusing to let go. Onwards and upwards!

Margot de Klerk is a British author who writes fantasy and science fiction for teens and adults, with a bit of comedy, a dash of romance, and a whole lot of plot. She is most often found in her favourite coffee shop typing furiously on her computer with an iced latte at hand. When not writing, she enjoys photography, travelling, sewing, and various sports.

Follow her on social media, subscribe to her mailing list, and get information on new books: